Avenging Heart
The Ignited Series
Book Four

Desni Dantone

Avenging Heart

This is a work of fiction. Names, characters, and incidents are either the product of the author's imagination or are used fictitiously. Any resemblance to actual persons, living or dead, or events is entirely coincidental.

The scanning, uploading, and distribution of this book via the Internet or via any other means without the permission of the author is illegal and punishable by law. Please purchase only authorized electronic editions, and do not participate in or encourage electronic piracy of copyrighted materials. Your support of the author's rights is appreciated.

Cover design by Najla Qambar Designs
Edited by Jennifer Leisenheimer at Beyond The Cover Editing

Printed in the United States of America

All rights reserved. Copyright © 2016 Desni Dantone

ISBN 13: 978-0-9895090-7-7

Books By Desni Dantone

Ignited Series:

Ignited
Sacrificed
Salvaged Soul
Avenging Heart

PROLOGUE

"In the modern day of man, one girl will rise above the rest. Her magic will bring an end to the race born in the war between good and evil. She will end it all."

This was the prophecy as we knew it. One thing was for certain. I was that girl.

One question remained. How bad would the fallout be?

For me? For everyone I loved and cared about? For anyone who crossed paths with me?

Micah was already gone. Though he had not been killed by my hand, his death certainly fell on my shoulders. He had died *because* of me.

I feared that death followed me, sparing me while taking those closest to me. Without Micah to stop me, I was free to cause the destruction I was created for. Those I loved the most would be the first victims.

Unless I stopped it. Stopped myself.

Free will had a hell of a way of throwing a kink into evil's plan. Fortunately, I was a strong-willed girl.

CHAPTER 1

Traveling permitted me too much time to think. I did a lot of thinking. Maybe too much.

Mostly my thoughts revolved around the prophecy, and my central role in it, what happened a week ago, and the unknown that awaited us.

I blamed myself for the attack on the Kala base last week, and for Micah's death. Though everyone tried to make me feel better about it, I couldn't shake the guilt that wrapped around me like a fat, life-extinguishing python.

I hadn't asked for this life, nor had I wanted all the bloodshed on my hands, but those were the cards I had been dealt. I chose to turn them all back over to the dealer in exchange for a new set of cards. A winning hand of freedom, determination, victory . . . and love.

The love I shared with Nathan was the one thing that brought me solace these days. I often thought about the possibility of returning to a normal life—as normal as I could live given my circumstances. Nathan was the central figure in those thoughts.

It didn't matter where we were—a dingy bus traveling across Central America, the dirty floor of a hotel room shared with our four travel companions, crammed into an airplane on a transatlantic flight, or on the pristine beaches of Greece—his mere presence enveloped me like a protective barrier, something I had been accustomed to nearly my entire life. I sought him, and his fiercely protective nature, with every move I made. Especially now, when the horizon of my future was at its bleakest.

Granted, not every day with him was rainbows and sunshine. Like when he went into that unbearable instructor mode I had once loathed, and I seriously contemplated kicking him between the legs so he would stop 'strictly coaching me' on my sparring techniques. That was his choice of words. To me, it strongly resembled 'being an asshole.'

Still, even those moments had a silver lining. While kissing Nathan was my absolute favorite extracurricular activity, fighting him came a close second.

"Good!" He flexed his fingers as he held his hands out to me. "Again."

I swung, and connected my fist with his open palm with a crack. God, it felt good.

"Combo," he instructed, and I jabbed both of his palms.

"Left is weak," he critiqued. "Again."

I struck him as he instructed, and winced from the sting to my knuckles.

"You can do better than that." I tried again, and he shook his head. "You call that a punch?"

"You know what?" I dropped my arms to my sides with a groan. "My arms feel like Jell-O. How do you expect me to punch with Jell-O arms?"

Nathan stared at me over his hands, which were still raised expectantly. "You done?"

"Yes, I'm done." I turned away with a sigh of relief. I was eager for a much needed break, and a shower. We had started over an hour ago with a run before the sun rose. After an ungodly number of sit-ups, push-ups, and fighting drills, I was so done.

"I meant . . . are you done complaining?" Nathan said, stopping me.

I glared at him over my shoulder, and he raised his eyebrows in challenge. I blew out a puff of air, and shook some life back into my arms as I turned to face him with narrowed eyes.

He was going to pay for that.

My right fist cracked his palm hard. As I rotated, I pulled my left arm back with the intention of giving him everything I had. Before I made contact, Nathan's hand shot out and clamped down on my wrist, stopping my follow through. My eyes lifted to his in time to see the smirk on his face before he twisted my arm behind my back and spun me around.

"Now what?" he murmured in my ear.

I ignored the shivers caused by his breath on my neck, and wrapped my right arm around his head as I twisted out of his hold. At the same time, I kicked my leg out. He grabbed it with his free hand before I could connect, and I lost my balance.

I'm going down . . .

And he's coming with me.

I attempted a twist that would land him beneath me, so that I could claim bragging rights, but it didn't happen. I ended up with my back on the sand, and Nathan kneeling over me in total control.

"Ugh!" I threw my head back with a groan. "How do you always manage to take me down first?"

Nathan brushed a speck of sand off my forehead with a grin. "You think too much. Just do it."

"Me? Think too much?" Had he forgotten who he was talking to? The girl who notoriously acted first, and thought second.

"You've got the potential. You're definitely a lot stronger than you were," he praised.

"Then why can't I take you down?" I whined. "I'm a demigod! I should be able to take you."

"I'm still more practiced than you," he returned with a small chuckle. "I don't think about my moves. I just do them. You're concentrating too much on getting everything perfect. That distracts you."

"Hmm." I bit my lip as I peered into his eyes, a silver-ringed blue that rivaled the most pristine of oceans. "You know what's distracting me right now?"

I watched as his eyes shifted from firm instructor mode . . . to sexy. His gaze dropped to my mouth, and the grin on his face grew as his head lowered.

I temporarily considered taking advantage of his guard being down. It might have been easy now, to grab him in a head lock and flip him over, but I would never know. While I would have loved to brag about it later, now I preferred for him to kiss me.

His lips skimmed cautiously over mine, as if he suspected my initial sneak attack plan. My arms wrapped possessively around his shoulders as I deepened the kiss, letting him know that was the last thing from my mind. The gravely noise that sounded from the back of his throat as he surrendered full-heartedly to me unraveled the pent up desire I had been forced to hold back all morning. From the way Nathan's grip tightened on my hip, I suspected it had been just as torturous for him.

His lips eased away from mine with a groan. "You really need to start wearing more clothes when we train."

I followed his gaze to my exposed hip. I was sporting short running shorts and a thin tank top that had drifted up to my navel. What was wrong with that?

"It's like a hundred degrees out here," I pointed out. Besides, he had no shirt on, so if anyone should be complaining about lack of clothing, it was me.

But I wasn't going to complain about that.

He grunted something unintelligible before claiming my mouth again. With our lips pressed together, he grumbled, "But it's really distracting."

"Didn't seem to affect you earlier," I returned between kisses.

He leaned back to pin me with a look. "Trust me. It does."

"Stop talking," I ordered, grabbing the back of his head as I pulled him to me.

The deliberate sound of a throat clearing behind us froze his descent. Nathan rolled away from me to peer over his shoulder, revealing Jared where he stood a few yards away with a shit-eating grin on his face.

"Interrupting something?" he asked.

"As a matter of fact . . ." I started as Nathan jumped to his feet.

He offered me a hand as I stood, then turned to Jared. "What's up?" He was so quick to leap back into mission mode. Much quicker than I was.

"Everyone's getting up," Jared explained as he waved his hand behind him, gesturing to the quaint hotel we had stayed in the night before. "We need to get an early start."

"Yeah, definitely," Nathan agreed.

Both of them had told us the night before that we would need to head out early this morning. Apparently, the climb to *The Hall of the Gods* was a brutal one, and required a good night's rest and an early start. Too bad I was exhausted now after training with Nathan.

But he had insisted on sticking to our routine, even this morning, because we never knew when we would encounter a demigod. Since I would technically have to be the one to destroy him or her, Nathan wanted me to be prepared.

Not that it was something easy to prepare for. Since I had fought Temulus, the demigod of manipulation, last week, and won, I realized that I had actually been lucky. Fortunately, I had the ability to use magic, which had given me a huge advantage in the fight. Regardless, I had been lucky to walk away mostly unscathed. I knew luck may not be on my side the next time.

Which was exactly why we were here, in the Greek tourist hub of Litochoro, and about to pay a visit to the gods. There were two other demigods, Isatan and Permna, who could help us, and we needed to join forces with them before any of the other nine demigods found us.

Nathan scooped his shirt off the ground and slipped it on. I fell into step alongside him and Jared as we walked back to the hotel.

"I hope they've figured out what that compound was that the Skotadi were using," Nathan mused along the way.

That was the other reason for our visit. During their mission to Greece last month, Jared and Nathan helped to rescue Isatan and Permna from a small army of Skotadi that had managed to hold them captive with the aid of a magical compound. It was apparently capable of weakening demigods' powers, and was something we could get a lot of use out of in our quest to destroy the other nine demigods. Not to mention, we didn't want it in the wrong hands, where it could be used against Isatan and Permna again . . . or me.

"I've been thinking about that," Jared said as we walked. "What are the chances that Circe came up with it?"

"You think Lillian might remember?" Nathan questioned.

"It sure would be nice if her memory came back a little faster," I muttered.

Not only was Lillian my old nemesis and Nathan's ex-girlfriend from seven years ago, when she was a Kala, but she had also been the Incantator created by Circe to put her curse into motion. Lillian's conversion back to a Kala had left her with a severe case of amnesia. Though bits and pieces of her memory had returned, it was coming back slowly. Too slowly to be of much help to us yet.

She had been the one to remember that Circe was behind the curse, and that Circe was counting on me to finish it. Apparently, neither Circe nor Lillian had the power that I had. As the daughter of the true goddess of magic, Hecate, I had the ability to do what they couldn't.

Not that I wanted to. Thousands of innocent humans would be sacrificed as a result, and my best friend, Callie, would be one of them. Not only was I on a quest to destroy the demigods who planned to benefit from this curse, but I was determined to stop the curse from being finalized to save Callie.

As an added benefit, there was a possibility that destroying Hades' three remaining demigods could sever the links Alec and I had to them, and thus our links to their evil influences. Since Temulus had been destroyed, we both have felt lighter and freer. It had been Alec's idea to go after the demigods to see if there was something to it, and I knew he couldn't wait to find out if his theory was right.

Even if that meant dragging his butt out of bed at the crack of dawn.

As we approached the hotel patio that overlooked the beach, I saw Alec sitting on one of the steps, leaning his head against the post with a gigantic cup of coffee in his hand, his eyes closed.

Nathan kicked the bottom of his foot, and one of Alec's eyes popped open.

"Watch it," he warned.

"Wow," Nathan chuckled. "You really don't take jet lag well."

"In all fairness, he did warn us," Jared said to Nathan.

I recalled a heated conversation between the three of them a few nights ago, with more foul language than I would have expected to hear in a sports bar during Monday Night Raw. And I would have described the conversation as threatening, rather than cautionary. But it was about flight times and wake up calls, nothing really important, so I hadn't stuck around long to get the details.

But yeah . . . Alec already wasn't much of a morning person. With the addition of jet lag, he was a downright grouch.

"Where are Bruce and Lillian?" Nathan asked him.

Alec didn't bother to open his eyes as he answered. "Restaurant. Breakfast."

My stomach grumbled, and I realized breakfast sounded like an excellent idea.

The patio was set off the back of the hotel. On the other side of the wide glass doors was a small restaurant. Already, I could smell the alluring combination of freshly brewed coffee, bacon, and maple syrup wafting outside.

Nathan turned to me. "What do you want?" I smiled at the thought of the many directions I could take that simple question, and

Nathan quickly amended, "To eat."

"I desperately want to shower," I returned as I plucked at my sweat-dampened and sand-covered shirt.

Nathan's eyes lowered to the sliver of exposed midriff I had created. "Yeah. You, uh . . . you go do that. I'll order something . . . for you. I know what you like so . . ."

Watching Nathan squirm was a secret guilty pleasure of mine. There was something adorable about a normally hard-nosed warrior being reduced to fumbled words just by being around me. It didn't happen often, but when it did, I loved him a little more.

I started to lean in to give him a kiss, but thought better of it. Even if his eyes were closed, Alec was right there. Though he had repeatedly told me he was fine with it, I cared too much about our friendship to throw my relationship with Nathan in his face.

Instead, I tousled Alec's hair as I passed him on the steps. He swatted at my legs, but missed, and I laughed as I crossed the patio to the glass door.

My smile faltered when I spotted our other two travel companions, Lillian and Bruce, sitting at a round table in the corner as they ate their breakfast. Though our travels over the past week had acclimated me somewhat to being around her all the time, I still found myself on edge around Lillian.

It was only partially because of the history between us. Sure, she had tried to kill Nathan a few times, tortured me, cursed my best friend . . . but I knew she was different now. She wasn't the same person who had done those horrible things. I knew that, even if the mere sight of her face gave me unwelcome flashbacks from time to time. I was slowly getting over that history we shared. Now, the awkwardness between us mostly stemmed from the very obvious fact that she was still in love with Nathan.

While Bruce flashed me a friendly smile as I approached, Lillian's face remained a blank canvas. I often caught her quietly studying me, and I wondered what she saw when she looked at me. The girl who had taken Nathan from her? The girl who stood in the way of her happily ever after? While I understood why she might have thought that, I knew that wasn't the way it had happened.

She looked away first and, as I pushed through the door, I turned to follow the direction of her distant gaze. From her seat, she had a clear view of the ocean . . . and the beach. I guessed she had been sitting there for some time, long enough that she had seen something that put that barely detectable frown on her face.

CHAPTER 2

As we climbed the mountain, Nathan reminded me again to steer clear of Zeus and Poseidon—especially Poseidon. Apparently, when he and Jared had talked with him before, Nathan had gotten a not-so-good vibe from him.

"Hera seems to be on your side," he said.

"Uh-huh."

"Don't go anywhere alone with any of the others," he continued.

"Nathan, I know," I puffed as I struggled up a particularly steep part in the trail. *Damn, this mountain is a bitch.* "Don't tell them anymore than I have to, don't be too trusting, don't . . ."

"Don't let them know you're the one Circe needs to complete the curse," he finished. He offered me a hand to help me up the final few steps to slightly more level ground.

"Right." How could I have forgotten? It was only the hundredth time he had warned me. I blamed the intense heat for my momentary lapse. "How much farther is it?"

"Seriously," Alec grumbled from behind me. "I really shouldn't have smoked that last cigarette before we left."

I shot Alec a grin. "Last one?"

He shrugged noncommittally as he hoisted himself up to a stand beside me.

Alec had quit smoking this morning . . . again. He had enjoyed several 'last cigarettes' this week. The longest he had made it without one was twelve hours. The rest of us had suffered that day just as much as he had, and we were all pretty relieved when he finally gave in to his cravings.

"This is it," Jared announced. He turned to Nathan. "Isn't that the tree?"

"Oh, thank God for shade!" Alec dropped to the ground under a single tree off the side of the path, and the rest of us followed him, eager for the break from the relentless sun.

"Where is the entrance?" Bruce asked as he brought a bottle of water to his lips.

Nathan pointed to the trail, where it narrowed between two rock walls. "Through there."

A warm buzzing sensation prickled my skin the moment my gaze landed on the spot he indicated. My feet took involuntary steps toward the gap in the rocks. With each step, the buzzing intensified. Unlike the strange pull I had felt toward the army of Skotadi that had invaded the Kala base the week prior, this sensation was a welcomed one. It filled me with a sense of longing.

Of hope. Joy. *Family*.

Someone behind me asked me what I was doing, but I didn't know who, nor did I know how to answer that question. I let my feet take me in the direction I instinctively wanted to go. I passed through the narrow gap, and approached a vertical rock wall. Though my eyes told me this was the end of the trail, I knew better.

I pressed my hand to the sun-warmed rock . . . and my arm slipped through like the wall was made of pudding. Though a blurry remnant of the wall remained, I could see my arm clearly on the other side. I found myself laughing softly as I wiggled my fingers.

"Holy shit," somebody muttered behind me, and I turned to find the others gaping at me.

I found Nathan's eyes. "This way?"

He nodded, confirming what I already knew. I didn't know how . . . but I knew.

"I guess we won't need one of the gods to lead us after all," Jared concluded with a chuckle.

The buzzing intensified as I stepped through the rock wall, passing into another realm. Once the rest of the group had joined me, I led them up a narrow flight of stairs. Though I had been winded and tired from the hike up the mountain only a few moments ago, I suddenly found myself full of energy. Perhaps it was excitement over what awaited me at the top. Maybe it was some previously unknown demigod superpower that I had suddenly channeled. Whatever it was, I was grateful. Not even the thick fog that blanketed us hampered me.

I knew the others weren't fairing as well as I was, and I slowed my ascent for their benefit. But the moment the golden doors appeared in front of me, I rushed forward without hesitation to push them open. I blinked against the sudden light that welcomed us as a chorus of complaints erupted from behind me.

Alec's voice reached my ears above the others. "Dammit, Kris! A little warning next time, huh?"

I opened my mouth to apologize, but the words were forgotten as the most magnificent sight I have ever seen appeared before me. The true Mount Olympus—*The Hall of the Gods*—was just as spectacular as Nathan had described it to be. Maybe even more so, I concluded as I gaped at the majestic waterfall that poured out of the side of the mountain.

As I craned my head to see where the water fell, a woman draped in a long white robe stepped forward, into my line of sight, with outstretched hands.

"Finally," she smiled. "Welcome to the home of the gods, my dear."

~ ~ ~

As Hera led us through the lush garden, she pointed out several highlights that she thought we might enjoy. We passed the ambrosia fields, from which the gods got their nectar; the fountain of prosperity; the springs of clarity and the majestic pool of love. We stopped there, at the base of the waterfall where it dumped into the pool, and tiny droplets of moisture beaded on my skin.

My jaw ached from having my mouth dropped in awe for so long. Hera offered me a warm smile as though she understood my sensory overload. Her kind eyes moved over the group.

"You will have to excuse my husband," she explained. "He and Poseidon are wreaking havoc in the Atlantic. I don't expect them to return for several more days."

"Wreaking havoc?" Jared pondered.

Hera's smile never faltered as she responded, "It's hurricane season."

I snorted as I unsuccessfully attempted to hold back a laugh. Nathan's elbow tapped my ribs, and I glanced over my shoulder to find his head bowed and a dimple in his cheek.

"We have recently discovered that Circe is behind the demigods' plot to overthrow us," Hera continued. "They were quite angry and needed to blow off some steam."

At least we now knew that they were aware of Circe's involvement. I wondered how much more they knew. Were they already aware that Circe was relying on me to complete the immortality curse? My shoulders were rigid as I waited for Hera to accuse me of being in allegiance with Circe, but she never did.

"We believe Circe has fled to her residence in Aeaea," Hera explained. "She has acquired quite an army to assist her and the ten demigods working with her, so I'm afraid you will meet considerable resistance in your quest to destroy them."

"Nine demigods now," Jared told her. "Kris destroyed Temulus last week."

Hera swung her gaze to me, and the surprise on her face shifted to admiration. "Zeus will be pleased to hear that."

"Circe's army?" Nathan questioned. "What do you know about them?"

"I'm sorry to say that it is composed of both Skotadi and Kala soldiers," Hera answered. "They have been promised immortality as well, in exchange for their loyalty to her."

"That explains the traitors," Jared grumbled from behind me.

The attack on the Kala base last week had partially been orchestrated by several members of Kala leadership. Nathan and Jared had been pondering the motive behind their deception since. I supposed the promise of immortality was a good enough reason for them to turn on their own.

Hera turned to me with a smile. "Isatan and Permna will be happy that you are here. I know they have been looking forward to having your help." She looked to Jared and Nathan, where they stood slightly behind me, and her voice lifted with uncertainty. "And the assistance of an army?"

"We hit a little snag in the preparations," Jared admitted glumly.

"So far it's just us," Nathan added.

Hera looked over our six-person group warily. Finally, her face brightened. "I suppose it is better to have trust than numbers. Now, please, come with me. I will take you to Isatan and Permna. They have been waiting for you."

She led us away from the pool. I felt as if I had swallowed a frog. It jumped around my stomach as she led us through a golden archway. We entered a room composed of grey walls and a high ceiling, all made of rock. Despite its grandness, the room felt small and cramped thanks to the enormous stone table that rested in the center. Shelves had been chiseled into the walls, and every inch was covered with an assortment of books and ivory-colored scrolls.

Hunched over the round table stood two individuals. They looked up from the scroll they had been examining as we entered.

"Isatan . . . Permna . . ." Hera placed her hands on my shoulders. "This is Kris, the thirteenth demigod. I will leave you all to talk."

When Hera retreated from the room, the two demigods approached us. Like Hera, they too wore long robes. His consisted of layers of several shades of green; hers a blend of yellow. While untamed black curls fell to his shoulders, her hair was slicked back into a tight auburn bun. Both hid their poise and emotion behind clear blue eyes.

I held back as Isatan shook hands with Nathan and Jared.

"Good to see you again," he said to them, then glanced over the rest of us. "I hope this isn't the army you promised. Though the addition of another demigod is certainly welcomed."

I felt small under his penetrating gaze. Then, as I remembered that I was equal to him, I squared my shoulders in confidence. Sure, I was way out of my league, but I could pretend.

"That is . . ." Isatan continued as he looked at me, "assuming you plan to aid us, and not Circe, of course."

I blanched as Nathan swung a concerned look at me.

Oh shit . . . Isatan knew?

"Isatan," Permna chided. "I told you what I saw before Circe put the bind on me." She turned to me with a reassuring smile. "We are aware of where your loyalties lie."

"My father doesn't know what Circe has intended for you," Isatan added with a warning ring. "I won't tell him as long as you remain on our side."

I had nearly forgotten that Permna was the demigod of prophecy. Now, I thanked the gods that she'd had a vision of me, and my intentions.

I swallowed the lump in my throat. "I'm not going to help Circe. I can guarantee that."

"Good," Isatan responded curtly, and I didn't know if I liked him or not. He turned to Nathan and Jared. "What of this army you were to gather for us?"

"We're short numbered now," Jared explained. "But I think we can gather more."

"We're going to need all the help we can get," Isatan said as he turned to the large table. "Permna and I have been searching for the locations of the other demigods. We know that three of the four sided with Hades are not venturing far from the Underworld. They will be difficult to get to. But we have located another four demigods hiding here." His finger landed on a map of Greece that was spread across the table, but I couldn't read the name of the town he pointed to. "Three others are unaccounted for."

"Temulus has been taken care of," Nathan offered.

"Really?" Permna studied me curiously. Over her shoulder, I caught the skeptical curve on Isatan's lips, and I decided that I definitely didn't like him.

"That leaves nine," Nathan continued. "Once we strike one, the rest will come for us. If we can take out those four before they realize our plans, we won't be as outnumbered later."

"The three of us against the four of them?" Isatan asked. "And with only the help of five hybrids?"

Nathan and Jared shared a look. "We'll get more hybrids," Jared promised. "But we were hoping to have another advantage."

"What do you know about that compound that the Skotadi used to hold the two of you?" Nathan asked Isatan and Permna. "If we could get our hands on it, we would have a huge advantage."

"We know that it's one of Circe's creations," Permna offered. "We believe she created it out of dried centaur blood, diamond, and a few other herbs. It does not affect hybrids, but will cause us to hallucinate and temporarily lose our powers. Once your Kala team removed it from our skin, the effects wore off within minutes."

"We've gone through her chamber here, but have found nothing. We believe she made it at her other residence in Aeaea," Isatan added.

Nathan and Jared shared another look that caused my stomach to twist . . . because I knew what they were thinking.

"Is there any way we can get to it?" Jared posed.

"We can get to Aeaea," Isatan said, "but I don't see how we can get past Circe."

Everyone was silent under the weight of disappointment. Then an idea hit me, and I turned to Permna, because I preferred her over

Isatan. "Is it something I could copy? If I knew how she made it, maybe I could find a way to make it."

I certainly should have the ability to do so. Since I'd reached my potential as an Incantator, I realized I was capable of far more than I ever thought possible. Granted, I spent most of my time concentrating on holding my powers back, and even then doors opened ahead of my approach, glass shattered when I was angry, and I flirted with a state of invisibility when distracted. Surely, I could recreate Circe's compound if I knew how she had done it.

"She's the only one who knows how," Isatan said dismissively.

"No." Permna's eyes were wide when they fell on me. "We can get past Circe. We can get the compound directly from her."

"How?" I asked hesitantly.

"We can bind her, like she did to me," Permna answered. "Well, *you* can bind her."

I glanced around at the group. From the number of confused faces I saw, I knew I wasn't the only one who didn't know what she was talking about.

"What does that mean, to bind her?" I questioned.

"It's a spell that can be placed on someone from a distance to limit their powers," Permna explained. "I suspect she placed one on me last week. I haven't been able to use my powers of prophecy like I used to. Binds are supposed to be temporary, but it doesn't seem to be wearing off yet."

"What if she binds Kris?" Alec spoke up from the back of the group. When I turned to him, he added, "No offense, but I don't think you can take on the demigods with nothing but your bare hands. You're going to need your powers."

He glanced at Nathan as if looking for confirmation, and I shot

Nathan a look that dared him to agree with Alec. Not that I didn't agree with Alec myself. I knew I never would have defeated Temulus if I hadn't used my powers. What good could I do without them?

"Your magic may be protecting you," Permna said to me. "Circe could never bind Hecate. Perhaps you're protected from being bound as well. For some reason, she cannot bind Isatan either."

"Likely because of my father," Isatan added.

I supposed that was reassuring, but one problem still remained. "I don't know how to bind. I've never even heard of it until now."

"I used to—" Lillian started to say, but was stopped with a look from Nathan.

The fact that Lillian had been an Incantator was something we didn't want the gods to know—especially that Lillian had been *the* Incantator that helped Circe spread the curse. Though she hadn't retained her Incantation powers since she had been converted back to a Kala, and she definitely wasn't evil like she had been, we didn't know how they would take the news of her involvement.

Lillian cleared her throat before she continued. "I used to have an interest in Incantation, and studied it for fun. I've learned about binding, and I think I can help with the process. But we will need certain materials to do it."

"Hecate left behind everything she had in her resting chamber," Permna offered as she looked between Lillian and me. "I'm sure you can find what you need in there."

"My mother has a room here?"

Permna nodded. "I'll show you."

I followed closely behind Permna as she led us out of the room, and into the garden. Nathan came up beside me, and took my hand in his as he leaned close enough to whisper, "Are you comfortable with this?"

"Absolutely."

So far, I had felt like little more than a pawn being moved around by others who knew so much more about the way this alternate world worked. I wanted to contribute more, and binding Circe so that we could get her compound was definitely a start to showing what I could do. I just hoped I could pull it off.

"I'm not so sure about Isatan, though," I added in a whisper. Fortunately, he had stayed in the room to strategize with Jared and Bruce. I was relieved to be free of his penetrating stare for a few moments.

Permna cast me a smile over her shoulder. "Don't you worry about Isatan. He's an insufferable creature with the temperament of his father."

I hadn't realized I had spoken loud enough for her to hear, and stared at the back of Permna's head in mortification before Nathan's hand squeezed mine reassuringly.

"See? That's just the way he is," Nathan offered. "Don't take offense to it."

I shot him a grateful smile as Permna led us through another golden doorway, and into the room that had been my mother's chamber. My feet stopped moving just inside the door as I took in the impressive sight.

While the size of the room was astonishing, that was not what caught my attention. The hundreds of candles that lined the walls and covered the floors did . . . for starters.

"Who keeps these candles lit?" Alec asked Permna.

"No one," she answered. "They've been burning for centuries. They never burn out."

"Her magic keeps them lit," Lillian added quietly. She had already moved farther into the room, and ran a hand over one of the many, many shelves covered with plants and herbs.

On another wall, shelves were filled with large glass containers filled with sands and liquids that encompassed every color of the rainbow, and books of all sizes. A large poster bed lay to the left of the room, and directly across from it was a large table covered with more candles and books. Above the table, a large wheel with lines crisscrossing in all directions was fixed to the wall.

It certainly appeared she had left everything behind, and I didn't doubt that the materials needed for a binding spell were here. Now, I only worried how we would find them.

CHAPTER 3

Permna returned to Isatan's planning room, and left us to sort through Hecate's belongings. *My mother's belongings.* I kept reminding myself of that, because it was still unbelievable to me. As I ran my hand over all the fascinating things we found, I ached with a sense of longing. I wanted to know this goddess . . . my mother.

In the midst of the emotion I didn't realize I had until now, I struggled to focus on our task. I found myself grateful for Lillian. She focused when I wavered, and she understood a lot more about this stuff than I did.

"Here." She dropped a thick ivory colored paper onto the table in front of Nathan and Alec. "This is the correct material."

I glanced over my shoulder. "What was the name of the ink again?"

Nathan looked down at the large book opened in front of him—at least four feet across and a foot thick. "Black nightshade ink," he read.

I plucked a jar containing a violet colored liquid from the shelf. "I found it."

I set the jar on the table beside the paper, and the rusty nail we had found earlier.

"That's everything we need, right?" Alec asked.

"It looks like it," Nathan agreed as he scanned the book again.

"And we have the spell right here, but I don't know how we can take this book with us."

We had decided not to perform the binding spell yet. According to what we had found in the spell book, the bind would wear off within a few days. Though the book didn't specify exactly what would happen to her, we wanted the bind to be at its strongest when we faced her.

"Maybe we can copy it into this one," Alec offered. He moved a few books to the side to reveal a small square shaped notepad we had flipped through earlier.

Only the first half of it had been written in and, though none of us had been able to understand the language, we suspected it had been used as a journal of sorts.

My mother's journal.

"Yeah," I agreed quickly. "I wanted to take that with me anyway."

Alec handed it to me, and I took a seat at the table to copy the spell from the big book onto a blank page in the journal. Some of the symbols were difficult to draw, and I had to concentrate on getting them right. Other than that, it wasn't all that challenging. The spell was composed of a few Greek words, Circe's name, and the symbols. I was nearly finished when Permna appeared in the doorway with Jared and Bruce.

"Have you had any luck finding what you need?" she asked.

"Yes," Lillian answered her. "Thank you. We have everything we will need to bind her."

"Excellent. Isatan would like to leave tomorrow," she said. "In the meantime, Hera insists that you all spend the remainder of the evening here."

"We really should get back to our hotel before it gets too late," Nathan objected.

"The sun has already started to set," Permna returned. "You won't make it off the mountain before darkness settles. We have a vacant chamber for you to rest in. That won't be a problem."

I met Nathan's eyes with a shrug. Though I was surprised to hear how late in the day it was, I didn't mind the idea of staying.

"And Kris," Permna continued. "I'm sure your mother would be happy for you to use her room for the night. The rest of you, come with me and I will show you where you will be staying."

Nathan paused by my chair. "I'll be back. Are you okay for now?"

I nodded. "I'm just going to finish copying the curse."

His lips grazed the top of my head. Then he was gone, along with the rest of the group, and I was left alone in my mother's room.

~ ~ ~

After I finished copying the binding spell into the notebook, I flipped through the pages of the spell book. A few of the spells I had heard mention of before. Some I was already capable of doing. Most, however, mystified me.

I skimmed over a levitation spell that I already knew, and was about to turn the page, when something caught my attention. *To Call A Mortal Into A Dream.* Micah had once mentioned that Incantators, like prophets, were capable of visiting people in their dreams. His prophetic specialty, meshed with my powers, had enabled us to share dreams. Until now, I hadn't known that there was a spell to enable me to do it with anyone else.

I jotted down the steps to the spell in the notebook. It required the use of rosemary, and I searched through Hecate's collection until I found what I needed. I plucked the star-shaped green leaf from the plant, and placed it and the notebook into my backpack where I had set it by the door.

"Where is everyone?" I muttered as I turned back to the room.

While I hated being left alone, I at least had some interesting things to keep me preoccupied. I was admiring the wheel pinned to the wall when Hera stepped into the doorway a few minutes later.

"That is the wheel of Hecate," she explained. "It holds much power, but only she can harness it."

"Everything in here fascinates me."

"She was a fascinating goddess," Hera returned. "And she is certainly missed."

"Has anyone ever tried to rescue her?"

Micah had explained that Hades imprisoned her in the Underworld. I understood she had been there for centuries, but didn't understand how the gods hadn't managed to get her back in all that time.

"Asclepius tried once. He was unable to get through the binds that hold her there."

"A bind? Like we're going to place on Circe?"

"Yes, but much, much stronger. We believe Hecate placed the bind herself so that she could not leave the Underworld."

Micah had also explained to me that Hades had placed a curse on Hecate, that if she were ever to escape the Underworld she would destroy her lover, Asclepius. That was one thing I had never understood.

"How could Hecate destroy Asclepius anyway? I thought gods

were immortal."

"It's a little difficult to understand," Hera started. "If Hecate were to destroy Asclepius, his outer shell, his body, would remain, but the essence of his being would be reabsorbed into the earth here at Mount Olympus. He would be reborn eventually, but it could take centuries. Being that Asclepius is the god of medicine and healing, the loss of his essence would be detrimental to the human world. Hecate would rather remain in the Underworld than let that happen."

I traced a finger over the wheel as I digested Hera's explanation. My mother chose humanity over herself. While noble on her part, I hated that the circumstances would prevent me from ever knowing her.

All I had was her room, and a journal I couldn't read.

"Now, come with me, dear," Hera ordered. "I have something to show you."

I followed Hera through the garden to a golden doorway near the waterfall. Once inside the room hidden there, the sound of rushing water surrounded me. Not only from the waterfall on the other side of the wall, but from a stream of water that snaked out of the wall and dumped into a large oval hole in the ground.

Lillian stood to the side of the pool in a flowing white gown as she wrung water from her long dark hair.

"Please enjoy a bath in the spring of clarity," Hera encouraged me with a wave of her hand.

She left, and it was just Lillian and me.

"The boys are using another one," she said to me. "I'm finished, so it's all yours."

I nodded as I surveyed the clear water. It was inviting, and after the grueling hike up the mountain earlier, a necessity. A cloud of steam hovered above the surface, and promised warmth to soothe my aching muscles. Another white gown that I assumed was for me lay on a spot of dry rock near the pool.

As Lillian walked past me on her way to the door, I called out to her. "Hey, Lillian. Thanks for your help with the binding spell. I would have never known what to do."

She offered me a small smile. "Anything to help our cause."

She left me to undress, and as I settled into the water, I replayed her words. *Our cause.* Not me. She hadn't meant to help me necessarily. Only what I was attempting to do. I supposed I shouldn't have been surprised, considering the man she was in love with had moved on . . . with me.

~ ~ ~

I returned to Hecate's room to find Nathan sprawled on the floor at the foot of the bed with the notebook in his lap . . . that he had dug through my backpack to find. Not that I cared. He was dressed in the same clothes he had worn earlier, his hair still slightly damp from his time in the springs.

I tossed my soiled clothes next to my bag as I approached him. "What are you doing?"

"Trying to interpret some of this." His eyes remained fixed on the journal as he answered. "I had to learn Greek during development, but I haven't had to use it since. I can't make much sense out of this now."

I dropped to the floor beside him, and took the opportunity to get close to him by looking over his shoulder. The writing looked like gibberish to me. I would love for someone to tell me what it meant.

But not now.

Now, I had something much different in mind.

"You being here right now . . ." I started as I rested my chin on his shoulder. "Does that mean you were planning to stay with me tonight?"

The corner of his mouth quirked up. "As if I would stay anywhere else."

"That's good." I plucked the book from his hands and set it to the side. In one fluid motion, I rose to my knees and climbed onto his lap. As I wrapped my arms around his neck, I murmured, "Because I wouldn't let you stay anywhere else."

Nathan's gaze dropped to finally take in the gown I wore, and a throaty sigh passed his lips. "What are you wearing?"

I shrugged. "Some gown Hera left for me."

"You look . . ." His eyes twinkled with admiration when they lifted to mine. "Kris, you're beautiful."

"Words every girl loves to hear."

Strands of wet hair framed my face as I dropped my head. His lips were waiting, and took mine hungrily as he gathered my hair in his hands. My fingers dug into his shoulders, which were taut with restraint, before moving lower. They grazed over the hem of his shirt.

It needed to go. Now.

I peeled my mouth away from his as I yanked the material over his head. I allowed myself a thorough gaze at his smooth chest, and when my eyes finally lifted to his, he grinned.

"So . . ." I started.

"So?"

I bit my lip. While we had been close to having sex just a week ago, we hadn't had another opportunity since. The knowledge that we were alone for the first time since then both excited and flustered me.

"I wish I knew if you were thinking what I'm thinking."

"Oh, I doubt you are." His eyes lit with mischief as they lowered to his hands, where they tightened around my waist. "Because right now all I can think about is what's under this gown."

My stomach flip-flopped. Well, his thoughts were definitely moving in the same direction mine were.

My voice, when I finally found it, sounded foreign to me. "Do you want to find out?"

His grip tightened around my waist as his gaze lifted to meet mine. I saw the fractional movement of his head as it bobbed up and down. His hands moved to my bare legs, and I melted under his touch when he slowly . . . oh, so slowly . . . pushed the gown higher. By the time he reached my hips, my breaths were coming in erratic bursts.

His movements were smooth and controlled, and though he didn't appear as rattled as I was, I knew he wanted this just as much as I did. Difference was, he knew what he was doing and what to expect, while I didn't. That, and that alone, was the source of my nervousness now.

I lifted my arms as he slid the gown over my head, and then I was in front of him in only my bra and panties. His eyes devoured me.

"Beautiful." His mouth seared a trail across my collarbone as he slid one strap off my shoulder.

I melted under his caress. I wanted more. As far as I was concerned, he wasn't going fast enough. My fingers trailed across the contours of his stomach, reaching lower. I fumbled to find the clasp of his jeans, and his hand came down on my wrist to still me.

"We're taking this slow," he ordered gruffly. "And if you ever want to stop, just say—"

"I won't."

His eyes met mine with a smile, and I knew I would never want to stop. Not now. Not with him.

His hands cupped my face and he pulled me to him. Just before we reconnected, I felt his back stiffen. My eyes popped open to find his wide as he peered over my shoulder.

"Uh . . . Kris?"

"What?" I turned my head to follow his gaze.

The table behind me was levitating off the ground. The books that had been scattered across it floated separately from the table, and swirled in a slow circle.

"Oh, no." I closed my eyes to pull my focus in. "This happens when . . ."

Nathan laughed, and I opened one eye to glare at him. He threw a hand up in surrender.

"Sorry, but . . ." He waved his hand at the blaring distraction behind me. "*That* is funny."

"Not the time," I muttered. Both eyes closed, I ground my teeth as I tried to concentrate on lowering the table to the floor with my mind. But trying to focus on anything other than what was happening—or what had been happening—between Nathan and me was impossible.

I opened my eyes to find him smiling as he watched me. "Maybe I can just leave it in the air?"

His smile grew. "I got you that worked up, huh?"

I nodded. I had no shame. He was insanely hot. Who wouldn't

have gotten a little . . . excited?

Nathan's smile dropped in response to the look on my face, his eyes hooded, and we were instantly back to where we had left off before the world's strangest mood ruining event happened—*almost* mood ruining event. But then, there were other ways to ruin it, and we found that out a moment later when there was a loud knock at the door.

Nathan nearly knocked me over as he scrambled to pick my gown up off the floor where it laid behind me because, well . . . there weren't locks on these doors. He handed it to me quickly before he stood, prepared to block me from the view of anyone who dared enter without permission.

Whoever it was didn't bust in, but was still on my shit list.

Another knock followed while Nathan scooped his shirt off the floor. He slipped it on as he walked to the door. He paused to make sure I was fully dressed before he swung it open.

Bruce lifted his hands up apologetically, and I could only imagine the look on Nathan's face that prompted his reaction. "I'm sorry," he gushed. His gaze swung to me, and he added, "Really sorry, but Jared needs you."

"Now?" Nathan growled.

"It's Lillian," Bruce muttered. "Something happened. He doesn't know what to do. And . . ."

"And what?"

Bruce glanced at me ruefully before answering Nathan. "She's asking for you."

~   ~   ~

I insisted on going along for two reasons. One, I didn't want to be alone. And two, I suspected that Lillian was up to something. How convenient was it for her to have a meltdown *now* of all times, when she knew Nathan and I were alone?

"She's muttering gibberish," Bruce explained along the way. "But I heard her tell Jared that she remembers everything."

"Everything?" I questioned with more than a trace of doubt.

Nathan shot me a look that equated to, *Be nice*, while Bruce shrugged. He hadn't mastered the ability to read me between the lines, not like Nathan had.

"From the way she was freaking out and crying," Bruce continued, "I think she really has."

We reached the guest room, and Bruce pushed the door open ahead of us. I entered last, and hovered near the door while Nathan approached the bed in the far right corner, where Jared was hunched down on his knees in front of a sobbing Lillian. Hera stood to the side, and turned as Nathan approached.

"I'm terribly sorry," she offered. "I wasn't aware that she had been suffering from amnesia."

"What happened?" Nathan asked her.

"The bath she took in the spring of clarity. It opened her mind to the truth far too suddenly for her to cope with. If I had known she was suppressing memories, I wouldn't have . . ."

"It's okay, Hera," Nathan muttered as he passed her, and stooped down beside Jared. His voice dropped, and I couldn't hear what he was saying from where I stood.

Not that I really cared to listen to him soothe Lillian. Hearing her cries, I couldn't help but feel bad for her. I couldn't imagine what it must have been like to remember seven years' worth of repressed memories at once. Especially when those memories weren't pleasant ones.

Though I only experienced the evil side of Lillian for a few months, it had been enough. She had done some terrible things to us, and I assumed the bulk of her time as a Skotadi had been spent doing similarly horrible acts to others. Including thousands of innocent humans.

Hera paused to wish me a peaceful night before she exited. I didn't have the heart to tell her that my night was pretty much ruined now, and smiled graciously before she slipped out the door behind me.

Alec stood from his bed on the other side of the room, and sauntered to my side. "So what do you think?"

"About?"

His response was interrupted by a loud growling noise. I spun toward the source in time to see Nathan grab a hold of Lillian as she attempted to launch herself off the bed. Her angry eyes were fixed on me.

"It was all because of you," she snarled. "Circe targeted me because of you! She used me so she could get to you!"

Eyes narrowed, I took a step toward her as she turned some of her rage on Nathan.

"And you," she continued. "Because you had to interfere in her life!"

"Lillian, calm down." Nathan forced her back onto the bed, and her eyes swung toward me again.

"I lost everything because of you," she rasped. "The things I have done . . . were all because of you!"

"Lillian," Nathan growled, drawing her attention from me to

him. "None of it was her fault. She's just as much a victim as you were."

Lillian's harsh laugh reminded me of . . . well, evil-Lillian. "A victim?" Tears rimmed her eyes when they leveled on Nathan. "How can you say that? I have lost *everything* because of her!"

I suspected Nathan was included in her definition of *everything*. And that did it. I snapped. I didn't miss the warning shake of Nathan's head. No, I saw it. And I chose to ignore it.

"You lost everything because of *me*?" I returned. "How about the fact that I never had anything? Except for him." I kept my eyes leveled on Lillian as I jabbed a finger in Nathan's direction. "But you didn't like that, did you? Even though I was only a kid at the time!"

Nathan stood to take a step toward me. "Kris, easy . . ."

"No!" I fired at him as I advanced on Lillian. "How dare you blame me—"

"I am blaming you!"

She shot to her feet. Jared wrapped his arms around her waist to keep her from rushing me. At the same time, Nathan moved to block me from doing the same. I had never been in a girl fight before. Never had the need or the desire . . . until now.

Nathan's arms encircled my shoulders. "Kris, you need to calm down," he whispered urgently into my ear.

"*I* need to calm down?" I shouted. "What about her? She's the one throwing around accusations."

"I know," he said gently. "But she's not the one I'm worried about right now."

Worried about? I narrowed my eyes at him. "Worried about me, or about what I might do?"

I answered my own question before Nathan could respond.

Over his shoulder, a stack of books flew off the shelves. One of the big ones smacked Jared in the back, and I grimaced because it looked like it hurt.

I closed my eyes in an attempt to pull myself together before I injured someone. I heard a thud, followed by a string of curses, and knew I wasn't doing a good job of controlling myself. Probably because I could still hear Lillian shouting at me. I didn't even know what she was saying anymore, because she was screaming like a lunatic.

Two hands came down on my shoulders, and pulled me back.

"I got her," I heard Alec say.

My eyes snapped open as I was hauled out the door, just in time to see Nathan turn away. He ventured farther into the room . . . toward Lillian.

Alec shut the door behind him as I yelled in protest, and he spun to me quickly. "You're letting your evil twin have too much control right now."

"Tell me something I don't already know."

"Do I need to kiss you to tame her down?" he asked. Though his eyes twinkled mischievously, I didn't doubt he was serious. "Whatever you need, I'm here. I'll take one for the team."

I snorted as a laugh erupted out of me. Already, I felt myself calming down.

"See? I'm so good I don't even have to kiss you." Alec placed a hand on my shoulder as he stooped to look me in the eyes. "Not even surging. I—" He broke off as his gaze dropped to his hand. His eyes trailed lower as he took me in. All of me. "What are you wearing?"

I groaned as I shifted my feet. With all the excitement, I had forgotten to change . . . and the gown wasn't exactly wearing-in-public acceptable.

"Don't get me wrong," he gushed. "You look hot as hell . . . kind of like a virgin goddess on her wedding night."

My eyebrows shot up on their own accord. I bit my tongue, but something about the look on my face must have told Alec that he wasn't that far off base.

His hand slid from my shoulder, and dropped to his side. "Oh. Yeah . . . I don't need to know that." He lowered his head with a grimace, and for a moment, I felt a twinge of guilt. Until I saw the hint of a smile on his face. "Man, I *really* wouldn't want to be Nathan right now."

The door swung open half way through Alec's statement, and Nathan stepped into the hallway. "What now?"

"Nothing," Alec and I both answered in unison. Alec glanced at me, and I snorted.

Nathan clearly didn't find it as amusing as we did. He looked at me. "You better?"

"Yep."

He frowned at my clipped tone. "I know you're mad at me, but I just didn't want you to aggravate the situation."

"What about her?" I thrust my chin at the door.

"Jared's working on calming her down."

"Huh. I thought she needed you for that?" His hesitation served as his answer. "You're going back in," I concluded.

His eyes met mine pleadingly. "I don't know what else to do. She's in bad shape."

"Didn't you hear what she said earlier?" I snapped. "She's not upset about the things she has done. She's only upset about losing . . .

everything. Her words. You think I don't know that everything means *you*?"

Nathan shook his head as he approached me. I took a step back, avoiding his touch.

"She's only here for you," I added.

"She's here to help," he countered.

"You really believe that?"

He didn't answer, but his eyes pleaded with me to understand.

I didn't. I couldn't. I knew she was up to something, regardless of her claim that she wanted to help. I wasn't stupid. I had been in high school long enough to know how girls worked.

"I'm going to the room," I muttered. "Alone."

My tone left no room for argument, and neither of them stopped me as I walked away.

Back in Hecate's room, I paced the floor for several minutes as I struggled to rein in my frustration. Objects moved with me as I fumed. When I thought I was calm enough, and I had things placed where they belonged, I crawled into bed. I stared restlessly at the ceiling for a long time before an idea slammed into me.

I bolted across the room to retrieve my backpack. Digging through the contents, I withdrew the rosemary leaf. I placed the herb under my pillow, and chanted the necessary words as I read them from the journal.

Nervous excitement kept me awake for a while before I eventually dropped off into a light, restless slumber. Sometime later, the bed shifted as someone slipped under the sheets behind me. A familiar arm wrapped around my middle, and pulled my back flush against a sturdy chest. I smiled into my pillow and, as his steady breath stirred the hair at my neck, I finally found a peaceful sleep.

~ ~ ~

The white Honda Civic pulls up as I step onto the curb. The passenger window rolls down, and Callie leans across the seat with a beaming smile.

"I got it," she declares proudly. "Get in!"

Oddly enough, I remember this. I am not dreaming so much as I am reliving something that already happened—the day Callie's older brother passed the family car on to her. I wonder if Callie is with me, sharing this dream with me from her hospital bed on the Kala island. Looking at her now, she seems oblivious of her current state.

Perhaps that is for the best. Though I had hoped to check up on her, and that is hard to do when she doesn't know what is happening.

As I did on that day, I climb into the passenger seat, bursting with excitement. The freedom is nice. The escape is nice. It had been that day, but it is even more so now.

As usual, we end up at the mall. I oblige Callie by purchasing a new outfit for the upcoming party this weekend. I want to tell her that the party will end up a bust—the drinks will be too strong, the cops will show up, and Callie will spend the majority of Saturday morning swearing off alcohol from my bathroom floor.

I don't tell her any of that, because she has no idea that we are sharing a dream and reliving a memory. She has no knowledge of where she is right now, what is happening to her body, or that her fate rests in my hands. I decide to keep her protected from that, so I happily relive that day.

Some things jumble together, and what had been an entire afternoon spent in the mall passes by in a matter of minutes. I suppose that is because I had never been a fan of shopping—not like Callie. Time slows down again as we cross the parking lot to the Civic, and that is when I notice him.

I hadn't noticed him that day, but now I cannot miss him. I wonder if his appearance is a byproduct of the dream . . . or if he had really been there that day.

Callie lets out a quiet appreciative whistle. "I would call dibs, but his eyes are all over you, Kris."

Nathan's lips curve into a grin as he pushes away from the familiar black Jeep. His stride is long and purposeful as he approaches us.

"That is the walk of a man who knows what he's doing." Callie grips my arm fiercely. "This is all you, girl. Don't screw it up, or I'm going to have to hurt you."

"I'm not . . ." I start, then stop once Nathan reaches us.

Does he know what this is? The look on his face tells me he does.

"Looks like you brought me with you," he says.

CHAPTER 4

A loud rap on the door startled me awake. Deep inside of a mountain, without windows, I could only assume that the knock indicated morning. Except I sure didn't feel well-rested. While seeing Callie happy and healthy had been awesome, the whole experience of dream-walking had left me feeling hung-over.

I grudgingly shifted to slide out of bed, but the arm wrapped around my waist tightened and held me in place.

"Not yet." A night of not enough sleep had turned Nathan's voice into the gruffest, sexiest sound I had ever heard that close to my ear.

Goosebumps danced across the back of my neck, effectively waking me completely.

I shifted just enough to roll my head over my shoulder. Nathan peered back at me with one eye. His arm tightened to pull me snugly into his chest as he grumbled, "They'll come back for us."

"And if they don't?"

His lips curled into a grin that suggested he wouldn't mind. He inched forward to brush them against mine in a soft and fleeting kiss. Enough to remind me of what we had been doing in this room just a few hours ago. Despite his firm grip, I managed to wiggle around so that I could face him.

"Stay still." Though his eyes were shut, the tease of a smile on his lips suggested that he was just as awake as I was. I planted a kiss to his scruffy chin, and was rewarded with a dimple. "You're really not going to go back to sleep, are you?" he grumbled.

"Nope. But I'm not getting out of this bed either."

Just in case he didn't already know my intentions, I gave his shoulder a shove, forcing him onto his back, as I propped myself on an elbow above him. As I moved in to kiss him, he did the next best thing. His arm snaked around my waist, and he pulled me on top of him so that my body was flush against his. His hands fisted into my hair as he drew my mouth to his. The kiss came with no preliminary warm ups. Oh, no. His kiss was hard, and full of demands and wants from the start.

And I was more than happy to give what he obviously wanted. My soft body wedged against his much more solid one, and we were wrapped up in the sheets like our very own unique Kris-and-Nathan burrito. As much as I enjoyed it, I had one complaint. I couldn't touch him.

I shifted until I was straddling his legs, and pushed myself up far enough to run my hands across his firm shoulders and chest. His grip on the back of my head wouldn't allow me to go any farther, but I managed to run an exploring hand across his rippled abdomen until I met the waistband of his boxers.

"Dammit, Kris," Nathan growled.

In one fluid motion, he flipped me onto my back. He rose above me, and trailed a line of kisses along my jaw as my hands gripped his shoulders tightly.

"They're going to come back," he murmured into my ear. Despite his warning, he gave no indication of stopping.

He was right. I knew we didn't have much time . . . not for what we both wanted to do. But that didn't mean I wanted to stop kissing him now. Especially when we hadn't had much time to be alone lately, and we likely wouldn't again for the unforeseeable future.

Reconnecting with Nathan was what I needed to face that future with confidence. It reminded me of why I needed to fight, and that I had something worth fighting for. That was exactly what he did for me now . . . especially after the disaster last night.

But we did have a mission to get to today, and someone reminded us of that with another series of knocks at the door. Louder than the last.

Nathan sighed as he dropped his forehead to mine. His eyes squeezed together tightly.

"Back to the real world," I whispered ruefully.

"I'm afraid so." His voice was deep and gruff, signaling his own remorse.

I traced my fingertips down the side of his face, forcing his eyes to flutter open. "It's nice to escape with you every now and again."

"Speaking of escape . . ." He shifted to reach a hand under my pillow. He withdrew the rosemary leaf, and shot me a curious look.

"I wanted to pull Callie into a dream," I shrugged.

And I had . . . sort of. Except it had been more of a memory, and she had no recollection of the current events. Maybe I hadn't done it right?

"How did I get there?" Nathan pondered.

"Because you're the man of my dreams, of course," I answered with a hint of sarcasm. While true, I wasn't corny enough to mutter that cliché without laughing.

"Smartass," Nathan muttered before kissing me again.

"You love it," I returned between kisses.

A few seconds later, another knock at the door broke us apart. I groaned my frustration as Nathan planted a fleeting kiss to my lips.

He stilled, and his eyes held mine intently. "*Soon.*"

The meaning behind that one word was evident, and sent the butterflies already in my stomach soaring. As Nathan and I finally parted to prepare for the long day ahead, I held on to his promise.

Soon. But not soon enough.

~ ~ ~

Our first stop upon returning to Litochoro was a cheap clothing store. Though they had both initially balked at the suggestion of wearing anything other than their robes, Isatan and Permna eventually understood the need to blend in. Not that the clothes necessarily helped them much.

I stifled a smile at the horror on their faces as they observed a teenage boy dressed in baggy jeans and a hoop in his nose dart past us on a skateboard. I suspected that they hadn't gotten out much lately and were not comfortable outside the walls of the mountain. Though Isatan was a born and skilled leader, he graciously took on a secondary role when it came to dealing with the humans we encountered.

With the rest of us, he was still his bossy self.

After shopping, we stopped at a small cafeteria-style restaurant on the coast for a late lunch. By the time Bruce, Lillian, and I collected the large order of food, the rest of our group were all engrossed in deep conversation at a table in the corner. Isatan's finger was pointed at a spot on the large map spread out in front of them.

"We've pinpointed four of the demigods here," he explained.

"Hades' demigods will be found somewhere near the Diros Caves, but we haven't determined an exact location on them yet."

"Diros Caves?" Alec questioned. "The entrance to the underworld, right?"

"One of the entrances," Isatan returned with a dismissive wave of his hand because, apparently, that wasn't important right now. Only the spot on the map covered by his finger was.

Alec hooked an eyebrow at me, and I barely restrained erupting in laughter. Isatan was an ass . . . but he was an ass to everyone. It wasn't just me.

"So where are we going now?" I asked as I slid into the bench seat next to Nathan.

"Corinth," he said to me as he claimed one of the sandwiches from my tray.

"In relation to Athens?" Considering that was the only Greek city I was familiar with, I used it as a starting point for all of our adventures.

"About an hour west of Athens."

Nathan gave my knee a gentle squeeze under the table before he ripped into his sandwich. Over his shoulder, I caught Isatan's impatient glare leveled on me. I chose to ignore him, in favor of my lunch.

"What about this help you mentioned getting?" Isatan barked as he swung his attention to Jared, who sat on the other side of him.

Jared glanced at Nathan. "I suppose we could gather up some Kala from the Australian base."

Nathan nodded. "No supervisors. Don't know who we can trust."

"Most of the members of the rogue army in allegiance with Circe should have left their bases by now," Permna volunteered. "We don't know where they are hiding since I can't use my powers, but I doubt you will encounter any traitors in your midst now."

"I could go to Australia and get some volunteers," Jared offered. "If Circe is going to be under the binding spell, it shouldn't take all of us to get the compound. We could split up to save some time."

"Isatan and Permna need to get us there," Nathan said. "Kris needs to do the bind. I'm going wherever she goes."

"Me too," Alec added around a bite of food in his mouth.

"I'll go with Jared," Bruce volunteered. "The rest of you can go on to Aeaea."

"Thank you." Jared said the words with emphasis as he glared at the others. Though it didn't look all that scary with his lips relaxed one step below a grin. He turned the map around to study it more closely. His finger skimmed over a spot not far from the spot on the map Isatan had indicated, and he looked up at Nathan. "Didn't the Kala used to have a safe house around here?"

Nathan chewed on his sandwich as he studied the map quietly for a moment. "I think so. But wasn't it abandoned after World War Two?"

"Abandoned, yes. But it should still be there."

"If it didn't crumble, or it wasn't demolished."

"We need a rendezvous point," Jared returned with a shrug, "and it is close to where the demigods are hiding."

After everyone agreed to Jared's suggestion, another thirty minutes were spent going over details as we finished our meals. It was decided that Jared and Bruce would go to Australia to gather soldiers while the rest of us went to Aeaea. Nathan and Jared pinpointed the location of the safe house, and plans were made for us all to meet there in a few days.

Jared and Bruce were dropped off at the bus station, where they would board the next bus to Athens, and the airport. Then the rest of us filed into our large rental vehicle for the long trip to Aeaea.

Along the way, Isatan and Permna gave us all a crash course in Greek history. I learned that Aeaea wasn't a real place . . . at least not in the human world.

In the human world, it was a mythical, magical place located near Cape Circeo, on the western coast of Italy. We spent the remainder of the day driving to the western coast of Greece, before stopping for the night. In the morning, we took a five-hour ferry ride to Italy, then continued the remaining five hours in the car to the tiny coastal village an hour south of Rome.

The isolated narrow strip of sand on the shore was deserted by the time we arrived at dusk. Half a mile from where we parked, the beach ended abruptly at a large rock formation that jutted out into the sea. According to Isatan, that was where the entrance to Aeaea would be found.

Nathan retrieved my backpack from the vehicle. "You should probably do the binding spell now," he suggested. "Before we get any closer."

I took the bag and sat in the front passenger seat as I removed the materials that I would need. I rolled the paper out on the dashboard, dipped the pen into the Black Nightshade Ink, and began to copy the spell down as I referenced the opened notebook in my lap. As I was writing Circe's name in the proper location, I heard a wrap on the window.

Lillian peered in at me as I rolled it down. "Do you need any help with it?"

My eyebrows shot up. "Seriously?"

She looked down at her feet with a sigh. "I'm sorry about the other night. I just . . ." She looked up with a defeated shrug. "A lot of hard memories hit me, and I thought I needed someone to blame. But I was wrong in blaming you. You were right. You were only a kid when this all started."

Despite the fact that she was apologizing, I didn't miss the slight undertone in her words. As if she were highlighting the fact that I was only a kid. Like she still considered me a kid.

And what right did some *kid* have to take away the most important person she had lost during her ordeal?

I acknowledged her backhanded apology with a nod before I returned my attention to the spell. Lillian hovered by the door as I finished and rolled the paper up.

I shot her a reluctant glance. "How specific does the nail placement have to be?"

"Through the center," she instructed. "As long as it pierces her name, it will work."

I followed her directions, and placed the nail precisely through the center of the scroll. After confirming that it was done correctly, we moved to the back of the vehicle where the others were waiting. From there, we walked down to the beach and dug a deep hole, into which I placed the scroll. I had to be the one to cover it up. Once finished, I stood to wipe the sand from my hands.

"Is that it?" I asked no one in particular.

"That should do it," Permna responded.

The walk to the rock formation took only minutes, but felt like an eternity thanks to the smothering silence that accompanied us. I knew I wasn't the only one nervously anticipating what came next.

This was the first real test of my abilities, and I really hoped I hadn't screwed it up.

The rocks were slick from moisture, which only worsened as we moved toward the point that jutted into the sea. The surf crashed into the rocks beneath our feet, creating a water spray that had dampened my hair and clothes by the time we rounded the corner. As we climbed across the rocks on the other side, I saw our destination.

Hidden between two boulders was the narrow entrance to a cave. Water lapped at the opening, and a few of the larger swells pushed water through.

"What about the tide?" I questioned.

I certainly didn't want to get trapped inside a cave as it filled with water. That would scare most people, but considering my intense fear of water, the thought nearly paralyzed me.

"It's waning right now," Permna told me. "We have about a two-hour window."

"And if we're not out in two hours?"

She glanced at me, but didn't respond.

"So we drown," I muttered her unspoken answer under my breath.

Night had crept up on us during the climb, and the faint glow from the moon spread only a few feet inside the entrance. Three flashlights clicked on simultaneously, allowing us to see the tunnel ahead and the trickle of water that seeped out of the walls and ran under our feet.

I had never been one to fear enclosed spaces before. Until now. I had never been in an enclosed space that could fill up with water before either.

Nathan's hand found mine, and he kept me close as we followed Isatan and Permna through the dark cavern. An eternity passed, and my breathing grew more labored with each step, before the first glimpse of light appeared in front of us.

"Circe would have placed wards to keep trespassers from entering her realm," Permna explained as she slowed at the opening. "The bind should have weakened them as well."

I held my breath, waiting to see if my magic had worked, as Permna stepped through the opening. She appeared on the other side of an invisible wall. Though she looked blurry to my eyes, she was unscathed, and ushered us through with a wave of her hand.

I felt a weak hum from the wards, and the zap of a faint electrical current, as I stepped across into Circe's realm of Aeaea.

Though night had fallen on this part of the world, the sky in Aeaea was lit in an unnatural orange glow as if permanently frozen in an impressive and vivid sunset. The oddly colored sky was curved, and I had the impression that we were tiny figurines placed inside of a snow globe—without the snow. There were no clouds, no moon, no sun . . . just orange, and a small cottage that sat atop a small island surrounded by marsh.

"Looks like we have to walk through the marsh?" Nathan's voice lifted as if questioning what he was seeing. I suspected we all were as confused—and amazed—as he was.

"She normally would have the marsh patrolled by her creatures," Permna stated, "but the bind should have rendered them powerless as well."

I exchanged a wary glance with Alec. "I better not get eaten by some sea creature, Kris," he muttered in my ear before he took a gigantic leap of faith . . . straight into the murky knee high water.

Sandwiched between Alec and Nathan, I pushed through the shoulder-high grass and clumps of floating algae. Our steps were slow and cautious, as if we all anticipated a sudden bite from a toothy, flesh-craving monster.

As we approached the other side without being eaten, my eyes settled on the cottage with trepidation. Getting through this marsh was one thing, but I feared what may await us inside.

Had the bind really worked, or were we walking into a trap? What about the two demigods who remained unaccounted for? Had they been hiding with Circe all along, and now waiting to ambush us?

All around me, weapons were drawn. I channeled the magic I had restrained, letting it slip a little closer to the surface. Just in case. Isatan entered the cottage first. The rest of us, all rigid with expectation, followed. But nothing ominous or dangerous waited for us inside.

The cottage looked like a cross between a charming vacation rental and a witch's lair. Tables covered with herbs, candles, and potions sat along one wall, which held more books than some small libraries. Between the tables were several comfortable-looking chairs that promised a relaxed read followed by an even better nap. Across the open room sat a small, neat bed adorned in black scarves and trinkets that I knew held magical properties. Beyond that was a kitchenette, and a small adjoining room.

Alec ventured through the open door first, and his eyes swept from the floor to the ceiling as he took in the mountain of organized potions and powders that lined the walls inside.

"If that compound is here, it's going to be in this room," he declared.

Isatan and Permna moved to join him. The room was too small

to accommodate all of us, so I turned to study the tables behind me, and the array of magical ingredients that covered them.

She had almost as much as Hecate had in her chambers. The things she could conjure here . . .

"See anything?" Nathan asked as he came up behind me.

"I don't know what I'm looking for."

"Me neither," he admitted wryly. One arm wrapped around me from behind as he pressed his lips to the top of my head. "Just look for a powder."

Though most of the containers I saw contained fluids, I also saw several that could qualify as a powder. Finding the exact one we were looking for would be impossible.

"It will be shiny red. Hard to miss." Lillian glided up alongside us, and Nathan's arm around me slipped away. Though he gave me a small squeeze first, I didn't overlook the distance he placed between us at her sudden appearance.

I told myself he did so only to not rub our relationship in her face . . . as I tried not to do around Alec. Regardless, I resented her a little bit for it.

"How do you know that?" I questioned her.

"The ingredients include diamond and centaur blood," she responded coolly, as if I should know that that combination would produce a shiny red powder.

And if I were a practiced Incantator, I probably would have known that.

"Like this?" Nathan lifted a container off of one of the tables and turned to us with it.

The powder inside it was a bright, perfect red, enhanced by tiny sparkles that reflected the candlelight. I instinctively reached for it, but he snatched it away before I could touch it.

"Don't even think about it," he said to me before turning toward the small room, where the others were still looking.

"He's very protective of you," Lillian muttered. "But then, he always has been."

Again, I picked up on her condescending tone. To her, I doubted I would ever be more than the little girl Nathan had taken upon himself to protect.

"Things change," I reminded her before walking away.

As I approached the room where the others gathered to look at the powder, I heard Isatan's deep voice.

"This looks like it."

"The only way to know for sure is to have one of us touch it," Permna added.

Nathan shook his head at me as I stepped into their circle. Before I could say anything—or volunteer—Permna took the powder out of Nathan's hands.

"Wipe it off right away," she said to no one in particular, and then she stuck her hand into the container.

The moment her fingers touched the powder inside, her knees wobbled. Isatan moved to break her fall, and tossed the container to Nathan. His eyes shot to mine with an order.

"Get a towel! Quickly!"

I hurried to the kitchenette and started opening cabinet doors in a frenzy. The first few I came to contained jars of things that didn't belong in a kitchen, but I didn't slow down to register what they were. Finally, in a drawer near the sink, I found a stack of towels. As I turned with one, I spotted a figure standing outside, behind the cottage, through the window.

"Where's that towel?" Isatan barked.

I rushed back to the room, and handed the towel to Isatan. He immediately wiped the substance from Permna's hand, and helped her into a sitting position. Her lips were parted, her eyes glazed, as she stared past me, at nothing.

"How long does it take to wear off?" Alec questioned.

"A few minutes," Isatan responded tersely.

I backed away from them, and bumped into Lillian as she stepped closer. I slid past her quietly, and no one noticed as I moved toward the back of the cottage, and opened the door I found there.

The woman I had seen was still standing in the same spot. Her back was to me, permitting me a view of her long black waves as they flitted in the light breeze. She wore a multi-layered dark gown, but the thin material left little to the imagination.

I maintained a safe radius as I came up beside her, and her porcelain face came into view. Her head and body remained frozen in place, but her eyes shifted to take me in and her lips curled into a sly smile.

"I'm pleased to know you have reached your potential," she said to me.

"Circe?" I rasped.

She nodded once. "As your dear sister, I'm deeply wounded by your bind."

"I'm sure you know why I found it necessary to do."

Her eyes penetrated mine with such an intensity, I was forced to look away. After a long moment, I glanced back to find her still staring at me.

"You confound me," she finally said. "Apparently, you have too much of our mother in you."

She said it as if that were a bad thing. To her, I supposed it was.

"Why are you doing this? What are you trying to achieve?"

The insincerity of her cold laugh sent a shiver down my spine. "I want it all, sister."

"All of what?"

"I'm tired of being known as the lesser goddess of magic," she explained. "I thought it would get better after I lured our mother into Hades' waiting arms, but it didn't. I gained nothing from it. Everyone pined for Hecate, and I got nothing."

I ground my teeth at her confession that she had been responsible for my mother being held captive by Hades. I couldn't let that revelation rattle me. I needed information first. Revenge could wait.

"You want power? Is that what you want?"

Circe smirked as her gaze drifted over my head, as if she were looking into her future—the future she desired. "Once my immortal army helps me to destroy the gods, and I arise into the role I deserve, I will have it all."

I scoffed, and her eyes hardened as they shifted to mine. "There's one problem with your plan," I told her. "You need me to help you get there."

"Yes. Unfortunately, you are more powerful than I. For now."

I didn't ask for her to elaborate. I knew that once Circe got what she wanted, she would get rid of me. With Hecate and me out of the picture, Circe would then be the most powerful manipulator of magic. That was exactly what she wanted.

"I'm not going to help you," I told her.

Circe's eyes lifted to the sky. "Yes. Well, I have a theory as to why you have managed to resist your evil influence thus far."

Sensing that we were no longer alone, I glanced over my shoulder to find Nathan and Alec in the doorway, watching us cautiously. I put a hand out to let them know I was okay, and stop them from coming any closer.

"I had no idea love between two evil souls could have the impact it has had. Of course, there are ways to fix that," Circe continued in a threatening voice.

I took a few steps toward her, and lowered my voice with a threat of my own. "I will destroy you before I ever let you hurt him."

"You can't destroy me, and you can't bind me forever." Circe laughed humorlessly. "No. Once he is gone, you will finally join me."

The breath I hadn't realized I was holding hissed as it slipped between my clenched teeth. Lillian had been right—Alec and I had a connection that kept us from succumbing to the evil within us. Worse, Alec's theory that Circe would set out to be rid of him as a result of that connection was right.

I dropped my chin to pin Circe with a hard glare. "You'll have to go through me first."

I turned and walked away without waiting for a response. Her icy laugh followed me to the door.

"You were right," I told Alec. "We're helping each other somehow, and she's going to come for you." I turned to Nathan. "We need to destroy these demigods *now*."

Nathan nodded as he cast an uneasy glance at Circe. "Permna just came to. She confirmed it's the right compound. We're ready to get out of here."

"Can't be soon enough," Alec muttered. "I hate looking like the victim of a cheap fake tan gone wrong."

Despite the sobering conversation I'd just had with Circe, Alec managed to force a laugh out of me as I entered the cottage ahead of him and Nathan. The faint smile on my lips fell as I came face to face with Isatan's taunting smirk.

"Family reunion?" he leered.

"Knock it off, Isatan," Permna reprimanded. "She's with us."

He turned away without another word, but I didn't miss the skeptical curve of his eyebrows.

"What's his problem with me?" I whispered to Nathan.

He slung an arm across my shoulders, and gave them a squeeze as we moved toward the front door. "He doesn't know your heart like I do," he murmured in my ear. "Don't let him rattle you."

"I'm trying," I muttered. But that was hard to do when he looked at me with visible disgust on a daily basis. I sure wouldn't trust him to have my back in any situation . . . yet we were supposed to be allies up against nine demigods.

Being rid of Isatan served as further motivation to destroy these demigods, and move on with my life. The simple life . . . free of evil, curses, death, and leering assholes.

"We have less than an hour before the tide turns," Permna reminded us all of our limited time.

A knot twisted in my gut as I recalled how long it had taken us to pass through the cavern to get here. Would we make it back in time, before the incoming tide filled it with water?

Nathan must have seen the concern on my face, because he offered me a comforting smile. "We'll get through in time," he assured me before he opened the door and stepped outside.

From directly behind him, I had an up-close view of the shiny blades that spiraled through the air toward us . . . and the two demigods who had thrown them.

I shot my hands out in front of me, stopping the first blade in midair, mere inches from Nathan's chest. The second blade kept coming, and I split my concentration between the two, managing to hold the first blade in place while I slowed the second one enough that it fell to the ground at Nathan's feet.

With another wave of my hand, I spun the blade suspended in the air around, and fired it back at the demigod who had thrown it. Someone shouted a warning behind me, and Isatan and Permna flew out the door, their own weapons drawn. They clashed with the second demigod as the first fell from the blade that had pierced his heart.

Nathan shoved me against the side of the cottage as diamond-coated metals clashed around us. From under his arm, I watched Isatan and Permna push the demigod to the edge of the marsh. There, the water rose up behind him until it towered over them like a small tsunami.

"Asleon," Lillian announced from the doorway.

Poseidon's son, the water manipulator.

"Nathan," I grunted as I tried to push past him. "They need my help."

His arm tightened, prevented me from getting any closer. As the wall of water spilled over top of Asleon and rushed toward Isatan and Permna, I let my magic slip free, and pushed against it. I couldn't stop the wave, but I did slow it down. Just enough to cause Asleon to dart a look in my direction.

That was the opening Isatan needed. He thrust his knife into Asleon a second before the wall of water washed over them. When the water receded into the marsh, only Isatan and Permna were left.

They were soaked and shaken, but alive. As Isatan rose to a

stand, he met my gaze, and for the first time since we had met, he didn't scowl. I supposed that was the limit of his appreciation of my help. Not much, but I would take it.

Besides . . . we had just taken out two demigods.

My triumphant smile faded the moment I turned and saw the ashen look on Nathan's face.

"What's wrong?" I asked him.

His hands rose to cup my face fiercely. "I love you," he gasped.

My brow wrinkled in confusion when he fell to my feet. His face buried in the dirt as he groaned and fisted the short blades of grass in agony. I dropped to a knee beside him in stunned confusion as he rolled onto his side. Only then did I see the tear in the leg of his pants, and the blood that oozed from a gash near his knee.

A gash made by a diamond-coated blade.

CHAPTER 5

The only sound I heard was that of the blood rushing to my head. Though everyone's lips were moving, I heard nothing as I stared in horror at the wound on Nathan's leg. I swayed slightly when Lillian dropped to her knees beside me, bumping me with her shoulder.

Finally, the sound of tearing fabric snapped me out of my daze. I fixated on Lillian's hands as she took a knife to Nathan's pants, fully exposing the wound in his leg. My eyes shifted to observe the signs of diamond poisoning that had already started to spread.

"Kris!" I looked up when Alec dropped to his knees across from me. "Focus, Kris!"

I shook my head to clear the lingering fog, and lifted my trembling hands to my neck. Despite the numbing fear that crippled me, I managed to remove the pendant Micah had left me from its chain. I dumped the powder into my hands, and tried not to think about the one and only time I had attempted to heal diamond injury . . . and failed.

Failure wasn't an option this time.

"What are you doing?" Lillian shrieked when I covered the wound with my hands.

Alec reached across Nathan to put a hand on Lillian's shoulder. "She's healing him," he told her. "Let her concentrate."

I squeezed my eyes shut to channel every ounce of energy I had left. I already felt weak from using my magic in the fight. Lillian's inconsolable sobs certainly didn't help my concentration.

I glanced up to find Permna hovering behind Alec. "Could you take her inside?" I pleaded.

Lillian started to protest as Permna took her by the arm. I blocked her, and Alec's reassurances to her, out as I lowered my head to concentrate. Once her terrified wails were silenced, I glanced up to meet Alec's eyes with a silent request.

His hand covered mine. "I'm here."

I closed my eyes with a nod, and channeled my powers. The sensation of free-falling through a pocket of hot air startled me at first, and I nearly pulled back, before I realized it indicated the energy I was pushing out. The heat encompassed the cold energy surrounding the wound, and I chanted the necessary words under my breath over and over while I focused on drawing the cold out. I found myself swaying from the dizzying effect it had on me, but I soon found my rhythm and I didn't stop.

I would never stop.

"Kris . . ."

I continued to chant, faster and louder, sure that I wasn't doing it right. Determination kept me going. Tears streamed down my cheeks and dripped onto my hands, reminding me of how much was at stake, as I pushed against the wound.

"Kris . . ."

I interrupted my chant only long enough to mutter, "No," before resuming.

"Kris, you're about to pass out," Alec warned, and his hand tightened on mine. "Take a break."

"I can't."

"You can," Alec ordered. "You've stopped the spread. If you're going to reverse the poison that has already set, you need to take a break."

"What?" I opened my eyes to peer down at Nathan.

He had lost consciousness at some point. A streak of black diamond poisoning had spread to his thigh, but stopped there. It was no longer spreading.

I glanced up at Alec in astonishment.

"You did it," he said with a nod. "But you need to take a break now."

I started to shake my head—what if it starts to spread again?—but Alec shut me down with a stern look.

"I watched Micah heal you," he told me. "I saw it, Kris. I saw how much it took out of him, and I saw how long it took. You're not going to do it all at once. Trust me. We'll get Nathan inside, and I'll watch him. But I want you to rest before you do any more."

I swatted at the fresh tears in my eyes as I nodded. I had done it. Partially. Though I hated to stop while the poison was still in Nathan's system, I did trust Alec. I knew he wouldn't let anything happen to Nathan.

Isatan helped Alec move Nathan inside. Once they had him lying in the bed, Alec pointed at one of the cozy chairs behind me.

"Rest. Now. I'll get you up in an hour or two," he ordered, and then pinched my lips together when I started to object. "Sooner if anything changes. I promise. Now go."

I turned toward the chairs, and nearly ran into Lillian where she had been standing behind me. Tears rimmed her eyes as she stared at me.

"Can you really heal him?" she asked.

"I'll die trying," I answered as I moved past her.

I fell into the first chair I came to. I realized how exhausted I was once the adrenaline started to abate.

My gaze drifted across the room and settled upon the face of the man who had repeatedly saved me. I had never been one to pray, but as my eyelids dropped, I prayed that, this time, I could manage to save him.

~ ~ ~

Alec woke me to perform the ritual three more times over the next several hours before all signs of diamond poisoning were completely gone. Nathan hadn't woken up yet, but Alec reminded me that I had slept for two days after I had been healed . . . so we assumed that was normal.

Isatan agreed to keep an eye on Circe, and watch for any signs that the bind was weakening. Alec suggested that I squeeze into the bed with Nathan—but only so he could get some sleep in my chair. While Lillian and Permna had succumbed to fatigue hours ago, Alec hadn't rested once.

"Hey, Alec . . ." I called out to him quietly as he crossed the room to the empty chair. "Thank you."

He flashed me a lopsided grin. "See how far we've come? A few months ago, I would have never . . ." He trailed off as a look of awe crossed his face. "Just tell him I only did it for you, okay?"

"Just admit you don't hate him anymore."

"Never," he tossed over his shoulder before he lowered himself into the chair with a satisfied sigh.

A knowing smile teased my lips as I crawled into bed beside Nathan. I doubted he knew I was there, but I felt better as I rested my head against his shoulder and finally gave in to the call of sleep.

~ ~ ~

~ Nathan ~

There was a brief moment I thought I might have been paralyzed after my eyes snapped open. The soreness I felt in every fiber of my body assured me that I was not. My muscles protested loudly as I shifted, and stretched the life back into them.

My arm hit something soft, and I rolled my head to the side to find Kris curled up alongside me. The soft snore that accompanied her steady breaths told me that she was deep in sleep. Nights of holding her while she slept had programmed me to know that.

Just like I knew to expect the tiny little whimper she made when I brushed my lips against her forehead. She stirred, but didn't wake. She never did.

I carefully positioned her head on the pillow as I sat up, and climbed out of the bed. Looking down at her, I was tempted to crawl back in, if only to be next to her. But my body was too sore to stay still.

I needed to move, and Kris needed to rest. And there was nothing like a brush with death to induce a bad case of insomnia.

With the aid of the candles spread throughout the cottage and the faint glow of orange spilling through the windows, I saw the others sleeping soundly on the chairs scattered across the room. I saw everyone . . . but one.

As I moved to the back door, I wondered how long I had been

out, and how much time we had before the bind on Circe wore off. I opened the door, and nearly tripped over Lillian, who sat with her back against the outer wall of the cottage.

She glanced up, and immediately shot to her feet. "Oh, my God! You're okay!"

Her arms circled my neck in a blink. My own arms moved hesitantly to return her generous hug.

"What are you doing out here?" I asked as I pushed her to arm's length. I grit my teeth at the pang I felt in my chest at the sight of the downward curve of her mouth that my distance had caused.

I couldn't help it sometimes. Though I was very much in love with someone else, I still cared about Lillian . . . and her feelings. Even if they were very different, and much stronger, than my feelings for her.

"Umm . . ." She shook her head against whatever thoughts were filling her head. "We were taking turns watching Circe. I couldn't sleep, so I volunteered."

I glanced at Circe, where she remained in the exact same spot I had last seen her. "No change?"

"No. But we're running out of time. It's a good thing you're recovered."

"Kris needs more rest," I returned a tad too defensively, but Lillian didn't seem to notice.

"Yeah. What she did . . ." She trailed off as she searched for the right words to say. Finally, with a shrug, she gushed, "It was impressive."

Well, Kris was an impressive girl. But I didn't say anything like that to Lillian. Instead, I said, "I'm up. Why don't you go lie down, and I'll watch Circe for a while. When Kris wakes up, we'll head out."

"Sure." Lillian attempted to cover her disappointment with a weak smile. She turned for the door, but stopped with her hand on the knob. "Nathan?"

"Yeah?"

"I'm glad you're okay," she murmured. "And I'm glad she loves you as much as she does, because she wouldn't . . ." Lillian trailed off with a shake of her head. When her eyes lifted to mine again, I saw the unshed tears that lined them. "She would have never given up on you."

She opened the door, to really leave this time, and I found my mouth opening before I could stop it. "Hey, Lil . . ." I swallowed the emotion I felt at seeing the hope in her eyes when they lifted to mine, because hope wasn't something I could give her. "For what it's worth, I'm sorry."

"Me too," she muttered with a sad smile.

She shut the door behind her, and I took her seat on the ground. Though my eyes settled firmly on Circe, my thoughts wandered.

This hadn't been my first brush with death, and I doubted it would be my last. But it had definitely been the *closest* I had ever come. Even a few months ago, when I was sure I would die in the back seat of Alec's car after escaping the Skotadi base in Kentucky, I hadn't been as sure as I had been this time.

How had I not known that Kris was capable of healing diamond poisoning? The moment the blade had sliced through my skin, I knew I was done for. I would have been, if not for her.

I remembered waking after that last incident to find Kris resting against me, my blood all over her hands, and her relief when we both realized I would survive. That was the moment I had accepted the feelings I had developed for her . . . feelings I had tried, unsuccessfully, to deny up until that point. It was then that I knew my intended future would come true, whether I had wanted it to or not.

I often wondered if I would have welcomed my feelings for her a little sooner if not for that prophet's words to me months before. And Gran's pestering . . .

Gran had definitely been the worst of the two. She had planned my future with Kris long before the prophet predicted it. Nothing like a nagging grandmother to give a guy a severe case of commitment phobia.

I shifted to retrieve the ring Gran had given me from my pants' pocket. It had once been hers, given to her by my grandfather. She insisted on keeping it in the family. Of course, I was the only option she had to ensure her wish was seen through.

I returned the ring, where it would continue to burn a hole in my pocket, as it had been for weeks. Not that I didn't know I wanted to spend my future with Kris. I did, very much so—prophetic vision, or not. It was just . . .

"So huge," I muttered.

The soft click of the door opening jolted me from my thoughts, and I looked up to find Kris peering at me from the doorway. Her face carried a mixture of amazement and disbelief that I was sure matched the look on my own face. She dropped to her knees in front of me, and I brushed away the single tear that had settled on her cheek.

"Don't cry," I ordered softly.

"I thought I had lost you," she admitted before circling her slender arms around my neck.

I pulled her against my chest as I murmured, "You couldn't lose me if you tried."

That earned me a soft laugh as she released her death grip on my neck. I guided her into a position between my legs, with her back pulled flush against my chest. I rested my chin on her shoulder and savored the feel of her in my arms while I wondered how someone so delicate could have managed to do what she had done.

"You amaze me, you know?" I whispered into her ear. "I don't think I ever gave you enough credit."

She shifted to gaze over her shoulder at me. "You believed in me when I didn't believe in myself."

"I didn't know you could heal diamond injury," I returned wryly.

"That was something Micah worked with me on. You were my first . . . successful attempt."

Her tone suggested the story behind her learning the skill wasn't one she wanted to revisit, so I didn't press. Instead, I planted a soft kiss to her lips. "Thank you for saving me," I murmured, though the words didn't feel like enough.

I felt her lips curve into a smile beneath mine. "Totally selfish on my part," she mumbled.

Then her arm curled around my neck, and I deepened the kiss with a hearty groan. She welcomed me with an eagerness I had come to recognize. And it drove me crazy. Wild with need . . . for her.

While I had taken special care to tread carefully with our physical relationship, she made it increasingly more difficult to do so. Though I knew we had reached the point that the protective barrier I had put between us would soon be torn down, I knew it wasn't going to happen on the ground outside Circe's residence in Aeaea.

That didn't stop me from kissing her like I intended to never stop kissing her. Because, right now, the thought of stopping hadn't registered a single bleep on my radar.

Spurred by my obvious need for her, Kris twisted in my arms to climb onto my lap. She must not have remembered to breathe, because her mouth slid from mine as she sucked in a sharp breath. I chuckled lightly as I took the opportunity to nuzzle her neck. Her perfect, supple neck. And her perfect, soft jaw.

My hands entwined in her silky, beautiful hair . . .

Her hands trailed across my shoulders and over my erratic, racing heart . . .

As her hands moved lower, I briefly entertained the idea that knocking that barrier down right here, right now, might not be that terrible. But no. I had exercised control with Kris from day one. That wasn't going to change now, in a moment of weakness. No matter how weak I was. She deserved a fairytale. Nothing less.

A soft cackling in the distance served as the effective bucket of cold water I needed, and I froze with my mouth an inch from hers.

Kris's eyes popped open and met mine warily. "What was that?"

"Ah . . . young love," Circe sang.

I peered over Kris's shoulder, expecting to find Circe looming over us, but found her still frozen in the same spot.

"Such a magical experience," she taunted from a distance. "However . . . not with the one I expected."

I involuntarily flinched from the rhetorical slap in the face. Though the movement was slight, Kris noticed. She clasped my face in her hands, and gave me a pointed look.

"No," she said, before she rose to a stand.

She spun toward Circe, and I saw her feisty side rearing its stubborn head. I clambered to my feet, and grabbed her hand to stop whatever quip she had planned for Circe's ears.

"Forget her," I ordered. With a fleeting glance in Circe's direction, I added, "Let's get out of here."

"Yes . . ." Circe goaded. "Go. Let your love grow. For now."

Kris didn't miss the hidden message behind Circe's words any more than I had, and she spun around to snarl, "You don't know what you're talking about!"

I pulled Kris behind me, into the relative safety of the cottage. I shut the door on Circe's taunting cackle before the situation worsened. She was trying to bait Kris for a reason, and I suspected the bind on her was weakening.

We woke the rest of our group, and within minutes we were prepared to leave this contorted realm behind. As long as the tide didn't trap us here for several more hours.

As we entered the dark cavern, Permna assured us that the tide was in our favor, and would remain so until we were safely back in Cape Circeo. How she was so sure of that, I wasn't certain, but I hoped it meant that the bind Circe had placed on her was weakening, and her powers of prophecy were returning. We sure could use the advantage of knowing what was coming.

Even then, considering the enormous feat before us, I wasn't sure even that would help.

~ ~ ~

We took turns driving through the night, and arrived at the location of the Kala safe house by late afternoon the next day. The abandoned hotel laid in the outskirts of Corinth, in the run-down part of the city that had not survived the economic changes following the Second World War. As I had feared, it didn't appear the most desirable of accommodations.

"There's no way in hell we can stay in there," Alec observed as he came up beside me where I stood in the parking lot, assessing the near-crumbling three story building from a safe distance.

I didn't respond, but something on my face must have given me away.

"Oh, God . . ." Alec grumbled as he retrieved several bags from the back of the vehicle. "Forget the demigods. We're all going to die under a pile of rubble in our sleep, aren't we?"

"You haven't seen anything yet," I warned.

The outward appearance of the hotel had me worried about the status of the section the Kala had claimed. I hoped it had survived the degeneration the rest of the building had been subjected to. If it hadn't, I didn't know where else we would go.

We gathered our bags, and I led the group through the unlocked front door, it's lock likely broken by kids looking for a cheap adventure a decade or more ago. Inside the lobby, we were greeted by an inch of dust that coated the floor and the sheets that covered the oddly shaped objects scattered around the grand room. I saw no fresh footprints, which meant two things. This was no longer a popular location for cheap thrills for bored kids, and Jared and Bruce hadn't arrived yet with a—hopefully—generous army of soldiers.

I tuned out Alec's complaints as I sought the door I needed. Finding it along the back wall, near the inoperable elevator, I shouted, "Over here!"

With the aid of the flashlight I had retrieved from my bag, I led the group down the cold, dark stairwell. An orange door, that might have been red at one time, waited at the bottom. A single padlock placed on the door—its key long gone—was all that prevented us from entry.

"We could blow it apart with a gun," Alec suggested.

I nodded my head, having already come to that conclusion. As I reached for the pistol secured in the waistband of my pants, Kris's hand stopped me.

"Or . . ." she started with a teasing smile. "Someone could maybe . . . magically unlock it, and save us all the headache?" With a pat on my arm, she added, "I know you like playing Rambo, but I got this one."

Playing Rambo? I made a face as she stepped past me to place her hands on the lock. I heard Alec's snicker behind me, and turned to shoot him a glare.

"Rambo," he repeated with a chuckle. "I think I've got a new nickname for you."

"What was the old nickname?" Lillian questioned Alec as she shot me an amused glance.

My mouth curved into a reluctant grin as Alec answered, "I had several names for him, actually." He grimaced at the apparent memory before smiling sheepishly at Lillian. "None of them were very nice."

Lillian glanced between the two of us. "What? You two weren't always friends?"

Kris snorted loudly as she tried unsuccessfully to contain her laughter. At the same time, Alec shrieked, "You think we're *friends?*"

Lillian shrugged. "It seems like it to me."

I heard a soft click behind me, and turned as Kris removed the padlock from the door. She handed it to me, before addressing Alec.

"Compared to the night the two of you first met, and the many clashes that followed after that,"—she patted Alec apologetically on the shoulder—"I'd say you're as close as brothers."

Now it was my turn to laugh. "I wouldn't go that far."

Kris lifted a shoulder as she smiled at me knowingly—like she knew something neither Alec nor I were aware of—before she gestured to the door. "Shall we?"

"Yes, please," Isatan grumbled from the bottom of the stairs. "I've heard enough bonding to last me the rest of this mission."

I met Kris's gaze with a nod. He *really* was an insufferable ass.

And something told me he wasn't going to be impressed with the accommodations awaiting us in the basement of the hotel. Not that any of us were, actually.

The amount of dust that the flashlights illuminated appeared triple that of what we had found upstairs. The enormous open space was damp and cold and, without any windows, especially dark.

Other than that, it had what we needed, which I realized when I opened one of the doors along the left wall. The large pantry contained shelf upon shelf of nonperishables to sustain the small army I expected . . . for a few days anyway. The storage room next to it was filled with enough blankets and pillows to permit us some comfort.

"So we sleep on the floor," Alec concluded glumly.

"Where else are we going to hide with a small army this close to the demigods?" I knew it sucked. We all did. But we also didn't have another option. Not if we wanted to remain undetected until we did what we came here to do. "We can get a new lock on the door. Set a look-out in one of the rooms upstairs. Get some radios to communicate . . ."

"We can make it work," Kris concluded.

She moved away from the group, disappearing into the shadows the flashlights didn't reach. I started to follow, wondering where she could possibly be going, when a bright orange glow flashed in front of me.

Kris held a small ball of fire between her hands. I watched as her hands separated, and the ball grew in size and strength. Even from several feet away, I felt the heat radiating from it.

She placed it in the center of the room, and turned to me with a satisfied smile. "Now we have light . . . and heat."

I glanced around to observe the open room—about half the size of a football field. Though the light was dim, it spread into every corner, illuminating the room perfectly in a soft glow.

I smiled as I wrapped her up in my arms, and planted a kiss to her temple. "You amaze me again."

CHAPTER 6

~ Kris ~

We spent the remainder of the day, and the entire next day, making the basement a habitable sanctuary. While Alec, Lillian, Isatan, and I swept and scrubbed our lives away, Nathan and Permna gathered the necessary gadgets for the look-out posts they planned to establish on the top floor of the hotel.

Far too many hours passed by with Isatan barking out orders, and I was one "you shouldn't do it like that" away from accidentally spontaneously combusting him.

"Natural leader my ass," I grumbled as I took the towel in my hands to the dirty wooden table in front of me.

"What about your ass?" Alec chuckled as he came up beside me. He made a show out of tilting his head to the side to examine my behind before lifting his eyebrows in approval.

I hurled the towel at his head. He caught it easily, and hopped up onto the table with a laugh while I grabbed another one.

"You know . . . I'm kind of in the middle of cleaning that," I pointed out.

"Who cares? What's he going to do?" Alec jutted his chin across the room in Isatan's direction. "Yell at us some more?"

"Good point," I muttered. But I didn't stop wiping the table around Alec. If I was expected to eat off of it at some point, I wanted it to be clean.

I felt his eyes on me as I moved around the table. When I came back to the spot Alec sat on, I glanced up and caught an uncertain look on his face before he covered it with a flashy smile.

Something was up. I inclined my head to the side with a silent question.

"Can I ask you something?" Alec wondered.

His suddenly sullen demeanor threw me, and I shifted uneasily under his gaze. But I would like to think that Alec could ask me anything, so I nodded.

"What would you think if I made a pass at Lillian?"

My mouth dropped without conscious thought before I could stop it. "Wh—what?"

Alec shrugged. "She's hot. She's single. I'm single. I'm just wondering how you would feel about it . . ."

I tossed a quick glance across the room to where Lillian was busy sweeping the floor. "I uh . . ."

"No words, huh?"

I shot him a sympathetic grimace. "I'm pretty sure she's still hung up on Nathan."

"Story of my life," he muttered under his breath, then grinned at the chastising look on my face. "I might not have been able to make *you* forget him, but I think I can make *her* forget him."

"Really?" I slid onto the table beside him, and tossed him a playful smile. "You think so?"

"Uh-huh." His eyes swung toward me, and the grin on his face dropped as he repeated, "I just want to know how you would feel about it first."

"I mean . . . I'm not a fan of hers by any—"

"No," Alec interrupted. "How would you *feel* about it?"

I decided that my legs swinging back and forth under the table were safer to look at, at that moment, than Alec. "What exactly are you asking, Alec?"

"Well . . ." he drew lazily, "the last time I hooked up with a girl, you got jealous."

I looked up quickly. "I did not—"

His eyes slid to mine knowingly, effectively cutting off my protest.

"Okay," I sighed. "*Maybe* I did a little bit. But . . ."

"But what?" Alec probed gently.

But nothing, I concluded. I had no argument, no hold on Alec, no reason to stop him from . . . being Alec. Even if that was with my old nemesis, if that was what Alec wanted.

I shifted to face Alec with a smile. "Go ahead. You don't need my permission."

Alec stared at me for a few heavy seconds, sans grin or smile. "I'm not asking for your permission, Kris."

"Then what are you asking?"

His eyes narrowed fractionally before he looked away with a heavy sigh. "Hell, I don't really know," he admitted with a chuckle.

I followed his gaze across the room, where it rested on Lillian. Oblivious to the conversation we were having about her, she rested the broom she was using against the wall and pulled out a hair-tie to pull her long brown hair into. As she turned to retrieve the broom, her eyes swept in our direction before darting away timidly.

Complete opposite of the scowls I had been used to seeing on her face.

Despite the negative history we had, I knew she wasn't a bad person. Not anymore. And I knew she was hurting . . . over a lot of things. Nathan had insisted that time would heal her. I was sure he was right, but . . . perhaps she needed a little push. Maybe she need to experience love again. Or whatever it was that Alec could offer her.

And, of course, I wanted only the best for Alec.

"Alec, I want you to be happy," I concluded. "And if she can make you happy, then I would feel . . ."

"Happy?" he teased.

I smiled brightly as I nodded. "That's all I want for you."

Alec stared at me for a moment before he groaned. "Shit, Kris. I'm not asking her to marry me, or anything."

It dawned on me exactly what he was saying. I smacked his arm hard. "You're a pig."

"I'm a guy," he returned with a shrug. "I have needs."

"Like I said . . . pig."

"What is with you girls, huh? There's nothing wrong with a little casual hook-up between two consenting adults."

I nodded thoughtfully. "You think she'll have the same opinion?"

"Well . . . she did just return from the dead to find her boyfriend is with someone else," he mused. "I'm thinking my chances are pretty good."

I waved a hand in her direction. "By all means . . . go get her, Tiger."

He shot me a sideways smile. "You're an adorable dork." I shrugged as Alec turned to watch Lillian again, and the smile on his face dropped. "Oh, shit."

"What?"

"Now I have to do something."

"I doubt that's a new experience for you," I pointed out.

"Yeah, but . . ." He turned to me with a wary grimace. "I've been out of practice for a while."

I patted his arm as I slid off the table. "I'm sure you'll do fine. Now, get off my table so I can finish cleaning it."

"Alright. I'm going in," Alec declared. He stretched his arms over his head, as if flirting required him to limber up first.

And he called me a dork?

I shook my head as I leaned across the table to clean the area Alec had been sitting on.

Alec bent down so that his mouth was near my ear. "I'm still here if you ever need help with your evil twin. Don't forget that." He started to leave, then came back as if remembering something else. "And I'll always think your ass is the nicest ass I've ever seen. That will *never* change."

As he turned to finally leave, his hand swatted my rear like he was a football player congratulating me on a great play. I jumped and spun around in time to watch Alec come to a sudden halt in front of Nathan. Despite his arms folded over his chest and the hardness of his jaw, I wasn't worried. I knew Nathan's mad face, and this wasn't it.

This was more . . . amused annoyance.

I turned back to the table with a small chuckle as Alec sidestepped the Nathan statue. A few seconds ticked by before he unfroze, and came up beside me to grab the towel I had thrown at Alec earlier.

"Should I even ask?"

My throat tightened as I recalled the initial purpose of Alec's visit. What would Nathan think of a possible romance—or fling—

between Alec and Lillian?

"I'm not sure you would want to know," I returned drily.

Obviously, that was the wrong thing to say, and I realized it the second the words tumbled out. Nathan turned toward me with a furrowed brow, and I realized I should to tell him the truth before he started to think something else.

"It's not . . ." I groaned at my own stupidity. "Alec's thinking about making a move on Lillian, and he was talking to me about it. That's all."

Nathan's head turned over his shoulder in Alec's direction. "That's it?"

"That's it?" I repeated a little more shrilly than I had intended.

He didn't sound bothered by the idea . . . at all. Nor did he look surprised. He turned back to the table with a dismissive shrug. "I figured it was bound to happen eventually."

"What have I missed?"

"Alec's been into her since . . . well, pretty much since she woke up," Nathan explained. He took in my dropped jaw. "You haven't noticed?"

I shook my head as I watched Alec pick up a broom and say something to Lillian that caused her to laugh. Huh. Though innocent enough, they certainly did seem friendly now that I was paying attention.

Nathan's eyes were on me. "You okay with it?"

Why was everyone asking me that? I threw my hands up. "Why wouldn't I be?"

Nathan studied me quietly, and it dawned on me that he was asking me the same thing Alec had asked me. Except neither of them knew exactly what they were asking. No more than I knew the answer.

Finally, I sighed, "I just don't want him to get hurt." I had done enough of that already.

"I don't think you have to worry about Lillian," Nathan replied. I followed his gaze across the room, where Alec and Lillian both stood with brooms in their hands and smiles on their faces. "The attraction is definitely mutual."

~ ~ ~

Nathan assisted me in cleaning while he filled me in on the progress he and Permna had made that morning. His hybrid crafting skills had enabled him to tap into the hotel's shut-down water supply, and we now had a slow trickle of running water in one of the rooms upstairs—enough to use the toilet and wash up on occasion. They had also prepared two rooms, on opposing corners of the hotel, as suitable look-out posts.

Though the demigods didn't know we were in town yet, we needed to be ready. Nathan and Permna had done all they could do to ensure that we were prepared for them.

When our stomachs started to growl, he helped me prepare a small meal—a disgusting powdery food that turned into something half-way edible with the addition of water—for the group. As we were cleaning up, a loud knock reverberated on the metal door.

"Weapons," Isatan barked as he withdrew a shiny blade from the sheath around his waist.

"Might be our guys," Nathan reminded him as we all moved cautiously to the door.

Nathan and Permna had also gotten a new lock for the door,

which they had placed inside to keep unwelcome visitors out. Now, Nathan quietly entered the four digit code—0416—to disengage it.

I smiled to myself when the significance of those numbers registered. *My birthday.*

With one last glance behind him to make sure the rest of us were ready, Nathan slowly eased the door open.

"You better not shoot my ass."

A familiar voice drifted through the crack, and Nathan opened it wider to reveal a grinning Jared.

Counting Jared and Bruce, a total of twenty hybrids spilled into the basement. I knew because I counted them. A few looked familiar to me, and I assumed that they were originally from the island that I had called home a few weeks ago. Seeing those faces now, after knowing that their base had been destroyed because of me, caused me to step back from the commotion.

Though Nathan insisted I had saved the base that night, I knew the truth. Temulus and the Skotadi had come there because of me. The Kala's base had been destroyed because of me. Micah had been murdered . . . because of me.

I hovered in the background as introductions were passed around. Watching Nathan, I realized that he knew many of the hybrids unfamiliar to me, from the Australian base. They were easy to pick out with their thick drawls.

One of them slipped through the wall of bodies, and approached me with a lopsided grin. Combined with chocolate brown eyes covered by the longest, thickest lashes I had ever seen on a guy and a head of perfect blonde hair, he resembled a model in a Calvin Klein ad.

"Hi," he drew.

Though his eyes appeared to be on me, I glanced over my shoulder to make sure he wasn't addressing someone else.

"I'm talking to you, Strawberry," he chuckled, and extended a hand. "I'm Jas."

I accepted his hand warily. "Strawberry?"

His eyes moved to my head, more precisely my hair, and his hand quickly followed to twirl a piece around his finger before I knew what he was doing. "I always liked a—"

The very purposeful sound of a throat clearing stopped him from finishing his thought, and I peeked over his shoulder to find Nathan, again with that amused annoyance look on his face.

Jas immediately took a step back. He looked from Nathan, to me, then back to Nathan again. "Ah . . . *this* is your girl?"

Nathan softened the purposeful nod of his head with a sly grin, and I suspected that the two of them knew each other fairly well. Jas stepped away, undeterred.

"Moving on . . ." he muttered before zoning in on another new face in the crowd.

Lillian.

I watched him in awe as Nathan came to a stand beside me. "Is he Alec's long lost brother, or something?"

"What?" Nathan chuckled.

"The need to hit on girls . . ." I nodded in Jas's direction as Lillian ventured away from him, and he was left scoping for another female to close in on. "Looks like the force is strong in that one."

The only new face left was Permna. Jas wrinkled his nose at her neatly-kept and reserved appearance, likely having come to the conclusion that he wasn't going to get anywhere with her either.

Glancing around at the rest of the hybrids, I spotted another face I recognized. I groaned inwardly. Why did *she* have to come?

As if sensing my eyes on her, Kira glanced up to meet my gaze. In contrast to the taunting smile on her face the last time I had seen her, she looked at me now with indifference as she emerged from the storage room with an armload of blankets.

She slowed as she passed by. "Nathan," she greeted with a sly smile. "I should have known you were involved in this vigilante suicide mission."

Nathan shifted his feet—the only hint he gave that he was uncomfortable. I didn't know the history between the two of them, and I was sure that I was probably better off not knowing. Especially considering the way Kira seemed determined to not go away.

"It's not a suicide mission," I sneered as I attempted to step around her.

She spun to catch my arm with her free hand. I glanced down at her hand in confusion, then turned to face her. Behind her, Nathan stiffened, visibly as confused about her intentions as I was.

"I heard what you did," she said to me.

I scoffed softly. "You're going to have to be more specific than that."

"My little brother was in the dorm that night," Kira explained quickly. "He was trapped by the fire. You got him out."

I nodded slowly as the realization of what this was hit me. She wasn't attacking me. She was thanking me.

"And . . . he survived that night?"

"Yes. I owe you for that."

"You don't owe me anything," I returned politely before I turned to walk away.

As relieved as I was to learn that my actions that night had benefited someone, Kira's gratitude only reminded me of the many others that had not survived the attack that night. Especially those that had been closest to me—Micah, Richie, and Kim. The tears that rimmed my eyes now started out of remorse for all the life lost. As I put distance between Kira and myself, and looked upon the familiar faces around me, those tears gave way to a wave of fresh, fat ones for the ones I had saved.

For the first time, I understood what Nathan had been trying to tell me. Though the attack had been spurred by my presence there, I had done *something* positive that night. While many had been lost, many more would have died without my help.

~ ~ ~

The basement was surprisingly quiet considering the two dozen bodies spread across the floor on makeshift beds made of blankets. It was perhaps the most uncomfortable situation I had ever been thrust into—well, aside from the days Nathan and I spent trudging through the Blue Ridge Mountains in the middle of winter.

Hushed whispers blended in with the low hum generated by the swirling ball of fire in the center of the room. It was peaceful, considering our purpose for being there.

The fireball lit the space with a dim glow, and provided just enough heat to keep us comfortable. Creating and maintaining the fire didn't drain much energy. Whatever energy I did expend was well worth the small luxury it permitted in the midst of overwhelming discomfort.

I rolled around on my bed in an attempt to get comfortable. It didn't matter what I did. Sleeping on a concrete floor was *never* comfortable.

The pile of blankets beside me was vacant. My gaze traveled across the room, to the cluster of tables in the corner, where Nathan stood with Jared and Isatan. Their voices were dropped and I couldn't hear what they were talking about. From their body language, I doubted I wanted to know.

But I wished Nathan would come back. I found it easier to sleep on his arm than the deflated pillow beneath my head now. I smacked the sides of it with my fists in an attempt to even out the lumps as someone dropped loudly onto the pile of blankets behind me. I spun around to find Alec.

"Where have you been?" I asked him.

"It was my turn to use the shower upstairs," he answered.

Isatan's idea: to schedule shower times. We had enough running water to accommodate a third of us each day. That meant we were permitted to shower every three days. Tomorrow was my designated day, and I couldn't wait. As long as I was one of the lucky ones who got warm water.

I'd heard the stories going around. Warm water wasn't a guarantee. But Alec looked refreshed, so I assumed he'd gotten lucky with the shower roulette.

"So how's it going, Romeo?" I nodded my head to the side, where Lillian slept on her own makeshift bed.

"It's a work in progress," Alec shrugged.

"You struck out, didn't you?"

Alec lifted a hand as if to say, *whoa*. "I don't strike out, Kris. I don't even know what that would be like."

My head tilted. "Umm . . ."

"I didn't strike out with you," he argued automatically. "As a matter of fact, I clearly remember getting safely to second base."

I groaned. "You are—"

"Sexy and you know it," he finished for me.

I contemplated throwing my pillow at him, but doubted it would have done any good. The thing only had like three feathers left in it. Instead, I rolled over with a sigh. I *had* to get some sleep.

"Hey." Alec shifted closer, and I felt his breath on my neck. "Nathan told me you've been visiting Callie in your dreams."

I rolled onto my back to peer up at him. "Since when have you two been into sharing secrets?"

"What?" His mouth twisted in disgust. "We're not. Sharing secrets? Definitely not. No way."

"Okay." His extreme reaction to my question spoke volumes, but I wasn't about to tell him that. They wanted to pretend they weren't friends? Go ahead. The rest of us knew better.

"Anyway,"—Alec started—"he said that you took him with you a few times."

"Yeah." I was afraid to ask where Alec was going with this.

His head lowered. Before his face was hidden, I swore I saw a flash of something I had never seen on Alec's face before—bashfulness. "Do you, uh . . . do you think you could take me with you?"

I stared at the top of his head in silence. Long enough for him to lift his eyes to mine. I saw it then. He was nervous. Like really, really nervous.

"What's going on, Alec?"

"Nothing," he answered quickly. "I just . . . I'd like to see how Callie is doing. That's all."

"She's not exactly aware of what's going on in the dreams," I explained, but quickly realized that wasn't all Alec was interested in. He simply wanted to see her. Like any good friend would.

"But, yeah," I added quickly. "I can try to take you. I don't really know how I was able to take Nathan, but it might be because he's been sleeping right beside me."

Alec's gaze shifted across the room, where Nathan was still talking to Jared and Isatan. I saw a glimpse of uncertainty flicker in his eyes.

"Come on." I patted the empty space between us before he talked himself out of it. "Pull your blankets closer. We'll give it a shot."

Though I had found that I didn't need to repeat the spell every night for it to work now, I did it again in Alec's presence for an extra boost. I placed the rosemary leaf between us after we laid down. Our shoulders just touched, and I hoped that was enough. I was usually wrapped all around Nathan when we slept, and I didn't know if that closeness had pulled him into some of the dreams with me. I hadn't been able to pinpoint the reason why he did some nights, and not others.

At some point, I felt Nathan's presence nearby, and assumed he had finally come to lay down. Normally, I would have nestled into his side. Tonight, I resisted that comfort for Alec's benefit.

If he wanted to see Callie, I would do my best to make sure he saw her.

~ ~ ~

She greets us on the sandy shore of Big Pine Lake. In Boone. At the last location the three of us were all together . . . before things got weird. Except this time, there is no raging party, and no bonfire. It is only us, meeting again on a warm summer day.

Callie slams into both of us with a cry of joy. Her slender arms wrap around our necks, and she pulls us in for a tight group hug.

I instantly know the difference. This Callie knows the truth.

I push her back to arm's length to get a better look at her. She looks like her healthy, normal self. Not the lifeless shell of my best friend—the vision that has haunted me since the day I left the island, and her, behind.

"It's about time you found a way to bring me into one of your dreams," she says. "I was starting to think Micah had overestimated your abilities."

I cringe at the mention of Micah, and Callie lays a gentle hand on my arm. "What's wrong?"

"You've been unconscious for a while. . ." I start tentatively. How do I tell her that one of our own is dead now, and she slept through it?

Callie glances between Alec and me, and a flicker of understanding registers on her face. "Oh. Is uh—is everyone else okay?"

"We lost Richie and Kim, too," I say.

"The rest of us are fine," Alec adds.

Callie nods thoughtfully. "You're all gone. I've woken enough to know that it's just me and Gran now. She didn't tell me what happened to the others."

"Is she taking care of you?" That had been one of my requests upon leaving the island—that someone I trust stay behind to watch over Callie. Gran had been more than happy to volunteer.

Callie beams. "Like a pesky grandmother. She told me you are going to save me."

"We are," Alec states firmly. His tone forces my gaze to shift to him, but his eyes rest determinedly on Callie. "When this is all over, we'll come back for you."

The smile Callie gives Alec tugs at my heartstrings. As her eyes search his face, I fear that, despite Alec's vow, she is preparing to say goodbye. That isn't something I'm going to let her do.

We aren't giving up. I'm not about to let her give up.

"How are you doing, Callie?" I interrupt. "Are you holding up okay?"

"I'm hanging in there, I guess." Callie shrugs as she gazes down at herself. "This dream body is a lot better than my real body, I know that much."

Alec snorts, earning curious looks from Callie and me. We both get the source of his amusement at the same time, and Callie smacks him in the chest with the back of her hand.

"Ow. That was a complimentary snort," he defends.

"Complimentary snort?" Callie repeats indignantly.

"Yeah . . . you know . . ." His hand waves up and down her body. "Because it's good. You're good. Your . . . body . . . is good. Total compliment. No reason to get violent."

Callie folds her arms in front of her as she stares him down. Several seconds tick by before her face breaks into a smile. "You have no idea how much I miss you."

She pulls him into another hug, and Alec mutters, "I think I know."

Callie's hand snags my shirt, and she yanks me into their hug.

My two best friends. It's sweet. It's perfect. It's heaven for a few hours.

CHAPTER 7

~ Nathan ~

The following days were spent brainstorming our next course of action, and fortifying our hideout against attack. Isatan took the reins, and did what he did best. He led. He bossed. He pissed everyone off.

Kris told me that he made me look like a softie.

After that, I pulled Jared aside to ask him to fill me in on whatever decisions he and Isatan reached later, because I was taking Kris outside for a few hours.

"Seriously?" she whined. "I thought you'd take that as a compliment, considering what an asshole he is."

I shrugged, and handed her a knife. Uncoated, of course, because I wasn't suicidal.

"Let's see what you've got," I told her.

She turned the knife around in her hand like it was the first time she had ever seen one up close.

I shifted my stance, momentarily letting my guard down at the worrisome look on her face. "What's wrong?"

"I hate using knives," she murmured.

"Why?"

"Because I've killed twice using one already," she answered softly. "I don't like it."

"Don't like what? Killing?" I ventured.

Her gaze lowered to the ground between us before she shook her head. "I'd rather use my magic." Her eyes were hopeful when they lifted to mine, and dammit, my chest tightened at the sight. A vulnerable Kris did me in every time.

I replanted my feet in an attempt to stand my ground. "You can't kill a demigod with your magic."

"I know," she returned quickly. She pulled her shoulders back, and met my eyes with a sudden fierce determination. "What do you want to show me?"

Before I could answer, Alec glided up beside me to offer his opinion. "For starters, you're holding the thing like you're about to butter up some bread with it." He shot me an accusatory look. "You didn't teach her how to fight with a knife?"

"I did," I told him before turning back to Kris. "She seems to have forgotten."

"Corn," Kris shot at me. "You made me stab bags of corn!"

I glanced at Alec. "She never got close to being ready for a real fight."

"Yeah? Well, that's about to change," Alec stated gruffly.

"I'm right here." Kris looked pointedly at each of us. "*Right here.*"

Alec laughed as he moved to Kris's side. "You're making me nervous with that thing. Here." He repositioned her hand so that she was gripping the handle properly. He stepped back to admire his work, then said, "Show me what you've got."

For some reason this elicited a full-on laugh from Kris, complete with hands on her knees as she attempted to compose herself. Alec and I shared bewildered glances as she sucked in a sharp breath.

"You . . ." She waved a finger at both of us. "You are so much alike!"

It was clear from the look on Alec's face that he didn't agree with her any more than I did. Nor did either of us find her comment half as amusing as she did, but we waited her out until she could breathe again. Not that the moment necessarily passed. Even as I was showing her the precise movements to inflict maximum damage to a target, an occasional giggle erupted from her.

I had her practice those movements over and over until she had them down perfect, and she forgot about anything being funny. We went over three primary techniques that all hybrids learned during training. I happened to know that she had not gotten that far in the class while living on the island, and she needed to be taught them from scratch. The fact that she was a demigod, and had a heavy concentration of Ares' blood flowing through her, made her a quick learner. By the end of the hour, she was still a novice, but I felt better about her holding her own in a knife fight.

Somewhere along the way, we had drawn a small audience. Not only had Alec's suggestions been in my ear the entire time, but I'd heard a few comments from Jas, Lillian, and eventually Kira as well. Glancing away from Kris's upward thrust, I spotted the four of them sitting on the chipped sidewalk, watching. All they were missing was a bag of popcorn.

Kris finished her set, and turned to me. "Okay. What now?"

I took in her slightly reddened cheeks. "I think we need to do some conditioning, then a few rounds of combat."

She groaned. "Can we skip the conditioning?"

"No."

I would have liked to go for a run through the city, but with four demigods hiding out somewhere nearby, I settled for running the hotel stairs. After five sets, Kris begged for a break.

The break consisted of a series of sit-ups and push-ups.

"Congratulations," she wheezed beside me. "You've officially made me hate you again. *Twenty*."

Her arms folded beneath her, and she collapsed to the floor, where she remained as I finished my set of push-ups. Once finished, I pushed to my feet and offered her a hand.

I took one look at her face, and called it quits for the day.

Maybe I was a softie?

We spent the next few days doing much of the same. I watched Kris grow stronger and more proficient every day. Once she realized it, she stopped complaining, and requested to be taught more difficult moves. The bulk of our time was spent either training or sleeping.

Every night, regardless of how mad she had been at me while training, she slid over onto my pile of blankets to sleep. I knew the simple act of being together like that was important to her. It was important to me too. Few things could top holding her while she slept. Those few things all involved her, too.

Nearly every night, she slept with her rosemary leaf, which enabled her to visit Callie in her dreams. I got dragged along a few times. As did Alec. Oddly, she had yet to share a dream with both of us. It seemed to be either one or the other, and either oblivious, alternate world Callie or real world Callie.

While I spent most of my time preparing Kris for battle, Isatan and Jared organized reconnaissance missions into the city to look for the demigods. Though no one had discovered their exact location yet, Isatan thought they were getting close. He assured me that we would have something to go on soon.

The next day, I worked Kris harder than ever—to the point that she started yelling at me again. I attempted to hide my smile, but realized I must have failed when she gave me her head tilt, narrowed eyes, and pursed lips combo. I took a step back before I got a knee to the groin.

"Can I make a suggestion?" Lillian called from her seat on the sidewalk.

"Please," Jas drew. "My body hurts just from watching this."

I waved a hand, inviting Lillian to offer whatever advice she had, and she approached with a calculating look in her eyes. To Kris, she asked, "You're not very comfortable throwing the knives are you?"

Kris glanced at me before shaking her head. It was easy for anyone to see that her discomfort with the knives was hindering her ability to master the use of them. Even after daily practice, she was stuck at a novice level.

"Remember what you did when the demigods attacked in Aeaea?" Lillian asked her. "You stopped that blade in midair, then threw it back like a rocket."

"Yeah, I pushed it with a wave of magic," Kris responded.

"Do you think you could do that again?" When Kris nodded, Lillian turned to me. "Got anything to make a target out of?"

Thirty minutes later, feathers littered the sidewalk under a pillow fastened to the wall. Kris pulled her arm back the way I had shown her, and the knife released from her grip as I had shown her. She caught the knife with her powers, and sailed it straight into the center of the pillow . . . again. And from a much farther distance than anyone I knew could hit it from.

I turned to Lillian with a grateful nod. Though I still worried about Kris's abilities in close combat situations, I felt better knowing that she could potentially take out a threat from a safe distance.

"What about the rest of your powers?" Lillian asked Kris. "Have you been working on them?"

"Some." Kris tossed a sheepish look in my direction. "Not that I've had much time lately."

Lillian spun to me. "She needs to work on her magic, too."

I threw my hands up in surrender, and was promptly dismissed to the sidelines while Lillian coached Kris on a few magical elements she had some knowledge of. I figured that was as good of a time as any to go check in with Jared and Isatan on the status of the reconnaissance mission from today.

I had seen the team return fifteen minutes ago, and was curious to hear what they had discovered, if anything. Walking into the basement, I quickly realized something positive had come from today's scouting.

Isatan's usual go-to soldiers buzzed around the room like bees in a field of daisies. I found Jared at the folded table that had served as mission control for the past few days.

"What's going on?" I asked him.

He glanced up from the map of Corinth, which had been dotted with red and blue marker—red for 'ruled out' and blue for 'potential' locations.

"One of the teams spotted a few hybrids here," his finger fell on a spot on the map near the coast. "They followed them to Archaia Korinthos, but lost them amongst all the tourists."

"The ruins?"

Jared buried his nose into the paper in his hand before he referenced the map again. He nodded his head at me distractedly.

"What are the chances they're hiding in there somewhere?" I ventured.

I wasn't as familiar with Archaia Korinthos as I was with some of the more popular Greek ruins, like the Acropolis and the Coliseum, but I knew most of them were known to have a lot of hidden spaces, and underground tunnels.

"We're going to look into it tomorrow," Jared responded. "I'd like you to go out tomorrow if you would. Isatan wants a bigger group around Archaia Korinthos, just in case, but there are three other locations we'd like to scout out too. I'm going to need all the willing bodies I can get."

"Fine. What's the plan?"

"Just blend in, act touristy, look for hybrids. Pretty basic." He looked up from the papers in front of him long enough to point to a box in the corner behind him. "Prepaid phones are there. Grab one, make sure everyone has your number. That'll be your only method of communication with the other teams."

I moved to collect a plain black phone from the box—an actual flip phone. They still sold these?

"Who am I partnering with?" I asked as I squinted at the small screen, trying to read the number assigned to this phone.

"Whoever you want. But most have already teamed up. Here." Jared threw a stack of papers at me, hitting me in the chest with a thud. "Go through the reports, and catch up on what we've been following."

Dismissed by Jared, I sat on my makeshift bed, and caught up on everything from the past few days. Despite the number of papers in my hands, nothing worthwhile had been noted until today. But sometimes even the mundane could turn out to be something in disguise, which was why Jared made me read through it all.

I was nearly finished when Kris plopped onto the blanket beside me. "I hear you're going out tomorrow."

"Yeah. Maybe you could just work with Lillian on your magic?" I turned to her when she didn't respond. I knew exactly what that hopeful look on her face was all about. "No. No way."

"Please?" She laid it on thick, complete with a sweet kiss to the corner of my mouth. "I'll listen to whatever Isatan says. I'll obey orders, and all that. I just need to do something different."

"You need to stay hidden and unseen," I insisted.

"If I go with you, I'll be safe," she returned with a too-sweet-to-be-innocent smile.

I narrowed my eyes. Dammit. When did she get so good at knowing exactly how to get to me? Now I knew what she had always complained about. She was right, it wasn't fair.

"Kris . . ." I started with warning shake of my head.

"I want to be more involved," she pleaded.

"You're involved enough. This whole thing revolves around you," I emphasized. "Which is exactly why you need to lay low."

"I'm doing all this training . . . and for what? I'm not doing anything real," she complained. "Come on. I heard you all were pretending to be tourists while you look for signs of the demigods. I can be a tourist!"

And then she did it. She ran her hand up my arm in a provocatively seductive way that made me wonder where she had learned that trick. Her lips grazed my chin, forcing my eyes to shut against the urge to turn toward her and make it more.

"Please?" she repeated.

Her hand gently squeezed my bicep . . .

Her lips feathered the corner of my mouth . . .

I sighed and, against my better judgment, found myself relenting.

"You stay with me the entire time," I warned. "Like a shadow."

She jumped to her feet, then stunned me her gorgeous smile. "That shouldn't be a problem."

In a flash, she collected her bag from the floor and scurried off to prepare. I stared after her with a scowl on my face as she approached Jared. I had never felt so . . . *used*.

"That was pathetic."

I turned to find Alec smirking at me. He shook his head as he dropped to the jumbled pile of sheets on the floor that had served as his bed the past few nights. He took his time, leaning against the wall to make himself comfortable, before he looked over at me again.

"You are the definition of whipped," he laughed. My eyes slanted to give him a semi-threatening glare, but that didn't stop him from continuing. "I bet if I Googled the word, your picture would pop up."

"Shut up, Alec," I muttered, though the words didn't come out with the usual bite I reserved for him.

Because, of course, I knew he was right.

~ ~ ~

Not that I didn't get something out of it return. I had been missing spending time with Kris, that didn't involve her scowling at me while I coached her. I got an entire day with her, though I spent more time on the phone than actually with her.

Five two-person teams were scattered around the city, and another six were camped throughout Archaia Korinthos. The phones enabled us to remain in constant contact with each other. Though no one had spotted anything significant yet, we all expected that it would happen soon.

The dark shades Kris and I both wore disguised our eyes from other hybrids. Besides, it was bright and hot as hell. Shades were necessary in every way.

"Our second date is a damn mission," Kris muttered as she picked up her second cheese tiropitakia from the plate set between us. She pointed it at me. "You're lucky you're cute."

I grinned as she nibbled on the flaky pastry. "Cute? I believe you once said I was *hot*."

"Oh, God," she groaned. "You remember that?"

How could I forget? That was the day I realized I hadn't been imagining the occasional lingering looks she had given me. That was the day I knew she was as attracted to me as I was to her . . . and that I might have gotten myself into trouble.

"I remember a lot more than you think," I returned.

She shrugged indifferently, and continued to pick at the assortment of food on our table. Her eyes lifted to skim the large flock of tourists that passed the crowded patio, reminding me that we were here for a reason.

Not even a real date.

"Come here." I hooked a hand around her waist and slid her across the smooth bench seat toward me. I planted a kiss to the side of her head. "I'll make it up to you when this is all over."

"You don't have to make anything up to me," she sighed as she buried her face into my neck. "I like—"

Her body stiffened, and I resisted the urge to whip around to find the source of her alarm.

"What is it?" I whispered.

"Four hybrids," she replied. "They just walked out of the

restaurant with to-go bags. I saw the one's eyes before he put his shades on. Definitely Kala."

I grumbled. We would have to determine if they were loyal Kala working here on some mission, or Kala working for Circe. Until we found out, they could not know that we were there.

Kris did a good job appearing inconspicuous . . . for her, though I had to chuckle at the panic on her face when the hybrids merged with the tourists on the street. She glanced at me with a look that questioned why we weren't on the move yet.

"As good as we are at tailing people,"—I explained as I casually stood to clean our table—"we're just as good at spotting tails."

"Have you seen the number of tourists? We're going to lose them."

My eyes darted to their retreating backs as I dumped the tray into the nearest garbage can. "I don't lose targets, Kris."

She harrumphed, clearly not impressed with my skills.

I grabbed her hand as we merged into the crowd. For one, because I wanted to. Two, to hold her back before she blew our cover. I realized her height disadvantage limited her ability to follow them, but I had a clear view of the back of their heads as we trailed from a distance of twenty yards.

"Trust me," I muttered before pulling out my phone to make a call to Jared.

He answered on the first ring. "Please tell me you have something."

I quickly filled him in, and relayed our location. He ended the call with a request for more details once I got it. I could tell from the sound of his voice that he hadn't seen anything remotely suspicious yet, and was getting a little stir-crazy from the lack of action.

Much like Kris was at my side. Both of them . . . the storm to my calm.

We followed the Kala for two blocks, moving closer to the coast, before they veered off the sidewalk, and entered through the front door of a tall, swank apartment complex.

Kris grumbled as I casually moved to follow them. She tugged on my hand, obviously eager to pick up the pace. I held her back easily. Though her shades covered her eyes, I felt the daggers I knew she was shooting at me.

"Trust me," I repeated with a gentle squeeze of her hand as I veered us toward the set of glass doors.

The air-conditioned lobby provided instant relief from the harsh summer heat, but didn't help the nerve-induced sweat that dampened my forehead. I settled my shades on top of my head, and motioned for Kris to do the same before we stuck out as the only people wearing them indoors. At her wary grimace, I nodded my head toward the wall lined with elevators, where our four Kala targets were waiting with their backs to us.

I steered Kris to a set of plush leather chairs set up in the lobby. "You're terrible at this," I chuckled.

"I just don't want to lose them," she returned heatedly, complete with the hands on hips stance that always made me smile.

"Well, sweetheart," I teased as I dropped into the chair that permitted me a view of the elevator, "I hate to tell you that we *are* going to lose them."

Her eyes narrowed, but I wasn't sure if it was because of the mocking pet name I knew she hated, or my claim that we would lose the Kala.

"The best we can do is watch what floor they get off on for

now," I explained as I pulled the phone from my pocket.

We couldn't risk stepping onto the elevator with them, and by the time we rode a separate car to that floor, they would be gone, hidden behind any number of possible doors. Finding out which room they were in would be simple, with some reinforcements . . . which was exactly who I planned to call.

Kris stood by my chair as I pulled up Jared's name on the phone. I glanced at her after I pushed the call button, and registered the determined gleam in her eyes a second too late.

Fortunately, the lobby wasn't packed with visitors, and I was the only one who witnessed her vanishing act.

"Kris," I whispered harshly at the spot she had just stood. But I knew she wasn't there anymore. All that remained of her was the breeze that rushed by me.

Jared picked up on the other end, and I greeted him with a few words that rendered even him speechless.

CHAPTER 8

~ Kris ~

The elevator doors opened as I hurried across the empty lobby. The four Kala stepped into the elevator, and I chanted the words to the invisibility spell under my breath to maintain my disguise.

I turned sideways to squeeze between the elevator doors before they shut. My arm bumped one of the doors, and they popped back open as I slid to the empty corner in the back.

"I hate these old buildings," one of the Kala grumbled as he impatiently pressed the 'door shut' button.

Before the doors closed, shutting me inside with the four Kala, I glimpsed Nathan's set jaw and the slight shake of his head across the lobby as he glared into the elevator. His phone was pressed to his ear as he exchanged what appeared to be heated words with whoever was on the other end.

If I made it out of this building alive, he was going to kill me. Best case scenario was house arrest for the remainder of our time here.

Now, I didn't care. I wanted to know where the demigods were hiding so we could eliminate them. Every day wasted looking for them was another day closer to Circe finding Alec, and Callie dying. I didn't know if it was bravery or stupidity on my part, but I valued their safety more than my own these days.

One of the Kala pressed the button to the last floor, then punched in a series of numbers to get the elevator to move. They were silent as we ascended, and I watched the numbers that lit up above the doors. We stopped on the eleventh floor. The top floor.

I hung back while they filed out, then slipped out behind them before the doors shut. I had expected to emerge into a hallway lined with doors, but instead found myself standing in the glorious marble floored entryway of a large suite.

The penthouse suite . . . and boy were they living in luxury.

As I trailed the Kala from a safe distance, an unsettling ache settled in my gut. I wasn't sure what the cause was, but I suspected I was about to find out.

The Kala stepped through a set of double doors, and into a grand sitting room with muted walls adorned in expensive-looking paintings, plush leather seating, and an impressive view of the coast through the adjoining balcony. Sitting in one of the chairs was a woman with a mane of coal black hair. Her head turned as the Kala entered the room, and I glimpsed half of her fire red lips and attractive face.

The ache in my stomach intensified at the sight of her. Though I had never seen her before in my life, I knew who she was. Or what she was.

A demigod, though I didn't know which one.

"What is the word from Phisma?" she questioned the four Kala.

Phisma? I dove into my memory banks to fish out one of the many things Nathan had given me a crash course in over the past few weeks. Phisma was . . . the demigod of wisdom, I thought. And if I remembered correctly, the demigod our small team feared the most. Phisma was especially brilliant at strategy, and I knew Isatan had wanted to take him out early, preferably before the demigods were aware of our plans.

But that hadn't happened.

"His team spotted several of them searching near the Archaia Korinthos hideout this morning," the burliest of the four Kala answered. "They are hidden well, but have ventured out, perhaps to search for us."

The demigod scoffed. "And Phisma and those fools that have stayed with him will be found. For being so wise, Phisma has made a terrible decision for them to stay together."

"They believe they have more strength together," the burly Kala responded. "And wish for you to join them."

"They expect to pinpoint the location of Hecate's daughter and her army by this evening," another Kala added. "It will be safe once the threat is eliminated."

Even if no one could see it, I shook my head rapidly. They were close to finding us? But we had seen no indication of them getting close. I hoped they were wrong, but feared they were right.

"Once she is subdued, I will join them," the demigod snarled. "But not before. I fear Phisma has severely underestimated their strength. I am less of a target alone."

"As you wish," the big Kala muttered. He set one of the bags of food on the table in front of her, and backed away timidly when she waved her hand in dismissal.

The four Kala shared uneasy glances as they moved toward the door. I wondered what they were concerned about. Her choice to remain alone, without the protection of the other three demigods in the city?

Because they had good reason to be concerned about that, I

thought with a smile. Not that anyone could see it.

I hadn't known what to expect when I stepped onto that elevator. To determine the loyalties of the four Kala? To find out how many of them there were? If I was lucky, to learn the locations of the demigods without getting busted?

I hit the jackpot. One demigod sat in front of me now, I'd learned the location of the other three in the city, *and* I knew that they were close to moving in on us. With the information I had gathered, we could take them all out within the next hour, and be well on our way to finding Hades' demigods tonight.

But first, I had to get out of there without being seen, and get some reinforcements.

Because, despite having killed in the past, it wasn't something I enjoyed. In fact, I hated it. So unless it was kill or be killed, I couldn't fathom walking up to this demigod and stabbing her in the heart without her knowing what hit her.

Despite having a perfectly suitable diamond-coated knife secured around my waist—something Nathan had insisted on before leaving our hideout this morning.

Nathan was probably worried sick by now. I wouldn't put it past him to have assembled the entire army to come get me by now. I needed to get back to the lobby before he blew our cover in an unnecessary rescue attempt.

I started for the door after the Kala, but froze when the demigod stiffened, and swung her head in my direction.

"Wait," she called after the Kala. I glanced down to confirm my invisibility spell was still working. Her next words froze the relieved sigh on my lips. "She's near."

One of the Kala stepped back into the room, forcing me to

hurry out of the way to avoid a collision. "Who is near?"

"The girl." The demigod's brow furrowed in confusion, and I wondered if she sensed me in the same manner I had sensed her—only she was thrown off by not being able to see me. "She's here. Search the building."

Oh, no. Nathan.

I was torn between dropping the invisibility right then and there so that I could call him with a warning, and trying to sneak out with the Kala on the elevator. But then, I didn't want to lose sight of the demigod. If she thought she was in danger, she might flee . . . and perhaps take the others with her. Who knew how long it would take us to find them again?

The four Kala hurried out of the room, leaving me alone with the demigod. She stood and approached a satchel set on top of a table on the opposite side of the room. She withdrew a vial filled with a sparkly red powder, and I cautiously backed away from the one thing that gave her an advantage over me.

She wouldn't attempt to kill me due to my important role in Circe's curse, but she could certainly subdue me with Circe's demigod-weakening compound in her hand.

In a sudden move, she spun and hurled a cloud of powder at me. Her aim was off, and I easily stepped out of the path of the compound as it landed on the floor beside me.

Her eyes lit up when they met mine. "There you are."

Her wrist snapped with another toss . . . straight at me, and I realized that I had dropped my invisibility in the chaos. In my hurry to get out of the powder's path, I bumped the table behind me, and sent a glass vase to the floor with a crash.

I sidestepped another blanket of red powder as I retrieved my knife from its hiding place. So much for getting out of this one with no more blood on my hands.

"Sneaky little witch," she growled as she tossed more powder at me, and missed. Her lips twisted into a sinister grin as she stared me down from across the room. Her arms dropped to her sides as if in defeat, but I knew better.

I just didn't know what she was up to.

Until a breeze swept through my hair, and I realized that I was dealing with the demigod of air manipulation. Ophe—something. I didn't have the time to remember as she collected the powder that had fallen to the floor into a sparkly red tornado in front of me.

Seconds from being doused in it, I sprang into action. I made it two steps before a powerful gust of wind knocked me into the table. Broken glass rained down around me as I fell to the floor.

I lifted my eyes, and sent her flying across the room with a nod of my head. An indent the size of her body was left in the wall when she crumbled to the floor. I was up and advancing on her before she managed to get to her knees.

A wall of wind stopped my pursuit. I pushed against it, to no avail, as she rose to a stand in front of me. I couldn't take a single step. Over my shoulder, the red tornado swirled closer.

"Circe will be pleased I have managed to subdue you," she taunted.

"You haven't done anything yet," I returned.

I lifted the knife in my hand as I pushed against the wind that had me trapped. Me . . . but not my magic.

I took control of the knife with my mind, which was much more powerful than my body could ever be. The knife hovered beside me, long enough for the demigod's eyes to widen in terror, before I thrust it forward, and straight into the center of her chest.

The wind died and the tornado dispersed at the exact moment she dissipated. Exhausted from our battle, and depleted of energy from using my magic, I crumpled to the floor, barely avoiding the mound of powder that lay behind me.

My hands shook as I retrieved the phone from my pocket and pulled up Nathan's number.

He answered on the first ring. "Kris?"

"Penthouse," I sighed. "Code is three-one-one."

"Kris!" He shouted as I dropped the phone to my lap.

I could barely keep my eyes open, let alone hold a phone. As I allowed my eyes to drift shut, I vaguely registered the sound of the door banging against the wall as it flew open.

That was fast . . .

I glanced up to face Nathan's wrath, but instead was met by the sneers of four Kala, and a red cloud tossed in my face.

I recognize where I am . . . because I have been here once before. Not in real life. In a dream, like this one. Only this time, I am not alone. Something waits for me in the shadows. Something I don't want to find me. Something I don't want to learn the identity of, because knowing will strike me down with fear.

Fog covers the ground at my feet, limiting my already restricted vision in the dark, cramped space. My hands on the cold stone wall guide me to where I know I need to go. I escape the enclosure, and avoid the pursuit of whatever hunts me. When the iron bars and her face appear before me, I know exactly who I am searching for.

"Mom?" I whisper.

"We can't move her like this..."

"We don't know how many more might show up..."

"We can't stay here..."

"Then leave! I'm staying with her!"

The hard edge to Nathan's voice pulled me through the haze, and back to the penthouse sitting room where he, Alec, Jared, and Isatan stood over me. Both Nathan and Isatan appeared ready to throw punches, so I figured it was a good time to make my newly awakened presence known.

"Hey..." I croaked.

Nathan immediately dropped to a knee by my head. "What happened?"

"I killed the demigod. Those four Kala are here somewhere," I warned.

"We took care of them."

"Oh. Good..."

I grip the bars that separate her from me. With my face pressed against the cool metal, I can see her warm smile.

"At last..." she says. "You have found me."

I pull on the bars as if my super-human strength can pull them apart. When that fails, I ask, "How can I get you out?"

"You cannot," she responds. "I cannot leave. I will not leave as long as the curse placed on me remains."

"But I need you! I can't do this alone."

Her hand slips between the bars to touch my face. "You can, and you will. It has been prophesized. You will bring an end to the hybrid race."

"Kris!"

I jerked back to the room, and blinked away the darkness.

"Which demigod did you destroy?" Isatan barked from behind Nathan.

"Wind . . ." I couldn't recall her name.

"How do you know?"

"Because she made a damn tornado in the room!" I fired at him, then winced from the stabbing pain behind my eyes. The room blurred, and I thought I was about to slip out again, but Nathan's voice held me there.

"It's okay," he crooned. "We're going to get you out of here."

"Wait. The other demigods," I started in a rush. "They're hiding . . . Archaia Korinthos. And they . . ."

The rest of my warning trailed off as the darkness returned, and this time I couldn't help but go to where I was called.

"We don't have much time," my mother says desperately.

"I have to go back," I plead. "I have to warn them . . ."

"Yes, but first . . . listen. You will be the one to end the war as the prophecy states."

"How?"

"Continue your present path."

I shake my head rapidly. My goal is not to end the war, but to save Callie. And free Alec and me from our destiny. "What about Circe? Her curse?"

My mother trailed a delicate finger over my face. "You must come for me. I can help you. That is the only way."

"I don't know how to find you."

Her beautiful face contorts into a frown. "The stars have aligned. The way will show itself to you soon."

I want to ask how I will know, but I am temporarily distracted. Her slender fingers graze my cheek in the way that I had witnessed other parents love their children. I always envied those children. Though Gran had been a fantastic caregiver to me, far better than all my foster parents combined, I still missed a mother's touch. Not just any mother's touch, but my mother's touch.

I sink into it like I don't want it to ever end . . . even if it is only in a fantasy dream world.

"You must go, child . . ."

"No . . ."

"You will know when it is time to come to me. You can succeed in freeing me where the others have failed."

"I don't want to go," I plead as the cell bars begin to warp and fade. I reach for her, but come up with nothing. She is already gone.

I am sitting in my old room in Boone, staring at the screen of my small television while the familiar scene from a romantic comedy plays out.

"What the hell?" I mutter to myself, then spin toward the voice beside me.

"Here . . ." Callie holds a vial of nail polish out to me. She's sitting beside me on the bed, her legs bent in front of her, and balls of cotton stuck between her newly polished toes.

I nearly tackle her out of pure excitement, but hold back. I am not sure if she is the real Callie, or the sheltered Callie, the one with no recollection of what has happened outside of dream-world.

"So how is your quest going?" she asks impassively. When I hesitate, she turns to smile at me. *"Have you saved me yet?"*

Okay. So I am with real Callie. *"Not yet,"* I respond. *"But we will."*

"I know you will." She wraps both arms around my neck in a tight embrace. Into my ear, she whispers, *"But right now, you need to wake up."*

My grip on her tightens. Not another person I love trying to kick me out of *my pleasant dreams.* "I want to stay here with you."

"You can't. You need to wake up, Kris," she repeats urgently. "Wake up . . ."

CHAPTER 9

There was a long terrifying moment after I woke up that I didn't know where I was. Dream-jumping could do that, I had come to realize.

As the familiar ache settled between my shoulder blades, and I registered the glow coming from my magically constructed fireball, I realized that I was back in the basement of the hotel. On my hastily prepared, and extremely uncomfortable, bed.

As I stretched to alleviate the stiffness that always followed sleeping on the floor, my eyes landed on Alec's, where he laid a few feet away on his own heap of blankets.

"You're awake," I whispered so as not to wake the others.

He shrugged. "You were talking in your sleep. Everything okay?"

I hesitated as I rolled his question around in my head. Once the fog of sleep lifted, the answer came to me, and I lurched forward to scan the bodies spread out across the basement floor. Several blanket piles were vacant, including the one on the other side of mine. "Where is everyone? Where's Nathan?"

Alec grimaced as he pushed himself into a sitting position. I recognized that face—the face of not wanting to tell me the truth.

"Alec? What's going on?"

He gazed at me with an intensity that only made my heart gallop faster. "A few of them went to attack the demigods where you said they were hiding. Isatan didn't want to wait any longer . . ." He shrugged as if to soften the blow he knew his words would have on me.

I could do the math. Our two demigods to their three . . . without the assistance of my magic to make up the difference. Nathan was with them—and virtually defenseless against demigods.

Damn that Isatan.

My head swirled from the gravity of the situation—so much so that I couldn't piece together the rest of what was floating around in there. Something else important. The fog from my vivid dream blanketed my mind, making it hard for me to concentrate, to remember.

One thing was certain. I knew we were in danger. Not only did I know it, but I felt it growing in my gut. Like a bad bellyache.

Lillian plopped down beside Alec. "Everything okay?" she asked as she glanced back and forth between Alec and me.

"Kris just woke up," Alec explained, while I muttered, "No. Nothing is okay."

I shook my head to break up the fog. Callie . . . my mother . . . I needed to find my mother? In the Underworld? Bits and pieces of my conversation with Nathan slowly came to the surface. Isatan knew where to find the demigods because I had told him where they were hiding . . .

But the dream had taken me before I could tell him that the demigods were close to finding us.

My head snapped up to meet Alec's eyes. "They're coming. We have to get everyone up, and get out of here!"

"What?" Despite the uncertainty in Alec's voice, he scrambled to his feet. He glanced around the room, at the shadowed lumps sleeping on the floor around us. "How do you know that, Kris?"

"They planned to have our location tonight. And . . ." I jumped to my feet beside him, then shook my head because I didn't know how I knew. I just did. "I can feel them."

No further explanation was needed. Alec sounded a warning that startled even me. But it worked. Around us, a dozen hybrids sprung to their feet, ready for action.

Several looked at me for explanation, but I didn't have one. All I had was instinct.

But then the ground beneath us shook, and I knew I didn't need to explain. The answer to all their unspoken questions had arrived.

~ ~ ~

~ Nathan ~

The ancient Corinth monuments lay on the coast, far from our own hideout. Twelve of us approached them in silence, with the aid of night vision goggles. We bypassed the visitor's information booth, which was shut down for the night, and stepped lightly across the pebble covered ground.

Three towers rose above us, immersing us in deep shadows. Beyond the towers, the monument opened into a partially erect, two-thousand-year-old amphitheater. Across the opening, archways were chiseled into what remained of the structure. Five tunnels . . . all led to the unknown.

We slowed to deliberate our best route.

Jared caught my gaze. "Take the lead as tracker," he commanded in a hushed voice.

With a nod, I began to search for traces of the demigods. Given my specialty in tracking, it didn't take me long to find footprints. Several led through the archway to the far right, while only three distinctive sets of tracks led to the archway in the middle.

I pointed them out to Isatan.

"This way," he ordered. "Nathan, keep the lead."

At the threshold, my hand shot up to stop the others behind me. Jared came to my side as I pointed out the tripwire at our feet. Bruce's hands followed it along the wall, to where it stopped.

"Device rigged with Circe's compound," Bruce announced quietly. "No explosives."

"Keep moving," Isatan barked. Even in a whisper, his voice was demanding.

I reclaimed the lead, and guided the team through the short tunnel and into a tight, enclosed room with three separate passageways for us to choose from. It took only seconds to find the tracks on the chipped concrete floor. We entered a smaller tunnel, and inched farther into the compound.

My eyes darted to the ground every few steps, constantly scanning for more traps, but I found none. For some reason, that only made me more nervous.

It was quiet. Too quiet.

We emerged single file into a grand circular room. The walls were created of a thick stone that had collapsed in parts, and piles of broken stone littered the ground around us. Opening from this room were seven more tunnels.

I moved to start my search for more tracks, but came up short when I spotted the wire at my feet. My fist shot up to halt the rest of the team behind me.

"Booby-trapped!" Someone shouted a warning from across the room. I turned just in time to see two members of our team blown apart by a bomb. As I jumped out of the way of falling rock, a wave of armed soldiers—a mix of Skotadi and Kala—swarmed us from all sides, filing out of the tunnels one after another.

"Defensive positions!" Isatan barked.

I dropped to one knee and let loose a burst of gunfire at the advancing wave. The sound of a dozen automatic weapons reverberated off the walls, rattling my teeth, as I kept my finger on the trigger. As the wall of soldiers in front of me fell, I glimpsed a demigod standing at the entrance to one of the tunnels. He maintained a safe distance while his eyes scanned the chaos around him.

"Isatan!" I called, and pointed out the demigod's location.

Isatan's eyes burned with murderous intent as he stalked toward the demigod. Though the demigod's gaze temporarily flicked in Isatan's direction, he didn't appear worried.

Instead, his eyes settled on someone behind me. He withdrew a crossbow from behind his back—my first clue that we were dealing with Cryteus, the son of Artemis. His diamond-tipped arrow sailed through the air, barely missing me as it passed with a sharp whoosh.

"Arrow!" I shouted as I twisted to follow its path.

The arrow slammed into Permna before she knew it was coming.

I caught Jared's stunned gaze from where he was hunkered down behind her.

"He shot it!" I motioned toward Cryteus before pulling myself across the ground on my forearms toward Permna. She had fallen onto her back. The arrow protruded from the center of her chest.

Her eyes shifted to mine as I rose above her. Blood poured from the wound, and her mouth, as she reached for me.

"It missed my heart," she rasped.

I gripped the end of the arrow with a nod. If I removed it quickly enough, she might stand a chance at living. She screamed in agony as I pulled on the arrow. I immediately stopped with a sigh of defeat.

"I don't . . ." I trailed off, and my head dropped when I saw that her eyes had glazed over. Her body dissipated beneath me, and I was left holding a bloody arrow in my hand.

"Dammit!" I shouted as I threw the arrow to the side.

I spun toward the sound of a soldier barreling down on me, and fired off a round that dissipated him immediately. I was left with a clear view of Isatan as he zeroed in on Cryteus. Isatan lifted his sword over his head at the same time Cryteus swung his crossbow on Isatan.

Jared fired off a shot that struck Cryteus in the gut. Not a kill shot, not for a demigod, but enough to alter his aim. The arrow struck Isatan's shoulder—a nonfatal blow.

Another shot from Jared dropped Cryteus to his knees. Isatan kept coming, his loud bellow rising above the shouting that echoed off the walls as he adjusted the aim of his swing on Cryteus's head. At the same time, Cryteus removed a hidden blade from near his ankle, and thrust it up and into the center of Isatan's chest.

Both demigods took fatal hits. They dissipated simultaneously.

"How do we always find ourselves in these situations?" Jared grumbled as he put his back to mine.

We moved together in a circle as we surveyed the rest of the chaos. Three enemy soldiers charged us from opposing directions. I cut one down with a burst of ammo before we were forced to tackle the other two with our knives. When it was over, we stood to face the next onslaught, only to discover that no one was left.

Only Bruce, who was withdrawing his knife from the body he currently straddled, remained. The body at his feet dissipated beneath him as he stood to face us.

"There's only one," Jared muttered. "Where are the other two demigods?"

My heart clenched when the answer came to me. Isatan, his soul rest in peace, despite his leadership skills had been duped by Phisma. They had known we were coming. This raid was little more than a diversion.

It was a goddam trap set for Kris.

~ ~ ~

~ Kris ~

No one knew what was happening—not even I knew—but they looked to me for the answer.

As the shaking beneath our feet intensified, creating a crack in the concrete that ran from one side of the room to the other, I shouted, "Get your weapons!"

It was all I could think of, because I had no idea where the shaking was coming from, or what was causing it, but I knew it wasn't naturally made.

"Eromna?" Lillian suggested warily.

The demigod of earth manipulation?

Alec and I eyed the widening crevice under our feet as concrete and dirt collapsed into the depths below.

"Looks about right," Alec muttered.

"Trapped in a basement with no way out," I sighed. How in the hell were we going to get out of this one?

I took tentative steps toward the door. Though I knew something incredibly unpleasant waited for us on the other side, it was our only way out. But damned if I would allow more blood to be shed over me. And that would surely happen if we stayed there.

As I approached the door on wobbly legs, Alec and Lillian by my side and the rest of the soldiers following closely behind, the door flew from its hinges with a loud crack. Blocking the entryway towered a broad man.

"Phisma!" someone shouted from behind me, earning a cold laugh from the demigod.

"I see my reputation precedes me." His eyes met mine with immediate recognition, then they shifted to the side, coming to a rest on Alec. His lips curled into a cunning smirk. "Two objectives at one time. How marvelous."

I moved to stand directly in front of Alec as a swarm of hybrids poured through the door behind Phisma. They fanned out, clashing with what remained of our small army. As gunshots and the clash of metal on metal erupted around us, I pushed Alec and Lillian back, keeping as much distance as I could between them and Phisma.

He wanted Alec gone. I knew that. And I would die before I ever let *anyone* get near him.

Phisma took careful, calculating steps toward us as we backed away from him, his eyes never leaving mine as he watched me for signs of attack.

Not yet. Attacking him would leave Alec unprotected. And I had a better idea. Or so I hoped.

The floor and ground opened beneath us as another stronger rumble shook the building around us. I glanced up to observe cracks in the ceiling as debris rained down on us.

"Is your friend going to bring the entire building down on all of us?" I questioned Phisma.

He shrugged. "You and I will survive. Can't say much for your friends."

"So where are your partners?" I asked, forcing my voice to remain light despite the fear running through me.

Just a few more steps . . .

"Eromna is here. Obviously." He waved his hand at the widening fissure beneath our feet. "Cryteus will join us once your other friends are dead."

I swallowed the newly formed lump in my throat. I knew that included Nathan, and the others who had gone with Isatan and Permna. Only one demigod had waited to ambush them. I hoped that meant they would be returning, instead of Cryteus. Surely they found a way to defeat him, and they would soon return to help me.

"None of this needed to happen," Phisma continued. "All you had to do was join us. Now, because you refuse to do so willingly, your friends will die."

His words made me pause, because he was right. My gaze lifted over Phisma's shoulder to observe the members of our small army fighting the hybrids who had accompanied Phisma. I hadn't had time to count exactly how many there had been, but a quick scan confirmed that there were noticeably fewer left standing.

Again, people were dying because of me. But many more would die if I gave in. Including Callie.

Behind me, Alec and Lillian crossed the threshold into the

storage room. I took special care as I backed in after them. I held Phisma's gaze steadily as he continued to advance on us.

He smirked at the sight of us trapped inside the room. His cockiness blinded him to the thin trip wire at his feet. Alec grabbed my shoulders to swing me into the farthest corner of the room as the blanket of red powder rained down on Phisma. Alec's body shielded me while Phisma shrieked in surprise.

"It's done!" Lillian exclaimed. "Take him now."

Alec stepped back to release me from the wall. He dropped to a knee in front of me, and withdrew my diamond-coated knife from its sheath around my ankle. He placed it in my hands with an encouraging nod.

I approached Phisma where he lay on the ground, his eyes rolled into the back of his head. As I knelt in front of him, I briefly wondered what dream he was walking in and if he would remain permanently in it, or be transported straight to his own corner in the underworld.

He didn't make a noise as I plunged the knife into his chest, and I had to look away from the blood that seeped through his robes. I held the knife there until his body dissipated. Once finished, I stood on wobbly legs and turned to find Alec and Lillian watching me.

The ground beneath us suddenly lurched. The earth screamed as it crumbled and shook beneath us.

"I guess Eromna got the memo that Phisma is gone," I shouted to Alec and Lillian.

Alec's eyes darted over my shoulder. "And he's pissed."

I turned to find Eromna standing in the doorway. His murderous glare was directed at me.

Beyond him, the floor split apart into two big chunks, and was swallowed up by the earth. Gone with the floor were all the remaining hybrids—ours and theirs—except two, who I couldn't recognize from the distance. They appeared trapped on a narrow sliver of concrete that was slowly eroding from beneath them.

Eromna approached us. Steps rose out of the wide crevice separating us from him as he walked across it, before disappearing behind him—like his own personal bridge.

We were trapped inside the storage room by the wide layer of powder that lay on the floor at the entrance. He could not step through it, but neither could I. He stopped just out of its reach, and I pushed Alec and Lillian behind me, to shield them the best I could.

"Got a plan?" Alec whispered.

"Nope," I returned.

Eromna's gaze lifted to the ceiling. His lips twisted into a sinister smile as a crack formed above us, sprinkling us with chips of plaster.

I needed a plan . . . before he brought the ceiling down on us. I eyed the wide crevice behind him, which had stopped expanding now that his concentration was elsewhere.

My hands fisted at my side as I let my powers flow closer to the surface. With a surge of concentration, I shot a wave of power into the center of his chest. The force flung him onto his back at the edge of the crevice. Another push with my mind tossed him over the side.

He disappeared from sight, but I doubted he was really gone. There was only one documented way to destroy a demigod that I knew of, and a fall into the center of the earth wasn't it. But then, I doubted this scenario had ever happened before.

Either way, he was gone for now.

Lillian scrambled to the doorway and began sweeping the red powder to the side with her hands so that I could step out of the room. Alec stopped her.

"This is quicker," he said, then proceeded to scoop me up, and carry me across the threshold. As he set me down, I saw two hands appear at the rim of the crevice, followed by the rest of Eromna as he climbed out.

I squared my shoulders as he stood, piercing me with a hard glare. I tightened my grip on the handle of the knife in my hand and took careful but steady steps toward him as the floor beneath me rolled and shook violently.

This was it. I knew it. He knew it.

A strong vibration threw me onto my knees. Standing was impossible. The floor cracked beneath me, and a bright orange glow seeped through the cracks from below, giving me the impression that I hovered above the fiery pits of hell.

A pair of hands grabbed me under my arms, and guided me to my feet. Catching the excited gleam in Eromna's eyes, I spun on Alec. "Get back!"

"I can help you, Kris," he shouted over the rumbling.

"Not if you're dead." I pushed him back and away with a wave of energy as a chunk of ground collapsed beneath us. Only an incredible burst of speed toward the edge kept me from falling into it while Alec landed on his back ten yards behind me, in relative safety.

I turned back to Eromna determinedly, the knife still firmly in my hands. I considered slipping into a state of invisibility so that I could sneak up on him, but feared he would collapse the entire floor beneath me once I disappeared from his sight.

I felt myself weakening from using so much of my powers already. I needed to end him now before I lost all ability to fight him. As I resumed my advance on Eromna, relief appeared in the doorway behind him.

Nathan, Jared, and Bruce lifted their guns in the air. This was my opportunity. While they fired an onslaught of bullets at Eromna, temporarily stunning him, I swiftly closed the distance between us. He spun toward them, his eyes fixed on the already cracked ceiling above them. They were forced to stop their assault as a large chunk of concrete crashed toward them. I watched long enough to make sure they had jumped out of the way before I focused my attention on Eromna.

He spun to face me as my hand thrust out, sinking the blade into his chest. The ground lurched, knocking both of us toward the wide chasm. With the last ounce of strength I had, I twisted the knife, finding his heart. His hand clamped down on my arm, pulling me with him as he tumbled into the crevice.

He dissipated beneath me, but my momentum kept me moving forward, toward the wide chasm.

A pair of hands clamped down on my ankles, stopping my plummet into the unknown depths below. I gasped as I rolled onto my back to find Alec sprawled on his stomach. The death-grip he had on my ankles released, and he crawled forward to pull me away from the edge.

"You okay?" he asked.

I nodded, not trusting my voice to work yet. Over Alec's head, Lillian hovered, terrified but unharmed.

The rumbling had stopped, and in its place, a deafening silence settled around us. I shifted to glance toward the door, and saw that Nathan, Jared, and Bruce were all safe. On the other side of the room, two more hybrids, whom I could now recognize as Jas and Kira, stood on a tiny island of concrete in the center of the chasm.

We were all that remained.

CHAPTER 10

Alec emerged from the storage room seconds later with a long rope in his hands. He tossed it across the chasm to Nathan.

"Get them first." He nodded his head at Jas and Kira, whose small platform continued to erode from beneath them.

Nathan handed the rope to Bruce. Built like a tree, he was the perfect anchor. While he held one end of the rope, and Jas held the other, Kira crawled across the void.

Nathan stepped to the edge of the crevice separating us. "Phisma?" he questioned warily.

"Dead. Cryteus?" I returned.

"Isatan killed him before . . ." He trailed off with a sorrowful grimace, and I filled in the blanks.

My heart sank, and my stomach clenched. "Permna too?"

"I tried to . . ." Nathan trailed off, but not before I detected the catch in his throat.

I wanted to jump across the chasm to give him the hug he needed to chase away the thoughts that haunted him. As difficult as it was to lose so many members of our army, the loss of the two other demigods in our group hit me the hardest. I would certainly miss Permna's kindness. Even Isatan, though he was an ass most of the time, would be missed as the glue that held us all together.

Now it was only me. My knees buckled slightly under the weight of the responsibility that now rested on my shoulders. Three more demigods—the most important to Alec and me—to get through yet. How in the hell was I going to pull that off by myself?

Behind Nathan, Kira reached safer, more stable ground. While Jared tended to Kira, Bruce planted his feet in preparation of Jas's weight on the rope, though I wasn't sure how Jas planned to climb across without anchoring the other end of the rope.

Without hesitation, Jas launched himself off the ledge. I gasped in horror when I lost sight of him.

"He's fine," Alec assured me. "He's climbing up."

Only then did I notice Bruce's stance. He leaned back on his heels, supporting Jas's weight as he used the rope to climb to safety. Fortunately, it only took a moment for his head to pop up, because I was sure I hadn't taken a single breath since the moment he had jumped off.

Then it was our turn. Nathan tossed one end of the rope across to us, and Alec caught it easily. He glanced between Lillian and me as he pulled the line tight, and anchored his feet.

"Who's going first?" he asked.

I turned to Lillian. "Go." Sure I could take down a few demigods, but I needed another minute to prepare myself for this.

I watched Lillian as she pulled herself across the rope. She appeared to be using her arms to pull her weight. She balanced herself with her feet curled around the rope as they trailed behind her. I doubted it was as simple as she made it look, which I found out a minute later, when it was my turn.

I kept my eyes up to avoid looking at what would swallow me if I screwed up and fell off the rope. Though I was blessed with strength as a demigod, I found myself tiring halfway across the divide. My energy was nearly expended from using my magic, and the rope pull was burning through what little I had left.

"You got it, Kris," Nathan called. "You're almost there."

I lowered my head and pulled hard three more times before a hand thrust out in front of me. I looked up into Bruce's warm eyes, and smiled in gratitude as he hoisted me the remaining two feet onto solid ground.

Behind him, Nathan let the rope sag as he ran a thorough eye over me, looking for any sign that I was hurt. I knew all he would find was exhaustion. Though that produced a small frown, he let it slide as he turned his attention back to Alec.

"Can you anchor it to something?" he shouted.

I eyed the distance separating us warily. This chasm was three times as wide as the one that Jas and Kira had crossed. If Alec did the same thing Jas had done, he'd have to climb a lot farther than Jas had climbed.

I would have used my powers to transport Alec safely across . . . if I could have. As weak as I was now, I feared I would drop him to his death.

Alec walked backward, unraveling the rope as he edged closer to the storage room. To give him more rope, Nathan walked closer to the lip of the chasm until pieces of earth gave way beneath his foot.

"Far enough," I warned sternly, earning a teasing grin from Nathan.

Apparently, he found it humorous for *me* to be protective of *him*.

Alec called back that the rope was secured on his end. "You got my weight?" he asked Nathan.

I grimaced when I saw the short piece of rope Nathan had left to hold on to. And he was already so close to the edge . . .

Why couldn't my magic be limitless?

Jared recognized the severity of the situation, and moved to stand behind Nathan. Knowing Jared would do everything he could to keep Nathan from falling provided me with some relief. Regardless, I held my breath as Alec climbed out onto the rope. Nathan grunted from the extra weight, far more than he had to hold for Lilian and me.

At least Alec moved a lot faster than we had, and had crossed halfway before Nathan muttered a pained, "Hurry!"

I pulled what little energy I had left to the surface. Jared's arms shot out to hold onto Nathan as he leaned dangerously forward. I heard the ground beneath him crack away.

I caught Alec first, and flung him across the remaining distance. He rolled to the ground at my feet. Beyond him, Jared and Nathan tumbled backwards from the sudden loss of Alec's weight on the rope.

Then I joined all three of them on the floor as I was zapped of all my energy.

"Turn the volume up," Callie squeals, waving her arms frantically at me. "This is my favorite part!"

I realize I am in possession of the remote control, and hit the volume button in time for Harry's infamous speech, and the following New Year's kiss, to play out loudly on the television in front of us. Scattered across the floor around us is an assortment of popcorn, chocolate, and sodas. It looks like every other sleep over we've had during our six years of friendship.

Except, this time, Alec is there. Yielding a nail polish brush.

He pauses to allow Callie ample time to settle down from her Harry Met

Sally swoon before taking the brush to her toes again. I glance down at my own feet, and find them smeared in still-wet, bright red polish. He even got it between my toes.

"Alec," Callie admonishes once she peels her eyes from the television. "You suck at this!"

"Not like I volunteered," he grumbles. He pulls his bottom lip between his teeth in concentration as he makes a swipe with the brush, catching more of the skin surrounding Callie's toenail than the nail itself.

"You love it," Callie returns, "almost as much as you love me."

Alec glances up, and blinks. His lips part in preparation to say something.

"Here!" Callie tosses me another video, silencing the words in Alec's mouth. "Let's reinvent ourselves like Julia Roberts next."

A glaring bright light ripped me from the dream. I opened my eyes in time to catch the oncoming headlights of a car before it passed. My head was resting on something warm and soft. I hissed from the stab of pain in my neck as I moved. As stiff as it was, I assumed I had been sleeping in this position for some time.

I was crammed into the middle seat of our vehicle, with Lillian, Bruce, and Alec. Alec stirred as I lifted my head from his shoulder. The headlights of another passing car illuminated his eyes as he stared down at me.

"Don't you dare say anything," he warned in a hushed voice. His finger tapped the tip of my nose. "And if you *ever* tell *anyone* I painted your toenails . . ."

I laughed softly. "You'll what? Paint them again as punishment?"

His eyes narrowed on me briefly before he cracked a smile. "What *was* that?"

"I don't know," I shrugged. "Apparently, one of us wanted to have a slumber party."

"Yeah, that was me," Alec answered without hesitation. He sounded so serious, I wasn't sure whether or not he was joking. "But I had hoped for a pillow fight in skimpy pajamas. Not painting toenails."

My eyes narrowed. "Is that what you think girls do at slumber parties?"

His face fell. "You don't?"

I shook my head, and earned a defeated sigh from Alec. "So . . . you paint nails and watch movies?"

"Two of Callie's favorite activities."

"Hey . . ." Nathan's head popped between the two front seats, and his eyes settled on me. "Everything okay back there?"

"Sure. Just dreaming," I answered.

His gaze swung to Alec, and he grimaced as if he felt sorry for him.

I nodded at the back of Jared's head, where he sat in the driver's seat. "Where are we going?"

"Areopoli. We've got a few hours of driving ahead of us yet. You should get some more rest."

"What's in Areopoli?" I asked.

"The Diros Caves," Nathan answered at the same time Alec said, "The entrance to the underworld."

~ ~ ~

~ Nathan ~

We took turns driving through the night to get to the

southernmost tip of Greece. We stopped there, in Areopoli, which was the closest town to the Diros Caves. It was the only place we could think of to start searching for the rest of the demigods. Isatan had suggested that they would be found near the entrance to the underworld, and the Diros Caves had long been considered the most commonly used of the few possible entrances.

The downside was that Areopoli was a much smaller town than Corinth, and that made blending in more difficult. However, the caves had made it a fairly popular tourist hub, so I knew we wouldn't be the only out-of-towners walking the streets.

Narrow homes constructed of stone towered over the smooth cobblestone streets. Broad windows displayed antiques and trinkets within the many shops that lined the sidewalk. Though I had done a lot of traveling, and had seen a lot of places, this little town quickly ascended to the top three, right behind Boone and Mount Olympus, simply for its charm and simplicity.

I found it hard to believe the demigods were there.

"Wouldn't you expect there to be some sign that they were near?" I mused as we navigated the local farmer's market in the town center.

The sign hanging outside the courthouse stated, population: 1656. That number had to have been wrong. If it were accurate, then every single resident had shown up at the market this morning. Along with all the tourists. This town was definitely flourishing. No signs of evil darkened the streets this bright and airy morning.

"I don't think they're here," Kris murmured in response.

"Maybe they haven't come out of the underworld yet," Alec suggested.

I sure hoped they had. Otherwise, our job was about to get a hell of a lot harder. Though Alec joked about it, taking a trip to the underworld wasn't something I wanted to do unless we absolutely had to. As far as I knew, no hybrid had ever ventured there. I didn't even know if we could return . . . or if our souls would be sucked up and forced to stay. That sounded like something Hades would do to unwelcome guests.

"Let's hope they have," I returned. "We just need to look harder."

Right on cue, Jared pushed his way through the crowd, and handed out the stack of brochures on the Diros Caves he had gathered from the front stoop of the courthouse. Flipping through, I saw the tour times, and consulted my watch.

"Next tour is in an hour," I volunteered.

"Enough time to check out the hostel," Alec pointed out.

"That's what I was thinking." As I nodded in agreement, I glimpsed Kris biting her lip to keep from smiling. "What?" I asked her.

Her eyes flicked between Alec and me, and her smile broke free. "You two are the only ones who don't see it."

I glanced at Alec, and he shrugged. "See what exactly?" I questioned Kris.

"Nothing. Absolutely nothing," she muttered as she pushed through the crowd in the general direction of the hostel. Despite her words, I knew she was pleased about something.

Damned if I knew what.

The hostel, on the other hand, wasn't much to be pleased about. Though we weren't in any position to complain. Not after we had all been forced to sleep in the cramped vehicle for a few measly hours earlier that morning. That miserable experience made the three-story hub for back-packers and tourists looking to save a few bucks look like the epitome of luxury.

Considering it was the weekend, the hostel didn't have many beds left. There were just enough to accommodate our eight-person team, though we were split between the two ten-bed rooms. Jared, Kira, and Jas joined those already roomed on the ground floor while the rest of us joined a family of five on the second floor.

This wasn't my first time using a hostel. I had a varied opinion of them. Some were better than hotels, while some were little better than squatting in an abandoned house, which I had also done at one time. This one fell somewhere in the middle. Crowded, with a poorly lit dingy communal bathroom on each floor, it was, at least, mostly clean and quiet. As an added bonus, the diner next door offered free breakfast to guests.

Though this hostel offered two private suites, they were both currently in use. I hung back to ask the concierge to let me know when either of them became available.

Being surrounded by the other guests limited our ability to communicate openly about the reason we were in town. Humans didn't handle the truth about our world very well, and the last thing I wanted to do was scare some kids on a family vacation with overheard whispered conversations about the dangers of the underworld.

The family we shared a room with was gone, on whatever adventure they were in town for, as we moved our bags in. I watched curiously as Kris removed the rosemary leaf from her backpack and placed it under her pillow on the narrow cot next to mine. Her eyes darted to mine, and I smiled.

"Come here." I sat on the edge of my bed, and pulled her to me.

I didn't have to do much coaxing. She snuggled into my chest like we were two connecting pieces of a puzzle, and breathed a content sigh.

"I know this is stupid, because I see you every day," she said, "but I miss you."

"It's not stupid," I returned. I knew exactly what she meant. We were together . . . but yet *not* together. Not in the way we both wanted.

Though this certainly helped.

"How are you doing?" I probed. "*Really* doing?"

She shrugged meekly, and I knew she didn't want to talk about everything that had happened the day before. At the risk of making her mad, I forced her back to give her a look that demanded an answer other than, *okay*.

"I don't really know," she admitted. "On one hand, I'm relieved that most of the demigods are gone. But the way it all played out will haunt me for a long time." She lowered her head, making it difficult to hear her as she muttered, "Too many have already died because of me."

"Not *because* of you," I returned. "Circe and the demigods started this. You're trying to stop them. There's a difference."

"But if I . . ."

"What? Join Circe to stop all this fighting?" I ventured. "Even more will die, Kris. Including Callie."

She sighed, looking utterly defeated. "But Permna . . . Isatan . . . all those soldiers. Maybe Phisma was right. All of this fighting is unnecessary."

"So what's the alternative? Give up?"

She shook her head at the floor. "I can't do that either. I don't know what to do."

"I know you, Kris. You're not going to bow down, and then let all those innocent humans die. You're not going to let Callie die. This is what the Kala does. We protect humans from the forces of evil, remember? We've trained and prepared to sacrifice for the good of the war against them. You shouldn't feel guilty about the sacrifices they've made."

"It's all going to end soon," she muttered softly. So quietly I wasn't sure I heard her right.

"What?"

"This war is coming to an end," she stated firmly. "You were right. I'm going to bring an end to it. My mother told me it has been prophesized."

"Your mother?"

"I saw her in a dream . . . or a vision? She says I can free her where the others have failed. She will help me defeat Circe's curse. I need to find her."

I choked on a laugh. "In the underworld?"

She nodded glumly, then shrugged. "We might have to track the demigods there anyway, right?"

"Still . . . Hecate will be . . ."

Significant measures had been taken to keep her there. What were the chances we could get through whatever traps had been set up to keep Hecate in? And then get back out with our souls intact?

"Destroying the demigods will take the pressure off of Alec and me," she added, "but it's not going to end the curse. We will need my mother's help."

I pondered the complexity of that task. The thought of getting in to the underworld seemed . . . impossible. Not to mention extremely dangerous.

"Why am I just now hearing about this?"

"I had the vision right before the demigods attacked the hideout," Kris explained. "I didn't have time to tell anyone about it until now."

I rubbed a hand over my face as if that could wipe away the pang of uncertainty that had settled into the pit of my stomach. It gave me no clarity. Only a brief episode of stars in my eyes.

"Do you know how to break Hades' curse on her? Did she explain that?"

Kris shook her head solemnly. "I have no idea. She said the stars have been aligned, and the path will show itself to me soon. That's all I know."

My eyebrows shot up. What kind of explanation was that?

"Okay," I forced. "We'll figure it out. We'll get rid of the demigods, then find your mother. Curses broken, life back to normal . . . then what?" I met Kris's curious eyes with a small smile. "Where do you want to go when this is all over?"

I watched the expression on her face change from curious, to understanding, to full-blown happy as it dawned on her what I was asking. What I was *saying*.

I could have said more, as the dainty ring burning a hole in the back pocket of my jeans demanded. While I knew I would give it to her eventually, it hadn't felt right yet. Considering we went from one troubling situation to another with little relief in between, I had decided to wait until our lives were back to normal. As normal as it could get after experiencing the things we had experienced.

Regardless, Kris smiled brightly at my question. The choices were limitless, and I would go anywhere she wanted to go.

Her arms tightened around my neck. "I thought maybe I'd want to be on a beach somewhere," she mused.

"As long as it's not the Kala base, I'm okay with that."

"But then, I thought maybe the mountains," she continued, her voice taking on a far-away quality. "I realized that I sort of miss Boone."

"That's okay, too."

"Which would you rather?"

I thought better of saying, *wherever you're at*, because I figured that would only add more ammo to Alec's claim that I was whipped. Instead, I said, "I like the mountains."

Kris's smile grew. "I didn't like the mountains when you made me walk through them for days." She scoffed softly. "God, you were unbearable then. Did you even realize how horrible you were?"

"I was trying not to feel what I felt for you," I admitted softly. "Even then."

Some self-control I'd had. Not that I cared now. I was with Kris, and there was no way I was about to give her up now.

Apparently, whatever I said was pretty good based on the kiss she gave me. The first few seconds, I even forgot that we weren't alone in the room, and I gripped her waist tight as I pulled her as close as I could get her to me. It wasn't enough.

It was never enough.

She pulled away with a smile on her face. "I heard you ask the guy at the front desk to let you know when a private room opened up."

I nodded. Yes, I had done that.

"It's ours, right?" she asked.

"Yeah, I figured we'd need a place to—"

"No . . ." Kris's gaze leveled on mine intently. "It's *ours*, right?"

And then I got it. I knew what she was asking. Though that actually hadn't been my intentions for requesting the private room, having some alone time with Kris was certainly a good enough reason in itself to have it.

"Yeah," I agreed. "It's ours."

CHAPTER 11

~ Kris ~

Diros Caves were a few minutes outside of town. We arrived with just enough time to purchase our tickets, and get in line with the other visitors. Though we had ulterior motives for exploring the cave, we blended in with the tourists as a group of friends looking for adventure.

After a few minutes, I lost myself in the tour as our guide pushed off away from the dock in our small eight-person boat. As one of the few caves in the world that was predominately under water, the only way to explore the caves was via boat. The path our boat took was illuminated by lights suspended by an overhead cable.

All the cables originated from a large black box near the entrance to the cave—something we would have to remember if we had to come back.

Everyone had their own list of things to pay attention to during the tour. Security, possible entry points after hours, and most importantly, anything that looked like an entrance to the underworld.

That was partly my job.

From my seat in the first row, directly behind the tour guide, I asked, "What do you think about the legend that the entrance to the underworld is here?"

Beside me, Nathan perked up, curious to hear what the

gentleman had to say. The rest of the boat fell silent in anticipation, but the guide didn't seem to notice.

Apparently, this was a common question, because he fell into a monotone explanation that included early Greek myths, and burial rituals that occurred at the caves thousands of years ago. All scientific explanation for why the cave was believed to have been a portal to the underworld.

But he didn't actually believe it.

A year ago, I probably wouldn't have either, but one thing I had learned was that these so-called Greek *myths* were usually real. Few knew the truth, and they were all in this boat right now.

The thirty-minute tour ended with us back where we started, and no closer to uncovering the hidden passageway to the underworld.

"Anyone see anything that looked like a possible entrance?" Jared questioned as we stepped outside.

"It could be anywhere." Nathan stopped in front of a large sign outside the cave museum. On it was a map of the caves. "The tour only covers a tenth of the actual cave. We can't get to the rest of it without scuba equipment."

A defeated silence settled over us as we stared at the expansive network of tunnels that made up the Diros Caves. Red dots marked the trail the boats took . . . and only dotted one tiny section of the caves. It continued for miles beyond where the guide had stopped the boat at a broad rock wall. Apparently, that had not been the end of the cave.

It wasn't close.

~ ~ ~

The following days were spent talking to locals and trying to dig up a trail on the demigods. While the guys focused predominantly on that, I practiced a few spells with Lillian's assistance. She remembered most of what she had known as an Incantator. Though I was a natural Incantator, I still had to learn how to perform the spells. Her guidance helped significantly.

Even my dream-walking improved. I could pull both Callie and Alec into dreams effortlessly now . . . without intending to most of the time. Both nights, since we had settled in Areopoli, the three of us shared a dream.

Nathan seemed relieved to have been left off the hook. He still insisted on keeping me on a rigorous conditioning and training regimen. Every. Single. Morning.

We usually broke for showers and lunch before he handed me over to Lillian. While we worked on Incantation, Nathan joined the rest of the guys in their research.

It was a nice routine. I was learning a lot.

"Hey, guys! Come check this out!" Lillian called, waving to the group where they had assembled near the parking lot adjacent to the beach after an afternoon of detective work. As they gathered around us, Lillian gave me a nod.

I channeled the power I needed, just as I had practiced, while I focused on a spot directly behind Alec. In a flash, I was staring at the back of his head. I tapped on his shoulder. His startled reaction caused everyone to spin around in my direction.

"Shit, Kris!" Alec's hand reached out to me as if he wanted to make sure I was real.

I blinked out again, and zapped myself directly in front of Nathan. He flinched from my sudden appearance, and I turned to

Lillian with a laugh.

"I could have some fun with this one," I told her.

Nathan's hands came down on my shoulders as if willing me to stop. "I'd bet you could."

"She's moving too fast for an invisibility spell," Jared mused.

"That's because it's not invisibility," Lillian returned. "She's teleporting."

Alec's eyes were wide when they met mine. "How far can you go?"

"It has to be somewhere I can see," I answered. "For now."

"For now?" Nathan spun me around. "Don't be going crazy, flying off to God knows where, just for the hell of it."

"I won't," I snapped a little too harshly.

"We wanted to see if she could take a passenger," Lillian said from behind me, breaking up my mini-showdown with Nathan.

"I volunteer!" Alec called.

I left Nathan's side to take a hold of Alec's hand. I glanced at Lillian. "Do I do anything special?"

"I don't know. Just try it, and see what happens," she shrugged.

So I did. I zeroed in on a spot of sand several yards away, where the water lapped with gentle waves. Then I was standing there, my feet just touching the water, with Alec beside me.

"That was awesome!" Alec hoisted me up, and spun me around with an excited whoop.

I patted his arm to get him to set me down. Dizziness and spells didn't work well together.

"How's your energy?" Lillian wondered.

"Still strong," I announced excitedly.

I tried it with everyone, just to make sure that I could. By doing some experimentation, we learned that I had to be touching someone to make them teleport. I also had to envision them coming with me. Though it took an extra second of concentration on my part, the reward was worth the small delay.

"How about glamour?" Lillian asked me after I had teleported everyone twice.

"I practiced it a little bit back on the base," I answered. "I was able to alter my appearance a little bit."

"And mine," Alec offered. "You gave me some wild hair a few times."

Lillian smiled at Alec before turning her attention back to me. "Have you tried doing more than one at a time?"

"I haven't tried it at all since we left the base."

Lillian gestured around to our group. "Try altering our appearances."

"That might come in handy," Jas muttered from the back of the group.

All eyes turned to me as the significance of Jas's words hit me. He was right. If I could alter our appearances, we could pull off just about anything. We could get close to Hades' demigods without them knowing. Unless, of course, they had that weird built-in demigod radar that I seemed to have. But the others . . .

They could be protected by my magic.

My eyes squeezed shut as I channeled my energy to the surface. I altered myself first, and stifled a smile at the gasps of surprise around me before I pushed the energy outward. I reached Lillian first, and knew I had succeeded in altering her appearance by the low whistle that came from Alec's direction.

I altered him next, giving him a blonde mullet and a flannel button-up shirt.

Jas's booming laugh nearly undid me, but I moved through the rest of the group quickly before my impatience at seeing the results made me lose my focus. By the time I finished, everyone was enjoying their own fits of laughter.

I opened my eyes to find Alec tugging on the wisps of blonde hair at his neck. He glanced down at the shirt he was wearing before hooking an eyebrow at me. "You made me look like Joe Dirt?"

I shrugged unapologetically before checking out the others. The spitting image of Rambo in the center of the group did me in, and I joined the others in laughter—all of them, the embodiment of nineties movie characters . . . and one famous billionaire with an unfortunate head of hair.

Jared folded his arms over his crisp business suit, his lips twitching as he fought to maintain his composure. "How long can you hold it?"

"The glamour?" I shrugged. It wasn't draining hardly any of my energy, despite glamourizing eight people. "I feel like I could hold it all day."

"Please don't," Alec begged. "I look ridiculous."

"We all look ridiculous," Kira—temporarily the lady from the movie, *Misery*—added vehemently.

"But look at our eyes," Bruce added thoughtfully. "They don't look like hybrid eyes."

For the first time, I looked directly at everyone's eyes. They all looked human—completely human. With no way for other hybrids to recognize us.

We would be stronger—we *were* stronger—as a team, with my powers at the center.

All we had to do was find the demigods.

~ ~ ~

We took a break for dinner. Jared spread a map of the area out on our table in the corner of the diner, and we all crowded around it.

"As you can see," he started, "there's not much around here. Only three small villages, each less than twenty minutes away. The next large city takes about an hour to reach."

"The demigods are not here," Nathan stated confidently. "If they were, we would know it by now."

"Could they be hiding in any of those nearby villages?" Alec questioned.

Jared nodded thoughtfully as he studied the map. "It's possible."

"They've got to be around here somewhere, right?" Kira mused. I glanced at her, and caught her gaze as it shifted from Nathan to me. Her lips curved into a snarky smile reserved for me.

I took the high road and ignored her. "Maybe we should check out the villages, work our way out."

"Move farther and farther from the caves," Nathan agreed. "They shouldn't have gone far."

"We'll make this ground zero for a few days, while we scope out the neighboring towns," Jared declared. "We'll find them."

I wondered about the other known entrances to the underworld. What if the demigods had chosen another route, and were nowhere near where we were looking? We would have to locate the other entrances, and search all over again.

I worried about how long it might take to find them. Each day wasted, I feared, put Alec in more danger of Circe's wrath. And Callie

. . .

What if Circe found a way to fulfill the curse without my help?

Time was our second biggest enemy, and there wasn't a damn thing we could do about it.

After dinner, Jared and Bruce took the vehicle for a quick trip to the next town over. It was only a ten-minute drive, and they planned to spend the rest of the evening looking for any signs of the demigods there.

Nathan held me back while the rest of our group retreated to the hostel. For a brief moment, I thought he had something nice planned for us. But no. He had an hour of hell planned.

"We already trained this morning, and I spent all afternoon working with Lillian," I whined. "Can't you give me a break this time?"

"We're this close to the demigods, and you want to take a break?" He folded his arms over his chest in a display of perseverance.

It was impossible to not notice the way the fabric stretched over his shoulders and arms. Even if he was a stubborn bull, he was a hot stubborn bull. And he was mine.

"What?" he asked guardedly, though from the slight twinkle in his eyes, I suspected he had caught me checking him out, and knew *exactly* what I was thinking.

"Nothing," I lied. "Let's go."

The only weapons we had at our disposal were our diamond-coated knives and the pistol Nathan carried with him everywhere. That meant no weapons training, which was perfectly fine with me. We fought in the traditional hand-to-hand sense. Fortunately, the beach was deserted. Otherwise, we would have had the police called on us for a domestic dispute within minutes of starting.

So I got a little vocal from time to time. Fortunately, Nathan never took any of the things I said in the heat of the moment to heart.

"Good," he praised after I practiced a particularly difficult set of moves. "Free style?"

"Ooh. My favorite. Bring. It. O—"

My taunt was cut off by a shoulder to my midsection as Nathan plowed into me. My elbow dug into his back as I rolled away from him. We got to our feet at the same time, but I was the first to strike. Low and fast, like Nathan had taught me.

I sent him flipping over top of me. I knew what he would do next. When he didn't disappoint, I was ready for him. I evaded his leg sweep, spun around with the speed of a demigod, and shoved an open palm into the center of his chest before he managed to get to his feet—the move that indicated a fatal strike during practice.

I must have hit him a little harder than I intended. He flew backwards several yards before landing with a thud on his back.

"Oh, my God!" I exclaimed as I hurried to his side. "Nathan . . . are you okay?"

I heard him groan as I dropped to my knees beside him. His head shook like he was trying to clear out of a daze, then his eyes landed on mine.

"You okay?" I repeated tentatively.

A few uneasy seconds passed before he answered me with a smile. Then he laughed—a laugh so deep, and full, and completely out of character for him, that I started to worry he had a head injury.

He sucked in a breath long enough to get out the words, "You kicked my ass," before laughing harder.

As I watched his amusement, a smile broke out on my face. I had finally done what he had wanted me to do all this time. I had used my demigod strength . . . and executed it well.

Go me.

Nathan pulled himself together with a sigh. When his eyes met mine again, all traces of amusement were gone. "I'm so proud of you right now. Come here," he ordered gruffly. His arm curled around my neck to pull me toward him.

My heart soared from his praising words as our lips met. What started off as a congratulatory kiss quickly evolved into something much, much more. Our fight had not caused the amount of breathlessness Nathan's demanding kiss caused me now. The more he coaxed, the more I wanted to give, and the more I wanted to demand for myself. Kneeling beside him with my head bent to his wasn't cutting it anymore.

I swung one leg over his hips and rose above him without breaking our kiss. It was easier to touch him with my hands. I started with his shoulders and moved down his arms, taking stock of every ripple under my fingers. By the time I reached his hands, where they gripped my waist tightly, I suspected both of us wanted to take this one step farther.

I peeled away long enough to scope out the rest of the beach. Still deserted. The sea was calm, the weather pleasant. The sun had recently dropped below the horizon behind me, creating a brilliant pink and orange sky. Honestly, it was kind of perfect.

The grin on Nathan's face told me that he knew exactly what the hook of my eyebrow meant. The smoldering look in his eyes as he pushed himself up into a seated position, with me in his lap and my legs curled around his waist, suggested that he, at least partially, liked where my thoughts were going. But the tender way he kissed me now also let me know that what I hoped to happen wasn't going to happen.

"Dog walker," he mumbled against my lips.

"What?" I pulled back with a laugh.

His head nodded to the side, and I turned to spy the distant silhouettes of a man and his dog down the beach.

"There will be others," he added between kisses. "Besides, the beach isn't as great as it's cracked up to be."

I supposed having sand stuck in unpleasant places didn't sound like an enjoyable way to spend the rest of my evening. Not that I knew anything about that.

I leaned away from another kiss. "You sound like you're speaking from experience."

Nathan tensed. His mouth opened, and shut again without a word.

"It's fine, Nathan." I smiled despite the twisty sensation in my stomach. "I get it. You were the one who once told me you weren't a saint."

He studied me peculiarly. "You remember that?"

"I remember everything we talked about."

One corner of his mouth tipped up. "Then you know my past doesn't matter. Not anymore."

I couldn't resist snuggling against him. It was impossible not to when he said the things he said sometimes—such a stark contrast to the times I wanted to kick him. Yet there was one thing that nagged me, and had for a while now.

With my face pressed into his neck, I asked, "Could you just tell me one thing?"

His heavy breath stirred my hair, and I suspected he was debating on which route was safer for him to take. Deny my request, and suffer my wrath. Or agree, and respond to my question with an answer that may also bring on my wrath.

I didn't give him a chance to agree or disagree. "Kira? Was she . . . ?" I pulled back to study his face as I trailed off.

He shook his head at the ground. "Kris, it doesn't matter."

"When she gives me her snotty little looks like she's keeping a secret from me, it matters. The next time I see it, she might end up getting hurt."

Nathan coughed to mask a laugh. When he looked at me, I tilted my head, silently repeating my question. He sighed warily.

"A fling," he admitted quickly. "After Lillian disappeared. That's it. That's all it was."

"A fling? Ew."

He shrugged. "You asked."

"Men," I muttered.

"Different," he emphasized.

I made a face that portrayed just how unimpressed I was. Ugh . . . what had I been thinking? I had known. Really, I had. Why had I needed to ask?

His finger under my chin forced my face up to his.

"I'm not about flings anymore," he said. Again, with the words. "I'm all about you."

"Keep talking."

He smiled tenderly. "I want to be with you, Kris, in every way. I know you know that. It's just . . ." He trailed off to feather my lips with a kiss. "I don't want to rush anything, and I don't want anything about it to be subjected to regret later."

"I would never regret—"

"I'm not saying you would," he interrupted quickly. "But if something were to happen, say a dog walker coming along at a bad time, that's not something we can do over."

I nodded when it clicked. He wanted it to be perfect . . . for me.

"But a private room all to ourselves?" I ventured.

His smile grew. "Now that's an idea."

I wondered what the chances were that one of the private rooms had opened. We hadn't returned to the hostel all day. For all we knew, we were missing the advantage of having a private room while talking about the advantage of having a private room.

I jumped to my feet. "Come on."

Nathan chuckled as he rose to a stand beside me. "And if it's not available yet?"

"Then we can make out in the common room for a while."

It was dark by the time we walked the two blocks back to the hostel. The street lights lit our way, which was surprisingly free of other pedestrians. One thing I had noticed about this town: it shut down at sunset.

"Do you think it's weird that this place turns into a ghost town at night?" I pondered as we turned the corner leading to our hostel.

Nathan glanced around as if noticing for the first time that the normally busy street was deserted, aside from us. "You're right."

"I know I'm right."

Nathan shot me an amused glance before he said, "Maybe we should ask some questions, find out if there's anything to it."

I was making a mental list of possibilities for the bizarre behavior when we rounded the corner in front of the hostel. Nathan and I both came up short when we saw the couple against the wall in the narrow breezeway between the street and the courtyard. A sconce fixated on the wall cast them in a dim light, just enough to make out their faces, which were passionately pressed together.

Alec and Lillian.

CHAPTER 12

Nathan was on my heels as I marched past them, and pushed through the entrance to the courtyard. The metal gate banged behind me, eliciting a curse from Nathan as he pushed it open. I was inside, and well on my way to the hostel's common room, by the time he caught up to me.

Someone had started a movie on the television, but the room was deserted. I dropped to the couch with a harrumph as Nathan appeared in the doorway. I felt his eyes on me while I read the subtitles scrolling across the bottom of the screen.

"What was that?" he asked in a clipped tone.

I scoffed. "Didn't you see them?"

"I do have eyes," he returned.

I ignored the obvious irritation in his voice, and silently mulled my own irritation at what I had just seen.

Nathan chuckled humorlessly from the doorway. "You might want to wipe the scowl off your face, Kris," he suggested coolly, "before anyone else sees how obviously jealous you—"

"I'm not jealous!"

"Yeah," he retorted. "I can see that."

I grimaced at the sound of disappointment that coated his words. He was reading the situation all wrong. It wasn't jealousy I felt, but an intense desire to protect Alec from harm. Not that I suspected Lillian capable of deliberately hurting him, but I wasn't stupid enough to believe she had gotten over Nathan this quickly.

Not to mention . . . had I completely misinterpreted the chemistry Alec seemed to have with someone else? I thought I had detected a little more than friendship between him and Callie, but maybe I hadn't?

Of course it had all been in la-la land. Perhaps what I had witnessed in the dreams had only been a byproduct of my own subconscious spurring what *I* wanted. I liked what I had seen between Alec and Callie . . . or thought I had seen. After imagining my two best friends together as more than friends, seeing one of them with someone else was a shock.

I wasn't *jealous* of Lillian and Alec. It was upsetting to realize I had read the situation wrong. When I turned toward the door to explain myself to Nathan, he was gone.

In his place, stood Lillian. I sunk into the couch as she moved farther into the room, and took a seat beside me. She stared at the television silently for a moment before turning toward me.

"Can we talk?" she asked.

"Sure." I swiveled in my seat, prepared to tell her exactly what I thought, when she cut me off.

"I know what you're thinking," she declared.

"If it's that you're using Alec to make Nathan jealous, then you are correct."

"It's not like that." I couldn't help but notice the sincerity of her words as she continued. "A part of me will always love Nathan, simply because he was my first love. I'm sure you can understand that."

I nodded, because I did. I supposed maybe that explained why I felt so protective of Alec's heart. Because it had been mine first, and I didn't want another girl to break it.

"Nathan's not the same guy I knew," Lillian added. "He's changed, and it took me a while to realize it. He's more mature now . . ." Her eyes shifted into a faraway gaze as she continued. "Even with me, he was restless. I didn't notice it then, but seeing him now, and seeing the two of you together, I know he's finally found exactly what he wants."

And now he was off stewing over what he considered a display of jealousy on my part. Lillian's words had a way of making me feel even crappier about the whole situation. I would make sure he understood everything before the night was over, but for now, I needed to make sure Alec's heart was safe.

"And what about Alec?" I asked Lillian.

"Alec . . ." She blew out a puff of air. "He's like a magnet. It's not love. I'm not naïve enough to think that. But he's a fun guy."

I recalled the conversation I had with Alec about Lillian. *I'm not asking her to marry me,'* he had said. Maybe they were both happy with their arrangement. Whatever it was.

I could deal with that, under one circumstance. I turned to Lillian with my warning. "Just don't break his heart like I did."

"Fair enough," she nodded. She let a comfortable silence stretch between us before she asked, "Can I ask what happened? You and Nathan? How . . ." She shook her head softly. "Never mind. It's none of my business."

"No, it's okay," I offered. "If you want to know, I have no problem telling you."

She sighed nervously, and her knee bounced against the sofa cushion hard enough that I felt the vibration from my seat. "I guess, um . . . when?"

When did it start? Gee, I had to think about that one. It was hard to explain, and I had lived it. We certainly hadn't experienced love at first sight, but the night he drove me out of Boone was the night it all started.

"I guess around January," I explained. "When the Skotadi came for me, and he took me away, hid me from them. We actually sort of hated each other at first, with the horrible situation and stress of everything. It changed somewhere along the way. I can't really pinpoint exactly when . . ."

Lillian chuckled like she understood exactly what I meant. "He's not exactly the romantic type, is he?"

"No, but he has his moments."

"And Alec?"

I explained to Lillian how everything transpired. From meeting Alec, to running with Nathan, to the reluctant partnership between the two of them, and how I had served as the catalyst in the feud between them. By the time I was finished, Lillian knew everything.

"And here they are," she concluded wistfully. "Working together, and actually *friendly*. I never would have guessed they had that history."

I laughed. "I think they were destined to be friends, whether they like it or not."

"They're actually a lot alike," Lillian mused. "Different in many ways, but still alike."

"Don't tell them that," I warned her light-heartedly, and she laughed.

After a moment, she sobered. "Maybe we could be like them?" I wrinkled my brow at her, and she added, "Many reasons to not be friends, but are anyway?"

Once I got what she was suggesting, I nodded. "Yeah, I'd like that."

Surprisingly, I meant it. Never thought the day would come that Lillian and I would be having this conversation, but I was glad that we were.

We talked some more about the guys, and shared laughs at their expense as the closing credits rolled across the television screen. We made plans to work together on my powers the next day, before parting ways.

Considering the late hour now, I wasn't surprised to find Nathan in bed, asleep. Across the room, Bruce snored softly. The family that had occupied the room earlier in the week was gone. As were Alec and Lillian.

I sat on the edge of my bed, facing Nathan, as I contemplated whether or not to wake him up to talk about earlier. Suddenly, his arm moved to fold the blanket over.

"Are you going to stare at me all night, or are you going to get in here?" His eyes shut, he lifted the sheets to create an opening for me to crawl into his bed with him.

I didn't hesitate. His arm hooked around me as I stretched out beside him, and I snuggled into his warm chest.

"I'm sorry," I mumbled.

"Me too," he returned with a kiss to the top of my head.

"It's not what you thought it was," I added.

"I know," he admitted. "Well . . . once I stopped and thought about it."

I pulled back so that I could see his face. "Then why didn't you come back, and let me know? All this time, I thought you were still mad."

"I did. You and Lillian were talking. I thought I'd let you two have that."

"Hmm." I returned to my cozy space under his chin.

Actually, my conversation with Lillian had been kind of fun. After tonight, I would say that our relationship had changed for the better. Finally, I could leave the past behind, and get to know her for who she was now.

"It's about time," Nathan sighed. "I'm glad to see the two of you finally getting along."

"Why is it so important to you?" I asked.

I felt his body move with a shrug. "I know her, and I think she could be a good friend to you. Once you both forget all the crap wedged between you," he added with a light chuckle.

"I think we finally have."

~ ~ ~

We slept late the next morning, choosing to cuddle in the small bed instead of training. We met the others for breakfast at the diner, where Jared and Bruce filled us in on what they had discovered the night before.

They had not *seen* much of anything, but talking to a few locals had gathered some intelligence. Reportedly, another nearby town, Vachos, had recently experienced an increase in criminal activity that had its residents nervous. Though nothing had happened yet in Areopoli, or any of the other small towns, the residents were nervous that the crime wave would soon expand to them as well.

"That explains why everyone stays inside at night," Nathan

volunteered.

"The people we talked to yesterday said that most of the villages around here have been enforcing a curfew," Jared said. "It hasn't really helped Vachos though."

"So what are we thinking?" Jas spoke up. "Skotadi? The demigods?"

"Well . . ." Jared spread out a map of the local area. He pointed to a dot that indicated the town of Vachos. "What's interesting is where this place is located."

"What's so interesting about it?" I asked tentatively, afraid I was the only one who didn't understand its significance.

Jared waved his hand over the wide open area between here and Vachos. No roads. No dots to indicate communities. Nothing.

"This is supposed to be the area over which the underworld is located. As you can see it's barren. And this river here . . ." His finger landed on a squiggly blue line that ran through Vachos. "It's one of the rivers that supposedly runs through the underworld."

"That's where the demigods came out," Nathan concluded. "Not here. Not the Diros Caves. But there."

Jared nodded once. "I think so."

"So what's the plan?" Alec asked.

No one spoke for a few moments as we all stared at the map, as if waiting for a resolution to materialize in front of us. Finally, Lillian's quiet voice broke the silence.

"I know that town," she whispered softly. All heads spun in her direction, and I noticed that her eyes appeared glazed as she stared at the map. From the horror-stricken expression on her face, I suspected she visualized something far more ominous than a map.

"I've been there." She blinked a few times as if to remember . .

. or to forget. "It's bad news, guys. The Skotadi have been there for years."

"What do you know about the demigods' influence there?" Jared asked.

Lillian shook her head solemnly. "They've been there. I never saw them, but many of the high-level Skotadi were in touch with them."

Nathan turned to look at Jared. "Maybe we should go check it out?"

"All of us," I added, earning an exasperated look from Nathan.

He spun back to Jared. "Dig up what you can before we go. In the meantime, we've got some work to do." His head nodded in my direction, and Jared smirked at me as I groaned.

It wouldn't have been so bad if he didn't make me go running first. We ran one way along the surf before stopping to do a series of sit-ups and push-ups. As we ran back, and approached the stretch of beach where we had started from an hour earlier, I spotted Alec sitting in the sand. He looked relaxed as he stared out at the surf crashing to the shore.

Today, the sea was angry. Kind of like my mood.

I dropped to my knees in utter exhaustion at Alec's feet.

"Glad you could make it," Nathan said to him as he gradually came to a stop beside me.

I glanced up at his form. Tall and sturdy, and not even a little winded from our workout.

"I can't say that I'm happy about it," Alec muttered as he rose to a slow stand. He took a long drink from the coffee mug in his hand. "I'd have rather gone back to bed, but you didn't really give me much of a choice."

"What's going on?" I glanced between the two of them.

Nathan looked down at me while I resisted the urge to curl into the fetal position on the sand—only because I didn't feel like digging sand out of my hair later. His eyes twinkled like he knew exactly what I was thinking.

"You're getting too strong for me," he told me.

"I am?"

"You need a bigger challenge than I can give you anymore."

I sighed. "No offense, but I have fought a few demigods, and I haven't used my fists once."

"Not yet," Alec countered.

I swiveled my head to find him in complete agreement with Nathan on this discussion.

"Hades' demigods are different from what you've seen so far," Nathan added. "Especially Sagriva. He'll fight the old fashioned way."

"Ares' son?"

Nathan nodded glumly. "He's going to be a tough one."

"In which case, I'll use my magic to gain the upper hand. Like I have been doing."

"What are you going to do when you're weak from using too much magic?" Alec strolled to my side, and offered a hand to help me up.

I resisted the urge to stick my tongue out at both of them. "Alright, fine." I waved my arms in the 'give it to me' signal. "Challenge me up then."

Alec grinned wickedly as he sized me up. I straightened my spine when he stalked me, as if I was his prey. Before I knew what he was planning, I found myself face down in the sand. And I had thought

Nathan was fast. Alec's nearly pure bloodlines gave him a significant advantage.

I pushed myself up, and shot Alec a hard glare as I swiped the sand from my face.

"Ooh, she's mad now," Alec teased, and tossed a grin in Nathan's direction.

"Careful," Nathan returned. "She fights dirty when she's mad."

And now they were ganging up on me . . . and enjoying it? What warped parallel universe had I stepped into?

"Just don't bite me." Alec pointed a warning finger at me. "I like to reserve that type of disturbing behavior for the bedroom."

He lunged for me again. This time, I allowed my demigod speed to take over, and I dodged his attack. I shoved him from behind as he whizzed by me, and sent him sprawling to the ground.

"Maybe we need to be training Alec instead," Nathan muttered to me, loud enough for Alec to hear.

"Shut it, Rocky!"

"Rambo," Nathan corrected.

"Same actor." Alec shrugged.

After that, Alec upped his game. But so did I.

Nathan stepped in a few times to point out a flaw in one of my moves, and to instruct me on a better way to do it. Though Alec was faster and stronger than I was used to, and I had a harder time keeping up with him than I had Nathan, I started to enjoy the new challenge. It didn't take long for me to adjust, and handle everything Alec threw at me.

I was happy to see how far I had come in such a short time. So much so that the two of them resorted to trading off on fighting me, to give themselves a break. I was consistently leveling both of them with ease by the time Jared showed up an hour later.

His loud clap of applause grabbed my attention, and I swiveled away from Alec, where he lay sprawled on the ground at my feet. Jared stood next to Nathan, where he sat, tending to his sore knee.

"As much fun as this has been to watch," Jared declared, "we have a trip to make."

Nathan slowly lifted to a stand. "What did you find out?"

"Twenty-three murders, seventy assaults, and over a hundred thefts in the past six months," Jared stated. "All in Vachos. There are two tourist-popular restaurants there, and three pubs that attract a good bit of business. But one of those pubs has recently been marked as a no-go spot. Locals advise tourists to steer clear of it. They don't always listen."

Of course, that was where the guys wanted to go, to find out what kind of shady business might be going on there. I was game for anything, if it led us to the demigods.

But first, I was in desperate need of a shower. Nathan and Alec needed one too, so we stopped by the hostel to clean up first. As the three of us passed through the door, the concierge called out to Nathan.

Though I couldn't hear the words that passed between them, I saw the transfer of keys from the concierge to Nathan. To the private room?

It must have been. If I had any doubt, it was squashed by the look on Nathan's face when he turned away from the desk.

If we didn't have somewhere to go right now, I would have led the way to the room. Once again, mission objectives trumped that idea.

But later?

We both knew. *Soon* had become *now*.

CHAPTER 13

Vachos was an hour from Areopoli, and a little larger in terms of population. I learned over the course of our drive that it was used as more of a travel pit-stop than a destination. Tourists stopped there for food and gas, and sometimes a place to rest, before moving on. It sounded like a carousel of unsuspecting humans served up on a platter for the Skotadi on a daily basis.

Typical Skotadi behavior . . . but were the demigods introducing a little of their own evil influence? That was what we needed to find out.

By the time we arrived around dinnertime, the pub we intended to scope out was crawling with thirsty tourists. We knew Skotadi would be present, so I disguised us all under a curtain of glamour. Nothing crazy like the last time. Just some eye and hair color changes in case they had descriptions of us. We didn't want to over-stretch my limit, and those little things were easier for me to hold for a longer period of time.

It worked. Aside from some leering looks from the three Skotadi at the bar, who regarded all the humans as pests, no one paid us much attention. After two beers and a few games of pool, I started to feel like we were just out for a night on the town.

That all changed when I excused myself to the bathroom. The doors were within sight of the pool tables, so no one gave my safety much thought. In retrospect, the dark hallway that led away from the bathroom's entrance should have been a giveaway.

When I exited a few minutes later, a cold hand clamped over my mouth, smothering my shrieks as I was pulled into the shadows. Within seconds, I was pushed out a back door and into an alley behind the building. Darkness had settled while we had been inside, so I couldn't make out the faces of the two men that advanced on me, but I suspected they were Skotadi.

If they thought I was human, they were in for a rude awakening.

One of them reached out to touch me, and I swatted his hand away.

"Ooh, we have a feisty one here," the other one said. He stepped into the eerie yellow glow cast from the street light at the end of the alley, and I caught the sly curve of his lips, which displayed the chipped tooth in his mouth.

My eyes darted between him and the touchy one, who I could now see looked like every high school girl's crush. Surprisingly attractive for a Skotadi . . . aside from the gold rings burning in his eyes.

"I happen to like feisty," he drew.

"Then you're in for a treat," I retorted before dropping my disguise.

Their eyes soaked me in, from head to foot, as they registered the change in my appearance. The first thing they probably noticed was my eyes, which carried faint golden rings. That made them pause temporarily. Then I saw the brief flash of recognition contort their faces—they knew exactly who I was. Their third surprise was my fists zeroing in on their faces.

I popped the touchy one first, since he was closer. He doubled over, his hands going to his face to catch the blood that squirted from his nose. As he groaned in agony, a perfectly executed upper cut launched Chipped Tooth into the side of the dumpster. I spun to launch a knee to the groin of Touchy when he straightened to look for his buddy. He dropped to his knees as the back door flung open.

I whirled around, ready to take on another one, but dropped my hands when I saw Nathan instead.

"What the—" His eyes hardened on the two bloody and moaning Skotadi on the ground before he turned to me with concern. "You okay?"

"I'm fine. I don't know about them."

The rest of our gang quickly filed out the door and crammed into the narrow alley—all of them in their true forms now. Bruce hauled Chipped Tooth to his feet while Jared and Jas stood Touchy up against the wall beside him.

Jas barked out a laugh. "Damn. She kicked both your asses! Look at all this blood."

Alec eyed me curiously. "Did you use your magic?"

I shook my head, and he turned to exchange a look with Nathan. Both of them regarded me with surprise.

"What? You *taught* me how to fight."

"Apparently, they did a good job too," Jared mused.

I watched while Jared patted down the Skotadi Jas was holding. He withdrew a pistol, a shiny blade, and a folded up card. The weapons he handed to Lillian, while he examined the card.

"*Club Red*," Jared read out loud. "What's this?"

When neither of them offered a prompt explanation, Bruce tapped Chipped Tooth's head against the wall to give him a little motivation to speak up.

Jared handed the card to Nathan, who angled it for me to see. It resembled a small postcard, depicting an alluring combination of dancing, alcohol, and a good time at this *Club Red*. Posted were an address and business hours.

"A Skotadi-run club," Nathan muttered under his breath. Turning to the Skotadi, he demanded, "You're luring humans here, aren't you?"

Neither of them answered.

"Let me see it," Lillian requested, and Nathan handed her the card before he drew closer to the Skotadi.

"You thought she was human," he jeered at them. "Big mistake."

"We know who she is," Chipped Tooth snarled, his eyes moving to me.

Nathan's arm shot out so fast I didn't realize what had happened until the Skotadi dropped to the ground, his face a little bloodier than it had already been. He rolled to spit up a mouthful of blood as Nathan turned his attention to the other one.

"You got anything to say?" he barked.

The Skotadi's eyes flicked in my direction.

"Look at her again, and you'll end up on the ground with your buddy," Nathan threatened. "Now, tell us what's going on at *Club Red*."

"They'll kill me if I tell you."

"We'll kill you if you don't," Nathan returned smoothly.

"*Slowly*," Jared added.

Damn, those two could be scary if they wanted to be. But the Skotadi still didn't speak.

Nathan casually withdrew his knife. The diamond that coated

the blade sparkled faintly in the dim light. He inspected it intently, holding it out for the Skotadi to get a good look at it.

"Do you have any idea what diamond poisoning feels like?"

The Skotadi shifted anxiously.

"It starts off as a burn," Nathan shared, his voice taking on that deep, threatening quality I hadn't heard in a long time. "You will want to tear your own flesh off, and pray for death to make the pain go away."

Chipped Tooth snorted. "Like you know."

"I do know," Nathan returned coldly. His head nodded in my direction. "She can cure it, did you know that? But I can guarantee, she will not cure you. You're going to feel every minute of it."

Both Skotadi eyed me suspiciously, and I maintained a stoic demeanor despite my unease at seeing this side of Nathan again. Chipped Tooth's gaze swung nervously between Nathan and Jared, and whatever he saw prompted him to open his mouth.

"It—it started off as a typical Skotadi establishment," he sputtered. "We've got them all over the world. You know how we work."

"So what is it now?" Jared pressed.

"The demigods came in a few months ago," he continued in a rush. "Started recruiting us for an army."

"Circe's army?" Nathan demanded.

The Skotadi's throat jumped before he nodded.

"And the humans?" Nathan snapped.

"We were instructed to lure every human we could find to the club." The Skotadi cast him a wary glance. "There was an Incantator. All the humans were cursed by the time they left."

Nathan turned to Lillian with a silent question. She nodded her head solemnly—she had been a part of it.

"Where are the demigods now?" Jared asked.

"I don't know," the Skotadi cried. "They haven't been there for a month or more."

"He's lying," Lillian declared.

The Skotadi did a double take, and finally settled his eyes on Lillian. His jaw dropped when he realized who she was.

"Yes, it was me," she confessed. "I did it. I did Circe's dirty work, and I'm here to stop it now." To Nathan, Lillian added, "We don't need them. I remember everything."

Nathan smirked as he took a menacing step toward the Skotadi.

"You'll never find them!" Chipped Tooth hollered. "They're hidden too well!"

"Then we'll draw them out," Alec offered quietly from my side.

"You can't. They're not stupid enough," the Skotadi insisted.

"Maybe, but we have something they want," Alec shrugged. He turned to me. "They want us."

~ ~ ~

We found *Club Red* on the outskirts of town—a large, brick building painted in a bright blood red, surrounded by a wide open parking lot and nothing else. A quarter mile from anything else remotely civilized, it presented the perfect isolated location for Circe's dirty work.

The card indicated that the doors would not open for another hour, yet I was anxious as we stood in the empty parking lot. The evil housed within the building's walls was palpable.

Certainly, if I were a human, I would never venture into a place like this. But I doubted the humans that showed up tonight would be of a sound mind. The whole operation probably feasted off the drunk and roofied.

Lillian was visibly tense where she stood against the vehicle, her eyes scanning the building with trepidation.

"What do you remember, Lil?" Nathan prompted softly.

"A back room," she murmured. "They brought me humans . . ." She trailed off to swat at the tear that rolled down her cheek. "There's a Skotadi—goes by the name Marcus—who runs the whole operation. He's the contact to the demigods."

"Do you think he's still here?" Jared questioned.

She nodded slowly. "Marcus opened this club decades ago. Even before Circe, he was preying on humans for the fun of it. Unless he's dead, I don't see him giving this place up. He'll be here."

"Tonight," I concluded.

"No, not tonight," Nathan countered.

I spun on him. "Why not?"

"Because we need a plan, that's why," he fired at me. "This isn't something we can just walk into and expect the result we want. It doesn't work like that."

"So we wait some more?" I straightened my back in defiance. "How long are we going to wait? For Circe to finish the curse herself? For her to find Alec? For Callie to die?"

"Kris . . ." His eyes softened as he took a step toward me.

"Don't." I backed away. "Who's going to have to die before we make a move? We need to strike first."

"We will," he insisted. "*After* we come up with a plan of action."

I felt a spark. My temper flared, and my other half rode it like an amusement park ride. She loved it, welcomed it. My eyes sought

Alec's, and he shifted to my side, recognizing that I needed him.

All he had to do was give me a look, and I started to calm down. But I was still mad. Mostly disappointed.

I hated waiting. Waiting risked the safety of everyone around me. Since no one understood my concerns, I had to bury my fear. Because I knew I couldn't do this by myself, I had to wait, even when every instinct told me to act now.

I passed Nathan as I moved to open the car door. "You better hope my best friend doesn't die first," I muttered before I climbed in.

~ ~ ~

~Nathan~

Kris was smoking mad. The tension between the two of us seeped out and infected the rest of the crew. It was the longest, quietest, and most uncomfortable car ride of my life.

The tension didn't alleviate once we arrived at the hostel, as I hoped it would. I thought a nice long car ride would have been enough to get over her anger. I was wrong.

Kris stomped off and slammed the door to the second floor, ten-bed room, while the rest of us stared after her from the hallway.

Alec turned to me with a snort. "Have fun sleeping in that big private room all by yourself tonight."

I withdrew the key from my pocket without a response. As I opened the door, I inclined my head, inviting the rest of them to enter.

Might as well. Not like I had any other use for the room now.

"I requested it so we had somewhere safe to talk," I eventually responded.

"Uh-huh."

Despite Alec's obvious skepticism, we did end up doing exactly what I had originally requested the room for. Thirty minutes into our heated discussion, we—minus the girls, who had disappeared at some point—came to one conclusion. Our best chance at getting to the demigods was to use the club to lure them out. Everyone had an opinion on how we would manage to do that, and no one agreed on any one idea.

I lost track of how much time had been spent discussing every scenario, when Lillian popped her head into the room.

"I'm going to grab a late snack at the diner," she announced. "Anyone want to join me?"

Alec immediately jumped to his feet. He shot a warning glare at the rest of us before he took off.

So he wanted alone time with Lillian. Alone time sounded nice.

Five minutes later, Kira popped in to invite us to watch a movie in the common room downstairs. Jas scampered off even faster than Alec had.

I shook my head. Was *everyone* hooking up around here?

Before Kira and Jas disappeared down the hall, I called out, "Hey, Kira! Where's Kris?"

"She was going to get a shower, then read something, I think."

Uh-huh. Sure she was.

I turned to Jared. "You still have the keys to the car, right?"

Jared grinned as he withdrew the set from his pocket. "She can't hotwire it, can she?"

"I wouldn't put it past her to try," I muttered.

"She'll come around." Jared patted me on the shoulder as he stood to let himself out. "We'll talk more tomorrow. I think Alec's suggestion might work the best, but let's all sleep on it, and talk in the morning."

"A shower and bed sounds good right about now," Bruce grumbled as he sniffed his shirt.

I agreed. After spending the afternoon in the bar, we all smelled like stale cigarette smoke.

At least I could take advantage of my newly acquired private shower. Apparently, my new room wouldn't be good for much else.

CHAPTER 14

~Kris~

I nearly ran into Bruce when I exited the communal bathroom. He held the door open for me, and gave me a shy smile as I passed.

"You really were taking a shower," he mused.

"What else would I be doing?"

"Somebody worried you might have tried to sneak off, return to the club to take matters into your own hands."

I dropped my chin to hide the smile on my face—because I knew it was a dead giveaway. I *had* thought about it. A lot. Though I had been tempted, I chose not to.

Somewhere along the way, I had come to realize that Nathan was right. Though waiting may put Callie and Alec in more danger, acting without a plan would put us *all* in danger.

Bruce shook his head. A grin tugged at the corners of his lips when I eventually looked up.

"What?" My arms fanned out. "I'm still here."

"Better keep it that way." Bruce winked before he pushed through the door, leaving me alone in the hallway.

I poked my head in the communal room. Neither Lillian nor Kira had returned yet. As much as I loathed Kira, I hated being alone more. Nathan's private room was just a few steps from there. No one answered my knock, but the door was unlocked, so I let myself in.

I covered my mouth to capture the laugh that bubbled up my throat. "Who would do this?"

The dim bedside lamp offered enough light to display the tacky décor, peeling flower printed wallpaper, and mismatched furniture spaced out on a faded yellow carpet. The bed was covered in a white eyelet bedspread and flower-adorned pillows.

"It's like a trip to the seventies in here," I muttered under my breath.

I got no response, of course. But the sound of the shower running in the adjoined bathroom let me know that I wasn't entirely alone.

I sat on the edge of the bed to wait. When the water shut off, I debated whether or not to announce my presence. Instead, I bit my lip as I listened to the sound of the shower curtain sliding open. More shuffling that sounded like clothing being pulled on, the thump of a wet towel hitting the floor, then the door swung open.

Nathan halted when his gaze landed on me. His messy, towel-dried hair looked darker in the poor light, and tiny water droplets had gathered at the nape, where they dripped onto the shoulder of his t-shirt. The five-o-clock shadow on his jaw added a hint of scruffiness to his otherwise refreshed appearance.

The mere sight of him twisted my insides, and momentarily caught my breath. Since I didn't trust my voice yet, I offered him a smile.

His eyebrows furrowed as he regarded me. "Hey."

"Surprised to see me?"

I thought I heard him grunt something, but couldn't make out what it was. He inclined his head as he moved to the lopsided table across from me. There, he stuffed the clothes he had worn earlier into a plastic bag.

"Thought I was going to take off, huh?" I said to his back, my voice lifting with a teasing ring.

He turned slowly. "The thought crossed my mind."

I smiled warily at my feet. "Mine too."

His heavy sigh filled the room, and dissuaded me from looking up. "Kris, I know you're mad at me, but—"

"I'm not mad." My head snapped up, and my eyes met his unflinchingly. "Not anymore. You were right."

One of his eyebrows shot up. "What?"

"I'm not mad," I repeated.

"No . . . after that."

A reluctant smile teased my lips. "Don't push it."

His eyes lit with amusement, a little bit of admiration . . . and something else that twisted me up a little more on the inside.

I inhaled a gulp of air before I continued, "I know you want to do what's best for me. You always have."

He nodded thoughtfully, and I stood to cross the short distance between us. Aside from the visible jump of his throat, he appeared relaxed with his arms folded across his chest.

"Everything you do is for me." His arms dropped to his sides as I stepped into his comfort zone, and one hand grazed my hip. "You've taught me everything I know." I kept my head down as my hand roamed across his ribcage. "You've made me a better, stronger person."

"You were strong long before I came along, Kris."

"Maybe," I shrugged, "but you're the one who taught me how to throw a left hook."

Nathan's chest vibrated with silent laughter. He sucked in a sharp breath when my hands moved to the hem of his shirt, and my fingers grazed his skin. I bunched the fabric in my hands.

"You taught me how to shoot a gun . . ."

I lifted the shirt over his head, and our eyes met.

"You were terrible at it," he murmured.

"You made me stab bags of corn," I continued wistfully while my hands explored him—every magnificent, exposed inch of him.

His hand slipped under my shirt, and his fingers traced over my lower back. "I was afraid you'd stab me instead."

"I considered it." Then, as if to show him just how far my opinion of him had come since those days, I pressed my lips to the faint scar above his heart. The scar created the night we had first kissed.

A staggered breath hissed between his teeth. "Kris . . ." My name was a warning. One I didn't need. Or want.

"Shh." I pressed my thumb to his lips to silence him before continuing, "And you never pressured me before I was ready. Not once."

Both of his hands were around my waist now, barely touching me, as if he was afraid to. He laughed softly, nervously. "Requesting a private room for us doesn't count as pressure?"

I shook my head. "No, because I'm ready now."

That must have been all he had needed to hear. All at once, his grip on me tightened, his mouth crushed mine, and my legs encircled his waist. My pulse soared, and butterflies took flight, as he flung us onto the bed behind me. We landed on possibly the most uncomfortable mattress ever made with a painful thud, and Nathan laughed against my lips.

"That didn't quite go the way I envisioned it in my head," he admitted.

"What is this thing made of? Cinder blocks?" I groaned.

Nathan's head lifted to pierce me with a look. A question burned in his eyes, along with understanding. I knew he had hoped for something more idyllic for our first time together, if only to satisfy my girly fantasies. But right now, I didn't care about any of that other stuff. It was only glitz and glitter.

My answer was to bury my fingers into his hair as I drew his mouth to mine. His hearty response told me that he wasn't going to question me again. He kissed me with the languid patience of a man who wanted to savor everything. He pulled and nipped at my lip, eliciting a sigh from me.

While my response turned his kiss into a demanding fury, his hands roamed leisurely. The balance of his control unraveled me, set me on fire. I thought I might combust by the time he slipped my shirt over my head.

The kiss that followed was gentle and promising. Though great as always, I had long moved past promising . . . to wanting. My hands slid greedily down his bare back to the flexible waistband of his pants. They froze there when Nathan's mouth ripped away from mine with a groan.

"Wait a minute," he sighed. "I need to tell you something."

I grumbled at the abrupt interruption, then pulled my lip between my teeth. "Is it just me, or has every bad conversation in history started with those words?"

"This isn't bad. I promise." His eyes shifted away, and his head shook once. I couldn't decipher the meaning behind his body language, but I did notice that it contradicted his words in every way.

"Then what is it?" I attempted to keep my voice light, but it came out sounding forced.

He seemed to pick up on the fact that he was worrying me, and cupped my face tenderly in his hand. "I want you to know that this is it for me. *You* are it for me." He paused to let those words sink in, and for a relieved smile to form on my lips, before he added, "You're my destiny."

Now it was my turn to shake my head. "I'm your what?"

Most girls would smile to hear such promising words from the man she loved—human girls, living a normal human life. But I had learned that, in my world, those words actually *meant* something.

He leaned back to give me some room as I pushed myself up onto my elbows, as if sitting up would help me understand what he was talking about. Because I honestly didn't know.

"Don't get mad, and don't take it the wrong way," he said in a rush. "Let me explain."

"You're going to have to . . ."

"Remember the prophet who I had watch out for you," he prompted, encouraging a nod from me. That I had known about. "She also had a habit of checking into my future, despite me not wanting her to. After I saved you from the car accident, she told me that my future had changed."

He paused, seemingly unsure about how to proceed. Or worried about my reaction?

"I want you to know that her telling me that had no impact on what has happened between us," he stated firmly. "I didn't like the idea of my future being predetermined like that, and I . . ." There was a silent apology in his eyes when they met mine now. "I fought it. Well, I *tried* to fight it."

Despite his surprising revelation, I felt a smile forming on my lips. "*That* I believe." The first few weeks of our time together hadn't exactly been the start of a beautiful romance.

"I fell in love with you anyway," he added without missing a beat. "And not because I felt like I was supposed to."

I nodded. "That's why you were so upset when Micah insisted that he was my soul mate," I concluded. "Because I was supposed to be yours."

"No. You *are* mine. I don't need a prophet to tell me that."

Since Micah's big revelation months ago, I'd had a varied opinion of soul mates, and destiny, and fate. Since the day I first discovered the life I was destined to live, I had tried to change it. I hoped I was close to succeeding. But this?

This was one thing I knew to be true, and the one thing I was okay with. Because whether a prophet predicted it or not, and whether it was meant to be or not, I knew Nathan was the one for me.

I pulled him into a kiss that I hoped let him know that. He responded slowly, hesitantly, like he had expected me to be upset with his revelation. Then he deepened the kiss with a hearty sigh, and my shoulders dropped to the mattress beneath his weight.

"There's more," he murmured against my lips.

He pulled away, and I barely refrained a groan of protest. He rolled onto his back to dig a hand into the pocket of his pants. I watched silently as his hand reappeared with a shiny object between his fingers.

"Gran has insisted that she's known all along, of course. Something about grandmotherly instinct, or something," he added with a soft chuckle. His eyes remained fixed on whatever he held in his hand, and if I didn't know him so well, I would have sworn that he was scared of it.

He turned to me with his hand outstretched, and I finally saw what he was holding. A delicate silver ring. My eyes darted between him and the ring, my jaw slack.

"She gave this to me a long time ago," Nathan continued. "To give to you when I was ready. It's been in the family for generations. Apparently, I'm her only hope of passing it on."

I sucked in a shaky breath. "How long have you had this?"

"Long enough." He made a noise that fell somewhere between a laugh and a sigh. My eyes moved from the ring to settle on Nathan as he gave me a half smile. "I was ready to make a promise to you a long time ago, but I wanted to make sure you were ready for it."

"Is it like . . . an engagement ring?"

He shrugged. "It seems like so much more than that, but . . . yeah."

I bit my lip, but it didn't stop me from grinning like a moron as I stuck my hand out. "Then what are you waiting for?"

His throat jumped as he shifted to kneel beside me. "When this is all over . . . we'll make it real."

"I can't wait."

He wasted no more time in slipping the ring onto my finger. His hand entwined with mine as our lips collided. I fell back onto the bed, taking him with me. Now that he had addressed everything that he needed to, he held nothing back.

His hands traced my skin delicately as he slowly undressed me. His touch was intoxicating. The more I got, the more I wanted. His controlled, deliberate actions wreaked havoc on my composure.

He must have noticed, because his head swung from side to side as he briefly took in the room. "Nothing floating?"

"Not this time." I shifted to give him more room as he nuzzled my neck, then sighed as he moved lower. "Nothing else you need to tell me, right?"

"Nuh-uh . . ." His head snapped up suddenly, as if he had realized something. "Except that . . . I love you."

I barely had time to repeat the same words before his mouth was on mine, stifling my response. The remaining fabric barriers between us disappeared at a rate that straddled the thin line between careful diligence and unadulterated urgency. His hand held mine, the ring and all that it promised, pressed between us, as we gave ourselves to each other in the only other way we had yet to do.

I had heard girls complain that their first times weren't the greatest of experiences. I had heard it all. It was awkward. It was unimpressive. It wasn't what they had expected.

I couldn't have disagreed with them more. If I could have gone back to school, I would tell them that I discovered the secret. It was all about finding the right guy. Because he made it everything I had hoped for. And then some.

I would have been lying if I said that there weren't some surprises. Good surprises.

Good surprises that I wanted to relive over, and over, and over again.

At some point, the lamp floated to the ceiling. At the time, I didn't care. I barely noticed when it crashed to the floor and shattered, right along with me.

~ ~ ~

The curtain of hair that covered my face didn't block the

morning sun any better than the hole-ridden blinds that covered the window. I stayed where I was, silent and still, as the previous night's events replayed in my head.

It all seemed surreal. Impossible. Nothing in real life could have been that amazing. Right?

My eyes shifted to the floor, and to the broken lamp that lay there. So I hadn't dreamt that part. That had really happened. *All* of it had really happened.

Holy crap. I buried my face into my pillow to stifle a scream of joy. Once I got that out of my system, nervousness crept in with reality. I had never had a 'morning after' before. I had heard that they were awkward.

Then again, that came from the same girls that claimed sex sucked the first time. They had definitely been wrong about that one.

Taking a calming breath to settle my nerves, I rolled lazily onto my side to face him, but he wasn't there. My eyes landed on the table across the room, where a plate of chocolate donuts and a steaming cup of coffee sat, waiting for me.

He certainly knew how to make me happy. In *every* way, I mentally added with a devious smile as I sat up.

I padded across the room to scoop Nathan's shirt off the floor, and slipped it on as I made my way to the donuts. I took a generous bite, then followed the sound of splashing water to the bathroom.

A shirtless Nathan stood at the sink, his back to me, as he ran a razor over his jaw. I stopped in the doorway to admire him while I nibbled on the donut. My eyes roamed appreciatively over his broad shoulders and back. By the time I found his eyes in the reflection, he was smiling at me.

"Good morning," he greeted.

"Morning." I bounced into the room, and plopped onto the counter next to the sink as he made another swipe with the razor. "You didn't wake me for our usual morning of torture."

His eyes darted to mine as he wiped the remnants of shaving cream from his face. "I thought you could use the extra sleep."

He winked, and I nearly slid off the counter into a puddle on the floor. The implied 'after last night' brought an unexpected flush to my cheeks. My mouth dried, and I gulped the last of my donut down.

"I thought we were meeting the others for breakfast," I finally managed to get out.

"It's still early." He shifted to stand in front of me. His hands gripped my waist to tug me forward while he wedged himself between my knees. "You're wearing my shirt."

"I'm wearing *only* your shirt."

Nathan's eyes darted to mine, and his chest rose and fell with a deep, controlled breath. "We're never going to make it to breakfast."

I mumbled something incoherently. Maybe something along the lines of, '*I don't care,*' but I couldn't be sure. He drew my lips to his, and all thought processes stopped.

My mouth slid from his long enough for me to mutter, "I'm not hungry anyway."

"We have donuts," he grunted.

My head rolled back as he nuzzled the sensitive spot beneath my ear. "Mmm. Good thinking."

Honestly, at that moment, I didn't care if we ever left this room. At some point, hunger and mission requirements would draw us out. But for now? I would happily postpone all of it for another hour—or two?—alone with Nathan.

~ ~ ~

The crew had decided to meet at nine. Nathan and I were twenty minutes late by the time we flew into the café, hand in hand.

"Well . . . well . . ." Alec consulted the imaginary watch on his wrist. "Look who finally decided to join us."

I attempted to shoot him a scathing look, but couldn't wipe the smile from my face long enough to make it believable.

"You seem happier than you were the last time I saw you," Alec said to me, then turned to Nathan. "And you're not scowling at me like you usually do . . ." He waited expectantly as Nathan took a seat at the table. When Nathan glanced up at him, he added, "Ah, there it is."

Nathan's head lowered to study the menu in front of him with forced concentration, effectively ignoring the eyes of everyone else at the table. I attempted to do the same, though I could feel the curiosity oozing off of them. His hand dropped beneath the table to squeeze my knee, effectively extinguishing the fire burning my cheeks from being the center of unwanted attention.

Honestly, who cared if they knew what we did last night?

Wasn't like it had been a random hook-up, like some of the others in our group. The ring on my finger proved that. As my thoughts drifted to the ring, and what it represented, the others saw it.

Jared snatched my hand, and shot a wide-eyed look at Nathan. "What's this?" he demanded.

Nathan didn't look up from the menu as he replied, "What's it look like?"

"Holy shit," Jared murmured as he gave me my hand back.

I glanced up to catch Alec's wide open mouth. He closed it slowly as his eyes lifted from my hand to my face. I held my breath as I waited for his reaction. In the past, I would have expected pain masquerading as contempt.

He showed no signs of either as his gaze shifted toward Nathan. "Can I please be in charge of planning the bachelor party?"

Nathan's stern response was immediate, and matched mine. "No," we replied in unison.

"Isn't that supposed to be the best man's job?" Jared's voice carried a teasing ring as he studied the steaming cup of coffee lifted to his lips. Behind it was a sly grin directed at Nathan, who had yet to lift his head out of the menu.

"Who says I can't be the best man?" Alec lifted a hand to his chest in mock heartbreak.

"Best man for what?" Lillian questioned as she settled into the empty chair beside Alec. Up until then, I hadn't realized her absence. She must have been in the bathroom.

My eyes darted to her as she slowly caught up. Her gaze settled on my hand, and a look of understanding crossed her face.

"Oh."

Nathan's head finally lifted at her softly spoken word. A silent conversation passed between the two of them while the rest of us sat, unmoving, in our seats. I barely breathed as I watched the gamut of emotions play across her face, from shock to resignation.

She finally settled on a small smile. "Not like we didn't all see this coming, right?"

The rest of us took a collective breath at her acceptance. Conversation reverted back to arguments over best men and bachelor parties, requests for an open bar at the reception, and bets over what month the deed would be done. It was a carefree breakfast, spent laughing and joking. But we all knew it couldn't last.

Before our plates were cleaned, conversation had shifted to our agenda for the day. We stayed long after our meals were finished, formulating a plan.

A loose plan, but a plan.

By noon, Nathan's private room was no longer a love nest, but a command center. Everything we had—weapons, ammo, papers and files on intelligence gathered, and maps—covered the tables and walls. Each detail was hammered out to everyone's satisfaction, though we all still felt a ripple of uncertainty.

It wasn't the best of plans, but it was all we had. I knew I was tired of waiting for another opportunity to arise, and I sensed the others were as eager to get this over with as I was. Because even after this was over, it wasn't really over.

We still had so much to do. I wanted to stop the curse without looking over my shoulder for the remaining demigods to find me, or kill Alec or anyone else I cared about.

This part of my life ended today.

Lillian left to go shopping for the things we didn't already have—specifically club appropriate attire for herself, Alec, and me. We would need to blend in, and her experience as a Skotadi provided her with the inside knowledge of how to do that.

After another few hours of strategy, objective, and contingency plans, I was actually glad when she returned, and it was time to get ready.

Until I saw the selection of outfits she had chosen.

CHAPTER 15

She tossed Alec a pair of skinny jeans and a black shirt with a skull on the front of it, then turned to me with a wary grimace.

"Uh, what the hell is this?" Alec interrupted whatever she had been about to say to me.

"Your outfit for tonight," she replied curtly.

"Yeah . . . I don't think so." He set the clothes aside with a shake of his head.

"You need to blend in," Lillian reminded him, "or you'll have every Skotadi in the club gunning for you."

I feared that might happen anyway, but I supposed Lillian's suggestions would give us the best chance at avoiding it. We only needed *one* Skotadi to recognize us. If we didn't dress the part and blend in, potentially hundreds of them could target us, and we'd never get the job done.

"Alec," I chided, forcing him to sigh in submission.

"Fine," he grumbled as he retrieved the clothes. Holding them like he suspected them to be laced with poison, he left the room to change.

Lillian led me into the bathroom, out of sight and earshot of the guys. "I picked out two outfits that will work. I wasn't sure which one you would be most comfortable with."

She laid them on the counter for me to inspect, and I chewed on my lip as my gaze swung back and forth between the short black skirt paired with a deep purple strapless top, and the shorter black skirt paired with a fire red blouse. I picked up the blouse, thinking it looked a little more concealing, but put it back when I noticed it didn't have a back—only two thin crisscrossing strings.

I was no prude, and had my fair share of party-approved skirts and blouses in my closet in Boone. But they were nothing like this.

"I'm thinking the purple?" Lillian suggested.

"Okay," I mumbled. It really didn't matter. Either outfit combined with the high black boots Lillian had set on the floor would make me look 'street corner on the wrong side of town' ready.

Five minutes later, I stood beside Lillian at the bathroom counter as we applied the layers of makeup she had also purchased. Every time I leaned to grab something from the kit, I was forced to tug the skirt back into place. Despite the fierceness with which it clung to me, it had a tendency to drift. I didn't doubt that my underwear would be visible to wandering eyes with a good angle.

As bad as the skirt was, the top was worse. As if having no straps wasn't bad enough, it was also sheer—a fact I hadn't realized until after I put it on. Apparently, in the Skotadi-fashion world, it was acceptable to wear a black bra underneath a practically see-thru shirt.

"I look like a hooker," I muttered to Lillian's reflection beside me.

"You look like a female Skotadi," she corrected.

I grumbled as I applied another layer of mascara. Lillian had suggested several layers. The darker the better, she had said, but I drew the line before I crossed into tarantula legs territory.

While she had suggested the fire red lipstick, I had opted for a slightly subtler shade. Still not my style, but not as bold. As I blotted my lips, I saw the door crack open behind me in the mirror's reflection.

I didn't want any of the guys to see me like this, but Nathan was the one I dreaded the most.

His eyes roamed over me before settling on my legs. "That's what you bought today?"

"Told you he'd hate it," I muttered to Lillian.

"He doesn't hate it," she whispered. "That's the problem."

Watching Nathan's face as his gaze swept up from my legs to other areas on display, I wasn't so sure I agreed with Lillian. Then his eyes turned to her.

"Did the shirt actually have to be see-thru?" he demanded.

She dropped the makeup brush she was using with a sigh, and turned to shove him out of the room while I peered down at myself.

"You said it wasn't that bad," I groaned once she returned.

"It's not," she promised. "He's just being . . ."

"Difficult?" I suggested when I saw that she was hung up on words.

"Concerned," she countered softly. A few heavy seconds ticked by as she dusted powder on her face before she added, "He's having a hard time with the plan for tonight."

"No kidding," I snorted.

There were too many what-ifs for any of us to feel completely comfortable with it. But it was all we had. Even backed into a corner, with no other options and everyone else against him, Nathan hadn't relented easily.

Not that I had expected him to, considering my central role. We were taking a risk. A big risk, but a necessary one. But there wasn't much I wouldn't do for Alec or Callie, and they both needed for tonight to be successful just as much as I did. Maybe more so.

I finished my makeup, and turned to Lillian for her approval. Her nod confirmed it. I looked Skotadi enough for the club.

As if they all knew how mortified I was to be seen looking like this, all the guys were waiting expectantly in the room when we finally emerged from the bathroom.

Alec whistled appreciatively. Jared's eyes nearly popped out of his head. Bruce's head tilted to the side as if in bewilderment. And Nathan . . .

His hand rubbed his jaw thoughtfully. Though I couldn't see his mouth, I imagined it was drawn into a tight line.

"Let's get this over with." I tugged on the skirt as I darted toward the door. As quickly as I possibly could in the hooker boots.

I hoped I wouldn't have to do much fighting tonight, because it certainly wouldn't be easy in these things. It wouldn't be easy without them.

Here's to hoping the plan works . . .

I said a silent prayer as we marched down the narrow steps, and into the street. The cooler night air hit my bare legs, and brought on a bad case of the goosebumps that didn't let up even in the car. The hour-long journey was spent checking and rechecking weapons and ammo, and going over our roles until we all knew them by heart. Despite all our preparations, my legs were shaking by the time we pulled up to the club. And it wasn't all because of the chill in the air.

Nathan grabbed my arm to hold me back when I climbed out of the car.

"Are you sure about this?" he asked softly.

"No," I admitted reluctantly. "But this is the only option we have right now."

His head dropped with a sigh, and I knew he had his own concerns over how this night may turn out. "I don't like being separated from you."

"It won't be for long," I returned, and hoped I was telling him the truth.

He nodded as if trying to convince himself. "You have your phone?"

"These boots are good for something." Though the rest of my ensemble didn't conceal much of anything, the boots proved an ideal location to hide both my phone and my sheathed diamond-coated knife.

He nodded before dropping his forehead to mine. I melted into the car at my back as I welcomed his lips. What started off as a soft brush quickly intensified into something fierce. It could have even been a heated goodbye, but I refused to believe that.

I smiled at the smudge of color left on the corner of Nathan's mouth when he withdrew, and wiped it away with my thumb. "Red is not your color."

I didn't even get a half-smile when he released me. That was how worried he was.

Behind him, Alec and Lillian were waiting, and I knew I had to go. It was harder than I had expected it to be. Perhaps that should have been my first clue that I wasn't entirely convinced tonight would go smoothly? I shook the negative feeling off before it took root.

My hand grazed Nathan's cheek. "I'll see you soon," I promised before I stepped around him to join Alec and Lillian.

Together, we rounded the corner to the front of the club. Before moving out of sight, I glanced over my shoulder to find Jared and

Bruce gathering what they needed from the back of the vehicle. Nathan stood frozen where I had left him.

"Focus." Alec grabbed my arm to pull me back to our task.

"I got it."

Alec and I trailed behind Lillian as we approached the entrance. One Skotadi stood at the door, beefy arms folded across his chest, and gold-ringed eyes peered down at us with disgust.

As Lillian stepped forward to greet him, Alec grabbed my hand. "Show time, sweetheart," he whispered.

And then he kissed me, hard and full, on the mouth. Though I knew it was coming—as per the plan— the way Alec jumped right in to a full-on steamy kiss with no build up whatsoever caught me off guard for a moment. Once my brain started firing on all cylinders again, I did my job of making it look believable.

I put up the glamour to make Alec and I appear human, if the Skotadi guard bothered to look closely enough. Our mindless groping, and apparent oblivion of our surroundings, made us optimal Skotadi prey. Lillian barely needed to say anything before he ushered us inside.

We stepped into a narrow hallway that overlooked a grand oval pit beneath us. Multi-colored strobe lights flashed to the beat of the music pouring from the speakers on the walls. Easily two hundred Skotadi and unsuspecting humans gyrated against each other on the dance floor. Another large group crowded around the long bar opposite of where we stood. Beyond that, the club darkened into shadows.

"Any last questions?" Lillian asked us.

Alec and I shook our heads in unison. We had gone over everything *extensively*.

With a nod, Lillian turned to leave, then stopped when Alec called out, "Hey Lillian, make sure they stick it out."

Code for: keep Nathan the hell out of here.

With nothing more than a calculating look, Lillian left Alec and me on the balcony.

I dropped the glamour so that Alec and I looked like our true selves. Alec grabbed my hand and steered me toward the flight of stairs that spiraled down to the pit. We bumped elbows with many Skotadi along the way, but no one gave us a second glance. I supposed no one expected the two Most Wanted Skotadi rebels to show up at *Club Red*.

The longer we went unseen, the more the bundle of nerves in my gut unfurled and I started to believe we might actually make it out of here. The plan might actually work. If a certain Skotadi was in attendance tonight.

At the bar, Alec handed me a glass of a light brown beverage . . . on the rocks. I took a sip, and forced myself not to make a face at the bitter taste.

Of course Skotadi would only drink the hard liquors. I wouldn't be getting any cocktails here.

But I also wasn't supposed to get drunk. Only . . . blending in.

Alec pulled out a stool for me to sit on, and leaned close to yell in my ear. "See anything yet?"

I swept my gaze around the pit, but only saw humans and Skotadi in various stages of foreplay on the dancefloor.

"Nothing." I tugged on the skirt in a desperate attempt to keep the dancers from catching a peek of my underwear, but the damn thing wouldn't budge.

Alec's gaze dropped, and he grinned wickedly.

"Don't you dare say anything," I warned.

His lips pressed together to hold back the words I knew he desperately wanted to say. Instead, he extended a hand to me, and shouted, "Maybe we should dance?"

I eyed him suspiciously as I sipped on my drink.

"I'm not going to lie, Kris. You sitting there in that skirt is messing with my ability to think clearly."

Because he had to lean in for me to hear him, I expected to feel his breath on my neck. I did not expect to feel his mouth press against the sensitive spot behind my ear. I nearly jumped off the stool before his hands came down on my hips to still me.

"We've got an audience," he murmured. "Come on."

I slid from the stool, and let Alec lead me out on the dance floor. Wedged between several couples, we fell into a rhythm that rivaled the other dancers. The music wasn't anything I recognized, but was fast and easy to move to. It didn't take me long to realize that Alec had dance skills.

One hand splayed possessively on my waist as we moved together, while the other moved to my neck to bring our heads together.

"Back wall . . ." he told me. "Beside the door."

As we spun to the beat, I caught a glimpse of the door, and the tall Skotadi standing next to it. I looked away quickly, because he was staring right at us.

Bingo.

He matched the description Lillian had given us of Marcus. But she had failed to mention just how freakishly scary he looked. With slick black hair, a tightly drawn mouth, and eyes narrowed on us in disgust, he looked the epitome of evil.

I snuck glances around the pit, searching for anyone else who may have recognized us, or a pack of beefy guards coming to apprehend us. Nothing. We went completely unnoticed, aside from Marcus.

As we continued to dance, Alec and I took turns watching him, waiting for him to make the move we were waiting for.

"Damn, Kris," Alec muttered.

"What?" I glanced away from the back wall to find Alec staring down at me.

"I had no idea you could dance like this." His grip on my waist tightened, and I knew he liked it.

"I had a slightly wild streak before you met me." Sneaking into clubs had been one of my and Callie's favorite after school activities. Though none of the clubs in Eastern Tennessee were like this.

He grinned. "Maybe that's why I liked you so much."

"You and your bad girls . . ." I shook my head.

His eyes shifted from the back wall, met and held mine. "You've made me reconsider my preferences. I kind of have a thing for the good girls now."

"So how is that working out with Lillian?"

He shrugged noncommittedly. "We had some fun . . ."

"But?"

"It ran its course," he replied simply.

"It's over? Just like that?"

"Not into it anymore."

"Lillian? Or meaningless relationships?"

He spun me around to the music, effectively avoiding a direct answer. I suspected I knew why. I also knew he wouldn't come right out and admit it without some trickery on my part. Clasping my hands behind his head, I swayed my hips to the beat, and pretended to not notice Alec's evasiveness.

"Do you think you will ever settle down?" I asked casually.

He lifted one shoulder. "For the right girl. Eventually."

Alec's eyes darted around as he looked everywhere but at me. A shy Alec was something I had never expected to witness. But there he was, standing in front of me, doing everything he could to avoid eye contact.

Alec's lips moved, but I couldn't hear what he said over the music. I pulled his head toward mine, and shouted, "What?"

His forehead bumped against mine. "It's almost over. We're almost free."

"We save Callie, and then it will be over," I added.

Our eyes met. I smiled brazenly. He frowned.

He realized I knew.

His grip on my waist tightened, and he focused on a series of dance moves as he avoided the direction our conversation had turned. Finally, I got a lopsided grin out of him. "I'm not going to say it."

"You don't have to," I returned. "But just so you know . . . I like it. A lot."

His head lowered as he absorbed my words. When his eyes lifted to peer up at me, he looked the most vulnerable I had ever seen him. "You do?"

"My two best friends? What's not to like?"

He chuckled as he pulled me closer—a feat I had thought impossible considering how close we already were. "Sunday dinners with you, Nathan, Callie, and me," he mused wistfully.

That was exactly what I wanted. I didn't care where I went, or what I did once this was over. All that mattered was that I got to share it with the most important people in my life.

"We've got action," Alec suddenly declared. It took me a moment to shake off my melancholy, and realize what he was referring to.

Alec retrieved the phone from his pocket and sent a swift text. I glanced at the back wall, and spotted Marcus with a phone to his ear.

"Done," Alec announced.

My eyes were wide when they met Alec's. Neither of us said anything. We didn't have to. We both knew. Everything was going down tonight.

CHAPTER 16

~ Nathan ~

Despite the steady ticking of the hands on my watch, time had stopped. Each slowly passing minute with no word on what was going on inside the club pushed me one step closer to irrational. I was seconds from tossing in the bag on this plan, and storming inside to drag Kris out here, where it was safe, when a click at the back door stopped me.

Lillian took one look at my face, and said, "It's done. They're okay."

Her reassurance didn't do much to calm my nerves. Kris was still in there. Alec was still in there. I wouldn't fully relax until we were all together again.

For now, I kept it together long enough to do what I needed to do. I needed to follow through on my end, I knew that. But dammit, I hated the thought of Kris and Alec at the mercy of hundreds of Skotadi. If something went wrong . . .

I hated being in a situation that rendered me powerless to help them. Maintaining my position outside the rear entrance, following through on my end, was the only way I could help them now. As long as everything transpired the way we hoped it would.

Sprawled on my stomach behind the dumpster, my eyes fixed on the door, all I could do now was wait for everything to play out, and hope it went our way.

I laid my head in my hands with a groan, causing Lillian to turn and look at me with concern.

"What if something goes wrong?" I asked her. I hated the desperation I heard in my voice, but I couldn't shake it.

I had never felt more desperate, more helpless.

Lillian said nothing. Because she knew as well as I did that there was a good chance of this blowing up in our faces.

Minutes passed as I stared at my phone, waiting for either *the sign*, or a call for help. I wasn't sure which I would prefer. To go through with our wildly unpredictable plan and hope it worked out in our favor, or cut our losses and fight our way out of here now.

Finally, my phone beeped as Alec's message came through.

Bait taken.

"It's happening," I told Lillian before sending a quick text to Jared's and Jas's phones.

Now we waited to find out who showed up, and what special talents they would bring for us to tackle. I wasn't sure which was worst out of fire manipulation, world's best fighter, or a run-in with the dead manipulator's minions.

And what if all three showed up? That was Kris's ideal, of course . . . assuming we were able to immobilize them.

I took a deep breath to steady myself. As I let the air out slowly, I felt the goosebumps prickle the back of my neck. A chill ran down the length of my spine as if the face of death himself hovered behind me. I turned slowly so as not to draw attention to myself, and took in the two rotting corpses that staggered toward Lillian and me.

"Lil."

She followed my gaze, and gasped in surprise at the sight of the nekros.

"Don't make eye contact," I reminded her of the golden rule when dealing with the walking dead.

"Where is he?" Lillian's eyes darted to the shadows behind the building.

Other than his minions, I saw no sign of Nakurlas, the demigod who had brought them here. But I knew he was near if he had sent his dead soldiers to scope out the area ahead of his arrival. If he sent them, he must not have realized yet that we were there.

Not like we needed him to.

Going against everything I had been taught about nekros, I stood and faced the two corpses.

"What are you doing?" Lillian gasped.

"Drawing him to us," I replied.

The nekros zeroed in on me, and shifted in front of my eyes. Into two men I knew and recognized . . . and whom I had lost years ago.

I knew that, of course. But they looked so real. Almost believable. It was hard not to feel the ache of loss.

"Come with us, brother," the first one said. The one who looked like my brother, Drew.

I faintly noted Lillian coming to a stand beside me, and grabbing my arm as I stared back at the illusion in front of me.

Only an illusion. But a believable illusion. And it had been so long since I had seen them both.

"You cannot win," the other one added, forcing me to turn my gaze on my other brother.

"Shawn?"

He looked so real as he nodded. "Yes. Join us now."

Lillian's grip on my arm tightened, stopping me from taking the step that I wanted to take. I dropped my head to the ground with a rapid shake.

"They're not my brothers," I muttered.

When I looked back at them, they shifted back into their true forms—with rotten flesh and fire red eyes. *Definitely* not my brothers.

Lillian and I took a collective step backwards. A loud clapping sound shattered the silence, and the nekros vanished.

The clapping grew louder, and was joined by a sinister laugh. We spun around to find the demigod of the dead, Nakurlas, emerge from the shadows.

"I must applaud your efforts," he taunted. "Really, good try. But this . . ." He tossed our booby-trapped blanket doused in Circe's demigod-weakening compound on the ground at our feet. "This is the work of amateurs."

I shrugged as he closed the distance between us. "We are only hybrids, right?"

"I expected more from you, considering your devotion to Hecate's daughter. Fortunately for me, you have failed."

My gaze swung up from his feet, and I met his eyes with a confident smirk. "You sure about that?"

A look of understanding crossed his face, a moment too late. Jared and Bruce sprung from their hiding place with an eruption of gunfire.

Nakurlas wasn't hit with just any bullet. Diamond-coated bullets wouldn't work on him. But empty shells filled with Circe's compound?

Those dropped him faster than a tranquilized elephant.

Jas and Kira emerged from their hiding spot, and we all crowded around Nakurlas as he rolled onto his back. His eyes glazed over as he mumbled incoherently. I darted a look toward the narrow alley from which he had come, then glanced around at the other confused faces in the group.

Jas was the first to ask the question we all wanted to know the answer to. "Where are the other two?"

~ ~ ~

~Kris~

Alec and I moved toward the back of the club as quickly as we could without drawing attention to ourselves. By the time we reached the hallway, Marcus was gone.

Alec gripped his phone tightly as he awaited word from Nathan that the demigods were secured, and ready for me. I was confident that it was all three of them too. I felt it. I knew they were all here. I told Alec what I felt. That revelation forced his feet to move a little faster.

The music faded as we passed through the empty hallway. We came to the end without finding an exit.

"Maybe this way?" Alec took a hold of my hand and steered me back the way we had come. Up ahead were two bathroom doors on the left. Across from them was another door with the letters VIP painted in big gold letters.

Alec pushed the door open cautiously, and we stepped into a dark room, illuminated only by the moonlight shining through the row of windows along one wall. A small bar took up one corner, and small round tables were scattered throughout, providing a sort of obstacle course for us to navigate as we hurried for the door illuminated by the bright exit sign on the opposite wall.

We were nearly there when Alec's phone buzzed. He glanced down at the message, then shot a puzzled look at me. "They only got one."

"One?" No. No way. I felt them. They were all here. I knew it.

So where were they?

I pulled on Alec's hand as a sense of doom whipped down my spine. I slowly turned toward the center of the room, where they now stood, masked in shadows.

"Oh, shit," Alec muttered from beside me.

"Which ones are they?" I whispered to Alec.

Before he could respond, one of the demigods answered my question by creating a ball of fire in his hand.

So Derona was one of them.

The growing light in his hand illuminated the second demigod, and permitted me a good look at his heavy body armor and crisscrossing blades strapped to his back. My guess was Sagriva, the son of Ares.

I really hadn't wanted to take on the best fighter in the world without the aid of Circe's compound. But so be it. Time to see how well my training had paid off.

Before I could come up with a plan of action, Derona shot the flames in his hands straight at us. More directly, at Alec.

My hand shot out to stop the ball of fire with a wave of magic. I didn't catch it in time, but slowed it considerably. Alec avoided a direct hit by rolling to the ground. The wrecking-ball-sized bundle of flames crashed into the wall behind us. The resulting fire spread rapidly, blocking the exit. The reaching flames and intense heat pushed us farther into the center of the room, closer to the demigods.

"Got a plan?" Alec asked.

"No. You?"

Alec's chin lowered, and his eyes hardened on the demigods. "Kill them. Not die."

Alec retrieved his diamond-coated knife from its hiding place as Sagriva charged, a dagger in each hand. The fire alarm wailed as Sagriva and Alec collided, drowning out the sounds of their weapons clashing. One of Sagriva's blades sliced through Alec's shoulder almost immediately. Fortunately, his weapons were not diamond-coated.

Perhaps so he didn't inadvertently kill me, and ruin Circe's plan? Whatever his reason, it was good for us. It wasn't a deep cut, and Alec held his own. But as strong as Alec was, he wasn't a match for the demigod blessed with unrivaled fighting skills. Eventually, Sagriva would win their battle.

He and Alec moved too quickly for me to offer much assistance with my magic. One wrong move on my part, and I could hurt Alec instead.

I was forced to turn my attention to Derona as he conjured yet another ball of fire. This one, he sent into the ceiling before I could stop it.

"Alec, watch out!"

Alec grunted as he jumped out of the path of a chunk of engulfed plaster.

In retaliation, I tossed a fireball of my own at Derona. It exploded upon contact with his chest, but he stepped through it unscathed.

"That was weak," he taunted.

In my periphery, I watched Sagriva launch himself at Alec with a whooping war cry. As they collided, the water sprinklers turned on, soaking us in seconds. That put a damper on Derona's primary weapon. I had other weapons in my arsenal.

I blasted him with an invisible wave of power, catapulting him into the wall. Using one hand, I froze him there, suspended in the air, as I retrieved the knife from my boot. Seconds from his own imminent death, he taunted me with a laugh . . . right up until the moment I thrust the knife into his chest. His eyes hardened on me in that brief moment before they flickered out.

I didn't wait to watch him dissipate before I spun toward the fight behind me. Sagriva had Alec pinned against an overturned table, the dagger pressed to his neck. Alec's arms shook as he struggled to hold the blade back. His eyes met mine from across the room.

"Do it, Kris!"

I squeezed my eyes shut, and instantly found myself standing behind Sagriva. He spun around, moments before my knife found its mark between his shoulder blades. His dagger met my raised arm, slicing through the skin above my wrist. At the same time, Alec's feet landed a solid kick to Sagriva's midsection that sent him sprawling to the ground.

Sagriva was on his feet instantly. He barreled toward me with a roar. His shoulder dropped, and I lowered to the floor, catching his legs the way Nathan had shown me. As he sailed over me, I stood.

I switched the knife over to my uninjured hand as I held the other out, pinning Sagriva with my powers while a steady stream of blood dripped from my fingers. Over the sound of the wailing fire alarm, the steady onslaught of the sprinklers, and my own victorious shout as I thrust the knife down, I heard the thunderous boom of a gun firing.

My head whipped toward the entrance as I withdrew the knife from Sagriva's chest. I flung the knife at Marcus, where he stood by the door. It wobbled end over end through the air before I took control of it with my mind, and sailed it straight into his chest. He dropped with a strangled cry, and dissipated along with Sagriva.

"We did it." I choked on a sob of relief as I stood. One more demigod to go, whom Nathan and the others were holding, waiting for me, but . . . it was over.

"Alec, we did it!" I couldn't contain my excitement as I spun around. My smile fell when I saw his face. "Alec?"

I took a step toward him, where he leaned on unsteady legs against the overturned table. I watched as his head lowered, and he coughed up a mouthful of blood.

"Alec!"

I closed the distance between us, and caught him as he fell to his knees. Blood darkened the front of his shirt, from a wound I found when I lifted the wet and sticky fabric. I sucked in a sharp breath at the sight of a small hole pierced through the center of his chest.

"Okay. It's fine. You're strong enough. You have enough pure blood in you to heal from this. No big deal, right? It'll heal . . ." I trailed off when I realized I was rambling in panic.

Panic wasn't going to help Alec right now.

His hand lifted to point behind me, to the gun Marcus had fired. "Let me see it," he gasped.

I shook my head. "No. That's not important. We need to—"

"*Kris.*"

Though my thoughts were on bandaging him up to slow the blood loss, I did as he asked. I jumped to the door, swiped the gun, and returned to Alec's side in a matter of seconds. I took my knife to the hem of Alec's shirt to create a makeshift bandage while he opened the chamber.

My hands froze when he retrieved a bullet—a shiny diamond-coated one.

"Oh, my God."

They were coated?

I forced my trembling fingers to the vial dangling around my neck. Alec's hand clamped down on mine, stopped me from removing it. My eyes met his as he shook his head once.

"Promise me . . ." He lurched forward with a grimace, and his hand tightened around mine. "Promise me you'll finish this. Promise me you will fix it."

"Stop it," I cried as I tried to wrestle the vial out of his grasp. "Let me save you."

His eyes were wild with pain when they met mine. "It's too late," he choked. "Save Callie. Promise me."

"Alec!" I caught his shoulders as another wave of pain ripped through him. His hand released mine, and I positioned him onto his back, his head cradled in my lap. My hands were free to finally twist the lid off the vial.

His breaths turned sharp and sporadic as I pressed a handful of powder to his wound—all that I had left. I choked down the sob rising in my throat long enough to chant the necessary words. Alec's body jerked under my hands, unaffected by the ritual.

It's not too late . . .

It can't be too late . . .

I tried again, but with each tremor that shook him, my tears fell faster and harder at the realization that my prayers were going unanswered.

It was too late. I was losing him.

Finally, he stilled. Not because I had succeeded, but because I had failed.

"Don't go," I pleaded. "Please . . . Alec, don't go."

My lips pressed to his forehead. His last breath slipped between his lips, warming my cheek, as my arms tightened around him. I held him with a strength I didn't know I possessed, as if I hoped that could keep him with me forever.

No amount of strength or love could hold him anymore. I knew the moment I lost him. I felt his soul leave. I felt him slip between my fingers, and out of my grasp.

I watched the wisps of his soul float away with tear-flooded eyes. "I promise," I cried, far too late for him to hear me now.

Alec was gone, and I was left with nothing but a promise.

CHAPTER 17

~Nathan~

"It's been too long." I turned on my heel, and paced the stretch of ground in front of the immobilized Nakurlas for what may have been the hundredth time.

"Give them another minute," Jared suggested calmly.

I was the opposite of calm. I was seconds from punching my friend in the face, and storming inside that club crawling with Skotadi. As wound up as I was, I needed to off a few of them just to get my heart rate back to normal.

"Thirty seconds," I countered between clenched teeth.

Beside me, Lillian sighed, and I shot her a hard glare. She opened her mouth, likely to argue with me, when the fire alarm sounded from inside.

"Why would they pull the alarm already?" Jared wondered.

I smelled it then. Smoke.

"They didn't!" Without hesitation, my feet carried me at full speed toward the back entrance.

"Nathan, wait!"

Ignoring Jared's protests, I flung the door open, and stepped into a dark hallway, lit only by the distant strobe lights from the dance floor at the other end. The faint scent of smoke hovered in the air, but there were no signs of a fire in the main area. A few confused-looking humans stumbled into the hallway, and passed us as they sought the exit. I pushed against them, barreling my way deeper into the club.

Four doors opened from the hallway, and I burst through them one after another, my gun leading the way. All empty. No sign of a fire. No sign of Kris or Alec.

I turned out of the last room to find Lillian behind me. "Where?"

"This way." She pulled me into one of the empty rooms I had already checked. As we hurried across what appeared to be some private party room with a dozen or so small round tables, the smoke thickened.

"There's another hallway on the other side," she explained along the way. "It connects to a few more rooms."

As we approached the second door, I heard a gunshot. I rushed into the hallway, but Lillian grabbed my arm to keep me from taking off in the direction of the shot.

While my training had taught me to proceed with caution, knowing that Kris and Alec were somewhere in this club, possibly in danger, squashed most of what I knew.

Fear drove me now. And nearly blinded me to the Skotadi who rushed us from the direction of the dance floor. Five of them coming to inspect the source of the gunshot. Five of them with their own guns now pointed at Lillian and me.

I shoved her to the side, and out of the way of a warning shot. They weren't trying to kill us . . . and that was the only reason we were still alive.

I took advantage of that knowledge, and fired off a spray of bullets that dissipated three, and wounded the other two. Lillian sprang to action, and finished them off while I covered the hallway. Fortunately, with all the commotion going on in the main part of the club in response to the fire alarm, no one seemed to be paying us much attention.

Lillian pointed behind me as she stood. "Bathrooms there." Her arm swung to the door across from the bathrooms. "VIP room there."

As I stepped toward the partially opened door marked VIP, I spotted a smudge of crimson on the floor at the threshold. I put a hand up to alert Lillian. She moved past me with a nod, and nudged the door open ahead of my entrance. Gun raised, my eyes scanned the room in one thorough sweep.

I sagged in relief when I saw her. And then I saw the blood.

"Kris!"

She didn't look up when I called her name. Nor did she look at me when I knelt in front of her. She flinched from my hand on her shoulder.

"Kris, what's—" I stopped when I saw the empty vial on the floor beside her. And all the blood—far more than I knew had come from the nearly-healed wound above her wrist. As fast as she healed, I knew the blood that covered her wasn't all hers.

Glancing around the room, and finding it otherwise empty, my stomach dropped. A strangely unfamiliar emotion bubbled up inside of me, and I squeezed my eyes shut to keep it from pouring out.

I knew. Just like I knew I had to get her out of there.

As I pulled Kris to her feet, I met Lillian's gaze. The unshed tears in her eyes told me that she had come to the same difficult realization I had. Her mouth worked, and I shook my head to keep her from saying anything.

It was too soon.

From the way Kris shook in my arms, and from the glimpse I had seen of her eyes, I knew it wouldn't take much to set her off. One mention of Alec might do it, and I would lose her. Without Alec, and with at least one demigod left alive, Kris was hanging on to herself by a thread.

I sure hoped that Alec's theory was right. I hoped killing Nakurlas would set Kris free. That was assuming Sagriva and Derona were already dead by her hand.

And if not . . .

I shook my head to stop the thought from taking root. I followed Lillian to the soot-covered exit along the back wall. Even with my arm supporting her, Kris wobbled. I suspected she had used a considerable amount of magic during her fight. A fight I hadn't been there for.

But I was here now. I picked her up to carry her the rest of the way.

I followed Lillian outside, and along the back wall of the building. Kris shook from what I, at first, thought was an intense fight for her soul. It took me a moment to realize that she was shaking from a violent onslaught of silent tears. Her face burrowed into my chest as they poured out, but she made no noise.

I would have preferred for her to cry out, to scream, to do *something*. Seeing her hurt so badly she couldn't make a sound terrified the hell out of me. I not only feared for her emotional state, but for her ability to fight her inner demons.

"Hurry," I muttered to Lillian.

"What if . . ." she started, but stopped at the sight of my scowl.

"He's it," I insisted as Nakurlas, and the rest of our crew, finally came within sight. "He has to be it."

Jared and Bruce looked from me, to Lillian, and then to Kris in my arms. A mixture of understanding and disbelief crossed their faces simultaneously. While Bruce turned his back to hide the anguish I had briefly glimpsed in his eyes, Jared struggled to put his game face on.

"Did they face both of them?" he asked.

"I don't know. I hope so. Without him, she's struggling."

I cradled Kris as I knelt to the ground near Nakurlas.

He was still under the effects of the compound, and oblivious to his fate—if we could persuade Kris to finish him. I hated to ask her to kill, especially now. But the alternative, the one that risked me losing her, wasn't an option.

I brushed aside the curtain of hair that covered her face. "Kris . . ."

She pulled her face out of my shirt far enough to meet my gaze. Though they darted away immediately, I glimpsed the surge in her eyes.

"Kris," I tried again, "you need to destroy Nakurlas."

"No." Her voice was ice cold, foreign. Almost evil.

I clasped her face between my hands. "No more fighting it, Kris. You can end it right now."

"I don't want to end it," she returned.

"That's your Skotadi side talking. Not you."

"How do you know? You don't know how to talk to my Skotadi side."

Her voice cracked on the word 'you,' and I knew why. Only Alec had understood her inner Skotadi. Kris was still in there, battling for control, and she was upset that the only one who understood wasn't here.

"And who did?" I asked softly. "Who understood like I can't, Kris?"

Her eyes narrowed, and I swore I heard her growl. Her body tensed in my arms. "Shut up," she sneered.

"Who, Kris?" I pressed.

"What are you doing?" Lillian whispered harshly.

I ignored her, and pressed Kris again. "Tell me who understood you, Kris. Who understood it all?"

"Al—" She lurched forward to scream—a shrill cry that signaled her pain. Finally.

"Alec," I said for her. "You want vengeance for what they did to Alec?"

"Yes," she hissed. Her head lowered. Her hands fisted her hair. She screamed again. This one ended with a sob.

I withdrew my knife, and held it out to her.

"Nathan," Jared warned. His eyes were on Kris, alert and concerned.

I understood. In her state, she could turn the knife on me, on any of us, in a heartbeat. But I believed she wouldn't. Her need to avenge Alec's death outweighed everything else.

I placed the knife into her hand. "Go get it, Kris."

She eyed me severely before she swung her attention toward Nakurlas. I released her, allowing her to crawl across the ground to where he lay. Jared tensed beside me, ready for her to spring on any one of us.

I wasn't worried. She had been so strong, from the beginning. She had the strength to fight back. This time, I knew she would finally find the freedom she sought.

When she thrust the knife down, finding Nakurlas's heart, I knew it was all over.

Her soul was finally free. But her heart was shattered.

~ ~ ~

Back in our room, I set Kris on the edge of the bed, and retrieved a towel from the bathroom. On my way back to her, I got stopped by a knock at the door.

Jared greeted me with a grimace. "How's she doing?"

I glanced over my shoulder. Kris's head was bent forward, her eyes fixed on the floor, but it was anyone's guess what she was actually seeing.

"How would you be doing right now?" I returned.

Jared nodded. He knew. We all knew.

We all felt the pain of Alec's death. But none of us more so than Kris.

I threw a thumb over my shoulder. "I've got to—"

"Yeah, yeah," Jared exclaimed. "Of course. Bruce and I will rotate shifts tonight, and we'll talk in the morning."

I hesitated before turning back to Kris. "You think there's something to worry about?"

Jared shrugged. "The demigods are gone, but the huge Skotadi presence in that town has me nervous. And we still have Circe out there. She's bound to be upset with us now."

I ran a hand down my face with a scoff. Understatement of the century.

"It'll be fine," Jared reassured me with a pat on the shoulder. "Bruce and I have got it under control. We'll leave in the morning."

Without Alec . . .

I held back my own emotion as I returned to Kris's side. Though I had come to like Alec, her devastation over his loss was a lot stronger than mine—stronger than any of ours. While we all wanted to know what had happened, I hadn't let any of them ask her. She was having a hard enough time right now, without being forced to relive the event.

She would talk when she was ready.

I knelt in front of her, and gently wiped the towel over her face, cleaning off as much of the makeup as I could. The hardest was her eyes, swollen from an endless stream of tears . . . and that black stuff that streaked her face didn't come off easily.

"Kris?" I probed gently.

Her eyes lifted slowly to meet mine, and she shrugged.

"Come here."

I pulled her to a stand, and escorted her to the bathroom. There, I started the shower. As the room filled with steam, I assisted her in removing her clothes.

The blank stare she gave me worried me more than anything. I expected her to be upset. I expected her to be angry, and sad, and frustrated. Right now, she resembled a zombie. She had cried all she could cry, and now she was left with . . .

I didn't even know. A hole in her heart? A piece of her soul missing?

"You're scaring me, Kris," I admitted softly.

Another blank stare.

"Do you want me to help?" I asked.

She turned toward the shower as if noticing for the first time that it was running. Her head shook once.

"Okay. I'll be right out here if you need me."

I saw her into the shower, then I took a seat on the floor. For nearly twenty minutes, I sat there, sneaking glances every so often to make sure she was okay. She washed her hair at least three times, from what I saw. A wall of bubbles clung to the shower curtain, and I imagined she had gotten a little overzealous with the soap. I would have too if I had my best friend's blood all over me.

Five entire minutes passed with her head in her hands. I watched, and waited, until I heard the sound of her sobs over the running water. I jumped to my feet, grabbed a towel, and shut the water off. She didn't fight me as I wrapped her up, and steered her into the bedroom.

"Do you want to talk to me?" I asked softly as I guided her to the edge of the bed.

She was silent for so long I assumed the answer was no. And that was okay. I understood.

I had experienced my fair share of loss over the years. My father . . . my brothers . . . countless friends . . . and even Lillian. Despite the hard-nosed mentality of being raised a Kala, I had struggled each and every time. But Kris? She hadn't been raised with that armor around her heart, and the ability to bounce back from life-shattering loss.

I gave her a kiss on the forehead to let her know it was okay if she didn't want to talk yet, but that I was there when she was ready, and I stood to find her some clothes to sleep in.

"I made him a promise," she whispered.

I stopped, and looked at the top of her lowered head as I waited for her to continue.

"I can't lose Callie, too," she cried. "I can't, but I don't know how to save her . . . and I made him a promise that I would. But I don't know what to do!"

I knelt in front of her in an attempt to ease the renewed surge of tears, but she only sobbed harder.

"I'm me now," she continued. "I'm free, but what was the cost?"

"Hey," I soothed. "Alec wanted this just as much as you did."

"But now what?" Her eyes met mine pleadingly, and I wished I had the answer.

But I didn't. I didn't know where to start.

"I don't know how to stop this curse," she admitted softly. "I don't know how to get to my mother to get the help I need. I don't know how to help Callie."

"We'll figure it out."

"What if Circe manages to go through with the curse without me?" Kris shot back in renewed panic. "She knows I'm not going to help her now that I'm free of the demigods' influence. She'll be desperate, she might find a way . . ."

"So we'll find your mother first," I returned convincingly. "You're going to keep that promise to Alec. *I* promise *you* that."

I didn't know how we would manage it. Not yet. But I knew I wasn't going to let her down. I wouldn't let Callie down, and I sure as hell wasn't going to let Alec down.

CHAPTER 18

~ Kris ~

My sense of smell is the first to develop. The scent of pine mixed with warm blacktop tells me where I am even before the old playground on the edge of Big Pine Lake materializes around me. A sad smile curves my lips at the not-so-distant memories I had created here.

We had created here.

My first kiss had happened here. On that battered old picnic table that still stands where I last remember it. On the night that I first realized Alec had secrets. On the night that my life changed forever.

I sit on the cracked blacktop, facing the basketball hoop, as I fully give myself to this dream. The melancholy is nice, and I find myself replaying the last time I was here with a smile. When I close my eyes, I can almost hear the soft thumps of the basketball striking the ground.

"I'm going to miss you," *I sigh into the breeze.*

"Is that so?" *The thumping stops, and I slowly turn to look over my shoulder, to find the source of the familiar voice behind me.*

Alec bounces the ball again, before tucking it under one of his arms with a grin. "One last game?" *A gasp escapes my open mouth. He shushes me with a sternly-pointed finger.* "No crying."

I sputter as I scramble to my feet, and finally utter one word. "How?"

"You can see the dead, remember?" *Alec sends the ball soaring toward the hoop. It goes through with a soft whoosh.* "I think I'm better at this dead. Divine powers and all that."

"But I destroyed Nakurlas," I argue. "I severed my ties to all of them. I'm . . . me."

"But you're still Hecate's daughter," Alec replies softly. His eyes meet mine tenderly. "Now, we have plenty of time to talk about business, and we will, but right now I want to play a game of basketball with you. Maybe I can finally beat you."

My eyes never leave Alec as he moves to retrieve the ball. I'm afraid he will disappear if I let him out of my sight. I want to hold onto this moment for as long as I possibly can. Real . . . or not.

So we play. We laugh. We tease. We are us, and I enjoy every minute of it.

And I win, once again.

"Are you sure you're not letting me win?" I playfully narrow my eyes at Alec when he places his hands on his knees to catch his breath—odd considering he's a . . . well, I'm not exactly sure what he is.

"Trust me," he gasps. "I'm not letting you win." He limps over to the picnic table, and stops short of sitting. He stares at it a moment, then glances at me. "This is where . . ."

I nod. "Yep."

"Huh." He runs a hand over the beaten wood as I come to a stand beside him. "I wondered why you picked this place."

"I picked this?" I glance around the battered playground.

"It must have meant more to you than I thought," Alec concludes, and finally turns to look at me.

I take the opportunity to memorize everything about him. From the way his hair sticks up a little on the top, to the magnificent green of his eyes, to the way he towers over me, and the feel of his arms around me when I move into them.

His cheek rests against my forehead. "We have work to do," he tells me, but gives no indication of moving anytime soon.

I don't want to work, or talk about anything. I want to stay right here, in his arms, in our spot. And I know he feels it too, which is evident from the sigh against my cheek when he reluctantly pushes me back. His eyes are soft with understanding, but with a hint of determination.

"You need to find your mother," he says.

"I know," I return quickly, "but I don't know how to—"

"I do. I can get you there."

"How?"

He stuns me with the carefree grin I am accustomed to seeing every day, and I swallow the emotion I feel at knowing I won't see it once I wake up from this dream.

"She's in the underworld, right?"

I nod. "But we don't know how to get there."

Alec spreads his arms wide. "I can tell you. I can't show you since you have to go there awake, but I can tell you. We get three days to make this happen."

"What happens after three days?"

"I get assigned to a side. Once that happens, I can't leave on my own. I'm only allowed out now since I'm in the in-between. Less security," *he adds with a wink.*

"After three days . . ." *I bite my lip to fight a new wave of emotion.* "Can you . . . will I be able . . ."

"To see me again?" *he finishes softly.* "I don't know. Something tells me I'm getting a special pass." *I nod slowly, then jump when Alec claps his hands together.* "But hey, we get three days together to make this happen. So let's do it."

Paper materializes out of nowhere, and Alec sets to drawing me sketches and instructions on how to get to the underworld. Though it looks easier than I thought it would be, assuming everything works right, it is still a multi-stepped process with a lot of what-ifs.

"Alec, I'm never going to remember all of this," *I tell him, waving a hand at* the elaborate details. It's nice to look at as he explains, but what good is writing it all down on paper inside of a dream?

"Kris, you repeatedly underestimate me. We dead work in mysterious ways. Trust me." He thrusts the paper into my hands. "It's going to work."

~ ~ ~

I woke with a start, to the sound of birds chirping, and the shower running in the next room. As I sat up to gather my bearings, my eyes lowered to the bed, and to the papers scattered beside me. I picked one up, and turned it over.

It was a map of the underworld, labeled in Alec's choppy handwriting. I frantically sifted through the other pages, and recognized it all. Alec had showed me all of it in the dream.

Excitement rolled off of me in waves. Unable to contain it, I bounced on the edge of the bed for what felt like an eternity—Alec's map and instructions in my hands—until the shower cut off. I barely gave Nathan enough time to dress before I barged into the bathroom.

He stood, back to me as he fastened his jeans, and turned his head over his shoulder at my noisy intrusion. With one look at my face, he knew something was up.

"What's going on?"

He twisted around as I launched myself at him. My momentum backed him up against the counter before he caught me.

"I saw Alec!" I exclaimed. "I had a dream . . . and he was there. He knows how to get to the underworld, and he's going to help us. He drew me a map!"

I started to squirm away to show it to him, and Nathan set me on my feet.

"Kris . . ."

"Here." I thrust the stack of papers out to him. "It's all here." I waved them under his nose when he didn't look at them. His eyes were on me, wary and concerned. "Nathan, look! Alec drew us a map to get to the underworld."

His eyes finally lowered to the papers, but he didn't look excited.

Why wasn't he excited? This was exactly what we needed. We finally knew the way.

"Kris, there's no map," he said softly. "They're blank pieces of paper."

"No . . ." I looked at them again. The map and instructions were as visible as before. It was all right there in my hands. "Oh, no . . ."

He couldn't see it.

"Dammit, Alec!" I shouted at the ceiling.

How was I going to convince the group that I knew the way into the underworld when I was the only one who could see the instructions?

"Kris?" Nathan's hands gripped my shoulders lightly. His eyes were lined with worry.

"Nathan, I'm not going crazy," I insisted. "I must be the only one who can see it."

He nodded slowly, his eyes lowering to the papers between us. "See what exactly?"

I breathed a sigh of relief. He believed me. Honestly, after all we had been through and had seen, how could he not? I stepped away from him to spread the papers out onto the counter.

"Here." I pointed to the first page. "Alec drew a rough map of the underworld—where things are in relation to each other. It's really pretty basic. The hardest part is going to be getting out . . ."

He had drawn the best route for escape, but warned me that he didn't know how dangerous it might be. He took another way out to come visit me, but it was only an option for souls. There was only one way out for mortals that he was aware of. No one knew what obstacles awaited those that navigated it.

"How do we get in?" Nathan asked.

"The Diros Caves." I shuffled the papers around until I found the one I needed. Scanning the instructions Alec had written there, I added, "We're going to need a few things first."

~ ~ ~

While Nathan believed me without solid proof, the others weren't as easy to convince.

"We have two and a half days left to get this done," I said as I scanned the eyes staring at me around the table. The café was busy that morning, forcing me to keep my voice lowered, despite my desire to shout my frustration.

"So says . . . a ghost?" Kira inquired.

"It's *Alec*," I corrected through clenched teeth.

"Right. A ghost." She rolled her eyes before turning to look out the window. Her guarded posture and undivided attention placed on her cup of steaming coffee made it clear that she had no interest in the rest of this conversation.

The Queen Bitch has spoken.

"It could happen," Lillian muttered from beside me. Her eyes scanned the others at the table as if daring them to challenge her. "We all know communication with the dead is a real part of our world."

Jared's arm struck the table with a thwack. "Okay," he declared. "I wish we all could see what you see, but . . ."

"You believe me?" I asked tentatively.

"I believe Alec would attempt to communicate with you, yes. I'm having a hard time with this method of entering the underworld, but if he says that's the way to do it . . ."

"Can we get what we need around here?" Jas questioned.

I started to answer when Queen Bitch's snort interrupted me.

"I can't believe you guys are buying this crap," she said. "The demigods are dead. We did what we came here to do. We should be boarding a plane, and getting out of this hellhole."

"The demigods are gone, but Circe's curse is still on," I explained. "My mother can help me to end it, and I need to find her. If you don't want to help, then you can leave."

My hard gaze shifted from Kira toward the slight movement across the table from me. Nathan leaned back in his seat, and lifted a cup to his lips to conceal the smile threatening to break his resolve. His eyes darted to mine long enough for me to see the gleam of pride in them.

To Jas, I answered, "It might take a few hours to gather everything we need, but we should be ready to go tonight after the caves close to the public."

Bruce cleared his throat as he leaned forward to place his elbows on the table. His eyes had been downcast since I arrived, but now, they lifted to meet mine. The sorrow in them was visible. Though everyone considered me the one who had taken Alec's death the hardest, I suspected Bruce had a good deal of his own grief to contend with.

"Can you communicate with him anytime, or only in a dream?" he asked me.

"I don't know. I know there are ways to communicate without using a dream, but I've never done it."

"You can do a spell," Nathan suggested quietly.

I started to tell Nathan that I had never been able to successfully contact the dead by using the conjuring spell I knew, but stopped when I remembered that I hadn't tried since I reached my potential as an Incantator. I was able to do things now that I had never been able to do before.

"I can try," I offered, "but I need to go back to the hostel to get something."

Though it was possible to do the spell without using an object belonging to the one you were attempting to conjure, having something personal of theirs made it easier.

Nathan went with me, and hovered in the door as I retrieved Alec's bag from under his bed. Reaching into it, I found mostly clothes, along with his toothbrush, cologne, and a pack of condoms.

I laughed as I tossed the square box onto the bed. "Why am I not surprised?"

Nathan sauntered across the room, and took a seat on the bed. "It's weird," he muttered.

I nodded. "I expected a bigger box."

"No. Him being gone . . . it's weird."

I froze with my hand in the bag, and peeked up at Nathan. His head was lowered, but with the angle I had from the floor, I saw the hint of emotion on his face.

It mirrored what I had felt yesterday. Seeing Alec last night, and knowing that I had the ability to see him again, had made his loss a little easier to handle today. But I still felt that tickle in the back of my throat at knowing he was really gone.

I swallowed the grief, grabbed Alec's toothbrush, and returned everything else to the bag before I stood. "I think this will work."

Nathan's head bobbed, his eyes glued to the object in my hand, but he gave no indication of moving.

"Nathan? Let's go. We have a lot of work to do today."

"Yeah." He took my outstretched hand as he stood. When I turned for the door, his grip tightened to hold me back. My eyes darted to his as he asked, "Are you okay?"

"I'm fine. I—"

"Kris, Alec is dead."

I wrenched my hand free of his. "I know that."

"Do you?"

"I watched him die," I hissed. I spun away from him with a strangled cry. "What is with you? What are you trying to do?"

He took slow, careful steps toward me. "I'm worried about you, that's all."

"You're worried, so you have to remind me that Alec is gone?"

"You're deflecting. You're not accepting it."

"I'm trying to get a job done," I countered his words. "I'm trying to save Callie before I lose her too. I made a promise to Alec that I would do it. If you don't want to help, that's your choice."

His bitter chuckle followed me to the door. He didn't try to stop me, and he didn't follow me—at least from what I saw—as I made my way downstairs and out onto the street.

My eyes stung with unshed tears, but I refused to let them fall. My stride was hard and fast from the effort to not cry, combined with my irritation with Nathan.

The others were on the beach, exactly where we had agreed to meet. They scattered as I approached the makeshift fire-pit I had instructed them to make.

It started off as a deep hole in the sand. The fire was my creation.

"Where's, uh . . ." Jared started, forcing me to look up from the flames. He took one look at my face, and dropped the rest of his question.

I held Alec's toothbrush in my hand as I chanted the words to the spell. Then I tossed the brush into the fire. The results were instant, and I took a step back as Alec's form filled the space in front of me.

"Was that really necessary?" He rubbed his eyes with a groan.

"What?" I asked him.

"You don't have to do all this. All you have to do is call for me, and I'll come to you. For the next two and a half days, that is. This . . ." He waved a hand at the fire behind him. "This is a little disorienting for me."

"Oh. I didn't know that," I admitted with a small smile. "Sorry."

I glanced around at the others for their reactions to Alec's appearance. I expected awe, but only saw confusion. And they were looking at me, not him. Nathan had joined us at some point. He hovered near the back, and watched me with visible concern.

"They can't see me," Alec explained. "Only you can."

"Why only me?"

"You're the one with the ability to see the dead."

Oh, great. Now they were really going to think I was going crazy.

"So what did you summon me for?" Alec asked.

I laughed humorlessly. "To prove to them that my dream was

real, and that you were able to come back and help. Apparently, that's not going to work now . . ." If anything, the group looked one step closer to tossing me into a padded room. To them, I announced, "Apparently, I'm the only one who can see and talk to him."

Bruce's eyebrows shot up. "So he's . . ." His finger waved around at the spot in front of me. "He's there now?"

I nodded.

"Honcho," Alec whispered to me, causing me to swivel toward him. "Call him 'Honcho.' I never called him that name around anyone else."

"Honcho?" I asked Alec with a laugh.

I heard Bruce's sharp breath. His eyes were wide when they settled on me. "Where did you hear that?"

"Alec just told me."

Alec's arm shot out from behind me, and he pointed a finger at Jared. "Maverick."

I made a face. "Maverick? Really?" I supposed it made sense, considering he looked like a young Tom Cruise.

Jared's jaw dropped, and I knew I had caught his attention.

I had no idea Alec had nicknames for everyone. But they all knew. Hell of a way to make them believe me . . . but it was working.

Alec's finger swung to Nathan next, and I held my breath as I waited for Alec to tell me his nickname. What followed was unexpected.

"Tell him that he's a lucky guy to have his mugshot on Google."

"What?" I laughed.

"Just say it," Alec insisted.

I repeated Alec's words to Nathan with a shrug. Though I had no idea what they meant, Nathan clearly did. He stared at me for several heavy seconds before his eyes darted to the spot beside me, where Alec stood.

His voice was thick when he finally responded. "I know."

His eyes shifted to me. Though I didn't know what had transpired between Alec and Nathan, I suspected it had something to do with me. That much was obvious from Nathan's steady gaze on me.

We may fight like an old married couple at times, but there was no doubt his love for me. Nor mine for him.

CHAPTER 19

To save time, we split up to go shopping for the items Alec suggested. By the time we all returned to the hostel later, we had an hour before the gates to the caves closed. It took us most of that time to gather our equipment, check and double check everything, and drive to the caves. We arrived when the last tour was leaving.

Another twenty minutes before the workers left, and we attempted to pull off the craziest—and perhaps stupidest—stunt yet. I bounced on my toes where we waited behind the shrubs. My eyes darted to the mostly empty parking lot behind us. We were well hidden, and the encroaching darkness aided our cover, but I feared getting caught before we had a chance to follow through with our plan.

And some plan it was. Wild . . . crazy . . . maybe even stupid. But necessary.

I was scared. Of failure, and of the unknown. The chance for success, as small as it may be, kept me moving forward. Regardless, my nerves were a jumbled mess. I jumped at every sound, and watched every movement. I nearly screamed my head off when something brushed against my arm.

"Kris?" Nathan whispered from behind me, and I put a hand to my galloping heart when I realized it had only been him.

I peered over my shoulder, and he gave me a 'come here' nod.

His hand took mine as he led me behind another shrub, out of ear shot of the others.

I didn't know what I expected. We hadn't spoken since our argument earlier. I bit my lip nervously as I stared at his back. Then he turned, and I found myself wrapped up in his arms.

I should have known I had no reason to be nervous. It *was* Nathan. Sure, I had seen him do some scary stuff, but he was always different with me. He rarely stayed mad at me long.

I melted into him with a contented sigh, and wondered how I hadn't found myself here hours ago. The answer came quickly—only because I was severely distracted. An impending trip to the underworld could do that. But now, I enjoyed the moment of bliss.

"I'm sorry about earlier," I mumbled into his shirt. "I shouldn't have said what I did. I want you with me."

"I know." His hand stroked my hair gently. "I shouldn't have pushed you about Alec. I just worry that . . ."

"I'm not dealing with it?" I finished his thought when he trailed off.

He was right, of course. I wasn't dealing with Alec's loss. I couldn't even say the words—dead or death. Instead, I said 'it' or chose words like 'gone' or 'lost.' Knowing that I could see him just by saying his name certainly wasn't helping me cope either.

"I'm not," I told Nathan honestly. "But I will."

He nodded, and pulled me back into his arms. We stayed there for several moments before he spoke. "Kris, don't think any less of me for saying this, but . . ." His grip on me tightened, and he exhaled slowly. "I've been in a lot of dangerous situations where the outcome could have gone either way, but this is the first time that I can honestly say I have no idea what might happen. I've never been more scared than I am right now."

I didn't respond. I didn't know what to say. I was scared too—terrified actually. But to hear him say that he was too? Unexpected wasn't a strong enough word.

"If this is it . . . I want you to know how much I love you."

"Don't," I muttered. "Don't you say goodbye to me."

His head lowered with a shake. "Right. We're going to do this." When he looked up again, all signs of doubt had vanished. In its place was the fierce determination I had come to know and recognize.

Warrior-mode had kicked in.

But a warrior could still kiss his girl. Which he did . . . well. With slow diligence, he gave me perhaps the best kiss of my life. A kiss I never wanted to end. When Jared called to us, alerting us that the entrance was clear, we only gripped each other tighter. We finally eased apart when we were ready, not because the time had come, not because the others were waiting for us, but because we had communicated to each other all that we needed to.

One final gaze into his eyes gave me the push I needed, and we turned toward the cave together.

Dressed head to toe in black, with bags strapped across our shoulders, we approached the entrance as a unified group. Fear was left behind in the shrubs. Determination rolled off of us in waves as we plunged headlong into the biggest unknown any of us would ever know.

The gate at the entrance was simple to breach—even for a minor criminal. For me, one touch with my hand unlocked and pushed it open. Once inside, Nathan turned his flashlight to the panel fixed to the wall. Wires ran out of the top, and snaked far out into the cave.

They attached to at least thirty switches.

"What section are we going to?" Nathan called out.

Jared moved to his side, carrying a map of the cave. Together, they referenced the map, then flicked the correct switch. Our destination was so far into the cave that the light they had turned on wasn't visible from where we stood.

A few more clicks, and lights began turning on in the distance. Enough to light our way to the section of the cave we needed to get to without drawing attention to the fact that the lights were on. The narrow steps to the base of the cave was left in the dark, and we used flashlights to navigate our way.

The boats were tied to the small dock, exactly where we had boarded them for our tour last week. Once we had all climbed in, Bruce took over paddling while I looked between the map and what the lights illuminated around us. Finally, near the end of the line, I saw it.

"There!" I pointed to the flat rock formation that jutted out of the water several yards away. Behind it, the smooth wall of the cave dropped beneath the water's surface as far as the clear water allowed me to see. I gulped as I wondered how deep it went.

Before we found out, we had to swim to the rock formation. Since the boats were anchored to the cables that ran above us, we were unable to reach the section of the cave we needed to with the boat. Why no one had thought to bring wire cutters baffled me now. It wasn't a long swim—perhaps fifty yards. Since I was the only one who couldn't swim, I supposed wire cutters hadn't been on anyone's priority list.

We all stripped out of our clothes, revealing the bathing suits we wore underneath. Our clothes went into the water-proof bags we all carried. One by one, the group jumped into the water and began the swim.

"Oh, shit, that's cold!" Jas shouted when he broke the surface. His arms sliced through the water as he sped toward the rock, passing Kira in a blink.

Nathan sucked in a breath as he lowered himself in. He held onto the side of the boat as he turned for me.

I shook my head. "How about I just teleport?"

"You need to save your energy. Come on. I'll get you there."

"You need to save your energy too," I pointed out. Carrying me through the water would only tire him out more, and I couldn't have that.

I eyed the rock formation, then him. His eyes narrowed when he realized my intentions. By the time his mouth opened with another argument, it was too late. I jumped to the rock formation, and glanced over my shoulder in time to see Nathan push off the boat with a shake of his head.

While he and the rest of the group cut through the water toward me, I emptied the contents of my bag. I had everything out and ready to go by the time Jas pulled himself onto the rock ledge beside me.

His lips looked a little blue. "Let's get this thing going," he shuddered.

I took the chalk, and began to draw the symbols on the wall above the water. By the time I was finished, the rest of the group had joined Jas on the ledge. Their chattering teeth greeted me when I turned away from my drawings.

"Who's got the non-coated knife?" I inquired. Lillian readily handed it to me, and I met everyone's eyes one at a time. "Everybody ready?"

Though they weren't the most enthusiastic bunch, no one protested. I took the blade to my thumb. A hiss slipped between my lips as it pierced my skin, and the blood bubbled to the surface.

"Aperuerit ianuam introibo," Alec had recited to me in the dream last night. *"I believe it loosely translates to 'open sesame.'"*

I chanted those words now as blood dripped from my finger. The clear water at my feet darkened to an unnatural crimson as it churned with my blood. Water from elsewhere in the cave rushed toward us, and lapped against the wall below the symbols. The group took collective steps back from the flood as it collected at our feet, and spiraled into a whirlpool.

The roar of the rushing water spiked my fear. I dreaded what came next.

Nathan's hand found mine. His voice was drowned out by the rumbling, but I didn't need to hear him to know what he said. It was time.

I nodded my head at the others. "Go!"

We had discussed this step earlier. I needed to jump into the whirlpool last, otherwise it would close and leave the others behind. Now that they had seen it, I suspected that some of them wouldn't mind being left behind.

They proved themselves far braver than I already knew, and stepped toward the swirling opening. Jared and Lillian took the leap first, jumping in together, hand in hand. Bruce, Jas, and Kira followed closely behind. The five of them tumbled around the whirlpool like giant goldfish flushed down a toilet. Nathan's gaze held mine as we stepped forward together.

My feet hit the water, and the current took me. Though I didn't fear death, the sensation of drowning paralyzed me as we swirled around and around, dropping lower and lower into the churning water. The few times my head broke the surface, I gulped small breaths of air before being submerged again. Nathan's hand never loosened its grip on mine as we spiraled toward the bottom of the pool.

The water suddenly calmed, and we floated freely, though still submerged at an unknown depth. My body collided with Nathan's, and I felt him tug me toward the surface . . . or what I hoped was the surface. Already, my lungs burned, and I longed to fill them with oxygen. I pinched my lips together, against the urge to take a satisfying breath.

A pair of legs bumped into me from behind, but I couldn't determine who they belonged to in the murky water. With a sudden jerk, they were ripped away from me. The current took Nathan next, and yanked his hand out of my grasp. My mouth involuntarily opened, and I choked on a mouthful of water as I was wrenched forward next, legs kicking ahead of me.

I was reminded of a water park ride I had once ridden with Callie—one filled with sudden twists, and turns, and drops. But with no raft, my head submerged under water, and no end in sight, this ride was far from fun.

My feet hit a rock wall, and my mouth opened to cry out from the jolt it sent up my legs. I pushed away from the wall as the current reclaimed me, now tossing me head first down the watery tunnel.

The water in my lungs burned.

Air. I needed air.

A bright light filtered through my eyelids, and I hoped it signaled the end of the journey. My mouth pressed together to stop myself from taking the breath I needed too soon. Then the feeling of free falling through empty space overcame me. My arms and legs flailed as I plummeted through a warm wall of water.

There was a brief relief, and then a splash as I hit water. I reached out for something to grab onto as I kicked my legs beneath me. I broke the surface and sucked in a gulp of air, only to choke on the water that had already filled my lungs.

Arms wrapped around me from behind, stopping me from going under again. My head dropped against Bruce's shoulder in relief as I sputtered.

"You're okay," he assured me. "I've got you."

He tucked me to his side, and pulled me effortlessly through the water with his big arms. I searched for signs of the others over his shoulder. I spotted Nathan and Jared as they each looped an arm around a limp bikini-clad body, and followed us to the nearby bank.

Bruce pushed me up first. Every breath I took resulted in a fit of coughing, and I dropped my head between my knees in an attempt to control it. Behind me, I heard Bruce assist Nathan and Jared.

"Give her to me," Bruce offered.

I swiveled to look over my shoulder as Bruce hauled Kira's lifeless body onto the stone bank beside me. Blood covered her face from a deep gash in her forehead. Her eyes were open, but stared blankly into the empty space above her.

My hand clamped over my mouth as Jas appeared at my side. Blood dripped from his chin, from the sizable cut in his lip. His head dropped with a sigh when he realized that she was dead.

"She hit that wall head first," he offered in explanation.

"We're missing Lillian," Nathan coughed. He had pulled himself to the edge of the bank, and turned to look out over the water. Blood oozed from his shoulder, from the scratches that marked his skin.

That damn rock wall had gotten all of us. Kira, unfortunately, had taken a fatal dive into it. Had Lillian suffered the same fate?

I moved around Jas, crawling toward the water's edge to look for her. The large black pool was calm. Steep rock walls lined the perimeter. There was no waterfall, as I had imagined falling from. No opening above from what I could see.

Where had we come from? Where could Lillian be?

As we all searched, Lillian silently floated to the surface in the middle of the pool. She came up peacefully, far too quietly for someone who needed air after being submerged for so long. Nathan saw her at the same time I did, and jumped into the water after her. Jared followed, and together they pulled her limp body back to us.

Not another, I thought as they hauled her onto the bank.

"Please, don't let her be dead," I muttered under my breath.

"She's not breathing," Jared declared. He immediately lowered his head, and delivered two short breaths into her. I watched as her chest rose slightly. Then Nathan's entwined hands compressed the center of her chest, forcing her heart to pump.

It was like reliving my own drowning months ago. Nathan had done this to me then. I had watched it in a dream. I had woken up; I had survived.

"Please, Lillian," I whispered as Jared and Nathan repeated the cycle. As an afterthought, I added, "Alec, help."

He was at my side instantly. His head swiveled as he took in the scene around us. "She'll be okay," he finally offered.

"How do you know?" I whispered so as not to distract the guys.

"The Collector isn't here."

"Collector?"

"He collects all the souls," Alec explained quickly. "Kira's is already gone."

I nodded, and waited. And waited. Two more breaths from Jared . . .

Lillian suddenly coughed, bringing an end to the smoldering silence. She rolled onto her side, fisting handfuls of stone as she struggled to catch her breath.

"Once she's able, you need to move," Alec advised.

Then he was gone. I wished he could stay, to walk us through this, but he had already explained to me that he couldn't. He couldn't take the passage again. It was up to us to follow his map, and find our own way.

No one wanted to leave Kira, where she lay dead on the hard ground, but we had no choice. We orchestrated a sort of burial, by covering her body under a mound of rocks. Then, once Lillian had her feet under her, and we had all redressed into dry clothes, we left.

The oval cave-like space we had emerged into was surrounded by slick black rock on all sides. The only opening was a small crack in one corner. We slipped into the crevice one by one. Nathan went first, and I followed. After several feet, I was forced to continue on my hands and knees.

It was dark, and tight. Reminiscent of the vision I'd had of my mother. Only I didn't sense something hunting me now. I felt entirely alone. Only Nathan's voice from ahead, the occasional graze of Lillian's hand on my foot, and the grunts of agony that echoed off the walls, let me know I had company.

"I see some light," Nathan announced. "Almost there."

"Thank God," Jared muttered from somewhere behind me.

I heard a pained grunt, followed by a vehemently spoken curse. From the last person I expected to hear it from.

"Bruce, you okay?" I called.

"Just fine," he returned.

He didn't sound fine. This tunnel was tight for me. I couldn't imagine how bad it was for Bruce.

I finally saw the light Nathan had mentioned. A moment later, I emerged from the tunnel with a sigh of relief. Coming to a stand beside Nathan, I saw it.

A thick cloud of fog enveloped us, and spread out in slowly moving, rolling waves. A deep reddish-orange glow far in the distance illuminated the two bodies of water that flowed toward us from the left, while a bright white glow illuminated the three separate rivers that flowed from the right. All five bodies of water met in the middle.

The six of us stood shoulder to shoulder on the bank overlooking the expansive lake. Through the fog, the sails of a ship were visible as it glided across the open water.

"That's the ferry," I pointed out.

Alec had told me about this part in detail. He had described the ferry as eerie. With its frayed sails, moss covered hull, and deck filled with the dead, I would have described it as terrifying.

"That's disturbing," Jared observed.

"We have to take that across?" Jas mused.

"Would you rather swim?" Nathan grunted.

The distance separating us from the other shore wasn't swimmable. I couldn't even see the bank on the other side. I couldn't teleport us without visualizing it. We were stuck riding the ferry with the other souls arriving to the underworld.

I dug the coin from my bag, which Alec had insisted that we each bring. "Time to pay up."

The ferry slowed at the dock as we stepped onto it. It creaked and groaned from the weight of all the souls awaiting passage. Around us hovered hundreds of the dead, lost in their own misery. Per Alec's suggestions, we followed their lead. Heads down, faces blank, slow and sullen steps as we boarded the ferry by means of a creaky wooden ramp.

I followed Nathan, and held my breath as he placed his coin into the waiting hand of Charon—the ferryman. Tall and lanky, and adorned in a long black gown with a hood that obscured most of his face, he was quite intimidating. I held my breath, tensed and ready for battle, as he regarded Nathan.

With a nod, Charon ushered Nathan forward. A set of red eyes swung toward me. I kept my head down as I pressed my coin into Charon's palm. My fingers brushed his during the transfer, and I flinched from the coolness of his skin. He didn't seem to notice, and sent me shuffling along after Nathan. We waited near the back of the ferry for the rest of the group to join us.

Jared gave a low whistle. "That went surprisingly well."

No one responded. We all knew the hardest part was yet to come.

The contrasting orange and white lights grew brighter as the ferry sliced through the water, and we drew closer to the gate to the underworld. Elysian Fields to the right, where the blessed and righteous spent their afterlife, and Tartarus to the left, where the evil were banished for an eternity of torture.

First we had to get past Cerberus, the gigantic three-headed watchdog at the entrance, pass through the Vale of Mourning, and find a way around the judges who awaited all souls inside. And that was all before we found a way to break into the palace from which

Hades oversaw it all.

I never thought this was going to be easy. But now, I wondered why I had ever thought it would be possible.

CHAPTER 20

"Anyone think to bring a dog treat?" Jas whispered as we approached the gate.

Looming over us, sitting on its haunches and reaching three stories in height, was Hades' watchdog. The three heads of Cerberus moved in all directions, missing nothing. One of the heads let out a toothy snarl, drawing the attention of the other two, who proceeded to snap at the snarling one. The sound of gnashing teeth—obviously big, sharp teeth—shot a ripple of fear down my spine.

The result was wobbly legs, and a tremor in my voice. "Alec said Cerberus will let us through," I assured Jas—and myself. The thought of being torn to pieces by a massive three-headed dog was enough to fuel a shred of doubt.

"He's there to keep souls in. Not keep us out," Nathan added.

His hand brushed against mine briefly, as if to let me know that he was there. Standing shoulder to shoulder with dead souls, I had never been more grateful to be reminded that I didn't belong here.

As promised, we slipped through the gate without as much as a growl from the beastly watchdog. However, the Vale of Mourning was much worse than I had anticipated.

The dead roamed freely there, taking their time moving along the dark and sullen path. The array of emotions that had followed them in death radiated from them in waves now. Some much stronger than others. Just by passing close to a soul, I was able to sense part of the story behind their deaths. I knew the murderers from the innocent, and the bitter from the accepting.

"You okay?" Nathan whispered.

So much sadness had brought tears to my eyes. I shook my head, because *no*, none of it was okay. Not the young girl victimized by her neighbor, not the man shot in an alley over ten dollars . . .

I drew in a ragged breath as a man passed me, the events of his death rolling off of him in vivid waves. Mass shooting . . . twenty dead . . . he had taken his own life. He had loved every minute of it.

"Kris?" Nathan shook me, pulling me back to him.

I watched the murderer slink away over Nathan's shoulder. "Don't you feel that?"

Nathan glanced at the rest of our group before shaking his head. "Feel what, Kris?"

"Can't you *see* them?"

Nathan hesitated, and his eyes narrowed in concern. "What do you see, Kris?"

My gaze shifted to observe a young woman as she passed. The details of her brutal murder at the hands of her boyfriend crashed into me, and my hand shot to my mouth to stifle the gasp of horror. Bile rose in my throat, and I choked it down.

"We need to move out of here," I heard Nathan tell the others.

Yes . . . yes, we did. The faster the better.

With Nathan's help, I forced my feet forward. I pressed against his side, and buried my face to shield myself from some of the more troubling souls that I passed. Apparently, I was the only one who could see them, or feel their mourning.

After what felt like an eternity, the sadness tapered. The Vale expanded, giving us some distance from the souls passing through. Some of them had been stuck on The Vale for a very long time, lost and confused. Those who were in denial were the worst to encounter. By the time we reached the end of the trail, I was forcing myself to not run. I couldn't get out of this place fast enough.

A shudder of relief rippled through me as we left The Vale of Mourning behind, and emerged into a dark, but massive, open space. The Judge's Hall, according to Alec's notes, appeared to go on and on forever. The shadowy outlines of souls stretched as far as I could see, though their emotions were not as distraught here as they had been on The Vale.

To the left, the orange-red glow of Tartarus was much brighter now. Just beyond the Judge's Throne, between us and Tartarus, rose a steep mountain-sized rock formation made of the smoothest, shiniest black stone I had ever seen. Set at the top was the palace.

"There." I nodded my head at the elaborate structure, which appeared to be chiseled out of the top part of the rock formation. Dark and massive, it looked exactly as I would expect the leader of the underworld's sanctuary to look.

"Here we go." Nathan laced his fingers with mine as we started toward the wall.

Getting to it would require walking through thousands of souls, which only I saw. Not something I wanted to repeat. Not to mention, we would have to pass close to the judges, and I didn't know what would happen if they realized we didn't belong here.

"Wait," I called to Nathan, tugging on his hand. "I can see the top. I can teleport us."

"I don't want you to drain your energy," Nathan returned.

"Climbing this thing . . ." I nodded my head at the steep wall.

"That'll expend a lot more energy, from *all* of us."

"She's got a point," Jared noted. "Not to mention the likeliness of at least one of us slipping."

Nathan pulled me to him with a nod. "Take me first."

Of course, he would volunteer to step into Hades' sanctuary first. His bravery was one of the things I both loved, and hated, about him.

I glanced at the lip of the cliff, and the sliver of flat ground visible at the top, before squeezing my eyes shut. My stomach hollowed, as it always did when I traveled, then a whoosh of hot air disrupted my hair and warmed my skin. My eyes popped open to find us standing on the cusp of a lava pit. It had been hidden from my view from the bottom, and we had nearly traveled into it.

I blew out a relieved breath as Nathan tilted his head at me.

"Sorry about that one," I muttered before closing my eyes.

A tug on my hand kept me from traveling, and I looked to find Nathan staring at me. He nodded his head to the safe zone behind him, free of skin-melting lava. "Look around," he suggested. "Maybe find a safer spot next time."

Despite the danger, I found myself smiling. My toes lifted me up to brush a fleeting kiss to his lips. I stepped back, breaking all contact with him, before I traveled back to the base.

Jared's transport went smoothly, as did Bruce's. Lillian and I landed a tad too close to the ledge. We were both saved from a tumble off the edge by the hands that shot out to grab us.

Nathan muttered a series of colorful words under his breath as he rubbed a hand down his face. He didn't do that often, only when he was particularly frustrated. I zapped off to get Jas before Nathan suggested leaving him to climb, to spare me from traveling again.

We landed close to another lava pit, and Jas jumped away from me with a series of ballet dancer moves. He dropped a few words that I assumed were Australian slang, because I had no idea what they were, or what they meant.

"That's everybody," I stated the obvious as I walked away from the edge of the pit to join the others.

"Thank the gods for that," Nathan muttered. His irritation over my close calls evaporated as a whole other reason to worry surfaced.

Hades' palace loomed above us. Separating us from the front entrance was a hundred yard obstacle course, a trail composed of crumbling stone bordered by pockets of lava. The languid fluid bubbled, firing bowling ball sized globs of skin melting lava into the air at random intervals.

Above our heads, a mirror image of the underworld reflected back at us. The rivers, the abyss, The Vale of Mourning . . . it was all visible. Breaking up the reflection were black dots that plummeted toward us. They looked like large birds as they swooped and flew above us.

I watched as one fell nearly to the surface, before it darted toward the palace. A streak of black. In its wake, a blast of ice cold air blew over us.

"Please tell me I'm not the only one who saw that," I gasped.

"No, you're not," Nathan assured me.

"What the hell was that?" Jas wondered.

"Alec," I called tentatively.

In an instant he stood in front of me. I flinched, and took a step back. My hand rose to my fluttering heart. "Don't do that."

The corners of his mouth quirked. "It's fun."

I realized how crazy I likely looked, talking to nobody, as far as the others were concerned. Though they knew he was there, and they believed that I was communicating with him, I realized our one-sided exchanges probably looked ridiculous to them. I ignored their stares as I focused on Alec.

"Any suggestions for what's next?" I asked him.

He spun to observe the palace with a calculating look, and it dawned on me that he hadn't seen it up close yet.

My stomach churned with unease. "Please tell me you know how to get in there."

"Sorry, sweetheart. Strictly off limits to all inhabitants," he responded. "Only his protection can enter. I'm talking about demons—*mean* sons of bitches."

"Is that what the black streak was?" I mused.

Alec's eyes were wide when they met mine. He nodded.

"So how do we get around them?"

He hadn't said anything to me about *demons*. As if this adventure wasn't already impossible enough.

He shrugged his shoulders, and I narrowed my eyes at him. To the others, I muttered, "He doesn't know how to get us in. That black streaky thing was a demon, the only thing allowed in the palace."

So close to my mother . . . yet so far away.

"What about a spell?" Jared suggested. "Could you make us invisible? Or glamorize us as demons?"

My head snapped up at the word *invisible*. I could make myself invisible, but had never tried to expand it to the others yet. Damn, why hadn't we thought to practice that?

"I can try," I muttered. If I could expand the glamour spell to include them, I couldn't think of a reason why I shouldn't be able to do it with invisibility as well.

I whispered the words to the spell under my breath, and closed my eyes as I surrendered to the magic. Once the buzzing sensation came over me, letting me know I had succeeded, I pushed the wave out toward the others. My skin hummed as it enveloped them, and I felt their energies merge with mine. I knew I had succeeded before I opened my eyes and saw the results.

Standing between me and Hades' palace were the blurry outlines of the members of the group. Based on their reactions to each other, I suspected I was the only one who saw their faint outlines. They were completely invisible to each other, and I hoped to the demons.

Already Jas and Jared were bumping into each other, while Bruce paced around with his arms stretched in front of him like he had lost his own sight. They looked like lost ducklings.

Alec shot me a grin. "This is going to be interesting."

"Yeah, a ball of fun," I returned wryly.

I worried that someone would get inadvertently bumped into the lava that surrounded us. I—hopefully—fixed that by positioning them all side by side in a straight line while explaining that I could partially see them all. I walked behind the group as we approached the palace, to thwart a fatal collision before it occurred.

The stony pathway was dangerous enough. Wide fissures below our feet permitted lava to bubble up in spots. Rocks crumbled beneath our feet, threatening to swallow the group whole. After several yards, we adjusted into a single file formation for safety.

Jared took the helm, with Nathan close behind. From the back, I watched with trepidation as they navigated the deadly terrain ahead of the rest of us. All it would take was one weak spot, and they would be gone, into the river of lava.

My attention was momentarily sidetracked as a flash of black flew toward us from the direction of the palace. I feared the invisibility spell had not hidden us from the demons. It was coming straight at us.

Jared halted, forcing the others to skid to a stop behind him.

"Alec?" My voice trembled as I searched for him. He was already there, watching the streak approach with fear in his eyes.

It wasn't slowing.

"Get down," Jared whispered urgently.

We all dropped to the ground as the streak flew over us. I rolled away from a bubble of lava inches from my face, and turned to watch as the demon rocketed straight up.

It disappeared into the abyss reflected above us.

"They've been coming and going," Alec offered in explanation. "Back and forth to earth. I know they're one step below a demigod. Very pure-blooded, and very strong. I don't know what they were like before, but they don't seem to be affected by the loss of the demigods like we were."

"Really?"

Alec nodded. "They've been extra busy lately. I've wondered if it has anything to do with the fact that the demigods are gone."

"No matter what happens, there will always be evil on earth," I concluded. Destroying the demigods hadn't gotten rid of all of it.

I supposed there was always supposed to be evil, as well as good. The demigods under Hades' rule had multiplied the amount of evil in the world. Perhaps now that I had destroyed the demigods, it would be more . . . normal? Not Hades-driven, without the use of the Skotadi to thrust unnecessary evil upon us.

"What?" Bruce turned to ask me.

I shook my head. "Nothing. Just talking to Alec."

His eyes swept over the spot beside me, where Alec stood, and he nodded.

With the demon gone, we were free to resume our hike. The rock under our feet grew less stable the closer we drew to the palace, forcing us to run the remaining few yards. As a large section gave way beneath Bruce and me, I wrapped my arms around him and jumped us to safety. We rolled to the ground, taking out Jas's legs in the process.

"Everybody make it?" Jared shouted.

I glanced around as a chorus of voices spoke up. It was impossible to pick them all out.

"Everybody's here," I confirmed.

We stood at the threshold of the palace. Towering over us was a large shiny black door. It was anyone's guess what awaited us inside.

"Where do we go once we're inside?" Jared pondered.

Good question. I turned to Alec for answers, only to remember that he didn't know. He hadn't figured out what spell Hades had used on my mother, let alone how to break it, nor where Hades was keeping my mother.

"Did your research turn anything up?" he asked me.

"I think so." I turned to Lillian for confirmation, only to remember that she had no idea what Alec and I were talking about. "Lillian thinks he probably used a coercion spell."

She nodded along as I continued to explain to Alec. A coercion spell was the only spell strong enough to give Hades the hold over Hecate that he had. With that spell, she would be forced to kill Asclepius if she were ever near him. During our research, we learned that Hades would have had to bury a wooden box containing objects belonging to the two subjects within the roots of a snakeroot plant. The plant required near constant nourishment to keep the spell alive.

That was when things got weird. It fed off the blood of Kobalos.

I, of course, had no idea what they were until Lillian described them to me—mischievous gnome-like creatures with a knack for tricking mortals.

Alec snorted softly. "Kobalos?"

I shrugged. "That's what the spell said. *If* that is the right spell."

"It's the right spell," Alec reassured me. He bypassed the door, and started around the side of the palace.

I dropped my invisibility briefly, for the benefit of the others. "This way," I called as I scurried after Alec.

The narrow strip of ground surrounding the side of the palace was loose and slippery, and gave way beneath us as we climbed over it. Below us was the judges' pit. A long fall awaited anyone who slipped. I rounded the corner of the palace behind Alec, and landed on solid ground. I spun to watch as the faded out images of the rest of the group clambered after us.

I didn't breathe until everyone had safely passed. Then I spun on Alec. "What was that all about?"

"This way," he responded.

He continued along the side of the palace, with us trailing after him. Our backs splayed to the cold, smooth wall as we avoided a small stream of lava that flowed through a crack in the ground. Again, small chunks of rock gave way beneath our feet.

"Alec," I pressed impatiently.

He ignored me, and we followed several more yards at a slow and steady pace. Finally, Alec stopped and pointed. I looked in the direction he indicated, and let out a small laugh.

"How did you know they were here?" I asked Alec.

"Gossip gets around in the underworld," he offered in explanation.

Behind me, Jas blurted, "Are those dwarfs?"

"Kobalos," I corrected.

At the sight of us, the two-foot tall creatures bounced off the side of the cage that held them. They moved like monkeys, but had old-man faces with stringy white hair and pointy elf ears. There were hundreds of them, all chattering at once.

"The snakeroot should be near," Lillian offered.

That made sense. Hades would want the plant near its source of nourishment. I eyed the Kobalos sorrowfully. If only we could rescue them . . .

"Don't even think about it," Alec warned. I turned to him with feigned innocence, and he shook his head. "I know what you're thinking."

"So? Look at them." A few had climbed the side of the cage. Their tiny claws held them up while their eyes penetrated mine. "They look so pathetic."

"They're devious little things," Alec returned quickly. "You can't—"

Alec's arm suddenly shot out to move me against the side of the palace. I spotted the source of his alarm over his shoulder. An incoming steak of black.

"I have to go," Alec told me urgently. "They can see me."

"What if they—" I started to ask what we should do if the demon saw through the invisibility spell, but Alec zapped out before I could finish my question.

I swiveled my head to make sure I had maintained invisibility over the rest of the group. So far, so good. Everyone's eyes were on the demon as it swooped down. A breeze of cold air followed as it struck the ground, and formed into a solid human shape. His back to us, the demon approached the cage on two feet while the Kobalos chirped and chattered in a frenzy.

Too terrified to move, I held my breath and watched as the demon withdrew one Kobalo from its prison. Shutting the door on the others, he walked past the cage and disappeared into a curtain of fog.

"Come on," I ordered the group.

I gave the cage a wide berth as I passed, not trusting the tiny creatures with their long, slender arms. As the fog enveloped us, I felt Nathan's fingers graze mine. A glance at his shape beside me showed a rigid jaw and determined, acute eyes.

A shrill cry arose in the distance, silencing the chatter from the Kobalos left in the cage. We turned in the direction it had come from, and emerged from the fog in time to witness the demon suspending the Kobalo's corpse on a wooden post. Its blood dripped to the ground, saturating the leaves of a plant with thick, twisted vines that rose ten feet into the air.

I recognized it from the picture I had studied earlier today. It was the snakeroot.

The demon's job done, he turned, shifted into a black cloud, and flew away.

"That's it," Lillian confirmed.

Bruce, Nathan, and Jared withdrew the small gardening shovels we had purchased that afternoon from their backpacks. They began the task of digging while the rest of us kept watch. Not that we had a plan if a demon came—other than run like hell.

We had no idea how often they fed the plant. I eyed the steady drip of blood from the dead Kobalo. It hadn't slowed yet. Hopefully that meant we had some time.

"The ground is too hard," Bruce muttered as he tossed a rock to the side.

We hadn't considered that the snakeroot would be planted within a bed of stone. The time spent digging through it was time lost. Time we didn't have.

"I hit soft ground," Jared grunted.

Nathan and Bruce moved closer to Jared. The three of them dug in a frenzy, taking turns tossing soil aside in a desperate attempt to uncover the box before we ran out of time.

Behind me, the Kobalos in the cage began to chatter loudly.

"Hurry up, guys," I pleaded.

I heard a soft thud as one of the shovels hit something. Nathan tossed his shovel to the side, and reached inside the hole. Behind me, a series of shrieks erupted from the cage. Either a demon was snatching another Kobalo, or something else had them riled up.

"Grab the other end," Nathan grunted to Bruce.

Together, they wrestled a large wooden box from the hole. They set it to the side, and I dropped to a knee in front of it.

"It's locked," I exclaimed.

"Burn the whole box," Lillian suggested urgently. Her head whipped over her shoulder at the shrill cry that came from behind us. "Something's coming."

I started to reach for my backpack—I was the one who carried the matches—when Nathan's hand stopped me.

"The lava," he suggested. "It will be faster."

He lifted one end of the box, Bruce grabbed the other, and we ran. We slipped into the cover of the fog, making sure to avoid the Kobalos' cage. Whether or not a demon came, whether or not it discovered the hole in the ground, we would never know.

We didn't stick around long enough to find out.

We tossed the box into the first pit of lava we found big enough to swallow it. No ceremony. No words to chant. The box, and its contents, needed to burn. That was what it took to free Hecate from Hades' curse.

I wondered if she would know that the spell was broken. Would Hades?

Would they *feel* it somehow?

I sighed, and leaned against the outer wall of the palace. Now that the deed was done, I realized how exhausted I was.

"You're losing energy," Nathan observed.

I nodded reluctantly. It wasn't luck that the demons hadn't spotted us yet. My magic was hiding us. Dropping the invisibility spell would leave us exposed. I wasn't sure how much longer I could hold it, but the group's safety wasn't something I was willing to gamble with.

"Drop it, Kris," Nathan insisted.

"Nathan . . ."

"Drop it," he repeated. "We'll be okay."

I shook my head, but dropped the invisibility spell—only because we were hidden along the back wall of the palace. Instantly, I felt a surge of relief. Maybe if I rested for a few minutes, I would be able to hold it for a while longer. At least long enough for us to find Hecate.

We needed an idea of where to go. I didn't have enough energy reserved to pull off a long search. The palace was too big to cover while maintaining invisibility for all of us.

Unless only I went in?

I didn't see that going over well with a certain someone. We needed a plan—a *good* plan.

"Alec," I called softly, then jumped at his sudden appearance. "Do you know where Hecate is being held?"

"I have a theory." He didn't look, or sound, convinced.

"How far is it?" I asked. "I'm losing steam fast."

"That's not good." He gave me a once over before frowning. "Come here. I'll show you."

He took my hand, and pulled me away from the group. At their grumblings, I explained, "Alec is showing me something."

He stopped us, and pointed to a section of the palace, only visible to us from the angle we had now. A large box-shaped section had been chiseled into the side of the rock. It was separated from the rest of the palace by a wide chasm. No steps, no bridge, nothing. Impossible to get to unless you were capable of flying, like demons, or teleporting . . . like me.

"Does that look like a good place to keep a prisoner to you?" Alec asked.

I nodded. "We'll start there," I agreed.

Alec turned toward the group, where they hovered along the wall of the palace. I trailed behind him as we passed a doorway hidden in shadows—perhaps a good point of entry? Alec suddenly stopped and turned to me, eyes wide with fear.

"Wha—" I started.

An arm reached out of the shadows to rip a handful of hair from my scalp. I glimpsed a black robe and long dark curls in the second before I was thrown into the wall head first.

CHAPTER 21

"You ungrateful little brat," Circe hissed. She loomed over me as I tried unsuccessfully to scramble to my feet. My vision blurred from the trickle of blood that dripped from my forehead. Regardless, her scowl was evident.

Behind her, the rest of the group lay scattered in a heap on the ground like knocked over bowling pins. Nathan and Bruce managed to get to their knees before Circe waved a hand behind her. She knocked them back down with an invisible blast of magic.

"I'm disappointed in you, sister," she sneered. "I have given up on waiting for you to come through for me. You may have taken the strongest members of my army, but I still have the miserable hybrids."

I scoffed. "What good can they do you without immortality? The gods will destroy you."

"The gods won't know what hit them," she returned vehemently. "I'm close to finishing the curse on my own. I don't need you, and I will not let you stand in my way anymore."

I bit down on my lip to keep from crying out as she wound another chunk of my hair into her fist. She led me by the hair toward the closest lava pit.

"Were you aware that there are actually three ways to kill a demigod?" she mocked. "A fatal wound with diamond is not the only way, my dear sister. Oh, no. A fall into a pool of Hades' lava will do it too. Don't worry . . ." She tugged my head to the side, forcing my gaze to land on Nathan and the others, where they were still held down by Circe's magic. Her breath was hot on my neck as she continued, "Your friends will be right behind you."

With a flick of her wrist, she sent me sailing over the rim of the pit. Heat blasted my face. My hair singed from the intensity as I fell. My gaze landed on the opposite ledge, and I squeezed my eyes shut to teleport myself to safety a second before it was too late.

Circe's back was to me—confident that I had been done away with—as she used her magic to toss the others toward another pit. Each of them struggled to catch their footing, or to grab a hold of something, as Circe rolled them across the ground, into and over each other.

I pushed my hands out in front of me, shooting a wave of power into Circe that knocked her to her knees. Her magic hold on the others dropped, enabling them to scamper away from the edge of the pit. She forgot about them as she turned toward me with a growl.

"I see I have underestimated the strength of your powers," she seethed.

"Your mistake," I returned brazenly.

"It's one I won't make again."

Her hand rose, and I hit her with another blast of power. She teetered on the edge of the lava pit behind her.

I didn't know what would happen if she fell in. She was a goddess. I couldn't exactly kill her . . .

Except Hera had told me that gods *could* be destroyed. In theory. At least, for a few centuries before they were reborn.

Could a fall into one of Hades' pits do it?

I gave her another nudge, stronger than the last one, which brought her to the cusp. Her eyes leveled on mine at the same time a blue streak shot from her hands. Whatever it was crashed into me, knocking me onto my back.

Lightning. I gasped as I rolled onto my side. *This is what it feels like to be struck by lightning.*

My eyes darted toward Nathan as he moved slowly across the ground toward me. Behind him, the rest of the gang struggled to move out of Circe's magical grasp.

Circe's head swung in Nathan's direction. I saw the decision in her eyes. She was done playing games.

"No!"

My scream fell on deaf ears. Circe held a hand out toward Nathan. She made a fist and rotated her hand. At the same time, Nathan's hands flew to his neck. A strangled gasp passed his lips.

My head spun with meaningless ideas for how to get us out of this alive. We were going up against a goddess, and a very powerful manipulator of magic. She was kicking our asses.

And Nathan was slowly suffocating to death.

I scrambled to my feet, and plowed into Circe the old-fashioned way. Her concentration on Nathan subsided as we rolled to the ground—I only knew because I took the time to look for him. That hesitation opened the door for Circe to shoot a hand out at me. I grabbed her wrist before whatever magic she had intended for me hit its mark.

"You may be a goddess," I grunted. "But I'm still a better fighter than you."

I drove an elbow into her nose with enough force to send her sprawling onto her back. As I crawled across the ground toward her,

I heard Nathan shout out to me.

He wanted me to stay away.

I wanted to end this . . . if I could. One thing was for certain, I would die trying.

Suddenly, a set of hands grabbed me around the shoulders, and hoisted me to my feet. Whoever it was pushed me behind them as they faced Circe. I got a glimpse of a porcelain face, smudged with dirt, and a curtain of long blonde hair. A shredded and stain-covered gown billowed around her tall and slender frame. Despite her beaten and vulnerable appearance, I knew she was anything but.

My eyes darted to Nathan's as he pushed to a stand. The look of awe on his face matched my own astonishment.

"Hello, Mother," Circe snarled. She dabbed the back of her hand to her nose, blotting the blood that had collected there from my elbow. "I wasn't aware that Hades let you out to play."

"He doesn't," Hecate returned smoothly. "Your sister broke the spell you and he placed on me."

Circe's glare shifted to me, where I stood behind the protection of Hecate. "Of course she did."

Nathan moved to my side, and pulled me back a few steps, out of the zone of the impending battle between the two goddesses. Behind us, the rest of our group hovered. Alec was with them, though none of them knew it.

His eyes met mine with a nod, and I knew what he had done. He had freed Hecate while I fought Circe.

As I stepped back to what I hoped was a safe distance, my eyes dropped to the impressive sword in Hecate's hands. Circe's gaze followed mine, and a flicker of fear crossed her face.

"You would destroy your own daughter?" Circe gulped.

Hecate answered by raising the sword. Circe's hands shot up, but not fast enough. Hecate thrust the blade into her chest, killing the magic on Circe's fingertips. Circe screamed as a bright white light exploded from her chest. Hecate withdrew the blade, and Circe's eyes lowered to the small speck of blood that spotted the front of her gown.

She was immortal, as a goddess. But Hecate had taken something more important to her than life. She had destroyed her essence, the very thing that made her a goddess. What remained was the shell of a goddess—a powerless immortal.

"Ga-rah-le-rah . . ." Hecate began to chant.

"No," Circe pleaded.

"Tierme garah peidor . . ." Hecate continued.

"No, Mother. Please."

"Biegharma," Hecate finished.

Circe's image flickered. With a whoosh, she disappeared. She was gone, but . . .

"Where is she?" I spun, expecting to find her leering smirk behind me. No Circe. Only the wary faces of my friends. All of them, wide-eyed with shock . . . but unharmed.

"Circe has taken my place in Hades' prison," Hecate replied. "We must go. Quickly, before he realizes I am gone."

She didn't give us time to prepare, or to ask questions. Her feet moved quickly, forcing us to run to keep up as she led us away from the palace, in the opposite direction from which we had come.

The flow of lava diminished as a steady cloud of fog rolled in. The lantern in Hecate's hand partially lit our way as we entered a dark and narrow tunnel. The fog was much thicker inside, and rolled over us in waves. The light from the lantern did little to cut through the heavy cloud. I had no idea what lay ahead of us.

The stench of sulfur grew stronger the deeper we went. It stung my nose, and brought tears to my eyes. My hands searched the cold stone wall as I pushed forward. With a start, I realized that I recognized the tunnel—the same as from my vision. Which meant . . .

"Oh, no," I gulped.

Something was after us. I sensed it now, just as I had in the vision.

"Quickly," Hecate urged. "They are coming."

Someone's hand brushed against mine in the dark. I assumed it was Nathan's, and took it eagerly. I had never told anyone about the sensation of being chased through the tunnel. I had never discovered from what I had been running. From the urgency of Hecate's warning, I doubted I wanted to find out.

A distant howl echoed off the walls around us, answering the question I had been too afraid to ask. A series of goose-bump inducing growls and toothy snaps followed. The tunnel carried the terrifying sounds to us. Whatever made them sounded close enough to nip at our heels.

My first guess was Cerberus, the three-headed watchdog. Except, the beast I had seen earlier couldn't fit into this narrow space. Instinct told me we were running from something far worse than Cerberus.

"Through here." Hecate shoved me through a small opening, into a more narrow extension of the tunnel.

Head bowed and shoulders hunched, I pushed blindly forward on fear-crippled legs. The uncertainty of not seeing where I was going had nothing on the terror I felt from what chased us.

I slammed into a stone wall nose first. Forced to a stop, I reached my hands out to search for an opening. Nothing. Only wet, cold stone, and Nathan's hands searching alongside mine.

"Where?" I asked breathlessly.

"I don't know," he returned.

I turned to look for Hecate, and saw the shadowy forms of the rest of the group behind me. Beyond them, Hecate stood with her lantern held out, facing the way we had come. A series of snarls bounced off the walls around us, much closer than before.

Hecate pushed through the group to come up alongside me.

"We're trapped?" I asked her.

"No, but I'm afraid we may not have enough time."

I watched as she moved her hand over the rock wall. Using only a finger, she began to draw a cluster of blood-red symbols.

More growling from what now sounded like a hundred unknown beasts echoed behind us.

"What is that?" Nathan asked.

"Cerberus's mutts," Hecate replied grimly. "They will not allow us to escape easily."

She moved on to another symbol quickly. I had no idea what Cerberus's mutts were, but her urgency, combined with the noises coming from behind us, and the string of heated words Nathan muttered under his breath suggested I never wanted to find out.

"Hellhounds?" Jas shrieked. "We have hellhounds after us?"

Nathan shifted to my side. "Can they kill a demigod?" he asked Hecate.

"They are an extension of Hades, and can strip me of my essence. So . . . yes, death by hellhound is one of the three known ways to kill a demigod."

A single low growl drifted to us from out of the shadows. Very close. Close enough that the hairs on the back of my neck stood on end. The clicking of claws on the hard ground drew closer as Hecate's hand flew across the stone wall.

I sensed them before I saw them.

Five sets of fire-red eyes stared back at us from the shadows. One slowly advanced, entering the circle of light cast by our single lantern, and I saw the one-headed miniature version of Cerberus—if the size of a grizzly bear could be considered 'miniature.' With black furless skin, long pointy ears, and a river of drool dripping from razor teeth, it was easily the most terrifying creature I had ever seen.

It was clear that we were on its dinner menu.

Jas stood the closest to the hound, and took several steps back, bumping into Bruce and Lillian. As a group, we pressed as tightly against the wall as we could.

"Almost finished," Hecate volunteered hastily. "Do what you can to keep them back, or we will all be trapped."

The leader of the pack growled, and I momentarily wondered if he understood her. But then he charged, and nothing else mattered besides the sound of Jas screaming.

Bruce lunged forward, knife raised and ready, to help. It quickly became obvious that no one could help Jas. A second beast growled, forcing Bruce to a stop. The lead hound's blood-curdling snarls peaked, then died along with Jas's screams.

"Is he dead?" Lillian shrieked.

Nathan cursed.

Bruce backpedaled while the rest of us pushed into the wall as if wiling it to absorb us. Each and every one of them were some of the bravest people I had ever known, but even the bravest could be reduced to cowering at the sight of the beast before us. It had killed Jas in seconds, and growled its intent to take the rest of us next.

Despite the cramped quarters, Nathan managed to push me behind him. "Stay back."

"Nathan, no!"

I reached for him, but he was already pushing between Jared and Lillian, to join Bruce where he now stood alone on the front line. Over the sound of gunfire, I heard a whimper—the telltale sign of a bullet hitting its mark. But then there were four more beasts prepared to take the leader's place.

Behind me, Hecate finished drawing her symbols and began to chant in a low, urgent voice. The wall warped as a blue light grew in the center, between the symbols. As the blue expanded, glimpses of a refreshing river of water, green trees, and sunshine appeared visible on the other side of the wall.

Over my shoulder, I heard Bruce's warning shout as one of the hounds howled. I turned to watch as Bruce impaled the beast barreling down on Nathan with his knife. It rolled to the ground as another took its place. Jared had also joined the fight, and placed a bullet into the head of the hellhound seconds before it ripped into Bruce.

Beyond them, and the river of blood that pooled under our feet, another cluster of red eyes drew closer in the tunnel. So many more of them.

"Now!" Hecate grabbed my arm, and shoved me through the warped wall. I popped out on the other side, standing in a stream with icy water up to my ankles. In front of me, a rock wall marked with graffiti bent and twisted, permitting me a fuzzy view of the tunnel, and the horror of what was transpiring inside it.

Lillian momentarily blocked my view as she followed me through the portal. On the other side, the three guys backed up, weapons held out in front of them to keep the hellhounds at bay. At Hecate's urging, they moved a little quicker. Jared reached the wall first, and threw himself out headfirst. He splashed facedown into the water beside me as Hecate followed.

It all happened in a matter of seconds, though it felt as if the world had come to a grinding halt. Bruce and Nathan broke for the portal simultaneously. One hellhound sprung. Its jaw enclosed on Nathan's shoulder as Bruce dove through the portal.

"No!"

I rushed toward the rock. Hecate blocked me from jumping through. I pushed against her, straining to get a glimpse of Nathan. Waiting to see him get up and step through. To join us.

All I saw were his shoes, and a giant paw pressed down onto his chest as a toothy beast knelt over him.

"No! Help him! Please!" I pleaded with Hecate. Her hand rose to my head, and I swatted it away. "What are you doing? Help him!"

Her hand touched my forehead, and I swayed unsteadily on my feet. As a calming warmth settled over me, I pictured the beach. Days ago, in Areopoli, with Nathan and Alec.

That was the last time I had been truly happy. Before I lost both of them, and my world shattered. As the black curtain dropped over my eyes, I envisioned us there. Together.

"Here. I like this one on you." Callie thrusts a light blue gown into my hands.

I run the fabric between my fingers, feeling its silky texture, as I examine it through a curtain of unshed tears.

"It'll match that boyfriend of yours's eyes beautifully," Callie continues, unaware of my distress.

"Who?" I choke.

She finally turns to me, sees me, my eyes. "Are you okay?" she asks. "Did you guys have a fight? The wedding is still on, right? Please tell me it's still on. I've already bought my dress, and the bachelorette party is going to be so much fun . . ."

I tune her out. She doesn't understand why her words are so painful. She doesn't know what's happened. She doesn't know that my world has just crashed around me.

How could I tell her that there is no wedding? There will never be a wedding now . . .

CHAPTER 22

I woke with a start—crying, gasping for air, and unable to catch my breath—as tears streamed down my face. I doubted they would ever stop. I wished for sleep, or for whatever Hecate had done to knock me out, because I feared the pain of being awake, without him, would kill me.

A gentle hand swept the hair from my face, and my eyes popped open to find Hecate staring down at me with concern. It was the way I always imagined a mother would look at her child when that child's entire world crumbled.

For some reason, that only made me cry harder—for Nathan, for Alec, for Jas and Kira, and for the mother I never had until now.

"I'm sorry, my dear," she whispered softly. "I will let you sleep."

"No," I exclaimed. No more dreams. As painful as it was to be awake, I couldn't handle another dream depicting the future I would never have.

The corner of Hecate's eyes wrinkled, and her mouth curved down. Despite the look on her face, her words were full of praise. "You should be proud. The prophecy has been fulfilled."

On some level, I knew what she was talking about. Yet, I found myself shaking my head. "What?"

"By destroying the demigods, you have freed the hybrids from their control," she explained. "They are no longer soldiers in the war between good and evil. They will lead normal human lives now."

"That is what I was meant to do?" I sniffed.

"Yes," Hecate confirmed with a nod.

The feared Incantator revealed in the prophecy wasn't meant to *end* the hybrids, but to *free* them? My destiny had not been as bad as I had feared all this time. Of course, Nathan had been right. And he wasn't here to know that. None of it mattered to me now anyway. What good was freedom without love?

Besides, I was still a demigod, and forced to go on without him for an eternity.

And Alec.

And possibly Callie . . .

"What about Circe's immortality curse?" I rasped.

Hecate smiled tenderly. "I believe I have nearly unraveled it. I have some more research to do, and only wanted to check on you. When you are capable, we will end it. Together."

I wanted to end it now. I pulled together as much bravado as I could muster, and started to pull myself up. Hecate stopped me with a gentle hand on my shoulder.

"You need to rest more, let the bind weaken," she protested.

"What bind?"

"I had to bind you," she explained softly. "I am sorry. It is only temporary. I did not want you to teleport your other friends."

I shook my head rapidly. Was it just me, or was the room spinning? And what was she talking about? Had I accidentally teleported myself here?

Where was I anyway?

For the first time since I had woken, I looked around the room I was in. I recognized it as Hecate's chamber. We were back in Mount

Olympus. Jared, Bruce, and Lillian hovered by the foot of the bed, watching me with worry-lined eyes. Lillian's were red and puffy, and I had to look away from the grief I saw in them.

"I am so sorry," Hecate whispered hoarsely, forcing my eyes to hers. "I have not been there for you, as a mother should be for her child."

I shrugged. Not like she had chosen to be kidnapped by Hades. Not like I had even known about her until a few months ago. Sadly, I had resigned myself to being motherless.

"They took you from me soon after you were born," she continued softly. "I should have tried harder to protect you. If you let me, I would like the chance to redeem myself, and be the mother that you deserve."

Eighteen years' worth of emotion caught in my throat, and prevented me from speaking—not that I knew what to say. It wasn't until recently that I realized I *wanted* a mother. Now that I had her, I had no words. I settled for a nod, and soon found myself resting against her shoulder, her hands cradling my head. A muffled sob erupted out of me as I buried my face into the layered fabric of her robe.

I had gained a mother, but lost two people I loved in the process. Two whose losses I would carry with me for an eternity.

Hecate pushed me back to regard the renewed surge of tears that rimmed my eyes with concern. "You love him, yes?"

I swallowed the cotton balls that had settled in my throat, and nodded. I had loved them both, yes.

"And this?" She lifted my hand to study the ring on my finger. "He gave you this?"

"Yes," I choked.

What would I do with it now? Give it back to Gran? Perhaps she would insist that I keep it. I liked that idea.

Hecate patted my hand tenderly. "Then you rest up, dear. Your groom will want to see you once he is well, and then we will undo the curse."

"What?" I pushed myself up, against Hecate's demands for me to stay still.

"You need your rest first," she insisted.

"No, he's . . ."

My eyes darted to Lillian. The tears in her eyes were highlighted by the slight curve of her smile. Happy tears.

Jared rounded the corner of the bed, stepping closer. "You teleported him just in time, Kris. You didn't know?"

I shook my head. "I saw . . ." Words jumbled in my throat at the recollection of the last thing I had seen. The beast's paw pressed down on Nathan's chest, its claws shredding his bloody shirt.

I didn't know how he was alive. At the moment, I didn't care. Nor did I care to know how I had managed to teleport him. All that mattered was that I had, and he was alive.

I pushed against Hecate's hand, and pulled myself out of bed despite her attempts to keep me there. I was dressed in a short, thin gown reminiscent of the paper sheets prevalent in doctor's offices. I didn't give a damn about the peep show I gave Jared and Bruce while scouring the floor for my clothes.

"I have to see him," I insisted. "Where is he?"

"He is in the healing chamber," Hecate replied. "He has to recover from his wounds yet. You do not—"

"I have to see him *now!*" I found my jeans, and nearly toppled over as I pulled them on. The gown was promptly replaced by my tattered and stained t-shirt. Finally dressed, I turned to Hecate. "Where do I go?"

She nodded compliantly. "I will show you."

"Kris?" Bruce's voice stopped me before I reached the door, and I turned to find him regarding me nervously. "Is Alec here?"

"No, but I can—" I gasped when an unwelcome thought occurred to me. I turned to Hecate. "How long was I out?"

How much time had passed while we were in the underworld? Had it been three days already? Had I lost the ability to summon Alec whenever I wanted to?

Would I ever see him again?

Hecate placed a comforting hand on my shoulder. "He is here." I looked around the room—still no Alec. "He is within the mountain, where he is protected. But he will not leave his post."

"What post?"

Hecate's lips curved into a ghost of a smile. "You will have to see for yourself."

"What about Jas? Or Kira?" Jared questioned.

My eyes lowered to the floor, and I shook my head. "No."

"Alec was the only soul who made it through the portal with us," Hecate added solemnly.

"So Kira and Jas?" I prompted.

"Will soon be receiving their judgement," Hecate finished.

They were gone. Unless they found a way to slip out, as Alec had done. Maybe I could try to summon them? But then what? I would be the only one capable of communicating with them . . . and it would only be temporary. It wouldn't bring them back.

That thought only saddened me, to know that my time with Alec would eventually run out. He would have to go back, to join Jas and

Kira, and Isatan and Permna, and everyone else lost along the way.

I shared mournful glances with Jared, Bruce, and Lillian. Jared nodded decidedly. The outcome could not be changed. We all knew that. Yet, as saddened as we were to lose so many, we still had much to be grateful for. The four of us had made it, and Nathan would make it. We still had each other.

I desperately needed to see Nathan, now more than ever. Jared noted the look on my face, and nodded his head at the door.

"Go get him," he ordered with a smile.

I didn't need to be told twice. I flew through the door, and Hecate followed to show me the way. It took mere seconds for the healing chamber's golden door to come into view. I couldn't believe he had been that close to me, and I hadn't known.

My excitement was temporarily put on hold when I spotted Alec, propped against the door like a sentry—at his post, as Hecate had described it—while he stood guard over Nathan. My cheeks ached from the wide grin on my face as I pulled him into a tight hug.

"I'm only here to catch a glimpse of Aphrodite when she stops by again," he explained to me in defense, as if he suspected my thoughts on why he was there.

"Aphrodite?" I laughed as I pulled away from him.

He nodded eagerly. "I wish I could get hurt so she would nurse me back to health. That Nathan's a lucky son of a bitch."

"You're a real charmer, you know that, Alec?" I shook my head, but couldn't hide the smile on my face.

"That's what you love about me." His finger tapped the tip of my nose to add a hint of playfulness to the heaviness that settled around us. But the longer our eyes remained locked on each other, the harder it became to ignore.

"I do love you," I croaked.

I should have been grateful that I had the opportunity to make sure he knew that, when so many never had the chance to say the things that needed to be said before death intervened. But all I could think about was that this wouldn't last.

I *would* have to say goodbye to him.

"How much longer do you have?" I asked, though I dreaded the answer.

His hand cupped the back of his neck as he gave Hecate a sheepish smile. "Actually, uh . . . my time is already up."

I started to smile—did that mean he could visit whenever he wanted, because that would be awesome—but stopped when I saw the look on his face. "What's wrong?"

"Your mother won't let me leave," he explained, nodding his head in her direction.

Her voice chimed in from behind me. "I apologize that I will not allow you to endure an eternity in Tartarus for your deception against Hades."

"You can see him, too?" I asked Hecate. She nodded, and I turned back to Alec.

From the look on his face, I suspected that he wished she couldn't see him. I wondered if she had forced her protective maternal instincts on him. Perhaps she was one of those overbearing mother types.

Which I was grateful for if that kept Alec out of Tartarus.

"She's got me warded from the hounds," Alec said. "For now."

"The hounds?" I shrieked as I looked between the two of them. And what was 'for now' supposed to mean anyway?

"Apparently Cerberus won't let them stop," Alec explained.

"They will never give up trying to drag me back."

"They cannot get you here," Hecate added decidedly.

As if accepting Alec's death wasn't enough. I couldn't bear the thought of him suffering in Tartarus for all eternity. One more thing to add to our to-do list—get Alec out of his prison sentence. I wondered if Hecate had an idea.

"Hey," Alec chided, interrupting my thoughts. "We'll figure something out. It's going to be fine. Go." He nodded his head at the door behind him. "I don't think he's awake yet, but I doubt you'll care."

"Not after just finding out he's alive."

With a parting smile for Alec and my mother, I slipped into the room. Seeing the wounds that Nathan had suffered, I concluded that he had been the lucky recipient of a miracle. One of the claws that had ripped his chest should have been enough to kill him. He had *three*. The bite that encompassed a large portion of his shoulder and neck should have severed major arteries.

He was pale, and still asleep, but alive. Perhaps thanks to the god that stood over him now.

He looked up as I approached the bed, and I saw that he was older, with dark hair and crinkly eyes that promised compassion.

He smiled, and extended a hand to me. "You must be Kris."

He looked familiar, but I couldn't place him. He must have noticed my struggle, because he volunteered, "I'm Asclepius."

I sucked in a sharp breath. My mother's lover . . . the healer . . . Micah's father. He looked precisely like I would have imagined Micah to look someday.

"It's nice to finally meet you," I managed before dropping my gaze to Nathan.

"He's recovering well, considering . . ." Asclepius offered.

"Considering what?"

"He has lost his supernatural ability to heal. Wounds like this would normally kill a mortal."

Because I had freed the hybrids. They were mere humans now, with no superior strength, special powers, or unnatural abilities to heal. No powers, no ties, no war. What I had been meant to do, though it could have contributed to Nathan's death.

Definitely a miracle.

"Your mother got him here just in time. Of course, being tended to by the god of healing doesn't hurt," Asclepius boasted, and I couldn't help but laugh at his joke.

The laugh quickly gave way to sobs, and I didn't even know why. I'd heard that people often cried happy tears. I had never had a reason. Until now.

Asclepius placed a hand on my shoulder as I sobbed over my relief. "I will leave you to have some time alone. Aphrodite or I may return to check on his progress periodically, but you may stay as long as you wish."

I nodded my gratitude, and Asclepius let himself out. Then I crawled into the bed beside Nathan, where I vowed to stay until he woke. However long it took.

~ ~ ~

I did fairly well, falling asleep myself for a few hours, until later, when the call of nature forced me to grudgingly leave the bed. Hera cornered me while I was searching for a bathroom. Despite my protests, she coerced me into the Spring of Clarity for a bath, and provided me with a clean pair of cotton pants and a comfortable t-shirt to change into.

When I returned to the healing room, Nathan was still asleep, but looked noticeably better. He even smelled good. Asclepius returned shortly after, and informed me that Aphrodite had cleaned him up in my absence. After checking the status of the wounds, Asclepius told me that Nathan would likely wake soon.

I watched the rise and fall of his chest, eagerly waiting for that moment. When it finally happened, I was on him before his eyes were fully opened.

"Thank the gods you're okay," I murmured against his neck before I kissed him.

My lips skimmed over his gently, tentatively, as I allowed him to come into his surroundings, and the fact that he had just woken up to me kissing him.

Within seconds, his arms snaked around my waist and he drew me to him with a grip impossible to escape. Not that I wanted to. I was exactly where I wanted to be.

"I think . . ." he mumbled against my lips between kisses, "I owe you . . . another thank you."

I pulled back long enough to ask, "For what?"

"You saved me again," he responded. "You got me out of there before the hound finished me off."

I grimaced at the images that flooded me at the mention of the hound. I had to remind myself that I had prevented the inevitable. Somehow.

"Where did I send you?" I asked curiously.

"The beach in Areopoli," Nathan chuckled. "I don't think anyone was around. I'm not sure how long I laid there before Hecate came for me. I don't know how she found me."

"She is the goddess of magic," I pointed out.

"I was pretty out of it," Nathan continued. "Asclepius came in, and gave me something. That's the last I remember."

"You lost your hybrid superpowers," I told him.

"So I've noticed." He smiled. "I guess that means it's over?"

"That's what Hecate told me," I shrugged. "Prophecy fulfilled. No more hybrids, no more war."

"We're all human," he mused quietly. His brow furrowed.

It didn't take me long to guess what troubled him. "You're going to age like a human now," I concluded. When his eyes darted to mine, I added, "And I won't."

"Kris . . ."

"You're going to turn twenty-three in a few months, then twenty-four, and then twenty-five . . ." My fears rushed to the surface, impossible to stop once they started. "And I'm going to be eighteen forever."

"Kris, stop." He was surprisingly calm despite the realization that our time together would be cut short. A lot shorter than it would have been when he was a hybrid. "We'll figure something out."

"How? There's nothing—"

His lips silenced the rest of my argument when they crushed mine. It was a damn good way to forget about everything, and I leaned into him with a content sigh. A laugh rumbled from deep in his chest, and he leaned back to give me a pointed look.

"That's all it takes to get you to quit arguing with me?" he wondered. "I'll have to remember that."

"Then why would you stop?"

My eyes narrowed playfully as I pulled Nathan in for another kiss. He froze an inch from my lips.

"Wait a minute." He lifted the sheets, and sniffed. "Why do I smell like flowers?"

"You were covered in blood," I explained. "Aphrodite washed you up. She must have used some special soap, or something. You do kind of smell like a girl."

"Aphrodite?"

The way he said her name caused me to roll my eyes. What was it with guys and Aphrodite?

"Let me get this straight. Aphrodite gave me a sponge bath . . . and I was *unconscious*?" He grinned at my narrowed eyes. "I'm surprised you let her."

"I didn't. She waited until after I left to find a bathroom."

"Huh." His eyes took on a distant, distracted look. When the start of a grin spread across his face, I smacked him on the arm. "What? You can't be mad at me. I wasn't even awake."

He edged closer to me, his dimple on full display.

"You're daydreaming about it," I grumbled, only half serious.

Regardless of the fact that we were talking about the most beautiful creature on earth, I had no worries. Especially not with the way Nathan looked at me now. His eyes traveled down from my face, soaking me in.

A deep rumble sounded from the back of his throat before he said, "You have no idea what I'm daydreaming about."

One hand hooked around my waist, tugging me toward him, before his mouth finally claimed mine. Pressed against him as he teased my lips with soft and sweet kisses that conflicted with the gruffness of his hands that roamed over me, I had an idea of what he was thinking.

A *very* good idea.

~ ~ ~

Much later, I rested my head in the crook of his arm. My eyes wandered around the room as I absorbed the melancholy. Though it wasn't as impressive as Hecate's, this room contained dozens of candles that cast a subtle light that was neither too bright, nor too dark. Romantic. Perfect.

This was how I wanted to spend my life. Comfortably with Nathan . . . anywhere, as long as we were safe. Carefree days, cuddly nights. Mornings when we didn't get out of bed until noon.

Speaking of which, I needed to find out what Aphrodite put in her soap. Whatever it had been, I wanted to bottle some of it up.

Because . . . *wow*.

Nathan chuckled, and his chest vibrated under my splayed hand.

"Did I say that out loud?" I gasped.

He planted a kiss to my temple. "Uh-huh."

"Oops."

He pulled me to his side, welcoming my head on his chest. His free hand took mine, and he held them up together. The ring shone brightly on my finger.

We were closer now. So close to the future we wanted. Just a few more hurdles, but after what we had just pulled off, they felt more like tiny bumps in the road.

Nathan took a deep breath, and I gathered his thoughts were merging with mine. "Should we go get this over with?" he asked.

"As nice as it is here, I can't wait to see Callie for real." The dreams had only been teases. They had only made me miss her more.

"I don't like it here," Nathan countered. "I worry about Poseidon and Zeus."

"They know I'm here," I offered. "I haven't seen them yet, but they haven't hinted at any aggression toward me. They were happy to hear the demigods were gone."

"All but one," Nathan pointed out.

He had told me once before that he suspected some of the gods wished to have *all* of the demigods eliminated, myself included, once the more problematic demigods were taken care of. Now that they had been, what were the gods' plans for me?

Nathan's obvious concern pushed him into getting up. He wanted to see how far Hecate had come, what needed to be done yet before the curse could be broken, and when we could get out of there.

On top of that, I planned to ask Hecate how to permanently protect Alec from the hellhounds and keep him out of Tartarus, and find out if she had a remedy for my aging dilemma.

Following Nathan's lead, I dressed quickly. Once finished, I turned to find him still shirtless as he fumbled with the clasp of his jeans. He must have sensed my eyes on him, because he tossed me a lopsided smile over his shoulder.

"It still hurts a little bit," he explained timidly.

My gaze followed his to what remained of the large wound that covered his shoulder, back, and neck. Nothing but puckered red tissue remained now, thanks to Asclepius. I wondered how much of the scar would be left a week from now . . . a year from now. It took nothing away from him. If anything, it gave him more of an edge.

An incredibly sexy edge.

"You didn't seem hurt a few minutes ago," I teased.

I scooped his shirt off the floor as I moved around the bed to help him. My incredibly sexy, hard-nosed man needed help. It was enough to make a girl swoon.

His head inclined at my insinuation, and his dimple popped. "It's called willpower."

Our eyes met, and I considered tossing the shirt where we would never find it. So what if we spent the rest of the day boarded up in here together? Hecate would find us when she was ready. I was sure of that.

"You keep looking at me like that . . ." Nathan took a step closer, forcing my chin up to keep my eyes on his, "and we're not going to go anywhere."

"I like the sound of that."

His hand grazed my hip, but didn't make it any farther before he dropped it to his side at the sound of a knock on the door. It swung open, and Aphrodite bustled into the room.

"Coming to check on the patient," she announced breezily. She froze, and clicked her tongue when her eyes landed on Nathan. "What are you doing out of bed?"

Nathan didn't respond, and it was clear from the expression on his face that an answer wouldn't be forthcoming. His brain had reverted to that of a fourteen-year-old boy's.

What was it about Aphrodite? Seriously? And why did *she* have to be his nurse?

Her hands ran brazenly over his back as she inspected the wound. Nathan's head turned to watch over his shoulder with a dropped jaw. His eyes darted to mine, and he grinned—actually *grinned* at me.

"It appears to have healed well," Aphrodite mused. She walked around to stand in front of Nathan, her back to me. "Anything else you will be needing? I am at your service while you are under our care."

My eyes nearly popped out of my head. Was she actually *flirting* with him? Was I invisible? And what the hell kind of *services* was she talking about in that sultry voice?

"I don't think the patient requires any further servicing," I quipped. I couldn't help it. She was lucky I hadn't already broken that hand that kept touching him.

Nathan shifted his amused gaze from me to Aphrodite. "The fiancée has spoken," he answered her with a shrug.

She spun around to regard me for the first time since walking into the room, her face lit with joy.

"Betrothed? Oh, how wonderful! I love when two destined souls find each other. It doesn't happen enough, in my opinion." As she gushed, she took each of our hands in both of hers. "Please, allow me to bless this union."

She didn't wait for either of us to respond before her head bowed and she began to chant a series of unfamiliar words—all of them Greek, but unknown to me. Nathan and I shared bewildered glances, but let her do her thing. It only took a moment, and I didn't feel any different when she finished. Nathan claimed he didn't either.

"I'm sure it doesn't hurt," he told me as we finally left the room, "to be blessed by the goddess of love. It can't be a bad thing."

CHAPTER 23

We found Hecate in her room. Books were strewn across the table in front of her, along with vials and bottles of the compounds she used to cast spells. The rest of the group had been put to work, and currently had their noses buried in books.

Jared glanced up when we entered. His lopsided grin couldn't hide the relief etched all over his face. "Well, well . . . the great Houdini has returned."

While Nathan exchanged greetings with everyone, my focus shifted to the back of the room, and to the lone person standing there. With his arms folded across his chest, his legs crossed at the ankles as he leaned casually against the bookshelf, he looked every bit the boy I knew. Death certainly hadn't taken away his personality, evidenced by the broad grin on his face as I approached.

But the simple fact that I was the only one who knew he was there reminded me that things weren't as they were.

"How's it going?" I asked him.

"I'm still here." His head nodded over my shoulder, at Hecate. "She's got me grounded."

"You are free to wander where you wish," Hecate chimed in from behind me, "*within* the walls of Mount Olympus."

Alec gave me a raised eyebrow look as if to say, *see?*

I turned to find the others watching me peculiarly. "Alec's here,"

I offered in explanation for the one-sided conversation they heard.

They accepted it so much easier now, as if it was a part of our daily lives to have a spirit hanging around. I supposed it had been lately.

"So what have you found out about the curse?" Nathan asked Hecate without missing a beat.

The goddess leaned back in her chair with a sigh. "Circe covered her steps well. I've discovered the spell she used, but I'm afraid it's a difficult one to break."

Her troubled gaze shot to me, and I swallowed. "It is possible though, right?"

Hecate nodded slowly. "A sacrificial ceremony is the only way I have found to break it."

My stomach hollowed. Though I feared the answer, I found myself asking, "What's the sacrifice?"

"You."

Silence settled amongst the group as her answer sunk in. Finally, Bruce broke it.

"But Circe tried to kill her," he pointed out. "Wouldn't she have broken her own curse?"

"No," Hecate answered. "It must be a self-sacrifice, and it must be done during a very specific ritual. Simply killing Kris would not have broken it."

"How was it supposed to be fulfilled?" I asked softly. Circe had been relying on me to do it, and I had no idea what would have been expected of me.

"Another self-sacrifice, using a different ritual."

"So I die either way," I summarized wryly.

"That's not going to happen," Nathan declared. To Hecate, he asked, "Are there any other alternatives?" His tone made it obvious that my sacrifice was not an option worth another second of discussion.

To him, I suspected it wasn't. But what about the thousands of humans that were wrapped up in the curse? Why should one life be more important than *all* of theirs? I bit my tongue on my thoughts, knowing they would get me nowhere with the people in this room.

"What if we do nothing?" Jared wondered.

"The human lives affected by the curse will eventually succumb if it is not broken," Hecate explained, "but their life forces will not be taken if Kris does not do the ritual to trap them."

"Is there any way for Circe to complete it?" Jared asked.

"No. I stripped her of her essence," Hecate replied. "She has no powers left with which to pull it off."

"What about Hades?" Bruce prompted. "Could he . . . help her somehow?"

Hecate scoffed. "Hardly. She has nothing to offer him now. He will likely imprison her until she can reclaim her essence, or until he finds me."

My mouth ran dry at the disgust that coated her words. "Will he come for you?"

"The mountain is protected. He cannot enter unless invited by Zeus," Hecate explained. "He will wait until I am vulnerable, as long as it takes. As long as I am the most powerful manipulator of magic, he will not give up searching for me."

"What are we going to do?" I fretted.

"Don't you worry about that, dear," she told me.

How could I *not* worry? I just got her back, and now I had to fear Hades coming to take her away from me again.

"We will deal with one problem at a time," Hecate commanded. "First, the immortality curse. There may be *one* other way to undo it, but I'm not sure if it will work."

"What is it?" Nathan asked. He was obviously game for anything that didn't call for my sacrifice.

"If I can pinpoint the moment the curse was initiated, I may be able to undo it by manipulating time. I'm not positive it will work. Circe may have thought about that, and protected the curse from manipulation."

"If she didn't, what will happen?" I asked.

"The curse will have never been started. Your lives will essentially start over from that exact time."

I laughed, only because I couldn't believe what I was hearing. "Like time travel?"

"Far from it," Hecate returned warily. "There may be significant side effects—memory lapses, your life could be very different from what you know now. There are no guarantees in time manipulation. There is no way to predict how much your new path may change from the one you are on now. Of course, the farther back I have to go, the bigger of a difference there may be."

My eyes met Nathan's from across the room. I was afraid to ask Hecate exactly what she meant by *no guarantees*. A new path? Would Nathan and I fall in love in another life? Or would altering Circe's master plan alter the events that led us to each other?

What about the rest of the people in this room, whom I had experienced so much with, and had also come to respect and love in my own special way? Would I even know them on another life path? Was losing the life I knew now a better option than sacrificing myself?

While I fought to contain the panic rising up my throat, Lillian turned to Hecate with the one answer we all needed.

"I started it," she admitted. Her eyes drifted to mine before lowering in shame. "Kris was twelve years old when Circe found me. She trained me for several years before we developed the curse. It started a little over a year ago. I remember the exact date, the first victim . . . everything."

As Lillian spoke, a dark, unwelcome thought planted and took root.

"What about Lillian?" I asked Hecate. "She was a Skotadi a year ago. What will manipulating time do to her?"

Hecate eyed Lillian carefully as she thought about her answer. "If she participates in the manipulation, I believe the version of her we see now will continue on the new life path. Again, I'm sorry to say, there are no guarantees."

"Kris . . ." My eyes shifted to Lillian at the sound of her voice. "I want to do this. I *need* to do this, to fix my mistakes."

I opened my mouth to argue, but she stopped me.

"I can't go on with the knowledge of what I have done," she insisted. "This is something I have to do, no matter the consequences." To Hecate, she added, "I want to help you with the spell."

Hecate nodded thoughtfully before inviting Lillian to sit with her. Their voices dropped as they discussed the details that Lillian remembered, and that Hecate needed. I couldn't stop thinking about what we were risking . . . for everyone.

"So much might change," I muttered under my breath.

A hand came down on my shoulder, and I swiveled to find Alec's mournful eyes. Circe's efforts to find me had ultimately brought him into my life. Without her, or her curse, would I even know Alec? Would I remember him at all on my new life path? The thought of losing the memories I had of him—when that was all I had left—produced a bubble of emotion to rise up my throat. I swallowed it down, but it had been too late. He had seen it.

He pulled me in for a hug. My head no sooner landed on his shoulder when a thought caused me to jump away.

I may lose the memories I had of Alec . . . but what about his life?

"What about Alec?" I called to Hecate. "If you manipulate time, the events that led to his death will never happen."

"I'm afraid some things cannot be undone, even with time manipulation," she explained softly. "However . . ."

I peeled my gaze away from Alec's to look pleadingly at Hecate. Please let it be a good 'however.'

"He is currently freed from the confines of the underworld," she mused.

I wasn't sure why that mattered, but I was hopeful. "So it's possible he . . ." I trailed off, unable to finish the thought.

As hard as losing Alec had been the first time around, I feared that allowing myself to have *too* much hope now, only to be disappointed with the outcome later, would crush me.

"I don't know," Hecate admitted before turning back to Lillian.

Alec's hand on mine forced me to turn my attention back to him. "I'm not the deciding factor here, Kris," he told me. "Callie is."

I nodded. "I know," I mumbled. But it would have been nice to know Alec would have another chance at life as well. Even if I might never know him.

"And you are," Alec added.

I lifted my eyes to his, and followed his gaze across the room to where Nathan stood. Our eyes met, and he took long and purposeful steps toward me.

"Do what's best for *you*, Kris," Alec advised.

But there were *no guarantees*.

I nodded glumly, and Alec wandered away to give me a moment alone with Nathan. His finger hooked under my chin, and with one look at my face, he knew my fears.

"I'll find you," he promised.

I shook my head. "What if—"

"I *will* find you," he repeated. "I've always managed to find you."

"We're about to rewrite the last year," I fretted. "The things that brought us together won't happen now. And even if we do meet again . . ." I pinned him with a heavy look. "Nathan, we *hated* each other when we first met."

Nathan's eyes narrowed slightly, and a grin curved his lips. "I never hated you. Never came close. I told you why I was . . . an asshole. I felt the exact *opposite* of hate, Kris."

I scoffed lightly. For some reason, that only made me feel worse. Would he feel the same way again?

He gave my shoulders a gentle shake to snap me out of my funk. "Besides, you didn't *really* hate me. Did you?"

"Well . . ." Yeah, kind of. But only because I had been so drawn to him at the same time.

"I promise I'll be nicer," he assured me.

"Less stubbornness would be good."

"Noted." He nodded with a smile. His eyes penetrated mine so deeply, so intimately, I feared he was using the opportunity to memorize what I looked like.

"Don't," I chided.

"Don't what?"

"Don't look at me like this is goodbye."

The lingering tease of a smile on his face dropped. "It's not. Because I am going to find you. No matter where we're at."

I knew he wouldn't stop until he did. As long as he remembered me...

Of course he would, I told myself. We were destined. We had just been blessed by the goddess of love. Surely *that* meant something.

My knuckles grazed his jaw tenderly. "I know you—"

My words were cut off by a crash at the door as it flew open. My hand dropped as Nathan's head swiveled toward the intrusion.

With one look at our uninvited guests, I knew all the hope in the world couldn't help us now. There were some things not even destiny, nor blessed unions, could overcome. Two angry gods ranked high on that list.

I had yet to officially meet Zeus and Poseidon, but I instantly knew that they were the two gods who stood in the doorway. Moving on their orders, three other gods I didn't recognize moved into the room. Two approached Hecate, while one stalked toward me.

I instantly found myself behind Nathan, his broad frame sandwiching me between him and the wall.

"What is going on here?" Hecate flew from her seat. She faced the doorway, where Zeus and Poseidon waited. "Zeus? Is this your doing?"

"We want no quarrel, Hecate," he returned calmly, despite the flicker of annoyance in his eyes. "The girl is a demigod. We have allowed them to exist for too long. We will not make the same mistake again."

"This is all because of a power-hungry goddess, and a few ill-advised children," Hecate retorted. She jabbed a finger in my direction. "*She* ended it all!"

"She is a danger to us all," Zeus countered.

The god sent to retrieve me reached Nathan and me where we stood against the wall. He halted a few steps away before removing a blade from its hiding place within his robes. He didn't have to say anything. The warning was clear.

"Nathan," I pleaded. I tried to push myself out from behind his cover, but his hold on me tightened.

"I'm not letting them take you," he snapped over his shoulder.

"Tell my mother to do it," I whispered urgently. "Have her manipulate time." I pressed my lips to his shoulder. "I'll wait for you to find me."

He started to turn, likely having realized my intentions, but it was too late for him to stop me. I squeezed my eyes tight, and jumped to the door in an instant.

Poseidon's lips curled into a snarl at my sudden appearance. I ignored him, in favor of Zeus.

"I'll go willingly," I vowed. "Don't hurt the others."

Zeus gave me a stoic nod before he gripped my elbow forcefully. His fingers dug into my skin as he led me away.

I glanced back into the room to find my friends watching me go with sorrow in their eyes. As if they knew we would never see each other again.

Nathan had not yet resigned himself to that conclusion. He strained against the god who held him to the wall, his eyes following me. I held his gaze for as long as I could, silently pleading with him to yield, while unable to shake the feeling that I might have been looking at him for the last time.

~ ~ ~

I was thrown into a small room near the pool of love. Water cascaded from the ceiling and walls. The limited space gave me few options in which to seek cover, and I was soaked within minutes.

Standing guard in the entryway was a god I didn't recognize. He surveyed me warily, as if he expected me to turn him into a frog any moment.

I probably could have—and maybe I should have—but I didn't doubt that at least one god had remained in Hecate's room with the rest of the group. The one who had restrained Nathan probably still had him pressed against the wall. Nathan and my friends would be the ones to suffer if I tried anything.

I didn't know what the gods intended for me. I suspected it wasn't good, but I would play nice in order to give Hecate the time to whip up the time manipulation spell.

Hopefully before it was too late for me.

"What's happening now?" I asked the god in the doorway. He eyed me silently, and I added, "I just want to know what to expect. Please?"

"The Olympians are assembling," he stated gruffly.

"For what reason?"

"To determine your fate."

"What's that supposed to mean?"

He didn't respond, but I got my answer a few moments later when another god came to retrieve me. I was led by the two of them to a large golden doorway, which opened ahead of our arrival. They ushered me through the entrance, and I emerged into the center of a large oval room. Above me, on seats chiseled out of the rock ledge that wrapped around the entire room, sat twelve gods and goddesses.

I recognized Hera and Aphrodite amongst them, but Zeus's booming voice demanded that I give him my undivided attention.

"The thirteenth demigod is all that remains from the uprising," he declared, inducing a series of murmurs amongst the others. Directly to me, he asked, "Do you stand before the twelve Olympians today to plead your case and beg for our mercy?"

I gulped. If I had known I would be begging for my life, I would have prepared a speech. But something told me it didn't matter what I said. My fate was already sealed.

"Um . . . I am the one who destroyed the other demigods," I started tentatively. "Like Isatan and Permna, I had no desire to be a part of the uprising. Though they did not survive, we all sought to stop it. We did succeed, and um . . ."

My thoughts ran together. Nothing came clearly to me. Anxiety bubbled as I fumbled over my words. Worst timing ever for a panic attack.

"We rescued Hecate," I added, though it sounded more like a question than a statement. I didn't know what they wanted, what they expected, or what might get me off the hook here.

"We have nearly stopped Circe's curse," I blurted suddenly. My breaths came in short bursts as a thought came to me. "I am needed to end the curse."

This statement brought another rumble of murmurs from the Olympians, and I wondered if that had been the magic get-out-of-jail phrase. Zeus's bellow brought an abrupt end to their chatter.

"In what way are you needed?" he demanded.

"Um . . . Hecate can explain it better," I stammered, "but it's my understanding that I need to perform a specific ritual for it to be stopped."

I chose to leave out the part about my sacrifice. Perhaps if they thought I needed to survive to break the curse, Hecate would have enough time to follow through with plan B.

Poseidon didn't buy my excuse. His voice rose above the murmurs. "It's a trick! Do not forget what she is capable of."

"Letting her live puts us at risk of another attack," a second god added.

"Just look at what her sister did," said another.

"Kris is nothing like Circe." Hera stood from her seat to address the rest of the Olympians. "She has stopped Circe, *and* the demigods. She has done nothing wrong, only what we have asked of her. I ask of you all to show her mercy."

With a subtle nod in my direction, Hera reclaimed her seat. As silence settled over the room, I chanced a peek at Zeus. His heavy gaze fell on me, making me feel like an ant on a crowded sidewalk—an ant doomed to be squashed by a dozen feet. I quickly averted my eyes, seeking relief from his obvious contempt.

Finally, he called, "Ares, your vote?"

"Death," came the swift response from the god to Zeus's left.

"Spare . . ."

"Death . . ."

"Spare . . ."

Around the ledge they went, one after another, voting on my fate. By the time they wound around to the last three—Hera, Poseidon, and Zeus—the vote was already in favor of my death five to four. Hera voted to spare me, as I knew she would, but it was too little too late.

Poseidon promptly countered her, and I settled my gaze on Zeus as I awaited his call. Would he kill me now? Or wait? Perhaps he would want me to suffer?

"Spare," he announced quietly.

I gasped in surprise, and swung my gaze to Hera. I expected to see relief, but only saw terror, in her eyes.

CHAPTER 24

I assumed Zeus's vote might have carried more weight, but apparently I had been wrong. The gods turned on each other. While their voices rose around me, I shrunk into myself in a poor attempt to hide. Stuck in the center of the room, I couldn't do much to avoid the fury of those who sought my death.

Poseidon appeared the most intent on seeing that through. Behind him, cracks snaked the walls. A trickle of water poured from the cracks, spilled over the ledge and into the pit in which I stood.

Beside Zeus, Ares withdrew a long black and silver spear. He vaulted over the ledge, and into the pit with me. I stumbled a retreat as he advanced on me.

Behind him, Hera shouted, "Ares, drop your weapon! Zeus has spoken!"

That didn't slow Ares, but a goddess jumping to my side did. I didn't recognize her, but she had a bow pointed at Ares' chest.

"What do you think you're going to do with that, Artemis?" Ares jeered.

"Do you intend to disobey our leader?" she returned.

Ares lifted the spear, its point directed at my chest. His eyes hardened on mine as he addressed Artemis. "The girl is a demigod. She must not be permitted to exist any longer."

He didn't wait for a response. His arm moved back in

preparation of throwing the spear. My eyes shifted over his shoulder, to a safe spot below Hera's chair. As the spear sailed through the air, I jumped to safety.

Ares spun to find me with a roar. "You see?" he bellowed. "She is a witch! She must not be permitted to live alongside us!"

A bolt of blue light struck the center of the pit, too suddenly for me to notice where it came from. The floor vibrated beneath me, and a crack ran up the wall to the ledge. It stopped at the base of Zeus's chair while he stood to peer into the pit.

My skin tingled and my hair stood on end as I watched him. The addition of the charred crater in the center of the pit suggested that the blue light had been a bolt of lightning. By Zeus's hand.

An angry Zeus's voice cut off all the others in the room, silencing them.

"You will restrain yourselves," he boomed. "The girl *will* die. But first, the curse against the humans must be broken."

I scoffed softly. So his 'spare' had only been a temporary 'spare.'

Zeus peered down at me. Despite my feistiness, I felt myself cowering under his wilting gaze. "Someone," he called, "go retrieve Hecate. We end this today."

~ ~ ~

~ Nathan ~

One god remained in Hecate's chambers with us. His presence put a damper on our ability to plot Kris's rescue, but not completely. Though none of us spoke out loud, we communicated plenty with our eyes.

We were all on the same page—no one was going to leave Kris

to her fate. Not that we knew exactly what that was.

"Do you mind telling us what's going on?" I asked the god.

His sword hadn't slipped from its deadly position against my neck since the others had left with Kris. He gave no indication of answering my question. Only Hecate's promising gaze kept me from shoving a fist into his face.

That and the knowledge that a fight now would not end well for me. Not since I had lost my speed and strength as a hybrid. I could still fight—years of training ensured that—but I knew better than to test my diminished skills against a god.

Besides, I knew Hecate had a plan. A brash move on my part would do nothing to help Kris.

Hecate flitted about the room as if the god wasn't there, and he did nothing to stop her. The rest of the group stood out of her way, silent but alert as they watched. The sack she carried with her was filled with various containers plucked from her shelves.

Finally, she turned to place a hand on the shoulder of the god that restrained me.

"Leave him alone," she scolded. "He is no threat to you."

"My orders are to contain all resistance," he returned. His sharp eyes roamed over me intently—he obviously considered me resistance.

"Which you have done," Hecate crooned as if she were addressing a child. "Now, take me to see Zeus."

The sword finally dropped from my neck as the god turned to Hecate. "I cannot. He is in court."

"Court?" I questioned.

"They're putting her on trial," Hecate explained to me quickly. To the god, she added, "Zeus does not know everything. I must speak with him."

The god shifted, visibly unnerved to be squaring up to a goddess with Hecate's abilities. The fire in her eyes reminded me of what I often saw in Kris's. Fierce determination, and a hint of stubbornness. Now I knew who she got it from.

Before the god could respond, the door swung open and two more entered. They ignored the rest of us as one of them addressed Hecate.

"Zeus has requested your presence," he announced. "He wishes for the immortality curse to be broken before the execution."

Execution? My panicked gaze swung to Hecate. Behind her, Bruce and Jared stiffened, while Lillian's hands flew to her mouth.

"I have everything I need in here," Hecate declared as she patted the sack in her hands—as if she had known their plans all along.

She turned to me. For all the similarities between Kris and her mother, and as practiced as I had become at reading Kris, I could not get a read on Hecate. Her eyes were trying to tell me something, but I didn't know what.

"It will be okay." Stepping closer to me, she reached a hand under her robe to remove an object. "Do not hesitate," she whispered as she placed the object into my hand.

She backed away, and my gaze lowered to what she had given me.

A flower? Why would she give me a flower? I rotated it in my hand as I pondered its significance. She left the room with two of the gods, leaving me panicked and confused.

Do not hesitate?

At what? What in the hell could I do with a damn flower?

My anxiety multiplied as the rest of us were led away from

Hecate's room by the remaining god. Though he had seen it, and didn't appear alarmed by it, I tucked the flower into my back pocket for safe-keeping. It meant *something*. I just had to determine what.

We were steered into a holding cell near the waterfall. The door banged shut behind us, and we were left there alone . . . and extremely puzzled.

Jared turned to me almost immediately. "Why did she give you a flower?"

"I don't know," I admitted. "She told me not to hesitate."

"What's that supposed to mean?" Bruce questioned.

"It's not a flower," Lillian exclaimed. Her eyes were wide when I turned to her. She waved a hand at my pocket, where the flower was safely tucked. "She glamorized something to look like a flower."

Everyone turned to watch as I reached into my pocket. Instead of white petals atop a green stem, I withdrew a shiny silver blade with a black handle.

"A dagger?" Bruce pondered.

"Not quite," I muttered.

It resembled the sword Hecate had used on Circe earlier—a miniature version of it. Now her words to me made sense.

Do not hesitate.

I wouldn't . . . once I knew who she intended for me to use it on.

~ ~ ~

~ Kris ~

Hecate burst into the room with purpose. Despite the two gods who flanked her, her head was held high as she approached Zeus's throne.

"You are a fool," she hissed at him.

His eyes flashed with anger before his chin lifted in a show of smug superiority. "The Olympians have voted. Your opinion is not valid."

"But I'm needed now?" Hecate returned. "For what, wise leader?"

"The curse is to be broken," Zeus answered stiffly.

"Ah," Hecate sighed. She swept a gaze around the room, at the other gods and goddesses sitting upon their thrones. "And none of the mighty Olympians know how to do it, is that correct?"

She spotted me where I stood, sandwiched between Ares and Artemis. One who had wanted me dead five minutes ago, and one who had protected me from the other's wrath. Hecate gauged the situation with one glance, and bowed a head at Artemis in gratitude.

To Ares, she growled, "You may leave now. Unless you wish to sacrifice yourself as well."

With a glance in Zeus's direction, Ares stomped off. Artemis retreated as well, leaving Hecate and me alone in the pit, and the center of everyone's unrivaled attention. As she began to remove items from the sack she carried with her, I panicked.

"Mother?" I whispered.

"It will be okay, dear," she returned before dropping to the ground at my feet. Without another word, she started to draw a series of symbols around me.

Was this really happening? Was I about to end the curse with my sacrifice?

I doubted that was what Hecate wanted, but the circumstances prevented her from doing anything else. With a heavy heart, I realized she hadn't had enough time to come up with another plan. Not even the time manipulation spell.

"I want you to listen to me," Hecate whispered from where she knelt at my feet. Despite the audible urgency in her voice, her attention appeared fixated on her drawings. Knowing we had an audience, I continued to watch her with a blank expression. "When the time comes, I want you to do what I tell you to do. Do not hesitate. Do not question."

My throat ran dry. Was she talking about my sacrifice . . . or something else?

"Where are the others?" I muttered under my breath.

"Your friends are safe."

A hand came out of nowhere, and took ahold of mine. I immediately recognized Alec's touch, and squeezed his hand in gratitude. A quick glance around the room confirmed that the Olympians could not see him.

Finally, Hecate stood. At my feet was an elaborate sketch of various symbols, none of which I recognized. In several spots, smudges of other magical compounds and powders marked the ground to give the spell Hecate intended to perform the boost it needed. I stood precisely in the center of it all—the glue that held it all together. Even with Alec at my side, I felt incredibly alone.

"We will be needing a glory blade," Hecate announced loudly.

"Where is yours?" Zeus returned, causing Hecate to slowly turn toward him.

"Lost in the underworld," she answered. "You wish to call upon Hades to return it to me?"

Alec's saucer eyes met mine. "I see where you got your smart mouth from," he chuckled.

Watching Poseidon's jaw drop, and Zeus's eyes nearly pop out of his head, did give me a twisted sense of pleasure. They deserved worse than to be sassed by an angry mother, but I would take it. Zeus was so flabbergasted he couldn't offer a response.

Instead, Artemis came forward to place a blade in Hecate's hand. "You may borrow mine."

"Thank you," Hecate nodded. To the rest of them, she shouted, "I ask you one more time to reconsider your decision. Spare my daughter, who rescued me from the confines of the underworld, who destroyed the demigods as you asked, and who ended the war between good and evil. She has done all you have asked for, and stands ready to carry out one more deed for you. She is not to be feared, but praised. Spare her from a sentence of death."

My breath caught as I peered up at Zeus. His face hardened, and his response came immediately. "No. She has been sentenced to death."

Hecate backpedaled slowly, coming to a stand on the other side of Alec. The three of us stood shoulder to shoulder as her eyes swung around the room once more. Though a few gods were visibly conflicted by the decision, none of them voiced an opposition to Zeus's final word.

Coming back to fix her murderous gaze on Zeus, Hecate declared, "Then I am afraid you have given me no other option."

She spun to take my hand in hers while she quickly chanted a string of words under her breath. As voices of alarm rang out around us, everything—the pit, the ledge, the thrones—faded from around me. In its place materialized the dreary walls of the holding cell.

And the faces I thought I would never see again.

~ ~ ~

~ Nathan ~

I thought Kris and Hecate were an illusion until Kris threw herself into my arms. As happy as we both were to be back together again, Hecate didn't give us much time to enjoy our reunion.

"Hurry," she ordered. "We need to move quickly."

"What's happening?" Jared wondered.

"I put a temporary bind on the Olympians," Hecate replied. "Come. We must go now."

She ushered us into a tight circle in the center of the room before chanting a series of words.

"Alec . . ." Kris shifted, leaving a gap between her mother and herself, which I assumed was occupied by the one member of our group the rest of us couldn't see. At my questioning glance, she explained, "I want him to stay with us. If there's a chance that he could—" Her head whipped around to the empty space beside her. "I don't want to hear it. You're coming with us."

I wanted to ask where we were going, but ran out of time to get the words out. Hecate's chants were drowned out by a sudden gust of wind that swirled around the room. There was a brief moment of absolute blackness, combined with the sensation of freefalling. My eyes involuntarily squeezed shut from the unexpected rush.

When they opened again, I found myself standing in the middle of the trail on the side of Mount Olympus—*outside* the mountain. The sun had started to set over the horizon, and the air had a slight chill in advance of the approaching night. We were all there.

Jared's dazed expression likely matched mine. Poor Bruce

looked a little on the green side. Lillian and Kris obviously handled it better than the rest of us.

Despite none of us having a clue as to why or what we were doing here, we all moved when Hecate ordered us to do so. She put us all to work, pouring and mixing compounds from her directions, while she drew symbols on the ground around us.

For what was anyone's guess.

"Hecate," I started tentatively. I didn't want to question her intentions, but I needed to know what we were doing. "Is this for the time manipulation spell?"

"There has been a slight change of plans," she responded quickly as she moved on to another symbol. "The gods will never let Kris go as long as she is a demigod. The time manipulation will only hide her for a short time. We must sever her from her powers to protect her indefinitely."

"There's a way to make me . . . not a demigod?" Kris questioned timidly.

Hecate's hesitation didn't give me a lot of confidence. Her words completely stomped out what little bit I had left. "It's never been successfully done before," she admitted.

Kris met my gaze warily. "How is it supposed to be done?" she asked.

"The glory blade. Used on a god, it will destroy his essence. It's been theorized to work on demigods as well."

I chuckled humorlessly. "We're going to go with a *theory*?"

"I have a plan," Hecate assured. "But we must be precise. No hesitation, or all could be lost." She stood from her newest set of symbols to look at me. "You still have the blade I gave you?"

As I nodded, Hecate's gaze swung over my shoulder, and her

eyes widened.

"They're coming," she announced. "We need to do this now."

Hecate turned and extended another blade to Kris, identical to the one in my possession. Kris's eyes hooded as they lowered to the weapon now in her hands. Her body shook from a fear that matched my own.

Something didn't feel right. To Hecate, I protested, "She can't . . ." I couldn't *let* her do this.

It had never successfully been done before. I couldn't stand back and watch while Kris risked her life to test Hecate's theory. Even if it was the only way.

No. There *had* to be another way.

"What do I do?" Kris's voice quavered as she questioned Hecate.

My gaze swung toward the group of gods descending on us while Hecate led Kris into the center of the circle drawn on the ground. The rest of our small group stood ready, useless weapons drawn, to defend Kris and ourselves. Mere humans standing toe to toe with immortals.

My gaze met Jared's, and he nodded. Of all the messes we had gotten ourselves into, this one trumped them all. Less than one minute before the gods reached us . . . and nowhere to go.

Hecate's hushed instructions to Kris reached my ears, and I forgot all about the gods. I spun around abruptly. "What?"

"She must sacrifice herself with the glory blade," Hecate repeated to me as she stepped out of the circle, leaving Kris alone in the center.

"No, that's not—" I took a step toward Kris. A blast of power struck me in the chest, and prevented me from coming any closer. I looked to Hecate, but it wasn't her.

It was Kris.

"I have to do this," she told me. "For Callie, and for me. For *us*."

The hand she used to hold me back lowered as she muttered a series of words. Freed from her magic, I lunged for her . . . but I was too late. Gripping the glory blade with both hands, she thrust the pointed end into her chest. Right in front of me.

A bright white light engulfed Kris. A burst of energy erupted from her body, shooting me to the ground several yards away as Kris dropped to her knees. She slouched forward, falling face down in the center of the circle.

Jared's hand on my shoulder prevented me from crawling to her. Hecate's chanting voice rose sharply over the shouts of the gods as they neared. I spun on her with murder in my eyes.

"It failed!" I snapped.

"No," Hecate returned calmly. "She is here. I have trapped her soul. You must use the glory blade in your hands to fight off The Collector."

"Where?" Jared asked.

Hecate's eyes darted from side to side before leveling on a spot over my shoulder. "There."

I followed her gaze, but saw nothing. Hecate chanted something quickly, and a ghastly illusion appeared in front of me. Adorned in the tattered shreds of a long black coat, his face hidden in the shadows of an oversized hood, The Collector moved past me with intent. I was insignificant to him. He had Kris's soul in his sights.

Do not hesitate.

I lifted the blade above my head, and thrust down, making

contact with The Collector between the shoulder blades. Like I had seen happen after Kris and Circe had been stabbed with it, a bright light exploded from the wound I created. The force that accompanied it knocked me back several steps. When the light faded, The Collector was gone.

Hecate gave me a nod of approval. "He's gone back to the underworld," she assured me.

"Kris?"

"She's here. I need another minute, and then we're all getting out of here."

I didn't have time to ask how she intended to make that happen. The gods had reached us.

A bolt of lightning that struck close enough to singe the tips of my hair served as our warning. One that we responded to with a unified stance of defiance. The second glory blade, which Kris had used, was now in Jared's hand. He and I stepped to the frontline together to face the gods.

Three of them—Zeus, Poseidon, and Ares—led the mob of eight. With a wave of Zeus's hand, the others' loudly voiced complaints quieted to that of a low rumble. His eyes were on Kris's body where it had fallen.

"What happened here?" Zeus demanded.

"What's it look like?" I returned curtly. Only Hecate's claim—that Kris's soul was still there, and the hope that Hecate had something up her sleeve—kept me from wanting to join Kris. Anger temporarily disguised my anguish.

"The curse?" Poseidon questioned.

"Her sacrifice broke it." I looked back and forth between the two gods who held the most power. "It's over. I don't suppose you plan to see the rest of us safely off the mountain, do you?"

Behind me, a low whirring noise started. A warm breeze developed, and intensified along with the whir. It brushed against the back of my neck like a soft kiss. I refrained from turning around to see what Hecate was doing, but I suspected the time had come for us to get out of there. If the gods permitted us to leave.

"It is done, Zeus," Hecate declared. "They are leaving."

Zeus's gaze slid over my shoulder to evaluate Hecate coolly. Beside me, Jared tensed, ready for a rebuttal. Though they were without productive weapons, Bruce and Lillian stood shoulder to shoulder on my other side.

"That cannot happen," Zeus returned. "These hybrids have worked in allegiance with—"

The breeze swirled behind me, and quickly strengthened. The hem of my shirt flapped from the force of the gust. The roar effectively cut off Zeus's argument, and prompted the other gods to take a unified step toward us. A wall of fire shot up in front of me, blocking them from our group.

"Now!" Hecate ordered. "We must go now!"

I backed away from Zeus's furious glare, barely visible through the flames, as the others retreated to Hecate's side. With a parting smirk directed at him and Poseidon, I turned to find Hecate's symbols replaced by a swirling blue hole in the ground.

"What is it?" I shouted above the roar of the wind as I approached.

"The portal to a new time." Hecate waved us forward. "Go. All of you. Quickly."

"What about Kris?"

"I have her soul," Hecate assured me.

"And her body?"

"Carry her through with you. But first . . ." Hecate touched my arm, which held the glory blade. "I need you to destroy my essence."

I took a step back. "What?"

A crack of lightening split the sky, illuminating the quickly developing black rain cloud that had rolled in over the mountain. As the resulting waves of thunder shook the ground, the cloud burst open, soaking my hair and clothes within seconds.

Another thirty seconds, and the rain would extinguish the fire. We didn't have time for questions, but I couldn't be sure I understood her correctly.

"Go! Go!" Hecate pushed Lillian and Bruce toward the portal.

I watched as they dove, hand in hand, into the hole in the ground, and disappeared from my sight. Jared stepped into my periphery, and gave me an encouraging nod as Hecate turned her attention back on me.

"I gave it to you because I knew you would do what was best for my daughter," Hecate told me. "The gods . . . Hades . . . they will never stop looking for me as long as I am the goddess of magic. I choose to be free. I choose my daughter."

This was my reason for having the glory blade. Not only to defend Kris from The Collector, but to take Hecate's essence—to render her a powerless immortal. *This* was the reason behind her words to me earlier.

Do not hesitate . . .

This was what she wanted.

I raised the blade, and did exactly what Hecate had asked of me. I thrust the blade into the center of her chest. The explosion rocked me, but I was prepared for it this time. Instead of flying backwards, I wobbled only a few steps.

Hecate's hands clamped down on my wrist to steady me. Behind her, Jared jumped into the portal. The blue swirling circles waned as he disappeared from my sight.

"Grab my daughter," she instructed me. "Quickly, before we lose the magic I created."

With Kris's limp body securely in my arms, I jumped into the fading portal with Hecate. The ground swallowed us up as we were transported into whatever life awaited us. The door slammed shut behind us, and there was no going back.

CHAPTER 25

~ Kris ~

I jumped with a start. My hand flew to my chest, to the spot where I last remembered stabbing myself. Nothing. No gaping wound. Not a drop of blood.

My arm reached out to touch the mirror I stood in front of, and the reflection of the girl that stared back at me. She looked . . . normal. Happy even.

What just happened?

And where was I?

Somewhere safe, I gathered by the muted walls adorned with tranquil landscape paintings, heaps of vases filled with colorful flowers, and set of matching plush chairs pointed out a large bay window in the room I stood alone in. The windows framed the vivid colors of an expansive garden that stretched across a long courtyard. At the other end stood a white gazebo, wreathed with more flowers. Three men arranged white fold-up chairs, all facing the gazebo steps.

A squeak jumped up my throat when a door banged open behind me. I turned to find Callie bustling into the room. In her hands was a white gown, but I barely noticed it.

I wasn't dreaming this time, I was sure of that. The dress's silky material bunched between us as I swept her into a tight hug. I only loosened my hold on her long enough to wipe away the single tear that had oozed onto my cheek.

"Kris, you're kind of suffocating me a little bit," Callie grunted in a strained voice.

"I'm so glad you're okay," I sighed into her elaborate up-do before releasing her . . . some. Not completely. I wasn't ready to let her stray too far yet.

She eyed me peculiarly. "Why wouldn't I be okay?"

I pushed her to arm's length to study her face. She squinted at me, and I realized that she didn't know. She had no knowledge of her ordeal, nor the trouble I had gone through to get her out of it.

I remembered it all. Minutes ago, I had been on Mount Olympus. I had sacrificed myself to save Callie and countless other humans, and to free myself from my role as a demigod. My mother had trapped my soul while Nathan fought off The Collector that had come to claim me. I had been pulled through the time manipulation portal with them. . .

And I ended up here. With Callie alive and well, and completely oblivious. After all she had seen and experienced, perhaps that was for the best.

"No reason," I finally muttered.

"You better not be getting cold feet," Callie reprimanded me.

"What?" My eyes dropped to the ball of white fabric in Callie's hand as she held it out to me. For the first time, I realized it was a wedding gown. "No freaking way."

Callie frowned. "Are you still drunk from last night?"

No, I was suffering from something far worse than a hangover right now. Instead of saying anything resembling the truth to Callie, I answered, "No. I think . . . I'm just . . . excited?"

Mostly confused.

"Good. Because it's time for you to get dressed."

Callie waved the gown under my nose, and I took it in my hands gingerly. Apparently, I had picked it out at some point, because it looked exactly like something I would wear. It bothered me that I had no memory of picking out my own wedding dress. While I stared at it with a furrowed brow, Callie bounced around the room like a hyper kangaroo, oblivious to my bewilderment.

"I can't wait to meet the best man," she gushed. "That groom of yours better have picked a cute one." She stopped buzzing long enough to flash me a grin. "Hot guys always have hot friends. At least that's what . . ."

I partially tuned Callie out as the significance of one word she had said slammed into me. *Groom.* With a rush of apprehension, it occurred to me that I was living an entirely different life than the one I had known only five minutes ago. According to Hecate's explanation of time manipulation, the past year had been a do-over.

Was the man I was marrying the man I loved, and the one I had intended to marry in another life?

A quick glance at the ring on my finger quieted my panicked thoughts. I *had* to be marrying Nathan. I was still wearing the ring he had given me.

A soft knock came from the door, and Callie shot me a warning look. "Hold up. Someone's here," she announced before bounding across the room to see who it was.

The open door blocked my view of the person Callie greeted. But I heard the voice that answered her. The sound of it sent a jolt straight to my heart, and carried my feet across the room to see with my eyes what I couldn't believe I had heard with my ears.

Green eyes rose over Callie's shoulder to meet mine, and my

hands flew to my mouth to muffle the cry of joy that rolled off my tongue. Callie moved to the side as I threw myself into his welcoming arms. His warm breath tickled my neck, and his light chuckle melted my heart.

"You're alive," I whispered.

"You should know by now that you can't get rid of me that easily," Alec returned. He squeezed me tight once before loosening his hold. Dropping his mouth to my ear, he asked, "Callie doesn't know, does she?"

I shook my head as I stepped back. While having no recollection of the events that had nearly led to her death was probably a good thing, it was a blow to realize she had no memory of *anything* we had gone through.

That included no memory of Alec, which was evident from the slight scowl on her face as she watched us. "Who's this?" she asked.

"Alec," I responded automatically.

Callie shot him a cursory glance before raising a dubious eyebrow at me.

"He's Nathan's brother. From Colorado. We weren't sure if he was going to be able to make it, or not," I gushed a quick excuse to explain my extreme reaction at seeing him, since Callie had definitely noticed. "There was some, uh . . ." I glanced at Alec for help, but only got an amused grin. "There was a mix-up with his travel arrangements."

That actually wasn't entirely a lie.

Though she still regarded him skeptically, Callie bought my explanation. "You're Nathan's brother?"

"Apparently," Alec returned.

"Then you must be the best man," Callie concluded.

Alec's grin grew to astronomical proportions. "Yes. Yes, I am the best man. A damn good one, too." To me, he added, "My *brother* asked me to give the bride a message before the ceremony."

"Ahh," Callie swooned. "I love him more and more every day." She squeezed between Alec and I, where we stood in the doorway. "I'm going to go get your mom. We'll be right back, and *then* you need to get dressed."

She added that last part with a warning glance at Alec—her polite way of saying, *'hurry up, because we have a wedding to get to.'* Like a maid of honor who took her position seriously.

After the door shut behind her, I asked Alec, "My mom?"

He shrugged. "I know as much as you do. Nathan actually sent me to find out who he was marrying. He was kind of hoping it was you, but none of us really know what the hell is going on right now."

"Kind of hoping?" I repeated indignantly.

"Oh, don't get your garter in a twist. Of course he hoped it was you." He paused to give me a calculating look. "He's going to kill you, you know?"

"What? Why?"

"Brothers?"

"Oh," I groaned. "Sorry. I couldn't think of anything else. You two always insisted that you weren't *friends* . . ."

"So you came up with *brothers* instead?" Alec returned. "Yeah, I don't think that's any better, Kris."

"He'll get over it," I replied. "And so will you."

Alec made a face like he wasn't convinced, and I had the sudden urge to hug him again. He was really there. Not a spirit, or ghost, or whatever it was he had been in death. He was real, and there was no countdown threatening to take him away again. Even so, after everything we had gone through, I couldn't believe he was standing in front of me.

I touched his shoulder gently, simply because I could. "I thought you were gone," I murmured.

Alec snorted softly. "So did I."

"What happened? I don't remember the last few moments."

Alec's brow wrinkled as he dug up his own memory of the events. "Nathan zapped Hecate with the blade, the portal started to die, and she took you all through it. It was kind of a last second thing, but she called to me as you all were falling through. So I jumped." He ended his story with a shrug, as if the decision to jump was no big deal.

It had brought him back to us, so it was a *very* big deal to me.

"I guess death can be undone, if you're not trapped in the underworld," I mused. That was the only way it was possible. Even that, Hecate had been unsure of, but it must have worked.

Because Alec was here. He was the best man in my wedding.

I sighed heavily as the realization hit me. With everything that had just happened, getting married shouldn't have been that big of a deal. But it was. I had always thought I would rather elope than have an official wedding. Why hadn't we thought of that?

Probably Callie's meddling. She was making me go through with the whole thing. No running away, no five minute courthouse procedure. The real deal—with the dress, an officiant, the walking down the aisle . . . and everyone watching me.

"Oh, God." I put my hand on the doorjamb to steady myself. Suddenly the room felt too warm, and Alec's face blurred through my crisscrossed eyes.

"What's wrong?" Alec asked urgently.

"I'm getting married," I squeaked.

"Huh. Nothing gets by you, does it?" Alec quipped as he slung my arm over his shoulder. I didn't have to tell him what I needed. He steered me to one of the chairs by the window, and sat me down. His hand gently guided my head down, between my knees. Amusement colored his voice as he instructed, "Deep, slow breaths."

"It's not funny," I gasped.

"It's a little funny."

I ignored Alec's chuckle as I concentrated on breathing. In. Out. Each breath blew away a layer of anxiety until my heart started beating at a normal rhythm again. My fingers felt a little numb. Other than that, I was okay.

"Feeling better?"

"Yeah. Thanks. I just realized what's happening."

It wasn't that I didn't want to marry Nathan. I did. Very much so. It was just crazy that this—our actual wedding day—was the day we had jumped to. This moment was the moment where our lives started anew. It was a lot to take in at one time. I wondered what Nathan thought of it.

"How's Nathan holding up?"

"He didn't have a panic attack," Alec laughed, "but I'm pretty sure he puked after I left."

I gave Alec a blank stare. My jaw worked, but I had no words.

"I'm kidding, Kris." Alec's hand covered mine when he realized his joke had nearly induced another attack. "He was only worried it wasn't you he was about to marry."

"Go tell him, will you?" I pleaded. I didn't want him to worry anymore. "Tell him I'll see him soon?"

Alec's gaze slid over my shoulder, and a grin graced his lips.

"You're not going to jump out the window, are you?"

"No. Of course not." Alec laughed boisterously, and I realized he was messing with me again. I gave his shoulder a playful shove. "Stop. Today is not the day for your antics."

"Fine. I'll go tease my brother." He stood, and turned for the door with a parting smile. "I never got to plan the bachelor party. I've got to get some fun out of this one way or another."

~ ~ ~

Callie returned shortly after Alec left with Hecate—or Mom, as she requested I call her now. Gran stopped by a few minutes later, and I flew into her arms before the door had shut behind her.

"Oh!" She laughed as I buried my face in her neck. I had missed her laugh, her smell, her touch. Mostly I had missed her hugs. "Now, now . . ." She pushed me back to give me a smile. "I just saw you yesterday, dear."

I blinked, and turned a questioning gaze on Hecate. Before she could offer a response, Gran whispered, "Even though I didn't go through it with you, I was told everything later. I know the truth, but that young one doesn't."

Her head nodded in Callie's direction, and I understood. Gran was playing it cool for Callie's benefit. But why was it that Gran and Callie had no memory of everything that had happened?

While Callie buzzed around the room like a hummingbird, Hecate and Gran did their best to answer my questions, and filled me in on what I had missed.

After the portal closed, we had all ended up in different locations. Though we all remembered everything that had happened, no one knew where to find the others in our group. Hecate had eventually brought us back together. Which had not been an easy task considering she had willingly given up her magical powers. Though she was still immortal, and would always be a goddess, she chose to live a human life. For me. For as long as I needed her.

"It was difficult," Hecate explained in a hushed voice. "But I managed to find them all, and bring you all together again. Lillian and Jared were the last. They had found each other before I found them."

"Lillian is . . ."

Hecate smiled warmly. "Her good self."

I breathed a sigh of relief. "Do they remember the past year of our new lives?"

"No." Hecate frowned as she adjusted the neckline of my dress. "The memory lapses are a side effect of the manipulation. I remember every day of the past year, but to you all, it feels as if you have woken up today, on the same day in which we left Mount Olympus. All of the do-overs that occurred in the past year have led you to this day, but you have no recollection of them."

"For Callie and me, it feels as if everything you went through never happened," Gran added. "I only know because I was told. My experiences as a hybrid prepared me for the wild tale your mother told me. But Callie . . ."

"She has no knowledge of that existence now," Hecate finished. "We thought it might be for the best to keep it that way."

I nodded thoughtfully. If only she remembered some of it. The good stuff, like her friendship with Alec, and the kindling of something more that had started between them.

I cheered when another thought came to me. "So I apparently met Nathan again in this life?"

Gran beamed. "Oh, yes. He actually found you before your mother tracked him down. It only took him two hours."

I laughed. "Two hours?"

"I'm sure it was the longest two hours of his life. Of course, it helped that the two of you ended up in the same town. Unlike the others."

"We were both here in Boone?"

Gran nodded. "You were living with me a year ago, weren't you? He knew where to start looking. Of course you weren't home when he came bursting in, scaring me nearly to death."

"Where was I?"

"The mall," Gran answered. "From what I understand, the two of you made quite a scene in the parking lot."

"Oh, I bet." My face hurt from smiling, but I couldn't help it. I wished I remembered like she did. At least I had all of my old memories.

"You learned to tone down your relationship with Nathan in front of Callie, and let it grow as a natural relationship would. That's why you weren't married sooner."

Though so much remained a mystery to me, the pieces of my missing year had aligned enough for me to understand. Perhaps someday I would get those memories back. Perhaps I never would. The important thing was that we all had ended up together, and we all knew the truth about how we had gotten here.

They were all here today, of course. I spotted them the moment I left the safety of my room, and began the walk toward the gazebo. Bruce and Lillian sat together in the last row, and smiled up at me as I neared. Fortunately, there weren't many other guests. Simple and small. Second only to eloping, it was perfect.

I gripped my mother's arm as we rounded the last white chair. I stepped into the aisle, and my gaze immediately sought Nathan's. He stood on the steps of the gazebo with Alec at his side. His eyes popped against the white button-up shirt and khaki slacks that he wore, and didn't waver from mine as I strolled toward him.

Few guests meant very few seats, and a very short walk down the aisle. Not that I cared about the dreaded walk anymore. From the moment I saw him, I knew I would have walked a mile if I had to.

I stood beside him, and sucked in a breath when his hand took mine. Finally.

"Told you I would find you," he whispered.

A soft, but intentional, throat-clearing sounded over my shoulder, and I peeled my gaze from Nathan's to find the source. Jared's eyes met mine, and he lifted a shoulder at the bewildered look on my face. I supposed he was just as surprised to find himself in the role of the officiant as I was.

So much of this day was a mystery. For all of us. As strange as it was, I honestly wouldn't have wanted it any other way.

The ceremony was short and sweet. There were some laughs, mostly over Jared's fumbling of his lines. I-dos and rings were exchanged, and everyone cheered when Nathan kissed me, for the first time, as his wife.

We didn't wait for Jared's announcement. We hurried past the rows of seats, hand in hand, until we were out of sight of the guests. There, hidden between a trellis of flowers and the building's brick wall, Nathan kissed me for real—a not for other's to witness kind of kiss. The kind that buckled my knees, and forced his arm to tighten around my waist to steady me.

I heard something that sounded like a bird squawking, and my eyes flew open long enough to witness the tail-end of Callie's reaction to finding us. I started to giggle when she spun around in a flurry, and collided with Alec.

Hearing the commotion behind him, Nathan pulled away with a reluctant groan.

"You do realize you're pressed up against the wall of a *hotel*, right?" Alec pondered.

Nathan's head dropped, but not before I caught the reluctant smile on his face. By the time he composed himself enough to offer a reply, Callie had started steering Alec in the direction of the gazebo. I heard the laughter in her voice as she reprimanded him.

Because she thought he was funny. I hoped that meant they would, again, have the relationship I remembered them having. Someday.

I looked away from the retreating backs of my two best friends to find Nathan watching me peculiarly.

"What?"

He shook his head once. "I can't believe you told Callie he was my brother."

~ ~ ~

The courtyard was quickly converted for a celebration. When the sun set, the hotel staff lit the torches that lined the walkways, illuminating our small group in a warm glow. Soft music played. We ate, and we danced. Callie caught the bouquet; Alec caught the garter.

"You think there's anything to those wedding myths?" I lifted my head off Nathan's shoulder long enough to ask. Couples danced around us, but my eyes were on one couple in particular.

His gaze followed mine. "What myth?"

"The one that says whomever catches the bouquet and the garter will be the next to get married."

I knew it didn't mean they necessarily had to marry *each other*, but it was nice to dream.

Gran bumped into me from behind, and she whispered loudly into my ear. "Yes, dear. There is definitely something to it."

"I never heard of that myth," Nathan countered drily.

"Oh, it's not our kind of myth," Gran dismissed with a wave of her hand. "But there is such a thing as instinct, and I have that. I predicted the two of you, didn't I?"

"Predicted, or hoped?" Nathan grunted.

"You see something there, Gran?" I asked her, my eyes on Alec and Callie.

While their relationship wasn't where it had been, they looked friendly enough. It was a start, I thought.

"Whatever was planted is still there," Gran winked. "Give it time."

She ventured off, swinging her hips to the mellow beat like a woman half her age. Nathan and I studied our friends while they danced, oblivious to our eyes on them. Alec leaned close to say something to Callie that prompted her to smile. I recognized that smile.

"She likes him," I determined.

Nathan nodded. "It might be even better the second time around."

"What do you mean?"

"Less drama. No history. Only a clean slate." Nathan's gaze held mine. "She might not remember everything. Things might be different than they were, but you never know . . . it might be better."

I wasn't sure if he intended for there to be a double meaning behind his words, but I applied them to us, and our situation, as well. It would be hard to make what we already had better . . . but we sure would try.

"Again with the words," I murmured before welcoming his lips with mine.

Surrounded by family and friends, it started off as an innocent enough kiss. In a matter of seconds, I started thinking about Alec's 'hotel' quip. Not so much a joke now.

A subtle throat-clearing came from behind me, and I reluctantly pulled away from Nathan to find Jared grinning at us.

"I've really got to stop catching you two like this," he grumbled, but with a smile on his face. He lifted an object in his hands, and it jingled as he passed it to Nathan. "All ready for you."

"Thank you," Nathan returned.

Jared gave a nod, but stopped before turning away. "You know . . . that should have been a job for the *best man* to do."

Nathan and I followed Jared's gaze across the courtyard, where Alec and Callie were still dancing, oblivious to the fact that we were staring at them. Actually . . . they looked oblivious to just about everything, but each other.

"Oh, my God," I exclaimed, and grabbed Nathan's arm tightly as excitement rippled through me.

"Relax," he told me. "Don't go planning their wedding already."

"Two years," Gran chimed in as she passed by. "Give it two years."

Nathan and I shared amused glances. We both knew there was no arguing with her. Besides, she *had* been right about Nathan and me. I hoped she was right about Alec and Callie.

"You going to watch them all night?" Nathan teased. "Or do you want to see your wedding gift?"

"You got me a gift?"

His head rolled. "Not really a *gift*, but I think you're going to like it. Want to say your goodbyes, and get out of here?"

"We're not staying here?" I hesitated, only because history had taught me to not separate from the people I cared about. Bad things happened then.

"We're going to see everybody tomorrow," he promised—again, knowing exactly what I was thinking.

"We are?"

He shrugged. "Apparently, we have plans for brunch."

I cast Alec and Callie a final glance—they never noticed—before making my way around the courtyard to say goodbye to the others. We confirmed brunch for eleven the next day. Everyone was smiling. Everyone was happy.

I found it was so much easier to be happy without the weight of war on my shoulders.

Forty-five minutes after we left the hotel, Nathan turned the Jeep onto a narrow dirt road. A feeling of déjà vu slammed into me, and I sat up straighter in my seat. Though it was dark, the road looked familiar.

"Nathan, where—"

The headlights swept over an open field, and illuminated a small cabin nestled against the tree line. A cabin I recognized. By the time the car came to a stop near the front porch, my knee was bouncing from excitement.

Nathan killed the engine, and turned to me. "You like?"

"Are you kidding me?" I exclaimed. I couldn't wait another minute. I pushed the passenger door open, and hurried up the porch steps to the front door.

This was where it all had begun.

This was where we had started to fall in love.

It felt like an eternity ago, but now we were back.

"It's ours, by the way," Nathan told me as he withdrew the key from his pocket.

"How?"

He shrugged. "No Kala system to monitor the old safe houses, and I was the only one who knew where the key was."

"What about Jared?"

"I told him where to find it, and asked him to come tidy up the inside for us."

He impressed me once again. "It's really ours?"

"If you want it to be." He slipped the key into the lock, and swung the door open.

Spread out in front of us was a dusting of red rose petals that covered the floors, the kitchen counter to the left, the love seat and chair to the right, and the bed in the corner. Though the late summer evening was warm, a small fire burned in the fireplace, creating a soft glow that illuminated the cabin I hadn't realized until now that I had missed.

Aside from the rose petals, it was exactly as I remembered it. A feeling of serenity washed over me. This was where my carefree days, snuggly nights, and mornings of sleeping in until noon would happen. We would add new memories to those already created here.

"I've never wanted anything more," I told Nathan. The double meaning was clear—him, the cabin, the whole package.

As we crossed the threshold, there was no doubt. I knew we were finally home.

EPILOGUE

~ 1 month later ~

There was much to be happy about these days—the promise of a future with the man I loved, days and nights spent in the cozy cabin we both treasured, the love and devotion of the mother I never had, and friends I wouldn't trade anything for. Sundays had quickly turned into one more thing to be happy about, because that was the one time I got to enjoy all the greatness in my life at one time.

It had just happened. One Sunday afternoon had become two, then three. Now it was a given—Sunday afternoon picnics at the cabin. Nathan grilled the burgers, Gran brought her infamous potato salad, and everyone else supplied the rest.

Alec brought the beer.

I grabbed two bottles from the cooler before I made my way to the grill. Behind me, set in the shade between the back porch and the trees, the picnic table was packed with the people I had come to know well over the past few months. My allies. My companions. *My friends.*

I paused to savor the sound of laughter that erupted from the table at a perfectly executed, if not a little dirty, joke. The laughing was amazing to hear, especially after all we had endured. One thing was for certain, our trials had turned us into a pretty tight-knit crew.

I glided up alongside Nathan, where he stood at the grill. I replenished his empty beer bottle with a new, cold one, and held my plate out in expectation. I received a juicy burger, and a kiss.

"You coming over?" I asked him.

"Be right there," he vowed, before returning his attention to the grill—a wedding gift from Gran.

I left him to gush over his new pride and joy, and took my seat at the table. Alec sat across from me, and nodded pointedly at the bottle I set down.

"What were you saying earlier about me never bringing anything good to the picnics?"

"How hard is it to buy beer?" I shot back with a smile. "Just once, I'd like to see you *make* something."

"Never going to happen, sweetheart," he returned. "Me and kitchens do not get along."

"Says the guy that just rented the nice apartment in town with a huge kitchen."

"That's only to impress the ladies."

"Oh, please," I groaned. "There's only *one* lady you're trying to impress. We all know it."

Alec didn't respond as the girl we were talking about slid into the seat beside me.

"Know what?" Callie asked.

"That Alec has good taste," I answered quickly. I raised the bottle in my hand, as if in explanation, but the look I gave Alec hinted at what I was *really* referring to.

He shook his head at me, but his grin was impossible to suppress.

He had it bad. We both knew it.

Callie sampled a drink, and nodded in agreement. "Much better than that crap you brought last weekend."

"Guinness?" Alec exclaimed. "Crap?" He looked at her like she had just kicked his puppy.

"Whatever it was." She waved off his reaction, and took a bite of her burger. "Oh, my God. These are getting better every weekend."

"He practices through the week," I volunteered with a smirk.

Alec choked on a laugh as Nathan finally joined us. He slid into the seat on the other side of Callie, and Alec teased, "Where's your apron, Martha?"

"Kris," Nathan grumbled.

I cowered behind Callie while Alec jabbed a finger at Nathan.

"Best nickname yet," he concluded. "No more Rambo. From now on, it's Martha."

"Rambo?" Callie questioned, and the laughter at the table faded.

Sometimes it was easy for us to forget that Callie had no memory of the truth. This wasn't the first that someone had let something slip.

"Alec has called Nathan Rambo since they were kids," Jared volunteered quickly. "Something about fighting over toys . . ."

The quick-thinking Jared was usually the one to bail us out. Again, Callie bought it, though I knew—I just knew—the day would come that she would see through our charade. On one hand, I looked forward to that day. On the other, I wanted to keep her protected from the truth.

Especially now, when things were finally normal for the rest of us.

"Speaking of toys," Alec chimed in casually. "How was your date the other night?"

Jared pointed a stern finger at Alec, while Bruce nearly spit out his beer. "Not funny."

"It was horrible," Lillian volunteered. "He ended up crashing at my place to avoid her."

"She apparently has stalker-like tendencies," Jared admitted.

"I tried to tell you." Alec shook his head. "I have built-in radar for the crazies."

"I'll listen to you the next time. Hopefully I won't be seeing her around again. Though . . ." Jared's eyes flicked between Callie and me. "She said she was starting at the school."

"The university?" Callie gasped.

Jared nodded glumly, and Callie shot me a determined look. No crazies were going to get to our boys—they would have to go through us first.

The decision to enroll at East Tennessee State University this fall with Callie had not been an easy one for me to make. Financially, I had no money. But Nathan did, and he had insisted that we put his life's savings to use.

He had found a job in nearby Johnson City—same town as the university—working as a personal trainer for some extra income, though we didn't really need it. He had been incredibly thrifty in his bachelor days.

Callie had been the deciding factor that pushed me into enrolling. Though we weren't going for the same majors—art history for her; undecided for me—she hadn't wanted to go at it alone. So starting in three days, I was attending my first class as a college student.

"That reminds me . . ." Alec dug into his pocket, and retrieved a folded up piece of paper. He tossed it onto the table in front of me, and Callie snatched it up.

Her eyes scanned the paper before lifting to Alec's in surprise. "You're enrolled too?"

"As of Thursday morning," he replied. "Late acceptance. They had some room."

"I think this calls for a toast," Hecate—*mom*, I had to keep reminding myself to call her that—declared. She lifted the bottle in her hand, and the rest of us followed suit. "For a wonderful bunch, given the gift of opportunity and new beginnings. May you all find your path to happiness."

I already found mine, I thought as I clunked my bottle against the others'. After taking our drinks, Callie leaned close to me.

"Your mom talks weird," she whispered.

I smiled. Callie had no idea how much weirder it could get.

We ate our fill, and I laughed until my stomach hurt. Afterwards, Hecate and Gran helped me to clear the table. Callie and Lillian brought out the chairs, and the guys worked on getting the fire started in the clearing. This was my favorite part of our Sundays—all of us, sitting under the stars, surrounding the fire. We would remain there for several more hours, joking and laughing like old friends.

I supposed we were now. Nothing like the things we had seen and done together to bring us all together. From my seat perched on Nathan's knee, I gazed around the group. Hecate and Gran conversed; Callie and Alec flirted; Jared, Lillian, and Bruce laughed.

Despite the difficulties we had experienced, I wouldn't had wanted it any other way. The things that had happened had led us here. This was where we belonged. All of us.

"What are you thinking?" Nathan murmured near my ear.

I turned to find his eyes on mine. The faint smile he gave me suggested he already knew my answer. I didn't waste time saying the words. My lips, when they met his, said it all.

I couldn't have dreamt a more perfect happily ever after.

AVENGING HEART

DESNI DANTONE

ACKNOWLEDGEMENTS

Writing and producing a novel—let alone a series—is a long and multi-stepped process that takes more than just an author willing to put words down. I'd like to thank my team for their dedication to making this series the best it can be. Najla Qamber—thanks for your patience and perseverance with the cover designs. You somehow take my rambled ideas, and turn them into gorgeous covers. Jennifer Leisenheimer—my editor, who never laughs at the silly typos that somehow get past my numerous editing attempts. Your polish makes my words shine extra bright. Beta readers—Sara Meadows, Nichole Fortin-Nelson, Taylor Johnson, Takeisha Spann Moore, Susan Friedlander—thank you so much for your invaluable input. You helped me to get everything right! Special thanks to Natalie Hughes—my favorite personal assistant, for tackling those 'extra' jobs that free me up for more writing time.

Big thank you to the fans of The Ignited Series. Your emails, messages, and kind words mean the world to me, and keep me going on days that I want to quit. Special shout out to the fans over at Club YA and We Are Ignited. It's fun hanging out with you guys every day.

WHERE TO FIND THE AUTHOR

Facebook: www.facebook.com/ignitedbooks
Twitter: www.twitter.com/ddantone
Instagram ID: d_dantone
Ignited Fan Group: www.facebook.com/groups/WeAreIgnited
Website: www.desnidantone.com

CPSIA information can be obtained
at www.ICGtesting.com
Printed in the USA
LVHW110623121218
600165LV00002B/400/P